BIO-FUTURES

BIO-
FUTURES

Science Fiction Stories About Biological Metamorphosis

Edited, with an introduction and notes, by

PAMELA SARGENT

VINTAGE BOOKS
A Division of Random House
New York

A VINTAGE ORIGINAL, June 1976
First Edition

ACKNOWLEDGMENTS

"The Planners" by Kate Wilhelm; copyright © 1968 by
Damon Knight. Originally appeared in *Orbit 3*. Reprinted by permission of the author.

"Slow Tuesday Night" by R. A. Lafferty; copyright ©
1965, 1970 by R. A. Lafferty. Reprinted by permission of
the author and his agent, Virginia Kidd.

"In Re Glover" by Leonard Tushnet; copyright © 1972
by Harlan Ellison. Originally appeared in *Again, Dangerous Visions*. Reprinted by permission of Fannie Tushnet.

These acknowledgments continued on facing page.

Library of Congress Cataloging in Publication Data

Main entry under title:

Bio-futures.

  Bibliography: p.
  CONTENTS: Wilhelm, K. The planners.—Lafferty, R.A.
Slow Tuesday night.—Tushnet, L. In re Glover. [etc.]
  1. Science fiction, American. I. Sargent, Pamela.
PZ1.B5   [PS648.S3]   813'.0876   75-39073
ISBN 0-394-71366-4

For Scott and Craig

CONTENTS

INTRODUCTION

PAMELA SARGENT

The chemical or physical inventor is always a Prometheus.
There is no great invention, from fire to flying, which has
not been hailed as an insult to some god. But if every
physical and chemical invention is a blasphemy, every
biological invention is a perversion.

> —J. B. S. Haldane, *Daedalus, or*
> *Science and the Future*

I

Joshua Lederberg, the noted geneticist, has written:
"Dilemmas about new knowledge, especially about our
own bodies, touch deep-rooted anxieties about man's
perception of himself." [1] The current pace of biological

---

[1] Joshua Lederberg, Foreword to Joseph Fletcher, *The Ethics of
Genetic Control: Ending Reproductive Roulette* (Garden City,
N.Y.: Doubleday Anchor Books, 1974), p. vi.

research suggests that we may soon have to alter our most fundamental beliefs about human life, human values, and human nature.

Developments in the physical sciences and the technologies that have grown out of them have made us question our relationship to nature. Biological innovations will undoubtedly raise even more basic questions about our presuppositions and values. In his book *The Ethics of Genetic Control*, Joseph Fletcher writes:

> At the same time, as we face up to our new powers, we should try to avoid two ethical errors that lurk near at hand. One is the capacity fallacy, the notion that because we can do something, such as genetic control, we ought to. It does not follow that because we can, we should. The other error is the necessity fallacy, the assumption of inevitability—that because we can do something we will.[2]

Even in an age during which the physical sciences have caused us to reexamine our relationship to the natural realm, we have remained fatalistic about certain biological facts. Mostly through hygienic measures and vaccination against infectious disease, we have extended the average human life span, but death remains a certainty. Children may have a chance of leading longer and healthier lives, but we have little control over the genetic diseases and disabilities they may inherit. Many of us still believe it is best not to meddle in the biological realm except for the purpose of treating or preventing illness or disability.

Unfortunately, for some, presuppositions take complete precedence over facts. One can, for example, view biological alteration as "unnatural," "wrong," or even

[2] Ibid., pp. 5–6.

"creepy," without examining either the facts or the reasons behind uneasy feelings. The facts, which do indeed present certain difficulties, also reveal many actual and potential benefits to be gained from biological developments. One cannot assume that because something can be misused, it will be misused.[3]

Discussions about biological innovations will of necessity involve conflicts among differing ethical systems. Objections to procedures such as abortion are often based on religious grounds. The presupposition here is that we are bound by a universal ethical law or by certain absolutes grounded in the existence of a Supreme Being who defines what is right for humanity. In the case of the Roman Catholic church, for example, a procedure designed to further "an end intended by nature" is allowed; a procedure which violates such an end is not. Abortion, therefore, is wrong; it is in fact considered murder on the additional ground that the fetus is believed to be a human being

---

[3] On this point, Fletcher writes:

We should note . . . that the . . . objection cuts both ways: If we refuse to do a thing which bears the possibility of abuse for fear we will find it easier and easier to tolerate the evil, then we will by the same token find it easier and easier to tolerate the loss of the good. If we will not pay a price or run a risk for the sake of making quality children we will soon be indifferent to their miseries. . . .

Hidden in this objection is a contempt for ordinary human beings, a belief that people have little or no value perception or capacity to discriminate. . . .

Actually this obstructionist device . . . has no place in standard works on philosophical ethics or moral theology. Yet it surfaces from time to time in the more conservative writers. Indeed, it is the quintessence of conservatism. . . . Prudence takes calculated risks in a trade-off spirit. It acts pragmatically for the sake of a proportionate good and does not flatly rule out all risks of undesired consequences regardless of the amount of good at stake. (Fletcher, pp. 33–45)

with a soul from the time of conception. Artificial insemination, however, is allowed if the husband is the donor of sperm. A person who adheres to a universal ethical system is not likely to give up opposition to various techniques unless he or she is persuaded that these procedures do not actually violate the code.

Another position is held by the French biologist Jean Rostand, who calls himself "vitalistic." Vitalism is based on the belief that life is caused and sustained by a vital principle that is distinct from chemical or physical forces. It is opposed to mechanism, which holds that life is entirely based on chemical and physical processes. Rostand does not espouse a system of absolutes. As he points out:

> We have seen that in some cases a total, inalterable respect for human life can lead to an impasse or a contradiction, and that in certain circumstances it can even result in advocating conduct that would be contrary to the true interests of human life. We have seen that even the most determined, intransigent vitalist must bring himself to make concessions when he is forced into the position of having to choose between two lives. . . .[4]

Yet having made that statement, Rostand goes on to say that respect for human life remains "the closest thing to an absolute in our civilization," [5] and worries that if, for instance, we allowed a life to end on the ground that it was not worth preserving, we would eventually reach the point of allowing only those who met certain standards to survive. This same objection

[4] Jean Rostand, *Humanly Possible*, translated by Lowell Blair (New York: Saturday Review Press, 1973), p. 88.
[5] Ibid., p. 89.

has been made to many possible biological advances.[6] This stance, although not absolutist, is similar to a position based on a universal ethical system. Rostand and those who believe as he does may allow for certain actions but wish us to understand that they are still wrong. This position is undoubtedly at the root of objections made by those who see in biological experimentation the erosion of ideas, principles, or feelings such as compassion that they have always valued.

Those who take what is termed a "utilitarian" approach to these issues will avoid certain problems but will also run into others. Traditionally, utilitarian philosophers have held that what maximizes pleasure for the greatest possible number of people is good, but have meant by the term "pleasure" that which promotes health, rationality, and social justice. The pursuit of physical pleasures, or a pure hedonism, can be seen as harmful in the long run if such pleasures are the only goal. The utilitarian will approve of a measure that benefits most people. Interpreted strictly, this means that a procedure harmful to a few might still be advocated, although many utilitarians have held that certain kinds of harm cannot be outweighed by any possible good result. Such an approach would also come into conflict with absolutist or vitalistic attitudes.

Another possible position, the "situational" ethical approach, is outlined by Joseph Fletcher. Here a person would be as informed as possible about the facts of a particular case and would reach a decision about what should be done based on those facts. This attitude is derived from naturalistic ethical systems, which have as an assumption that any workable ethical

[6] One possible reply to this objection has already been noted in footnote 3.

system must be based on the knowledge of certain
facts: what we are, what we can be, and what we can
do.[7] What we *should* do can vary from case to case. A
procedure such as cloning, for example, can be right
in one case and wrong in another. The situational approach is difficult in practice, since it requires that we
attempt to be well-informed and make difficult decisions which might be glossed over or avoided under
another system. It can also conflict with recommended
courses of action by those adhering to any of the previously mentioned systems of ethics.

These ethical questions will raise new legal problems
as well. The recent case of Karen Quinlan is an example of some of the difficulties we will face. Some feel
we should keep such issues out of the courts; that the
fate of Karen Quinlan should be decided by her doctors and that the law has no business stating either
that life must be prolonged by extraordinary means
or that it can be terminated in certain cases. But it
is not likely that people will refrain from using the
courts to resolve problems they cannot solve themselves.

Many of us, obviously, are not consistent in our beliefs and have mixed feelings about scientific advances
in general. Fletcher writes of those who "are ready to

[7] The traditional objection to naturalistic ethics has been that
one "cannot derive *ought* from *is*," that facts alone cannot tell
us how we should act. This objection oversimplifies the naturalistic approach. Aristotle, for example, believed that actions which
promote the exercise of one's rational faculties were "good"
because man's rationality is the quality that distinguishes him
from other forms of life. He believed also that the path between
extremes (termed "the golden mean") should be pursued,
though he admitted that in certain cases, one might have to
lean toward an extreme. These principles, although naturalistic
and derived from various observations, do involve certain value
judgments as well.

approve of the therapeutic uses of the new biology but oppose anything like genetic engineering or designing. They can find a moral defense for remedial treatments but not for constructive manipulations of the elemental genetic 'stuff' of a human being." [8] It is perhaps understandable that we should be fearful of biological advances in an age which has shown us some of the horrors the physical sciences can bring about—better to leave our biological selves alone. One should recall, however, that it is often those in power who decide how to use science and technology. Our apprehensions might better be directed toward what governments and various agencies might do, rather than toward the developments themselves. Even so, perhaps evolution should be allowed to take its course. Who knows what undesired consequences, possibly irreversible ones, uncontrolled biological research might help to bring about?

In spite of these feelings, many of us do retain an ambivalent attitude toward biological developments. There is an inconsistency in our assumptions. We will meddle—up to a point. Sterile people seek to bear children; pregnant women seek abortions. Some of those with genetic disabilities seek genetic counseling or make use of the technique of amniocentesis, an analysis of the embryonic fluid surrounding a fetus in the womb, which can reveal severe genetic defects. The transplantation of kidneys, hearts, and other organs is an accepted fact. Cosmetic surgery is almost commonplace among those who can afford it. Arti-

[8] Fletcher, p. 82. This position is not unlike a typically American approach to the practice of medicine, where a great deal of attention is paid to techniques for curing ailments and less is paid to prevention. The attitude is, however, probably derived from a belief that the "end nature intended" should be aided rather than altered.

ficial replacements for damaged limbs and joints have helped many. Almost no one wishes to return to a situation in which nature alone decides our biological destiny.

Even so, we have come to accept our bodies, with relatively minor alterations, as constants. Thus we are apt to view biological changes, in the words of J. B. S. Haldane, as "perversions." [9] Most of our institutions are based on certain facts which we have taken for granted. If we live long enough, then we shall age. Many if not most of us bear certain genetic traits about which we can do little. Women, not men, have always borne children. Our appearance and body type can be altered only up to a point. We shall all die. Anything which challenges existing institutions can be seen as threatening. Developments which challenge such basic assumptions will be feared, especially if people believe that they have little control over such developments.

Unless we deliberately turn our backs on biological innovation or restrict research, biological advances will change our institutions and our attitudes. We may lose experiences that have value, but we may also gain

[9] Perhaps we should not view our human nature and form as being quite so sacrosanct. R. C. W. Ettinger points out that "it should be clear . . . man is an accident, not only his body but his psyche a patchwork of makeshift adaptive compromises. His attributes do not fit any apparent grand design or rational blueprint, but represent only the current, tentative result of the endless tugging and hauling of evolutionary forces, including random elements and self-contradictions." Having offered some examples of these characteristics, Ettinger concludes that "man . . . can be considered only a beginning and a dubious compromise, in both mind and body. In the course of 'natural' development, he might or might not eventually attain a higher and more harmonious state; but the race cannot depend on that, and the individual cannot wait for it. We must remake ourselves. . . ." (R. C. W. Ettinger, Man Into Superman, New York: St. Martin's Press, 1972, pp. 21–22)

others of equal or greater value. Some institutions may crumble; others may be strengthened. The bond between parent and child, for instance, could become stronger through the employment of biological techniques. Those who wish to have children but are sterile or have a genetic problem could be aided. Those who do not want children could make use of safer and more reliable contraceptive methods than we now have. Children would be the result of conscious desire and planning and consequently might be valued more intelligently by their parents.

What is the extent of possible biological change? It can involve new ways of reproducing ourselves, a use of techniques such as cloning, ectogenesis (the use of an artificial womb), in vitro or "test-tube" fertilization, hybridization of animal species and humans, and others. Other possibilities are somatic alteration (a change in a grown person's biological construction) and genetic manipulation, thus eliminating the "reproductive roulette" which at present leaves us little control over what we and our children will be. Research into the mechanism of aging and an understanding of how and why it takes place could lead to an extension of the human life span. Work in cryonics (the freezing of tissues and organs) might enable us to preserve a seriously ill person until he or she could be treated. A more speculative possibility is that people now alive might be frozen and revived in a future where immortality is a reality. Immortality itself, or a greatly extended life span, may be realized in the future. Biological change could in time affect our notions of what a human being *is*. We could become many different and divergent species, each designed for different tasks.

Or we could all transcend our present limitations

and have a variety of options open to each of us. Perhaps a human being is an intelligent creature who has the plasticity to transcend himself or herself constantly, combined with an open projective nature that is conscious of itself. Because we have the ability to change ourselves, we are capable of *participant evolution*.[10]

II

The treatment of biological change shown in science fiction describes a line of development that moves from individual cases and accidents to a view of a future in which biological change is normal and creative. This suggests the analogy of evolution, in which sports or mutations appear, most fail, and viable organisms survive as a common occurrence. As far as science fiction is concerned, we are talking about both the evolution of ideas (some of which are sports and do not survive) and the larger reality of biological innovation. Most readers of science fiction have come to accept the idea of biological change, suggesting that wider public acceptance is a possible line of development. Science fiction has warned us of the dangers of such change and at the same time legitimized the concept.

One common theme of the biological sf story and of science fiction in general is that of the lone scientist who uses a particular discovery for his or her own purposes. Mary Shelley's *Frankenstein* (1814) set the pattern for this type of story; the legend of Faust provided a model as well. Shelley's scientist succeeds in

---

[10] The term "participant evolution" was coined by Manfred Clynes and Nathan S. Kline in an article, "Cyborgs and Space," published in *Astronautics*, September 1960.

his work, but his accomplishment also brings him to a bad end.

This type of story can be used by the science fiction writer to introduce a new idea. In later stories, a group of scientists, rather than a lone researcher, is sometimes shown, thus reflecting the realities of much current research. The effect of the biological development on society is viewed conservatively; these stories are often dubious about the possible results of a discovery or a new technique. Instead, the emphasis is on the development itself and the scientific or pseudo-scientific ideas used to support the central idea, as well as the use to which the central character will put the technique.

H. G. Wells's *The Island of Dr. Moreau* (1896) is a fine example of this theme. Moreau, who lives on an isolated island, experiments with animals, giving them human forms and habits. He dies at the hands of one of his creations, and the animals quickly revert to their bestial ways. In the novel, human civilization is seen as a veneer which cloaks our animal instincts. Wells, who called this work "a youthful exercise in blasphemy," was expressing his doubts about humanity's ability to change its own nature.

Waldemar Kaempffert's "The Diminishing Draft" (1918) shows us a scientist who uses his discovery, a potion which will shrink and solidify a person who can then be restored to life by submersion in water, in order to arrange meetings with his mistress. When his wife discovers this technique, she uses it to destroy the woman her husband loves. In Donald Wandrei's "A Scientist Divides" (1934), a man experimenting with mitosis begins to undergo the process himself. In Stanley G. Weinbaum's "Proteus Island" (1936), a geneticist's manipulations on a small island result in a complete differentiation of individual animals and plants; no two living things on the island are of the same species. The implication of such stories is that the scientist is too concerned with his personal reasons for doing research, and this contributes to his downfall. This implies that an excessive concern with the personal can be socially harmful. These stories prefigure current debates about the impact of biology on society and the scientist's responsibility to others.[11]

Stories of the lone scientist display another interesting similarity. At their conclusions, the scientist's work is destroyed, and the world in most cases returns to normal. This serves the purpose of assuring the reader that the story is an imaginative exercise that never really happened, while asserting that some things are better left alone. If the reader cares to do so, he or she can then dismiss the disturbing, "perverted" biological technique. In his novel *Gladiator* (1930), Philip Wylie even has his hero, Hugo Danner, struck by lightning at the end of the book. Hugo, who has superhuman strength, is the product of his biologist father's research. The story begins by using the lone scientist theme; in its treatment of Hugo's difficulties with normal humans, however, it resembles stories about mutants.

The theme of the mutant has been explored by

[11] We should also consider the image of the scientist projected by such works. Historically, the labors of the scientist and technologist have been misused by those in power rather than by scientists themselves. Often the scientist has little control over how his or her work will be used. This should be kept in mind even when justifiable criticism, much of it made by scientists themselves, is leveled at those who ignore the possible consequences of their research. Julian Huxley's story "The Tissue-Culture King" (1927), in which a biologist's work aids an African theocracy, presents some of these issues in a satirical and clever way.

many science fiction writers. The mutant is an accidental by-product of circumstances, either a "sport" of nature or the inadvertent result of human actions (such as a nuclear war). Often the mutant has superhuman abilities. He or she can become an outcast or can be shown as benevolent in spite of these abilities.

In Olaf Stapledon's novel *Odd John* (1935), John and his fellow mutants are seen as a threat. In *Re-Birth* by John Wyndham (1955), the mutants must keep their telepathic abilities a secret. The other members of their post-holocaust world fear even minor mutations, such as extra fingers or toes. Wilmar Shiras's *Children of the Atom* (1953) is a moving novel about a group of brilliant mutant children whose parents were exposed to radiation during an accident at an atomic energy plant. Shiras presents several problems facing these children, among them the question of whether the children should develop their genius apart from society or live among normal children. Theodore Sturgeon's "Maturity" (1947) shows us a mutant during his adolescent phase. The emotional problems his abilities create for him and for others are vividly presented.

Often a mutant story will depict the fear we have of those unlike ourselves. Many such stories also make a plea for understanding such differences. In Stapledon's *Odd John*, in which the mutants are wiped out by humans who are afraid that the superhumans may replace our own species, one still feels sympathy for the outcasts. Stories about mutants, in contrast to those about the lone scientist, often are concerned with the societal and personal consequences of these biological differences. They can present some of the issues that might face those produced by deliberate biological innovations.

Other stories and novels deal with change that is consciously planned and that affects the society as a whole. Alternate modes of reproduction have been a concern of science fiction for some time. Aldous Huxley's *Brave New World* (1932) describes a society in which the breeding of specialized types of humans is combined with artificial gestation. Huxley may have helped set the tone for later works discussing these topics. His characters, members of a hedonistic yet controlled society, are vapid and dehumanized. To them, the very idea of "normal" reproduction is an obscene joke.

There is, however, no inherent reason for assuming that alternate modes of reproduction will be dehumanizing. It would of course be wrong to force these techniques on people, just as it is wrong to coerce women into bearing children which they may not want. One example of a more optimistic treatment of future child-bearing can be found in Robert A. Heinlein's *Podkayne of Mars* (1963). In this novel, women bear their children in youth. The infants are then frozen cryonically. They are revived when their parents, having established themselves in their careers, have the time to raise them. Except for a few errors, one of which involves the heroine's mother whose three children are revived at one time by mistake, the system seems to work relatively well.[12]

[12] Stories of overpopulation, in which we reproduce ourselves excessively in the normal fashion, may be considered a branch of biological science fiction. An overpopulated world serves as the background for Walter M. Miller's "Conditionally Human" (1952) and Isaac Asimov's *The Caves of Steel* (1953). "Billenium" (1960) by J. G. Ballard shows us a world so crowded that the protagonist, upon discovering a small empty room behind one of his walls, thinks of the room as almost unimaginably spacious. More recent works include Harry Harrison's *Make Room! Make Room!* (1966), in which a future New York City resembling Calcutta is shown; Robert Silverberg's *The World*

One possible means of reproduction, cloning, has often been dealt with pessimistically. Even in works where cloning is not the central theme, the writer often assumes that clones would act almost as one person, that others would treat them as interchangeable parts, or that in fact there would be no difference between them. In Kate Wilhelm's novel *Where Late the Sweet Birds Sang* (1976), an interesting and original picture of a possible clone society is presented. These clones are the descendants of a large family, the Sumners. In the aftermath of a world-wide ecological disaster, the Sumners had discovered that, with few exceptions, they were sterile. Reproduction by cloning was their one option. The mores, customs, and relationships among the various clonal groups are vividly portrayed. But the author feels that such a society is ultimately not viable.

Stories of medical cures and techniques have produced both humorous and gloomy fiction. One of the humorous stories is Alan E. Nourse's "The Coffin Cure" (1951) in which a new vaccine cures the common cold but has the side effect of improving one's sense of smell to the point where everyday odors become unbearable. Larry Niven's "The Jigsaw Man" (1967) is a grim view of a world in which organ transplants have become commonplace. The need for organs has brought about a society which has a death

---

Inside (1971), in which each person spends his or her entire life inside a tall urban "monad" and is encouraged to have many children; and John Brunner's *Stand on Zanzibar* (1968). Usually the overpopulated world is seen as an extremely unpleasant place; Asimov's *The Caves of Steel* may be an exception. Asimov's crowded world seems almost homey; his characters have adapted to it, have developed various customs for the preservation of their privacy, and seem relatively comfortable in their large cities. It is obvious that a confirmed city dweller wrote the novel.

penalty for reckless driving. A vast criminal establishment deals in organs acquired by murder. Brain surgery is another technique often presented pessimistically. In Michael Crichton's *The Terminal Man* (1972), an epileptic's condition is worsened by an electronic implant meant to control his seizures.[13] Distrust of the medical profession is often an undercurrent in such stories.

The possibility of genetic engineering has also been the cause of some depressing speculations. Vonda N. McIntyre's "The Genius Freaks" (1973), a moving story about a young girl whose genius is a product of genetic alteration, shows us an unhappy outcast. Damon Knight's "The Country of the Kind" (1955) describes a society of gentle people. Traits such as aggressiveness and hostility have been bred out. Yet the main character, a throwback who is sociopathic and cruel, is the only member of his society able to produce great art. C. M. Kornbluth's "The Marching Morons" (1951), on the other hand, is a bleak, sardonic view of a world where there have been no genetic controls. In his story, Kornbluth assumes that if less intelligent people breed in greater numbers than the more intelligent, the inhabitants of a future world will be near-morons. Although Kornbluth's premise is far from certain, recent research on the effects of malnutrition on intelligence during infancy raises the possibility that his future could come to pass as a result of environmental influences.

Other stories, particularly those about the possible

[13] A related theme is that of the cyborg, a person who is part human and part machine. This concept is the subject of an anthology of stories, *Human-Machines: The Cyborg in Science Fiction*, edited by Thomas N. Scortia and George Zebrowski (Vintage, 1975).

consequences of genetic engineering in the far future, have presented a different picture. Of particular interest is James Blish's "pantropy" series, a group of stories published in book form as *The Seedling Stars* (1957). Blish assumes that we may wish to settle other worlds on which we could not live in our present form. His characters, who have been created through genetic alteration and are the descendants of humans, belong to different species. In Olaf Stapledon's *Last and First Men* (1930), a work which covers hundreds of thousands of years of humanity's possible future, humans are transformed into many different physical types. *A Torrent of Faces* (1967) by James Blish and Norman L. Knight, a novel set against the background of an overpopulated world, describes altered people capable of living in the oceans.

A related topic is covered in stories that deal with the alteration of other forms of life. In Robert A. Heinlein's "Jerry Was a Man" (1947), a court must decide if an intelligent, genetically altered chimpanzee should be granted the rights of a human citizen. In "Conditionally Human" (1952) by Walter M. Miller, Jr., an overpopulated world is shown in which only a few are given permission to reproduce. Other couples can adopt artificially created beings called "neutroids." The neutroids mimic the behavior of human infants, but remain immature and unintelligent. It is discovered, however, that some of these beings are in fact intelligent and will grow to maturity. In Cordwainer Smith's *Nostrilia* (1975), as well as in stories by this author, several of the characters are beings with human appearances who are the descendants of dogs, cats, cattle, and other animals. These beings, called "under-people," are intelligent but do not have the rights accorded humans.

In the case of altered people, we might ask if such changed beings are still human. If another form of life is altered or a new form created, we might ask if such a being should be treated as a human. Science fiction, which has often dealt sympathetically with alien characters, is inclined to display the notion that any form of life which shows intelligence, rationality, and ethical concerns is essentially "human." In fact, in James Blish's "Seeding Program," a part of his pantropy series, those who have our familiar form are more inhumane than the sympathetically drawn altered people of Ganymede, Jupiter's moon.

There is also, however, a body of work in which such notions are regarded more skeptically. If we alter ourselves biologically, then it follows that our minds, perceptions, and values may also change. In Theodore Sturgeon's *Venus Plus X* (1960), a man of our time finds himself in the future, where he discovers a single-sexed culture. The man is repelled when he learns that these people, descendants of humans, have voluntarily made themselves hermaphrodites. In Damon Knight's "Masks" (1968), a man whose brain is encased in a mechanical body becomes alienated from other people. It is simple-minded to assume that changed people would be either completely malevolent or basically just like us.

It sometimes seems as though stories dealing with this topic and the near future are more grim and fearful than those set comfortably in a distant time. It is as if we can understand the problem of altered humans quite rationally—unless it hits too close to home. On the other hand, it is natural that a writer concerned with the near future will tend to concentrate on possible problems, since he or she will be setting the story in a period of transition. Stories of the near future are also often meant as warnings to the present-day reader. They may therefore focus on pessimistic possibilities.

A story set in the far future can be more speculative. We would not expect the characters in such a story to feel about things exactly the way we do, any more than we would expect a contemporary to hold beliefs common among ancient Egyptians. We can therefore understand why a character in a far-future story would accept biological change or choose to be an altered person. By reading about such a fictional character, we might even free ourselves of some of the attitudes imposed on us by our own temporal provincialism.[14]

Immortality, an age-old dream, has been the subject of a variety of stories. In keeping with our cultural traditions, and perhaps with certain postulated evolutionary mechanisms for the acceptance of death built into all living things, the prospect of immortality has been regarded fearfully by many writers. It is often asserted that the immortal person would of necessity become bored or might seek to cling to life regardless of the consequences to others.

One of the few humorous treatments of this theme is "The Big Trip Up Yonder" (1954) by Kurt Vonnegut, Jr., in which an old grandfather, to the dismay of his family, insists on postponing the day of his death, an option in his society. Damon Knight's "Dio" (1957) shows us a man who begins to age in a world where everyone is youthful and immortal. The price these people have paid for their longevity is that they remain in an adolescent state. Clifford Simak's "Eter-

[14] The noted sf author Arthur C. Clarke has written: "Pope's aphorism gave only part of the truth, for the proper study of mankind is not merely Man, but Intelligence" (Arthur C. Clarke, *The Promise of Space*, New York: Harper & Row, 1968, p. 307). Clarke was discussing the possibility of life on other planets, but his dictum could also be applied to the idea of biological change.

nity Lost" (1950) shows us a senator running for reelection in a society where the powerful control the secret of immortality. If the man loses the election, he will also lose extended life, as he will no longer be needed. Kate Wilhelm, in "April Fool's Day Forever" (1970), hypothesizes that immortal people might be cut off from humankind's collective unconscious.

Any discussion of immortality will involve two essentially different attitudes. One may view immortality as merely "extended old age." This can apply even to stories peopled by characters who remain physically youthful if the characters get bored, apathetic, childish, or set in their ways. On the other hand, one can take a creative, open view of extended life. Here immortality can be seen as opening up new experiences. The immortal might be a person who will have the time to change, grow, and explore many things.

Which of these attitudes one holds will depend in part upon whether one thinks of death as a prod which forces us to achieve as much as we can in this life, or as an inevitable restriction which limits our accomplishments. One's view may also be determined by one's feelings about old age. Relatively little gerontological research has been done, so we do not know how many of our opinions about old age and old people are the result of the perceived physiological effects of aging, and how many are caused by our own societal attitudes toward the elderly. Many old people remain healthy, vigorous, and alert. They engage in activities for which they previously had little time. A change in our feelings about the old could mean a different attitude toward extended life.

Often a biological idea, although central to a particular piece, may be used symbolically or metaphorically. The concern of such a story is not with a realistic development of the idea, even in cases where known scientific facts are not violated. Two important and successful examples of such a story are Gene Wolfe's "The Fifth Head of Cerberus" (1972) and Robert Silverberg's "Born With the Dead" (1974). The protagonist of Wolfe's story is a boy who is a clone of his father. Silverberg shows us a society of people who have died and been revived. The biological ideas used are necessary parts of each story. Yet neither is really *about* these biological themes.

III

There is of course nothing wrong with using biological ideas symbolically and metaphorically. Much of the best science fiction has been written this way. A fine realistic piece will also have levels and meanings beyond simply a development of its ideas. A story about clones, for example, will almost inevitably concern itself with the theme of identity.

Many authors shy away from concentrating on the realistic treatment of an idea for various reasons. Some prefer to use scientific notions and props to enrich a story which is actually concerned with present-day issues and problems. Others believe that the non-realistic work is aesthetically more pleasing than the realistic one. Still others feel that science fiction writers should direct their efforts to evoking the experience of transcendence by concentrating on the fantastic.[15] It is important to remember that authors belong to their time. The future can only be mimicked or imagined, not produced.

There is nothing inherently wrong with using fanciful biological ideas. The rich and detailed background

[15] This particular approach has been developed by the sf writers and critics Alexei and Cory Panshin in a series of essays written for *Amazing* magazine.

in the works of Cordwainer Smith is an example of the successful use of highly imaginative ideas. Even if an idea is scientifically dubious, the author's treatment of the theme can serve to illuminate possible issues, as well as human reactions to the forms of scientific discoveries and possible future changes.

There is also the possibility that the imaginative idea may in time not be quite so fanciful. This may be true some day of immortality. It is certainly true of organ transplantation and parts replacement. A flight of fancy, as long as it does not capriciously violate known science, may turn out to be closer to future realities than a straightforwardly realistic depiction that is limited by what we know today.

James Blish, in commenting on the role of science in science fiction, has written:

> In my opinion . . . it is the duty of the conscientious science fiction writer not to falsify what he believes to be known fact. It is an even more important function for him to suggest new paradigms, by suggesting to the reader, over and over again, that X, Y, and Z are not impossible. Every time a story appears with a faster-than-light drive, it expresses somebody's faith . . . that such a thing is accomplishable, and some day will be accomplished. . . . It seems to me that the most important scientific content in modern science fiction is the impossibilities.[16]

As Blish makes clear, his conclusion should not be used as an excuse for ignoring known scientific theory and fact. The science fiction writer must mimic the creative cutting edge of scientific speculation. Better still, he or she should be able to speculate seriously in the manner of the scientist, but without the scien-

[16] James Blish, "The Science in Science Fiction," in Vector 69, The Journal of the British Science Fiction Association, Summer 1975, p. 10.

tist's empirical restrictions, which are those of evidence and empirical proof. The science fiction writer is bound only by the consistency of his or her hypotheses.

The well-known author Isaac Asimov has said that *science fiction is a literature which deals with the human response to changes in science and technology. It is realistic fiction in the sense that future changes in science and technology are connected to the present changes in these areas.* Present-day knowledge can serve as a platform from which the writer can take off in a speculative flight. It can enrich the story by giving it more than a purely imaginative function; the projected impossibility can be presented in the guise of a real innovation, which it may be.[17]

---

[17] Generally a pattern, although not necessarily a chronological one, can be discerned in science fictional works about a particular idea. Take, for example, the theme of cloning. Novels such as the excellent *Rogue Moon* (1960) by Algis Budrys, *A for Anything* (1959) by Damon Knight, *Four-Sided Triangle* (1951) by William F. Temple, and *The Duplicated Man* (1959) by Robert W. Lowndes and James Blish, although not about cloning, suggest it through their use of the notion of duplicated human beings. Fritz Leiber's "Yesterday House" (1952) is about a man who replaces his lost love by using parthenogenesis, or stimulation of the dead woman's ovum, thus producing a child genetically identical to her mother. Although the term "cloning" is never used, the technique shown in Leiber's story is similar to it. Damon Knight's "Mary" (1964) shows us a society divided into clans of specialized people. Knight nowhere calls these clans of identical people clones, although we can assume that they are. Leiber's story focuses on a new scientific idea; Knight's concentrates on telling a love story within the context of a strange future society which could be the result of human duplication on a wide scale. Ursula K. Le Guin's "Nine Lives" (1969) is a more realistic story than either. Le Guin deals with the possible reasons for cloning and how cloned people might be viewed by others. Clones have since become common currency. They have been used as details in works as different as Joe Haldeman's *The Forever War* (1974) and Woody Allen's film *Sleeper* (1973).

Science fiction on biological themes, then, has often taken a grim view of these ideas. It is true that a pessimistic story will often have more dramatic impact than a positively oriented one. Many writers have used *Frankenstein* as a model, toyed with an unusual or original idea, and then ended with the notion that such tampering with nature's plan would destroy the tamperer. Thus the use of a biological idea, and other ideas as well, can often become a prop in a horror story. Societal consequences, if any, are either viewed negatively or are ignored.

Writers who do concern themselves with these consequences may remain cynical or pessimistic about human beings. Distrustful of those who hold power in particular, these writers may assume that almost any discovery will be perverted or misused. To a degree, they may be right. But a study of history will show that many biological developments, once feared, have also improved our lives; vaccination against infectious disease is only one such example. A crucial distinction is not aways drawn in such works. One can too easily go from depicting a misuse of a technique to concluding that the technique itself is wrong or evil.

Another problem with much science fiction on biological themes is a tendency to derive ideas from other science fictional works instead of from the research and speculation of scientists. A related problem involves writers who may use a new idea to dress up an old sf plot. However interesting such stories may be, the result is that either interesting ideas remain unused, or new ones, and their possibly far-reaching implications, are not explored.

In spite of the amount and variety of science fiction on biological themes, there is still much to be done.

Many nonfictional works, such as Gordon Rattray Taylor's well-known *The Biological Time Bomb*, are as speculative as some science fiction. The pace of biological research and its results can suggest many new avenues of thought not dealt with previously. The interface between biological research and society can be explored in more detail. We can speculate about our possible biological limitations and how these may be discovered. We can consider the biological tools we might use to overcome these limitations. Such ideas can bring about science fictional works that will be truly innovative, uniquely unlike each other, rather than belonging to the formulas of genre fiction.

This anthology shows some of the best of what has been done in the past, and suggests new areas of exploration. Each story illustrates particular biological ideas and depicts their possible effects.

BIO-FUTURES

THE PLANNERS

KATE WILHELM

For my part, I believe that there is no life so degraded,
deteriorated, debased, or impoverished that it does not
deserve respect and is not worth defending with zeal and
conviction.

—Jean Rostand, *Humanly Possible* *

*Any discussion of biological research must consider its
ethics. Recent public disclosures have presented the issue
forcefully. The Central Intelligence Agency and the U.S.
Army have tested the effects of various drugs on unwitting subjects; the Tuskegee syphilis study, which involved withholding treatment from victims of the disease
in order to trace its effects, was clearly unethical. Experimental subjects are supposed to be informed of possible
risks and are not to be coerced into giving their consent.*

* New York: Saturday Review Press, 1973, p. 89.

Yet mentally retarded children and adults have been used
as subjects, and the quality of the consent obtained from
convicts used in experiments is questionable. In at least
four experiments cited by Robert M. Veatch and Shar-
mon Sollitto in the June 1973 Report of the Institute of
Society, Ethics and the Life Sciences (in Hastings-on-
Hudson, New York), subjects were not even told that
they were part of an experiment.

Biological experimentation raises many questions. Have
the subjects given their informed consent? Are the possible risks to subjects outweighed by the potential benefits of a new discovery? Is the experiment a useless duplication of previous efforts? What is the purpose of the
research? Objections to various experimental procedures
have been made by assorted groups for different reasons.
When the film Primate was shown on public television,
several viewers were upset by what they saw as needless
cruelty to apes used as subjects by the Yerkes research
center. The purposes and possible benefits of the research,
however, were not shown in the film. Other groups, particularly those who believe abortion is wrong, have objected to fetal research; yet such work might aid infants
in the future. Some might object to biological research
by the military, but work funded by the armed forces has
helped defeat yellow fever and given us penicillin.

Some scientists, concerned about the effects of certain
experiments, have sought to regulate themselves. An inter-
national conference of molecular biologists, meeting at
Asilomar in California at the beginning of 1975, set up
guidelines limiting or banning experiments involving
techniques for transplanting genetic information from one
unrelated organism to another. A self-imposed moratorium
had been in effect in the United States since the summer
of 1974. The transplantation of genes could be beneficial; in time, defective genes could be replaced with
working ones which would cure or prevent disease. But
such work could also result in biological warfare agents or
an accidental epidemic.

Where do we draw the line? What is allowable and what is not? Darin, the scientist in Kate Wilhelm's story, is suffering doubts about his work, its effects on his subjects, and its purposes.

Rae stopped before the one-way glass, stooped and peered at the gibbon infant in the cage. Darin watched her bitterly. She straightened after a moment, hands in smock pockets, face innocent of any expression what-so-goddam-ever, and continued to saunter toward him through the aisle between the cages.

"You still think it is cruel, and worthless?"

"Do you, Dr. Darin?"

"Why do you always do that? Answer my question with one of your own?"

"Does it infuriate you?"

He shrugged and turned away. His lab coat was on the chair where he had tossed it. He pulled it on over his sky-blue sport shirt.

"How is the Driscoll boy?" Rae asked.

He stiffened, then relaxed again. Still not facing her, he said, "Same as last week, last year. Same as he'll be until he dies."

The hall door opened and a very large, very homely face appeared. Stu Evers looked past Darin, down the aisle. "You alone? Thought I heard voices."

"Talking to myself," Darin said. "The committee ready yet?"

"Just about. Dr. Jacobsen is stalling with his nose-throat spray routine, as usual." He hesitated a moment, glancing again down the row of cages, then at Darin. "Wouldn't you think a guy allergic to monkeys would find some other line of research?"

Darin looked, but Rae was gone. What had it been this time: the Driscoll boy, the trend of the project itself? He wondered if she had a life of her own when

5

she was away. "I'll be out at the compound," he said.
He passed Stu in the doorway and headed toward the
livid greenery of Florida forests.

The cacophony hit him at the door. There were four
hundred sixty-nine monkeys on the thirty-six acres of
wooded ground the research department was using.
Each monkey was screeching, howling, singing, curs-
ing, or otherwise making its presence known. Darin
grunted and headed toward the compound. THE HAP-
PIEST MONKEYS IN THE WORLD, a newspaper article
had called them. Singing Monkeys, a subhead announced. MONKEYS GIVEN SMARTNESS PILLS, the most
enterprising paper had proclaimed. CRUELTY CHARGED,
added another in subdued, sorrowful tones.

The compound was three acres of carefully planned
and maintained wilderness, completely enclosed with
thirty-foot-high, smooth plastic walls. A transparent
dome covered the area. There were one-way windows
at intervals along the wall. A small group stood before
one of the windows: the committee.

Darin stopped and gazed over the interior of the
compound through one of the windows. He saw
Heloise and Skitter contentedly picking nonexistent
fleas from one another. Adam was munching on a
banana; Homer was lying on his back idly touching his
feet to his nose. A couple of the chimps were at the
water fountain, not drinking, merely pressing the
pedal and watching the fountain, now and then im-
mersing a head or hand in the bowl of cold water. Dr.
Jacobsen appeared and Darin joined the group.

"Good morning, Mrs. Bellbottom," Darin said politely. "Did you know your skirt has fallen off?" He
turned from her to Major Dormouse. "Ah, Major, and
how many of the enemy have you swatted to death
today with your pretty little yellow rag?" He smiled
pleasantly at a pimply young man with a camera.

"Major, you've brought a professional peeping tom. More stories in the paper, with pictures this time?" The pimply young man shifted his position, fidgeted with the camera. The major was fiery; Mrs. Bellbottom was on her knees peering under a bush, looking for her skirt. Darin blinked. None of them had on any clothing. He turned toward the window. The chimps were drawing up a table, laden with tea things, silver, china, tiny finger sandwiches. The chimps were all wearing flowered shirts and dresses. Hortense had on a ridiculous flop-brimmed sun hat of pale green straw. Darin leaned against the fence to control his laughter.

"Soluble ribonucleic acid," Dr. Johnson was saying when Darin recovered, "sRNA for short. So from the gross beginnings when entire worms were trained and fed to other worms that seemed to benefit from the original training, we have come to these more refined methods. We now extract the sRNA molecule from the trained animals and feed it, the sRNA molecules in solution, to untrained specimens and observe the results."

The young man was snapping pictures as Jacobsen talked. Mrs. Whoosis was making notes, her mouth a lipless line, the sun hat tinging her skin with green. The sun on her patterned red and yellow dress made it appear to jiggle, giving her fleshy hips a constant rippling motion. Darin watched, fascinated. She was about sixty.

". . . my colleague, who proposed this line of experimentation, Dr. Darin," Jacobsen said finally, and Darin bowed slightly. He wondered what Jacobsen had said about him, decided to wait for any questions before he said anything.

"Dr. Darin, is it true that you also extract this substance from people?"

"Every time you scratch yourself, you lose this substance," Darin said. "Every time you lose a drop of blood, you lose it. It is in every cell of your body. Sometimes we take a sample of human blood for study, yes."

"And inject it into those animals?"

"Sometimes we do that," Darin said. He waited for the next, the inevitable question, wondering how he would answer it. Jacobsen had briefed them on what to answer, but he couldn't remember what Jacobsen had said. The question didn't come. Mrs. Whoosis stepped forward, staring at the window.

Darin turned his attention to her; she averted her eyes, quickly fixed her stare again on the chimps in the compound. "Yes, Mrs. uh . . . Ma'am?" Darin prompted her. She didn't look at him.

"Why? What is the purpose of all this?" she asked. Her voice sounded strangled. The pimpled young man was inching toward the next window.

"Well," Darin said, "our theory is simple. We believe that learning ability can be improved drastically in nearly every species. The learning curve is the normal, expected bell-shaped curve, with a few at one end who have the ability to learn quite rapidly, with the majority in the center who learn at an average rate, and a few at the other end who learn quite slowly. With our experiments we are able to increase the ability of those in the broad middle, as well as those in the deficient end of the curve so that their learning abilities match those of the fastest learners of any given group. . . ."

No one was listening to him. It didn't matter. They would be given the press release he had prepared for them, written in simple language, no polysyllables, no complicated sentences. They were all watching the chimps through the windows. He said, "So we gabbled the gazooka three times wretchedly until the spirit of camping fired the girls." One of the committee members glanced at him. "Whether intravenously or orally, it seems to be equally effective," Darin said, and the perspiring man turned again to the window. "Injections every morning . . . rejections, planned diet, planned parenthood, planned plans planning plans." Jacobsen eyed him suspiciously. Darin stopped talking and lighted a cigarette. The woman with the unquiet hips turned from the window, her face very red. "I've seen enough," she said. "This sun is too hot out here. May we see the inside laboratories now?"

Darin turned them over to Stu Evers inside the building. He walked back slowly to the compound. There was a grin on his lips when he spotted Adam on the far side, swaggering triumphantly, paying no attention to Hortense who was rocking back and forth on her haunches, looking very dazed. Darin saluted Adam, then, whistling, returned to his office. Mrs. Driscoll was due with Sonny at 1 P.M.

Sonny Driscoll was fourteen. He was five feet nine inches, weighed one hundred sixty pounds. His male nurse was six feet two inches and weighed two hundred twenty-seven pounds. Sonny had broken his mother's arm when he was twelve; he had broken his father's arm and leg when he was thirteen. So far the male nurse was intact. Every morning Mrs. Driscoll lovingly washed and dressed her baby, fed him, walked him in the yard, spoke happily to him of plans for the coming months, or sang nursery songs to him. He never seemed to see her. The male nurse, Johnny, was never farther than three feet from his charge when he was on duty.

Mrs. Driscoll refused to think of the day when she would have to turn her child over to an institution. Instead she placed her faith and hope in Darin.

They arrived at two-fifteen, earlier than he had expected them, later than they had promised to be there.

"The kid kept taking his clothes off," Johnny said morosely. The kid was taking them off again in the office. Johnny started toward him, but Darin shook his head. It didn't matter. Darin got his blood sample from one of the muscular arms, shot the injection into the other one. Sonny didn't seem to notice what he was doing. He never seemed to notice. Sonny refused to be tested. They got him to the chair and table, but he sat staring at nothing, ignoring the blocks, the bright balls, the crayons, the candy. Nothing Darin did or said had any discernible effect. Finally the time was up. Mrs. Driscoll thanked Darin for helping her boy.

Stu and Darin held class from four to five daily. Kelly O'Grady had the monkeys tagged and ready for them when they showed up at the schoolroom. Kelly was very tall, very slender, and red-haired. Stu shivered if she accidentally brushed him in passing; Darin hoped one day Stu would pull an Adam on her. She sat primly on her high stool with her notebook on her knee, unaware of the change that came over Stu during school hours, or, if aware, uncaring. Darin wondered if she was really a Barbie doll fully programmed to perform laboratory duties, and nothing else.

He thought of the Finishing School for Barbies where long-legged, high-breasted, stomachless girls went to get shaved clean, get their toenails painted pink, their nipples removed, and all body openings sewn shut, except for their mouths, which curved in perpetual smiles and led nowhere.

The class consisted of six black spider-monkeys who had not been fed yet. They had to do six tasks in order: 1) pull a rope; 2) cross the cage and get a stick that was released by the rope; 3) pull the rope again;

4) get the second stick that would fit into the first;
5) join the sticks together; 6) using the lengthened
stick, pull a bunch of bananas close enough to the bars
of the cage to reach them and take them inside where
they could eat them. At five the monkeys were returned
to Kelly, who wheeled them away one by one back to
the stockroom. None of them had performed all the
tasks, although two had gone through part of them
before the time ran out.

Waiting for the last of the monkeys to be taken back
to its quarters, Stu asked, "What did you do to that
bunch of idiots this morning? By the time I got them,
they all acted dazed."

Darin told him about Adam's performance; they
were both laughing when Kelly returned. Stu's laugh
turned to something that sounded almost like a sob.
Darin wanted to tell him about the school Kelly must
have attended, thought better of it, and walked away
instead.

His drive home was through the darkening forests
of interior Florida for sixteen miles on a narrow straight
road.

"Of course, I don't mind living here," Lea had said
once, nine years ago when the Florida appointment
had come through. And she didn't mind. The house
was air-conditioned; the family car, Lea's car, was air-
conditioned; the back yard had a swimming pool big
enough to float the Queen Mary. A frightened, large-
eyed Florida girl did the housework, and Lea gained
weight and painted sporadically, wrote sporadically—
poetry—and entertained faculty wives regularly. Darin
suspected that sometimes she entertained faculty hus-
bands also.

"Oh, Professor Dimples, one hour this evening?
That will be fifteen dollars, you know." He jotted

down the appointment and turned to Lea. "Just two more today and you will have your car payment. How about that!" She twined slinky arms about his neck, pressing tight high breasts hard against him. She had to tilt her head slightly for his kiss. "Then your turn, darling. For free." He tried to kiss her; something stopped his tongue, and he realized that the smile was on the outside only, that the opening didn't really exist at all.

He parked next to an MG, not Lea's, and went inside the house where the martinis were always snapping cold.

"Darling, you remember Greta, don't you? She is going to give me lessons twice a week. Isn't that exciting?"

"But you already graduated," Darin murmured. Greta was not tall and not long-legged. She was a little bit of a thing. He thought probably he did remember her from somewhere or other, vaguely. Her hand was cool in his.

"Greta has moved in; she is going to lecture on modern art for the spring semester. I asked her for private lessons and she said yes."

"Greta Farrel," Darin said, still holding her small hand. They moved away from Lea and wandered through the open windows to the patio where the scent of orange blossoms was heavy in the air.

"Greta thinks it must be heavenly to be married to a psychologist." Lea's voice followed them. "Where are you two?"

"What makes you say a thing like that?" Darin asked.

"Oh, when I think of how you must understand a woman, know her moods and the reasons for them. You must know just what to do and when, and when to do something else . . . Yes, just like that."

His hands on her body were hot, her skin cool. Lea's petulant voice drew closer. He held Greta in his arms and stepped into the pool where they sank to the bottom, still together. She hadn't gone to the Barbie school. His hands learned her body; then his body learned hers. After they made love, Greta drew back from him regretfully.

"I do have to go now. You are a lucky man, Dr. Darin. No doubts about yourself, complete understanding of what makes you tick."

He lay back on the leather couch staring at the ceiling. "It's always that way, Doctor. Fantasies, dreams, illusions. I know it is because this investigation is hanging over us right now, but even when things are going relatively well, I still go off on a tangent like that for no real reason." He stopped talking.

In his chair Darin stirred slightly, his fingers drumming softly on the arm, his gaze on the clock whose hands were stuck. He said, "Before this recent pressure, did you have such intense fantasies?"

"I don't think so," Darin said thoughtfully, trying to remember.

The other didn't give him time. He asked, "And can you break out of them now when you have to, or want to?"

"Oh, sure," Darin said.

Laughing, he got out of his car, patted the MG, and walked into his house. He could hear voices from the living room and he remembered that on Thursdays Lea really did have her painting lesson.

Dr. Lacey left five minutes after Darin arrived. Lacey said vague things about Lea's great promise and untapped talent, and Darin nodded sober agreement. If she had talent, it certainly was untapped so far. He didn't say so.

Lea was wearing a hostess suit, flowing sheer panels of pale blue net over a skin-tight leotard that was midnight blue. Darin wondered if she realized that she had gained weight in the past few years. He thought not.

"Oh, that man is getting impossible," she said when the MG blasted away from their house. "Two years now, and he still doesn't want to put my things on show."

Looking at her, Darin wondered how much more her things could be on show.

"Don't dawdle too long with your martini," she said. "We're due at the Ritters' at seven for clams."

The telephone rang for him while he was showering. It was Stu Evers. Darin stood dripping water while he listened.

"Have you seen the evening paper yet? That broad made the statement that conditions are extreme at the station, that our animals are made to suffer unnecessarily."

Darin groaned softly. Stu went on, "She is bringing her entire women's group out tomorrow to show proof of her claims. She's a bigwig in the SPCA, or something."

Darin began to laugh then. Mrs. Whoosis had her face pressed against one of the windows, other fat women in flowered dresses had their faces against the rest. None of them breathed or moved. Inside the compound Adam laid Hortense, then moved on to Esmeralda, to Hilda . . .

"God damn it, Darin, it isn't funny!" Stu said.

"But it is. It is."

Clams at the Ritters' were delicious. Clams, hammers, buckets of butter, a mountainous salad, beer, and finally coffee liberally laced with brandy. Darin felt cheerful and contented when the evening was over. Ritter was in Med. Eng. Lit. but he didn't talk about it, which was merciful. He was sympathetic about the stink with the SPCA. He thought scientists had no imagination. Darin agreed with him and soon he and Lea were on their way home.

"I am so glad that you didn't decide to stay late," Lea said, passing over the yellow line with a blast of the horn. "There is a movie on tonight that I am dying to see."

She talked, but he didn't listen, training of twelve years drawing out an occasional grunt at what must have been appropriate times. "Ritter is such a bore," she said. They were nearly home. "As if you had anything to do with that incredible statement in tonight's paper."

"What statement?"

"Didn't you even read the article? For heaven's sake, why not? Everyone will be talking about it . . ." She sighed theatrically. "Someone quoted a reliable source who said that within the foreseeable future, simply by developing the leads you now have, you will be able to produce monkeys that are as smart as normal human beings." She laughed, a brittle meaningless sound.

"I'll read the article when we get home," he said. She didn't ask about the statement, didn't care if it was true or false, if he had made it or not. He read the article while she settled down before the television. Then he went for a swim. The water was warm, the breeze cool on his skin. Mosquitoes found him as soon as he got out of the pool, so he sat behind the screening of the verandah. The bluish light from the living room went off after a time and there was only the dark night. Lea didn't call him when she went to bed.

He knew she went very softly, closing the door with care so that the click of the latch wouldn't disturb him if he was dozing on the verandah.

He knew why he didn't break it off. Pity. The most corrosive emotion endogenous to man. She was the product of the doll school that taught that the trip down the aisle was the end, the fulfillment of a maiden's dreams; shocked and horrified to learn that it was another beginning, some of them never recovered. Lea never had. Never would. At sixty she would purse her lips at the sexual display of uncivilized animals, whether human or not, and she would be disgusted and help formulate laws to ban such activities. Long ago he had hoped a child would be the answer, but the school did something to them on the inside too. They didn't conceive, or if conception took place, they didn't carry the fruit, and if they carried it, the birth was of a stillborn thing. The ones that did live were usually the ones to be pitied more than those who fought and were defeated *in utero*.

A bat swooped low over the quiet pool and was gone again against the black of the azaleas. Soon the moon would appear, and the chimps would stir restlessly for a while, then return to deep untroubled slumber. The chimps slept companionably close to one another, without thought of sex. Only the nocturnal creatures, and the human creatures, performed coitus in the dark. He wondered if Adam remembered his human captors. The colony in the compound had been started almost twenty years ago, and since then none of the chimps had seen a human being. When it was necessary to enter the grounds, the chimps were fed narcotics in the evening to insure against their waking. Props were changed then, new obstacles added to the old conquered ones. Now and then a chimp was removed for study, usually ending up in dissection. But not Adam. He was father of the world. Darin grinned in the darkness.

Adam took his bride aside from the other beasts and knew that she was lovely. She was his own true bride, created for him, intelligence to match his own burning intelligence. Together they scaled the smooth walls and glimpsed the great world that lay beyond their garden. Together they found the opening that led to the world that was to be theirs, and they left behind them the lesser beings. And the god searched for them and finding them not, cursed them and sealed the opening so that none of the others could follow. So it was that Adam and his bride became the first man and woman and from them flowed the progeny that was to inhabit the entire world. And one day Adam said, for shame woman, seest thou that thou art naked? And the woman answered, so are you, big boy, so are you. So they covered their nakedness with leaves from the trees, and thereafter they performed their sexual act in the dark of night so that man could not look on his woman, nor she on him. And they were thus cleansed of shame. Forever and ever. Amen. Hallelujah.

Darin shivered. He had drowsed after all, and the night wind had grown chill. He went to bed. Lea drew away from him in her sleep. She felt hot to his touch. He turned to his left side, his back to her, and he slept.

"There is potential x," Darin said to Lea the next morning at breakfast. "We don't know where x is actually. It represents the highest intellectual achievement possible for the monkeys, for example. We test each batch of monkeys that we get and sort them— x-1, x-2, x-3, suppose, and then we breed for more x-1's. Also we feed the other two groups the sRNA that we extract from the original x-1's. Eventually we get a monkey that is higher than our original x-1, and we reclassify right down the line and start over, using his sRNA to bring the others up to his level. We make constant checks to be sure we aren't allowing inferior strains to mingle with our highest achievers, and we keep control groups that are given the same training, the same food, the same sorting process, but no sRNA. We test them against each other."

Lea was watching his face with some interest as he talked. He thought he had got through, until she said, "Did you realize that your hair is almost solid white at the temples? All at once it is turning white."

Carefully he put his cup back on the saucer. He smiled at her and got up. "See you tonight," he said.

They also had two separate compounds of chimps that had started out identically. Neither had received any training whatever through the years; they had been kept isolated from each other and from man. Adam's group had been fed sRNA daily from the most intelligent chimps they had found. The control group had been fed none. The control-group chimps had yet to master the intricacies of the fountain with its ice-cold water; they used the small stream that flowed through the compound. The control group had yet to learn that fruit on the high, fragile branches could be had, if one used the telescoping sticks to knock them down. The control group huddled without protection, or under the scant cover of palm trees when it rained and the dome was opened. Adam long ago had led his group in the construction of a rude but functional hut where they gathered when it rained.

Darin saw the women's committee filing past the compound when he parked his car. He went straight to the console in his office, flicked on a switch and manipulated buttons and dials, leading the group through the paths, opening one, closing another to them, until he led them to the newest of the compounds, where he opened the gate and let them inside. Quickly he closed the gate again and watched their frantic efforts to get out. Later he turned the chimps loose on them, and his grin grew broader as he watched the new-men ravage the old women. Some of the offspring were black and hairy, others pink and hairless, some intermediate. They grew rapidly, lined up with arms extended to receive their daily doses, stood before a machine that tested them instantaneously, and were sorted. Some of them went into a disintegration room, others out into the world.

A car horn blasted in his ears. He switched off his ignition and he got out as Stu Evers parked next to his car. "I see the old bats got here," Stu said. He walked toward the lab with Darin. "How's the Driscoll kid coming along?"

"Negative," Darin said. Stu knew they had tried using human sRNA on the boy, and failed consistently. It was too big a step for his body to cope with. "So far he has shown total intolerance to A-127. Throws it off almost instantly."

Stuart was sympathetic and noncommittal. No one else had any faith whatever in Darin's own experiment. A-127 might be too great a step upward, Darin thought. The *Ateles* spider monkey from Brazil was too bright.

He called Kelly from his office and asked about the newly arrived spider monkeys they had tested the day before. Blood had been processed; a sample was available. He looked over his notes and chose one that had shown interest in the tasks without finishing any of them. Kelly promised him the prepared syringe by 1 P.M.

What no one connected with the project could any longer doubt was that those simians, and the men that had been injected with sRNA from the Driscoll boy, had actually had their learning capacities inhibited, some of them apparently permanently.

Darin didn't want to think about Mrs. Driscoll's reaction if ever she learned how they had been using her boy. Rae sat at the corner of his desk and drawled insolently, "I might tell her myself, Dr. Darin. I'll say, Sorry, ma'am, you'll have to keep your idiot out of here; you're damaging the brains of our monkeys with his polluted blood. Okay, Darin?"

"My God, what are you doing back again?"

"Testing," she said. "That's all, just testing."

Stu called him to observe the latest challenge to Adam's group, to take place in forty minutes. Darin had forgotten that he was to be present. During the night a tree had been felled in each compound, its trunk crossing the small stream, damming it. At eleven the water fountains were to be turned off for the rest of the day. The tree had been felled at the far end of the compound, close to the wall where the stream entered, so that the trickle of water that flowed past the hut was cut off. Already the group not taking sRNA was showing signs of thirst. Adam's group was unaware of the interrupted flow.

Darin met Stu and they walked together to the far side where they would have a good view of the entire compound. The women had left by then. "It was too quiet for them this morning," Stu said. "Adam was making his rounds; he squatted on the felled tree for nearly an hour before he left it and went back to the others."

They could see the spreading pool of water. It was muddy, uninviting looking. At eleven-ten it was generally known within the compound that the water supply had failed. Some of the old chimps tried the fountain; Adam tried it several times. He hit it with a stick and tried it again. Then he sat on his haunches and stared at it. One of the young chimps whimpered pitiably. He wasn't thirsty yet, merely puzzled and perhaps frightened. Adam scowled at him. The chimp cowered behind Hortense, who bared her fangs at Adam. He waved menacingly at her, and she began picking fleas from her offspring. When he whimpered again, she cuffed him. The young chimp looked from her to Adam, stuck his forefinger in his mouth and ambled away. Adam continued to stare at the useless fountain. An hour passed. At last Adam rose and wandered nonchalantly toward the drying stream. Here and there a shrinking pool of muddy water steamed in the sun. The other chimps followed Adam. He followed the stream through the compound toward the wall that was its source. When he came to the pool he squatted again. One of the young chimps circled the pool cautiously, reached down and touched the dirty water, drew back, reached for it again, and then drank. Several of the others drank also. Adam continued to squat. At twelve-forty Adam moved again. Grunting and gesturing to several younger males, he approached the tree trunk. With much noise and meaningless gestures, they shifted the trunk. They strained, shifted it again. The water was released and poured over the heaving chimps. Two of them dropped the trunk and ran. Adam and the other two held. The two returned.

They were still working when Darin had to leave, to keep his appointment with Mrs. Driscoll and Sonny. They arrived at one-ten. Kelly had left the syringe with the new formula in Darin's small refrigerator.

He injected Sonny, took his sample, and started the tests. Sometimes Sonny cooperated to the extent of lifting one of the articles from the table and throwing it. Today he cleaned the table within ten minutes. Darin put a piece of candy in his hand; Sonny threw it from him. Patiently Darin put another piece in the boy's hand. He managed to keep the eighth piece in the clenched hand long enough to guide the hand to Sonny's mouth. When it was gone, Sonny opened his mouth for more. His hands lay idly on the table. He didn't seem to relate the hands to the candy with the pleasant taste. Darin tried to guide a second to his mouth, but Sonny refused to hold a piece a second time.

When the hour was over and Sonny was showing definite signs of fatigue, Mrs. Driscoll clutched Darin's hands in hers. Tears stood in her eyes. "You actually got him to feed himself a little bit," she said brokenly. "God bless you, Dr. Darin. God bless you!" She kissed his hand and turned away as the tears started to spill down her cheeks.

Kelly was waiting for him when the group left. She collected the new sample of blood to be processed. "Did you hear about the excitement down at the compound? Adam's building a dam of his own."

Darin stared at her for a moment. The breakthrough? He ran back to the compound. The near side this time was where the windows were being used. It seemed that the entire staff was there, watching silently. He saw Stu and edged in by him. The stream twisted and curved through the compound, less than ten inches deep, not over two feet anywhere. At one spot stones lay under it; elsewhere the bottom was of hardpacked sand. Adam and his crew were piling up stones at the one suitable place for their dam, very near

their hut. The dam they were building was two feet
thick. It was less than five feet from the wall, fifteen
feet from where Darin and Stu shared the window.
When the dam was completed, Adam looked along
the wall. Darin thought the chimp's eyes paused momentarily on his own. Later he heard that nearly every
other person watching felt the same momentary pause
as those black, intelligent eyes sought out and held
other intelligence.

". . . next thunderstorm. Adam and the flood . . ."

". . . eventually seeds instead of food . . ."

". . . his brain. Convolutions as complex as any
man's."

Darin walked away from them, snatches of future
plans in his ears. There was a memo on his desk. Jacobsen was turning over the SPCA investigatory committee to him. He was to meet with the university representatives, the local SPCA group, and the legal
representatives of all concerned on Monday next at
10 A.M. He wrote out his daily report on Sonny Driscoll. Sonny had been on too good behavior for too
long. Would this last injection give him just the spark
of determination he needed to go on a rampage? Darin
had alerted Johnny, the bodyguard, whoops, male
nurse, for just such a possibility, but he knew Johnny
didn't think there was any danger from the kid. He
hoped Sonny wouldn't kill Johnny, then turn on his
mother and father. He'd probably rape his mother, if
that much goal-directedness ever flowed through him.
And the three men who had volunteered for the injections from Sonny's blood? He didn't want to think
of them at all, therefore couldn't get them out of his
mind as he sat at his desk staring at nothing. Three
convicts. That's all, just convicts hoping to get a parole
for helping science along. He laughed abruptly. They

weren't planning anything now. Not that trio. Not planning for a thing. Sitting, waiting for something to happen, not thinking about what it might be, or when, or how they would be affected. Not thinking. Period.

"But you can always console yourself that your motives were pure, that it was all for Science, can't you, Dr. Darin?" Rae asked mockingly.

He looked at her. "Go to hell," he said.

It was late when he turned off his light. Kelly met him in the corridor that led to the main entrance. "Hard day, Dr. Darin?"

He nodded. Her hand lingered momentarily on his arm. "Good night," she said, turning in to her own office. He stared at the door for a long time before he let himself out and started toward his car. Lea would be furious with him for not calling. Probably she wouldn't speak at all until nearly bedtime, when she would explode into tears and accusations. He could see the time when her tears and accusations would strike home, when Kelly's body would still be a tangible memory, her words lingering in his ears. And he would lie to Lea, not because he would care actually if she knew, but because it would be expected. She wouldn't know how to cope with the truth. It would entangle her to the point where she would have to try an abortive suicide, a screaming-for-attention attempt that would ultimately tie him in tear-soaked knots that would never be loosened. No, he would lie, and she would know he was lying, and they would get by. He started the car, aimed down the long sixteen miles that lay before him. He wondered where Kelly lived. What it would do to Stu when he realized. What it would do to his job if Kelly should get nasty, eventually. He shrugged. Barbie dolls never got nasty. It wasn't built in.

Lea met him at the door, dressed only in a sheer gown, her hair loose and unsprayed. Her body flowed into his, so that he didn't need Kelly at all. And he was best man when Stu and Kelly were married. He called to Rae, "Would that satisfy you?" but she didn't answer. Maybe she was gone for good this time. He parked the car outside his darkened house and leaned his head on the steering wheel for a moment before getting out. If not gone for good, at least for a long time. He hoped she would stay away for a long time.

SLOW TUESDAY NIGHT

R. A. LAFFERTY

A Portuguese physician, Antonio Caetano de Abren Freire Egas Moniz, in 1935 introduced the operation known as prefrontal lobotomy. . . .

Though Moniz won the Nobel Prize in medicine, he paid a high price for his pioneering excursions into the brain. He was shot five times by a lobotomized patient. . . .
    —Lee Edson, "The Psyche and the Surgeon" *

Psychosurgery, often a last resort for severely disturbed or pathologically violent people, is a subject of controversy. Although violent tendencies have been removed in many cases, there is evidence that rational and emotional functions are impaired by such surgery. In cases where the corpus callosum was severed, the patient's left side literally did not know what the right side was doing; one famous example was that of a man who would try to harm his

* New York Times Magazine, September 30, 1973, pp. 78–79.

wife with one hand while restraining himself with the other.

Related to psychosurgery are procedures involving the electrical stimulation of the brain. One well-publicized experiment was performed by José Delgado of Yale. By transmitting an electrical current to the brain of a charging bull, he stopped the animal in its tracks. Such experiments raise fears that electronic devices planted in human brains might be used to control any behavior seen as undesirable.

R. A. Lafferty shows us an entire society affected by one form of psychosurgery. Although his story can be seen as a humorous flight of fancy, it makes an important point: the results of research on the brain, made available on a large scale, might forever alter us and our society.

A panhandler intercepted the young couple as they strolled down the night street.

"Preserve us this night," he said as he touched his hat to them, "and could you good people advance me a thousand dollars to be about the recouping of my fortunes?"

"I gave you a thousand last Friday," said the young man.

"Indeed you did," the panhandler replied, "and I paid you back tenfold by messenger before midnight."

"That's right, George, he did," said the young woman. "Give it to him, dear. I believe he's a good sort."

So the young man gave the panhandler a thousand dollars, and the panhandler touched his hat to them in thanks and went on to the recouping of his fortunes.

As he went into Money Market, the panhandler passed Ildefonsa Impala, the most beautiful woman in the city.

"Will you marry me this night, Ildy?" he asked cheerfully.

"Oh, I don't believe so, Basil," she said. "I marry you pretty often, but tonight I don't seem to have any plans at all. You may make me a gift on your first or second, however. I always like that."

But when they had parted she asked herself: "But whom will I marry tonight?"

The panhandler was Basil Bagelbaker, who would be the richest man in the world within an hour and a half. He would make and lose four fortunes within eight hours; and these not the little fortunes that ordinary men acquire, but titanic things.

When the Abebaios block had been removed from human minds, people began to make decisions faster, and often better. It had been the mental stutter. When it was understood what it was, and that it had no useful function, it was removed by simple childhood metasurgery.

Transportation and manufacturing had then become practically instantaneous. Things that had once taken months and years now took only minutes and hours. A person could have one or several pretty intricate careers within an eight-hour period.

Freddy Fixico had just invented a manus module. Freddy was a Nyctalops, and the modules were characteristic of these people. The people had then divided themselves—according to their natures and inclinations—into the Auroreans, the Hemerobians, and the Nyctalops—or the Dawners, who had their most active hours from 4 A.M. till noon; the Day Flies, who obtained from noon to 8 P.M.; and the Night Seers, whose civilization thrived from 8 P.M. to 4 A.M. The cultures, inventions, markets and activities of these three folk were a little different. As a Nyctalops, Freddy had just begun his working day at 8 P.M. on a slow Tuesday night.

Freddy rented an office and had it furnished. This took one minute, negotiation, selection and installation being almost instantaneous. Then he invented the manus module; that took another minute. He then had it manufactured and marketed; in three minutes it was in the hands of key buyers.

It caught on. It was an attractive module. The flow of orders began within thirty seconds. By ten minutes after eight every important person had one of the new manus modules, and the trend had been set. The module began to sell in the millions. It was one of the

most interesting fads of the night, or at least the early part of the night.

Manus modules had no practical function, no more than had Sameki verses. They were attractive, of a psychologically satisfying size and shape, and could be held in the hands, set on a table, or installed in a module niche of any wall.

Naturally Freddy became very rich. Ildefonsa Impala, the most beautiful woman in the city, was always interested in newly rich men. She came to see Freddy about eight-thirty. People made up their minds fast, and Ildefonsa had hers made up when she came. Freddy made his own up quickly and divorced Judy Fixico in Small Claims Court. Freddy and Ildefonsa went honeymooning to Paraiso Dorado, a resort.

It was wonderful. All of Ildy's marriages were. There was the wonderful floodlighted scenery. The recirculated water of the famous falls was tinted gold; the immediate rocks had been done by Rambles; and the hills had been contoured by Spall. The beach was a perfect copy of that at Merevale, and the popular drink that first part of the night was blue absinthe.

But scenery—whether seen for the first time or revisited after an interval—is striking for the sudden intense view of it. It is not meant to be lingered over. Food, selected and prepared instantly, is eaten with swift enjoyment; and blue absinthe lasts no longer than its own novelty. Loving, for Ildefonsa and her paramours, was quick and consuming; and repetition would have been pointless to her. Besides, Ildefonsa and Freddy had taken only the one-hour luxury honeymoon.

Freddy wished to continue the relationship, but Ildefonsa glanced at a trend indicator. The manus module would hold its popularity for only the first

third of the night. Already it had been discarded by
people who mattered. And Freddy Fixico was not one
of the regular successes. He enjoyed a full career only
about one night a week.

They were back in the city and divorced in Small
Claims Court by nine thirty-five. The stock of manus
modules was remaindered, and the last of it would be
disposed of to bargain hunters among the Dawners,
who will buy anything.

"Whom shall I marry next?" Ildefonsa asked herself. "It looks like a slow night."

"Bagelbaker is buying" ran the word through Money
Market, but Bagelbaker was selling again before the
word had made its rounds. Basil Bagelbaker enjoyed
making money, and it was a pleasure to watch him
work as he dominated the floor of the Market and
assembled runners and a competent staff out of the
corner of his mouth. Helpers stripped the panhandler
rags off him and wrapped him in a tycoon toga. He
sent one runner to pay back twentyfold the young
couple who had advanced him a thousand dollars. He
sent another with a more substantial gift to Ildefonsa
Impala, for Basil cherished their relationship. Basil acquired title to the Trend Indication Complex and had
certain falsifications set into it. He caused to collapse
certain industrial empires that had grown up within
the last two hours, and made a good thing of recom-
bining their wreckage. He had been the richest man
in the world for some minutes now. He became so
money-heavy that he could not maneuver with the
agility he had shown an hour before. He became a
great fat buck, and the pack of expert wolves circled
him to bring him down.

Very soon he would lose that first fortune of the
evening. The secret of Basil Bagelbaker was that he

enjoyed losing money spectacularly after he was full of it to the bursting point.

A thoughtful man named Maxwell Mouser had just produced a work of actinic philosophy. It took him seven minutes to write it. To write works of philosophy one used the flexible outlines and the idea indexes; one set the activator for such a wordage in each subsection; an adept would use the paradox feed-in and the striking-analogy blender; one calibrated the particular-slant and the personality-signature. It had to come out a good work, for excellence had become the automatic minimum for such productions.

"I will scatter a few nuts on the frosting," said Maxwell, and he pushed the level for that. This sifted handfuls of words like *chthonic* and *heuristic* and *prozymeides* through the thing so that nobody could doubt it was a work of philosophy.

Maxwell Mouser sent the work out to publishers, and received it back each time in about three minutes. An analysis of it and reason for rejection were always given—mostly that the thing had been done before and better. Maxwell received it back ten times in thirty minutes, and was discouraged. Then there was a break.

Ladion's work had become a hit within the last ten minutes, and it was now recognized that Mouser's monograph was both an answer and a supplement to it. It was accepted and published in less than a minute after this break. The reviews of the first five minutes were cautious ones; then real enthusiasm was shown. This was truly one of the greatest works of philosophy to appear during the early and medium hours of the night. There were those who said it might be one of the enduring works and even have a holdover appeal to the Dawners the next morning.

Naturally Maxwell became very rich, and naturally Ildefonsa came to see him about midnight. Being a revolutionary philosopher, Maxwell thought that they might make some free arrangement, but Ildefonsa insisted it must be marriage. So Maxwell divorced Judy Mouser in Small Claims Court and went off with Ildefonsa.

This Judy herself, though not so beautiful as Ildefonsa, was the fastest taker in the city. She only wanted the men of the moment for a moment, and she was always there before even Ildefonsa. Ildefonsa believed that she took the men away from Judy; Judy said that Ildy had her leavings and nothing else.

"I had him first," Judy would always mock as she raced through Small Claims Court.

"Oh, that damned urchin!" Ildefonsa would moan. "She wears my very hair before I do."

Maxwell Mouser and Ildefonsa Impala went honeymooning to Musicbox Mountain, a resort. It was wonderful. The peaks were done with green snow by Dunbar and Fittle. (Back at Money Market Basil Bagelbaker was putting together his third and greatest fortune of the night, which might surpass in magnitude even his fourth fortune of the Thursday before.) The chalets were Switzier than the real Swiss and had live goats in every room. (And Stanley Skuldugger was emerging as the top actor-imago of the middle hours of the night.) The popular drink for that middle part of the night was Glotzenglubber, ewe cheese and Rhine wine over pink ice. (And back in the city the leading Nyctalops were taking their midnight break at the Toppers' Club.)

Of course it was wonderful, as were all of Ildefonsa's —but she had never been really up on philosophy so

she had scheduled only the special thirty-five-minute honeymoon. She looked at the trend indicator to be sure. She found that her current husband had been obsoleted, and his opus was now referred to sneeringly as Mouser's Mouse. They went back to the city and were divorced in Small Claims Court.

The membership of the Toppers' Club varied. Success was the requisite of membership. Basil Bagelbaker might be accepted as a member, elevated to the presidency and expelled from it as a dirty pauper from three to six times a night. But only important persons could belong to it, or those enjoying brief moments of importance.

"I believe I will sleep during the Dawner period in the morning," Overcall said. "I may go up to this new place, Koimopolis, for an hour of it. They're said to be good. Where will you sleep, Basil?"

"Flophouse."

"I believe I will sleep an hour by the Midian Method," said Burnbanner. "They have a fine new clinic. And perhaps I'll sleep an hour by the Prasenka Process, and an hour by the Dormidio."

"Crackle has been sleeping an hour every period by the natural method," said Overcall.

"I did that for half an hour not long since," said Burnbanner. "I believe an hour is too long to give it. Have you tried the natural method, Basil?"

"Always. Natural method and a bottle of red-eye."

Stanley Skuldugger had become the most meteoric actor-imago for a week. Naturally he became very rich, and Ildefonsa Impala went to see him about 3 A.M.

"I had him first!" rang the mocking voice of Judy Skuldugger as she skipped through her divorce in Small Claims Court. And Ildefonsa and Stanley boy went off honeymooning. It is always fun to finish up

a period with an actor-imago who is the hottest property in the business. There is something so adolescent
and boorish about them.

Besides, there was the publicity, and Ildefonsa liked
that. The rumor mills ground. Would it last ten minutes? Thirty? An hour? Would it be one of those rare
Nyctalops marriages that lasted through the rest of the
night and into the daylight off-hours? Would it even
last into the next night as some had been known to
do?

Actually it lasted nearly forty minutes, which was
almost to the end of the period.

It had been a slow Tuesday night. A few hundred
new products had run their course on the markets.
There had been a score of dramatic hits, three-minute
and five-minute capsule dramas, and several of the six-
minute long-play affairs. *Night Street Nine*—a solidly
sordid offering—seemed to be in as the drama of the
night unless there should be a late hit.

Hundred-story buildings had been erected, occupied,
obsoleted, and demolished again to make room for
more contemporary structures. Only the mediocre
would use a building that had been left over from the
Day Flies or the Dawners, or even the Nyctalops of
the night before. The city was rebuilt pretty completely at least three times during an eight-hour period.

The period drew near its end. Basil Bagelbaker, the
richest man in the world, the reigning president of the
Toppers' Club, was enjoying himself with his cronies.
His fourth fortune of the night was a paper pyramid
that had risen to incredible heights; but Basil laughed
to himself as he savored the manipulation it was
founded on.

Three ushers of the Toppers' Club came in with
firm step.

"Get out of here, you dirty bum!" they told Basil savagely. They tore the tycoon's toga off him and then tossed him his seedy panhandler's rags with a three-man sneer.

"All gone?" Basil asked. "I gave it another five minutes."

"All gone," said a messenger from Money Market. "Nine billion gone in five minutes, and it really pulled some others down with it."

"Pitch the busted bum out!" howled Overcall and Burnbanner and the other cronies.

"Wait, Basil," said Overcall. "Turn in the President's Crosier before we kick you downstairs. After all, you'll have it several times again tomorrow night."

The period was over. The Nyctalops drifted off to sleep clinics or leisure-hour hideouts to pass their ebb time. The Auroreans, the Dawners, took over the vital stuff.

Now you would see some action! Those Dawners really made fast decisions. You wouldn't catch them wasting a full minute setting up a business.

A sleepy panhandler met Ildefonsa Impala on the way.

"Preserve us this morning, Ildy," he said, "and will you marry me the coming night?"

"Likely I will, Basil," she told him. "Did you marry Judy during the night past?"

"I'm not sure. Could you let me have two dollars, Ildy?"

"Out of the question. I believe a Judy Bagelbaker was named one of the ten best-dressed women during the frou-frou fashion period about two o'clock. Why do you need two dollars?"

"A dollar for a bed and a dollar for red-eye. After all, I sent you two million out of my second."

"I keep my two sorts of accounts separate. Here's a dollar, Basil. Now be off! I can't be seen talking to a dirty panhandler."

"Thank you, Ildy. I'll get the red-eye and sleep in an alley. Preserve us this morning."

Bagelbaker shuffled off whistling "Slow Tuesday Night.".

And already the Dawners had set Wednesday morning to jumping.

IN RE GLOVER

LEONARD TUSHNET

The proposal that human beings could be preserved alive by freezing would, it is pointed out, offer the possibility to people suffering from an incurable disease of waiting around until a cure was discovered. . . . Among the problems one can see arising are those of inheritance of property. Children expecting to inherit would be irked at being bilked of their inheritance. . . . A son who had taken over the management of a business owned by his frozen father . . . would not want to be ousted by the old man. . . . One might ask too whether the law could insist on reviving a frozen individual required to give evidence in court. . . .

—Gordon Rattray Taylor,
The Biological Time Bomb *

We may go to court and seek a declaratory judgment that will allow freezing before death, under carefully specified

* New York: New American Library, 1968, pp. 102–103.

conditions, arguing that it is *desirable* because it improves the patient's overall chances, and that it is *permissible* both for this reason and because the patient . . . may still be "alive" after freezing.

—R. C. W. Ettinger, *Man Into Superman* *

Cryonically preserved or "frozen" people are already among us. Cryonics societies have been formed. Facilities for freezing are available, although few people have made use of them. It does not appear likely that those now preserved can ever be revived, but they are betting that the future will have ways of restoring them to life. Small as their chance may be, it is greater than that of the inhabitants of cemeteries.

There have been some advances in cryobiological research. In one experiment, cited by R. C. W. Ettinger in his book Man Into Superman, Isamu Suda of Kobe University froze the brains of several cats, one for over six months. A corticogram or brain wave tracing was present after thawing. Dog kidneys have also survived after freezing. The revival of a human being, especially one who is clinically dead at the time of freezing, presents a complex difficulty: some believe that the restoration of such a person will never be possible.

Because so few people have been frozen, most of us are not concerned with the procedure's implications. There has been little objection to cryonic interment on religious grounds; two frozen people, Steven Mandell and Ann DeBlasio, had Orthodox Jewish and Roman Catholic memorial services. The procedure is expensive, but within the reach of middle-class people willing to plan for it. No doubt economic and religious problems would come up if more people were frozen; the poor would rightly want the option, and clergymen might become apprehensive. Few of us are likely to concern ourselves with freezing until there has been more successful research, or maybe even until someone has been frozen and revived.

* New York: St. Martin's Press, 1972, p. 260.

Legal complications have not yet arisen; there is no reason to assume that cryonic suspension is illegal, as it does not as yet differ from burial. But what if someone were to be frozen before death? What legal status would he or she have? Leonard Tushnet raises this possibility in a humorous yet realistic way. Indeed, legal questions like the ones he raises could come up in connection with other biological advances.

n re Glover finally reached the Supreme Court. The nine Justices, in their Friday conference, were unanimous that a writ of certiorari be granted and that the case be heard. Unanimous on those points, they had already made up their separate minds about various phases of the case and each of them was already preparing a memorandum for his opinion. In re Glover would set landmarks in law, in a new field of law as well as in the laws of wills, mortmain, trusts, and homicide, with overtones to be subtly discussed in obiter dicta bearing on euthanasia and medical and legal malpractice.

It looked, on the surface, like a simple case of merely determining the facts, ordinarily not in the purview of such an august body as the Supreme Court of the United States. Ralph Glover, the brilliant and dynamic founder of the many-sided business empire bearing his name, had died—or had he? If he were dead, his four sons by his first wife and his two daughters by his second (both wives having predeceased him, if that term could be used without prejudice) were due to inherit the entire estate, share and share alike, after a number of relatively minor bequests had been paid; the great Glover Foundation, the internationally known medical research institution, was to get nothing, having been the recipient of munificent gifts during its founder's lifetime; the federal government and the states of residence of the heirs were eagerly anticipating the considerable inheritance taxes. If he were not dead, the trustees of the tax-free Glover Foundation would continue to receive, as they had for five years now, all revenues from the many corporations constituting the Glover enterprises; the children were to fend for themselves, meaning that the sons and sons-in-law would have to find jobs; and the federal and state governments would have to wait until Glover's actual demise to collect.

Mr. Allen Freundlich, J., in the succinct manner for which he was noted, summarized the scientific background thus: (1) When living tissues are frozen, the ice crystals formed by the frozen intracellular water occupy a larger space than liquid water; hence the cell walls are ruptured and tissue death ensues. (2) The chemical, dimethylsulfoxide, commonly known as DMSO, had the remarkable property of being able to bind to itself intracellular water, so that below 0° Centigrade no ice crystals are formed and cell structure, except for its physical state, remains unchanged. (3) When DMSO is injected intravenously into the body of a small mammal, that mammal by a quick-freezing process could withstand the lowering of its body temperature to well below the freezing point of water and could then remain in that frozen state, like packaged meat in a supermarket, without tissue damage and with suspension of all vital functions. (4) It could then be slowly returned to its normal temperature and those functions would return, including resumption of activity in the higher cerebral centers. Rats, so frozen and later thawed out, ate and drank and copulated and ran easily through the paths of mazes they had previously learned, just as they had before the artificially induced hibernation or state of suspended animation. Experiments had demonstrated that such hibernation was without harm for at least ten years and probably longer, but it was only ten years ago that the first batch of animals had been frozen. (5) What was true of rats was true of larger mammals, including primates. Rhesus monkeys, a gibbon, and two chimpanzees had successfully survived the process; the chimpanzees had thereafter been mated and been shown to be fertile. (6) The procedure had no ill effects on the animals other than that they developed cataracts, opacification of the lenses of the eyes, a condition easily correctible by surgery. (7) Once thawed out, however, refreezing could not take place without damage to vital organs; why this should occur was not known.

Mr. Henry Gibson, J., gave the stipulated facts: Mr. Ralph Glover, aged sixty-two, in full possession of his faculties, suffering from an inoperable cancer of the pancreas which had spread to his liver, had had DMSO injected and had been artificially frozen. He (or his body) was now lying in the freezer vaults of the Abby C. Glover Memorial Hospital in New York City; the vaults ordinarily were used to preserve cadavers for dissection. The injection and the subsequent freezing had been done by a medical team headed by Doctors Green and Hankey, who assumed full responsibility for their actions. They had acted under instructions of Mr. Ralph Glover himself. The letter of instructions was in the exhibits; it had been carefully drawn up by the highly reputable firm of Shires, Band, and Jarvis, and Mr. Glover's signature had been witnessed by the senior partners. The letter, in the form of a contract between Doctors Green and Hankey and Ralph Glover, gave full and free permission to carry out the procedure, its purpose being the maintenance of Glover's life; he (or his body) was to remain in suspended animation until such time as a cure for cancer was discovered; he was then to be thawed out and restored to activity (or life?). During the period of hibernation Doctors Green and Hankey or successors appointed by them were to be joint agents with full powers of attorney to act for Ralph Glover in any and all capacities and were to use the net profits of all the Glover enterprises for intensive cancer research.

The case had first been brought up in Surrogate's Court in New York, where Adolf Brun, Glover's chauffeur, had sued for a declaration that his employer was dead and had demanded that his will be admitted to probate so that he could receive the $1000 bequest his (ex-?) employer had informed him he was to have. Then the complications started. The Glover Foundation said that Ralph Glover was still alive and that to probate the will was premature, to say the least. Three of the heirs (?) sued in a lower federal court (because of the diversity of citizenship) for distribution of the assets of the estate of their deceased (?) father. Doctors Green and Hankey were indicted and found guilty of wilful homicide in that they knowingly caused death by the injection of a noxious drug. They appealed their convictions on the ground that error had been committed by the trial judge when he admitted evidence (?) that Ralph Glover was indeed dead when he was not, that evidence having consisted of the inspection by the medical examiner of the body (?) in the freezer vault. The five man Court of Appeals, sitting en banc, upheld the conviction, but Judge Minglin dissented strongly, saying that the supposed decedent was in posse alive and that no corpus delicti was produced.

The ordinance requiring an autopsy to be performed on all persons suspected of having died by violence was invoked by Archibald Smythe, a son-in-law, but a temporary injunction against such an autopsy was granted on petition of Luke Glover, a son. He challenged the city's right to order the mutilation of a corpse (?) without permission of the near relatives, especially since such a corpse (?) was not available, as Judge Minglin had pointed out.

The heirs (?), in addition, brought suit for medical malpractice against Doctors Green and Hankey and the Abby C. Glover Memorial Hospital, where the procedure was carried out. They won a very large award, which was being contested by the Caducean Medical Liability Insurance Company, which said that the heirs (?) had no substantive right to sue on the behalf of an adult individual who was alive and who was capable, when he was restored to full consciousness, of saying whether or not he had been injured by the procedure.

Certain members of the New York State Bar Association had asked for a vote of censure of the firm of Shires, Band, and Jarvis for violation of ethical standards of the bar, in that the firm participated in the drawing up of a contract that was grossly immoral and fraudulent. By a very narrow margin the vote was held up pending the report of an *ad hoc* committee. The committee was seeking from the courts an opinion whether the contract was fraudulent in its statement of purpose, which implied human immortality, a state inconsistent with fact and contrary to the Blasphemy Act passed during the early days of the sovereign State of New York and never repealed. The Society for the Advancement of Atheism asked leave to submit a brief *amicus curiae* to show that the Act contravened the First Amendment to the Constitution.

Furthermore, the firm of Shires, Band, and Jarvis was being charged by the Attorney General of the State of New York with entering into a conspiracy against public policy, that policy being that no man had a right to commit suicide. The doctors, as well, were accused of spreading a vile and pernicious doctrine, one that had been condemned in the American courts in *Wiggins v. Moore* and internationally in the Nuremberg trials, to wit, that the lives of hopelessly ill patients could be taken without impunity under the guise of easing their suffering and pain.

The State Tax Commissions of the sovereign states of California, New York, Ohio, and Florida also sued for distribution of the assets of the Glover estate because acceptance of the continued existence of Ralph Glover in his present state (alive or dead) would be a novel evasion of the laws regarding mortmain, in that a corporation controlling land and property was preventing the just payment of taxes due to the states.

The federal government brought action to void the tax-exempt status of the Glover Foundation on the basis that it existed solely for the purpose of keeping a man alive (?), a laudable goal but not one covered by existing tax laws regarding charitable trusts.

The Glover Foundation itself, through motion by a majority of its trustees, sought to have Doctors Green and Hankey removed from their posts because they were convicted felons and hence had no legal right to act as agents for Ralph Glover. In this they were supported by the directors of General Diatronics and Magnolia Consolidated, Glover subsidiaries, who refused to obey a court order to turn over the net profits of the companies to the doctors.

Doctors Green and Hankey, furthermore, sued to set aside the ruling of the New York State Board of Health that the body (?) of Ralph Glover be buried or cremated according to local ordinances and state law, five years being too long and too repugnant to good taste and morals to keep a corpse (?) on ice, so to speak.

The doctors also sought a declaratory judgment

from the Food and Drug Administration that DMSO was a harmless drug incapable of causing death in the dosage used on Glover; the judgment was refused on the tenuous ground that the Administration, as a branch of the Executive, never intervened in a matter before the judicial arm of the government.

An injunction was sought and obtained by Agnes Litinsky, one of the minor legatees, against any attempt at thawing out, on the ground that she had a vested interest in the estate and until final adjudication should be made she was not to be disturbed in that right. The injunction was put aside on petition of Countess de Croix, one of Glover's daughters. She, in turn, wanted a legal guardian appointed for her father, he being incapable and incompetent in his present state of health of managing his own affairs; that plea was fought by two of her brothers and one sister, whose lawyers argued that it was absurd to appoint a guardian for a dead man.

The tangled web was now before the Court. By agreement of the parties concerned, all the cases were consolidated for final judgment, hinging as they did on the question of the quick or dead status of Ralph Glover. To the voluminous briefs of the pleaders were appended those of the organizations given leave to participate as *amici curiae*, the most important of which were the Society of Experimental Biologists and the American Cryologic Association. The former argued that judgment adverse to the doctors would set back developments in organ transplantation techniques because of the fear physicians would then have were there untoward results. The latter protested that to characterize freezing of living persons as murder was to invade the liberty of an individual to do with his body as he pleased.

The Chief Justice ordered the Gordian knot to be

cut. He was proud of his suggestion: that the body (?) of Ralph Glover be inspected by a special master who would then give his opinion whether Ralph Glover was dead. He was chagrined at the report of the special master, who had taken a team of medical forensic experts with him for the inspection. The special master said that the electroencephalograms were equivocal; they showed none of the brain waves normally present in living persons, nor did the electrocardiograms show any evidence of electrical current in the heart muscle; however, he pointed out, at the very low temperature at which the body (?) was maintained, electrical conductivity was expected to be minimal, if present at all. No pulse nor heart beat nor respiratory movements were found. Those findings were of equally little value because, as had been shown in the famous Warsaw Hunger Project, the time when life departed was difficult to ascertain when metabolism was close to zero. Blood, because it was frozen, could not be drawn for oxygen level determination. Examination of the eye grounds to see the state of the blood vessels was impossible because of the clouding of the lenses and the opacification of the aqueous and vitreous humors. No lividity of the dependent tissues was found, a condition which should have occurred a few hours after death, not to say five years. To further confuse the picture, a small section of skin was taken for biopsy (or autopsy); when thawed out its microscopic detail showed cloudy swelling of the cells, a common sign of death but also, alas! present in cachectic or wasting states such as advanced cancer.

The Justices read the report and looked at each other glumly. Mr. Robert Gordon, J., an irascible old man who refused to retire and who had no use for newfangled ideas, snorted, "Well, that gets us nowhere. All right, let's issue a writ of habeas corpus. Let the body be brought into court." He chuckled. "That way it'll have to be unfrozen. If the man's alive, all the cases fall out. If he's permanently dead—what an expression!—judgment will be easy in every case."

Mr. William Cluney, J., the most junior member of the Bench, pursed his lips and said, "I wish to remind my learned brother that we cannot issue the writ as an original matter except in the sharply delimited areas within our jurisdiction. Also, even as an appellate court, we can issue it only to determine if the corpus is detained by an inferior court that has acted without jurisdiction or in excess of authority. To do otherwise would require an act of Congress extending our power. Can you imagine the uproar if we asked for that after our segregation and civil rights decisions?"

The Chief Justice nodded. "I agree. That we cannot do. But my brother's suggestion has merit. Let us order that the corpus be thawed out for the purpose of determining his (or its) intentions in the letter of instructions. We have an out there. Glover said that the purpose of the procedure was to maintain his life until a cure for cancer was found. That is too indeterminate a date. It is the equivalent of the establishment of a trust in perpetuity. We can say a term must be put to the period of refrigeration and that term must be stated viva voce or by sworn affidavit by Glover himself."

Justice Freundlich shook his head. "That won't do. If we order the thawing out we shall be interfering with the terms of the contract with the doctors. He cannot be refrozen. We can order the contract broken only if it is contrary to public policy or to a specific statute. Otherwise we are in effect condemning Glover to a real death—if he's not dead already."

"Furthermore," Justice Gibson broke in, "we cannot order the doctors, who have been found guilty of homicide, to carry out the thawing process without the tacit assumption that they are not guilty and that the corpus is revivable. That is the same as our finding that Glover is indeed alive without any evidence to prove our belief. And, if we feel that he is alive, then there is no need for the thawing out. Something else. If we issue such an order we are returning to trial by ordeal. If the man's alive, the doctors are free of the homicide charge but exposed to suits for enormous damages by the Glover Foundation and by Glover himself for breach of contract. If the man is dead, they are incriminating themselves by their failure to—to—to resurrect him."

The meeting was adjourned without a decision. To put on a show to indicate that they knew what they were doing, they assigned their bright young law clerks to the preparation of memoranda on the nature of contracts made in anticipation of death, on the responsibility of lunatics (specifically those with a pathologic *horror mortis*) in the making of agreements, and on the laws concerning the duties of physicians to their patients in the presence of certain death.

On the following Monday the union of stationary firemen and operating engineers went on strike in New York City. It was an inopportune time for hospitals and other institutions depending on auxiliary generators in an emergency, for on Wednesday came the tremendous lightning storm on the upper East Coast that blew down power lines and knocked out electrical grids. New York City had no electricity for fourteen hours.

Naturally, all refrigerating systems were affected. No ice was available for highballs, meat spoiled in food lockers, and vaccines and other biological supplies were ruined.

The Abby C. Glover Memorial Hospital and its freezing vaults did not escape the effects of the power failure. All the animals in suspended animation died. So finally did Ralph Glover, as Doctors Hankey and Green sadly reported to their attorneys, who promptly telegraphed the news to Washington.

On Friday the Justices met again. The Chief Justice heaved a sigh of relief when his very brief opinion *In re Glover* was read and when for the first time in six years the Court was unanimous in supporting him. They agreed, 9–0, to accept as their judgment, "This Court finds that Ralph Glover died by an act of God on an indeterminable date." Thereby they sidestepped all issues raised in the pleadings before the Court. There followed a series of orders remanding the disputed cases back to the lower courts for final disposition.

The Countess de Croix, out of a sense of filial duty and to take advantage of loopholes in the tax regulations, organized a nonprofit corporation, called the DMSO-Cryobiologic Institute, under the laws of the State of Delaware. Its stated purpose was to repeat the same procedure as was used for her father on human volunteers. A permanent injunction against such experimentation was sought by the Anti-Vivisection Society in spite of the fact that to date no one has yet volunteered, an indication of lack of faith in the American power industry.

EMANCIPATION
A Romance of the Times to Come

THOMAS M. DISCH

How far do we want to depart from the conventional and familiar marriage syndrome—monogamous, permanent, exclusive, heterosexual? With the separation of love making from baby making, plus the reduction of progeny numbers and the escape of women from the baby-machine role, the family is losing some of its pragmatic importance. Historically marriage and the family, which "began as a physical union and then became a legal one—to give men property rights in women and their offspring—has now reached the threshold of a moral union: a free one, elective to start, and elective to stop."

—Joseph Fletcher, *The Ethics of Genetic Control* *

A feat that many science fiction writers have been predicting for many years and that many members of the public have feared now appears to be a reality. One baby in

* Garden City, N.Y.: Doubleday Anchor Books, 1974, p. 167.

England and two in Western Europe have been conceived during the past 18 months in test tubes from ova removed from the would-be mother and then placed back in her womb to develop to birth.

—*Science News*, July 20, 1974 *

When Douglas Bevis of Leeds University in England told the press that "test-tube babies" were apparently a reality, yet refused to disclose further information, both the public and other biologists were alarmed. The scientists were concerned about the lack of information as well as the potential dangers of the technique. The public had to come to terms with more evidence of disturbing scientific advances.

Yet the procedure mentioned by Leeds is only one of a number of possible ways we may reproduce in the future. Artificial insemination has been used for some time. Egg transfer to a host mother, artificial gestation outside the womb, and cloning are other possibilities. The effect of these methods of reproduction will be great. Our attitudes toward the family, parenthood, and sex will be altered. There will be beneficial effects; sterile people will be able to have children, the fetus in an artificial womb can be monitored before birth. How we will deal with these possibilities is another question.

Thomas M. Disch shows us a young married couple with familiar problems who come to terms with their difficulties in a very familiar way. But the methods they use differ from our own.

* Vol. 106, No. 3, p. 37.

Summer mornings the balcony would fill up with bona-fide sunshine and Boz would spread open the recliner and lie there languid as something tropical in their own little basin of private air and ultraviolet fifteen floors above entrance level. Just watching, half-awake, the vague geometries of jet trails that formed and disappeared, formed and disappeared in the pale cerulean haze. Sometimes you could hear the dinky preschoolers on the roof piping their nursery rhymes in thin, drugged voices.

> A Boeing buzzing from the west
> brings the boy that I love best.
> But a Boeing from the east . . .

Just nonsense, but it taught directions, like north and south. Boz, who had no patience with Science, always confused north and south. Onc was uptown, one was downtown—why not just call them that? Of the two, uptown was preferable. Who wants to be MOD, after all? Though it was no disgrace: his own mother, for instance. Human dignity is more than a Zipcode number, or so they say.

Tabbycat, who was just as fond of sunshine and out-of-doors as Boz, would stalk along the prestressed ledge as far as the rubber plant and then back to the geraniums, very sinister, just back and forth all morning long, and every so often Boz would reach up to stroke the soft sexy down of her throat, and sometimes when he did that he would think of Milly. Boz liked the mornings best of all.

But in the afternoons the balcony fell into the

shadow of the next building, and though it remained almost as warm it didn't do anything for his tan, so in the afternoon Boz had to find something else to do.

Once he had studied cooking on television, but it had nearly doubled the grocery bills, and Milly didn't seem to care whether Boz or Betty Crocker made her omelette fines herbes, and he had to admit himself that really there wasn't that much difference. Still, the spice shelf and the two copperbottom pans he had given himself for Christmas made an unusual decorator contribution. The nice names spices have—rosemary, thyme, ginger, cinnamon—like fairies in a ballet, all gauze wings and toe shoes. He could see her now, his own little niecelette Amparo Martinez as Oregano Queen of the Willies. And he'd be Basil a doomed lover. So much for the spice shelf.

Of course he could always read a book, he liked books. His favorite author was Norman Mailer, and then Gene Stratton Porter, he'd read everything they'd ever written. But lately when he'd read for more than a few minutes he would develop really epic headaches and then be a complete tyrant to Milly when she came home from work. What she called work.

At four o'clock art movies on Channel 5. Sometimes he used the electromassage and sometimes just his hands to jerk off with. He'd read in the Sunday facs that if all the semen from all the Metropolitan Area viewers of Channel 5 were put all together in one single place it would fill a medium-sized swimming pool. Fantastic? Then imagine swimming in it!

Afterwards he would lay spread out on the sofa that looked like a giant Baggie, his own little contribution to the municipal swimming pool drooling down the clear plastic, and he would think glumly: *There's something wrong. Something is missing.*

There was no romance in their marriage any more, that's what was wrong. It had been leaking out slowly, like air from a punctured Baggie chair, and one of these days she would mean it when she started talking about a divorce, or he would kill her with his own bare hands, or with the electromassage, when she was ribbing him in bed, or something dreadful would happen, he knew it.

Something really dreadful.

At dusk, in bed, her breasts hung above him, swaying. Just the smell of her is enough, sometimes, to drive him up the walls. He brought his thighs up against the sweaty backside of her legs. Knees pressed against buttocks. One breast, then the other, brushed his forehead; he arched his neck to kiss one breast, then the other.

"Mm," she said. "Continue."

Obediently Boz slid his arms between her legs and pulled her forward. As he wriggled down on the damp sheets his own legs went over the edge of the mattress, and his toes touched her Antron slip, a puddle of coolness on the desert-beige rug.

The smell of her, the rotting sweetness, like a suet pudding gone bad in a warm refrigerator, the warm jungle of it turned him on more than anything else, and way down there at the edge of the bed, a continent away from these events, his prick swelled and arched. Just wait your turn, he told it, and rubbed his stubbly cheek against her thigh while she mumbled and cooed. If only pricks were noses. Or if noses . . .

The smell of her now with the damp furze of her veldt pressed into his nostrils, grazing his lips, and then the first taste of her, and then the second. But most of all the smell—he floats on it into her ripest darknesses, the soft and endless corridor of pure pollened cunt, Milly, or Africa, or Tristan and Isolde on the tape recorder, rolling in rosebushes.

His teeth scraped against hair, snagged, his tongue pressed farther in and Milly tried to pull away just from the pleasure of it, and she said, "Oh, Birdie! Don't!"

And he said, "Oh shit."

The erection receded quickly as the image sinks back into the screen when the set is switched off. He slid out from under her and stood in the puddle, looking at her uplifted sweating ass.

She turned over and brushed the hair out of her eyes. "Oh, Birdie, I didn't mean to . . ."

"Like hell you didn't. Jack."

She sniffed amusement. "Well, now you're one up."

He flipped the limp organ at her self-deprecatingly. "Am I?"

"Honestly, Boz, the first time I really didn't mean it. It just slipped out."

"Indeed it did. But is that supposed to make me feel *better?*" He began dressing. His shoes were inside out.

"For heaven's sake, I haven't thought of Birdie Ludd for years. Literally. He's dead now, for all I know."

"Is that the new kick at your tutorials?"

"You're just being bitter."

"I'm just being bitter, yes."

"Well, fuck you! I'm going out." She began feeling around on the rug for her slip.

"Maybe you can get your father to warm up some of his stiffs for you. Maybe he's got Birdie there on ice."

"You can be so sarcastic sometimes. And you're

standing on my slip. Thank you. Where are you going now?"

"I am going around the room divider to the other
side of the room." Boz went around the room divider
to the other side of the room. He sat down beside the
dining ledge.

"What are you writing?" she asked, pulling the slip
on.

"A poem. That's what *I* was thinking about at the
time."

"Shit." She had started her blouse on the wrong
buttonhole.

"What?" He laid the pen down.

"Nothing. My buttons. Let me see your poem."

> Pricks are noses.
> Cunts are roses.
> Watch the pretty petals fall.

"Why are you so damn hung up on buttons?
They're unfunctional." He handed her the poem!

"It's lovely," she said. "You should send it to *Time*."

"*Time* doesn't print poetry."

"Some place that does, then. It's pretty." Milly had
three basic superlatives: funny, pretty, and nice. Was
she relenting? Or laying a trap?

"Pretty things are a dime a dozen. Twelve for one
dime."

"I'm only trying to be nice, shithead."

"Then learn how. Where are you going?"

"Out." She stopped at the door, frowning. "I do
love you, you know."

"Sure. And I love you."

"Do you want to come along?"

"I'm tired. Give them my love."

She shrugged. She left. He went out on the veranda and watched her as she walked over the bridge across the electric moat and down 48th Street to the corner of 9th. She never looked up once.

And the hell of it was she *did* love him. And he loved her. So why did they always end up like this, with spitting and kicking and gnashing of teeth and the going of their own ways?

Questions, he hated questions. He went into the toilet and swallowed three Oralines, one just nicely too many, and then he sat back and watched the round things with colored edges slide along an endless neon corridor, zippety zippety zippety, spaceships and satellites. The corridor smelled half like a hospital and half like heaven, and Boz began to cry.

The Hansons, Boz and Milly, had been happily unhappily married for a year and a half. Boz was twenty-one and Milly was twenty-six. They had grown up in the same MODICUM building at opposite ends of a long glazed green-tile corridor, but because of the age difference they never really noticed each other until just three years ago. Once they did notice each other though, it was love at first sight, for they were, Boz as much as Milly, of the type that can be, even at a glance, ravishing: flesh molded with that ideal classic plumpness and tinged with those porcelain pink pastels we can admire in the divine Guido, which, at least, *they* admired; eyes hazel, flecked with gold; auburn hair that falls with a slight curl to the round shoulders; and the habit, acquired by each of them so young that it could almost be called natural, of striking poses eloquently superfluous, as when, sitting down to dinner, Boz would throw his head back suddenly, flip-flop of auburn, his ripe lips slightly parted, like a saint (Guido again) in ecstasy—Theresa, Francis, Ganymede—or like, which was almost the same thing, a singer, singing

> I am you
> and you are me
> and we are just two
> sides
> of the same coin.

Three years and Boz was still as hung up on Milly as he had been on the first morning (it was March but it had seemed more like April or May) they'd had sex, and if that wasn't love then Boz didn't know what love meant.

Of course it wasn't just sex, because sex didn't mean that much to Milly, as it was part of her regular work. They also had a very intense spiritual relationship. Boz was basically a spiritual-type person. On the Skinner-Waxman C-P profile he had scored way at the top of the scale by thinking of one hundred and thirty-one different ways to a brick in ten minutes. Milly, though not as creative as Boz according to the Skinner-Waxman, was every bit as smart in terms of IQ (Milly, 136; Boz, 134), and she also had leadership potential, while Boz was content to be a follower as long as things went more or less his own way. Brain surgery aside, they could not have been more compatible, and all of their friends agreed (or they had until very recently) that Boz and Milly, Milly and Boz, made a perfect couple.

So what was it then? Was it jealousy? Boz didn't think it was jealousy, but you can never be sure. He might be jealous unconsciously. But you can't be jealous just because someone was having sex, if that was only a mechanical act and there was no love involved. That would be about as reasonable as getting uptight because Milly *talked* to someone else. Anyhow he had had sex with other people and it never bothered Milly. No, it wasn't sex, it was something psychological, which meant it could be almost anything at all. Every day Boz got more and more depressed trying to analyze it all out. Sometimes he thought of suicide. He bought a razor blade and hid it in *The Naked and the Dead*. He grew a mustache. He shaved off the mustache and had his hair cut short. He let his hair grow long again. It was September and then it was March. Milly said she really did want a divorce, it wasn't working out and she could not stand him nagging at her any more.

Him nagging at *her?*

"Yes, morning and night, nag, nag, nag."

"But you're never even home in the morning, and you're usually not home at night."

"There, you're doing it again? You're nagging now. And when you don't come right out and nag openly, you do it silently. You've been nagging me ever since dinner without saying a word."

"I've been reading a book." He wagged the book at her accusingly. "I wasn't even thinking about you. Unless I nag you just by *existing*." He had meant this to sound pathetic.

"You can, you do."

They were both too pooped and tired to make it a really fun argument, and so just to keep it interesting they had to keep raising the stakes. It ended with Milly screaming and Boz in tears and Boz packing his things into a cupboard, which he took in a taxi to East 11th Street. His mother was delighted to see him. She had been fighting with Lottie and expected Boz to take her side. Boz was given his old bed in the living room, and Amparo had to sleep with her mother. The air was full of smoke from Mrs. Hanson's cigarettes and Boz felt more and more sick. It was all he could do to keep from phoning Milly. Shrimp didn't come home and Lottie was zonked out as usual on Oraline. It was not a life for human beings.

II

The Sacred Heart, gold beard, pink cheeks, blue blue eyes, gazed intently across twelve feet of living space and out the window unit at long recessions of yellow brick. Beside him a Conservation Corporation calendar blinked now BEFORE and then AFTER views of the Grand Canyon. Boz turned over so as not to have to look at Jesus, the Grand Canyon, Jesus. The tuckaway lurched to port side. Mrs. Hanson had been thinking of having someone in to fix the sofa (the missing leg led an independent existence in the cabinet below the sink) ever since the Welfare people had busted it on the day how many years ago that the Hansons had moved in to 334. She would discuss with her family, or with the nice Mrs. Miller from the MOD office, the obstacles in the way of this undertaking, which proved upon examination so ramiform and finally so formidable as very nearly to defeat her most energetic hopes. Nevertheless, some day.

Her nephew, Lottie's youngest, was watching the war on the TV. It was unusual for Boz to sleep so late. U.S. gorillas were burning down a fishing village somewhere. The camera followed the path of the flames along the string of fishing boats, then held for a long time on the empty blue of the water. Then a slow zoom back that took in all the boats together. The horizon warped and flickered through a haze of flame. Gorgeous. Was it a rerun? Boz seemed to think he'd seen that last shot before.

"Hi there, Mickey."

"Hi, Uncle Boz. Grandma says you're getting divorced. Are you going to live with us again?"

"Your grandma needs a decongestant. I'm only here for a few days. On a visit."

The apple pie colophon signaling the end of the war for that Wednesday morning splattered and the decibels were boosted for the April Ford commercial, "Come and Get Me, Cop."

Come and get me, Cop,
'Cause I'm not gonna stop
At your red light.

It was a happy little song, but how could he feel happy when he knew that Milly was probably watching it too and enjoying it in a faculty lounge somewhere, never even giving a thought for Boz, or where he was, or how he felt. Milly studied all the commercials and could play them back to you verbatim, every tremor and inflection just so. And not a milligram of her own punch. Creative? As a parrot.

Now, what if he were to tell her that? What if he told her that she would never be anything more than a second-string Grade-Z hygiene demonstrator for the Board of Education. Cruel? Boz was supposed to be cruel?

He shook his head, flip-flop of auburn. "Baby, you don't know what cruel is."

Mickey switched off the TV. "Oh, if you think this was something today you should have seen them yesterday. They were in this school. Pakistanis, I think.

Yeah. You should have seen it. That was cruel. They
wiped them out."

"Who did?"

"Company A." Mickey came to attention and saluted the air. Kids his age (six) always wanted to be
gorillas or firemen. At ten it was pop singers. At fourteen, if they were bright (and somehow all the Hansons were bright), they wanted to write. Boz still had
a whole scrapbook of the advertisements he'd written
in high school. And then, at twenty . . . ?

Don't think about it.

"You didn't care?" Boz asked.

"Care?"

"About the kids in the school."

"They were insurgents," Mickey explained. "It was
in Pakistan." Even Mars was more real than Pakistan,
and no one gets upset about schools burning on
Mars.

A flop flop flop of slippers and Mrs. Hanson sham-
bled in with a cup of Koffee. "Politics, you'd try and
argue politics with a six-year-old! Here. Go ahead,
drink it."

He sipped the sweet thickened Koffee and it was as
though every stale essence in the building, garbage
rotting in bins and grease turning yellow on kitchen
walls, tobacco smoke and stale beer and Synthamon
candies, everything ersatz, everything he'd thought he
had escaped, had flooded back into the core of his
body with just that one mouthful.

"He's become too good for us now, Mickey. Look
at him."

"It's sweeter than I'm used to. Otherwise it's fine,
Mom."

"It's no different than you used to have it. Three

tablets. I'll drink this one and make you another. You
came here to stay."

"No, I told you last night that—"

She waved a hand at him, shouted to her grandson:
"Where you going?"

"Down to the street."

"Take the key and bring the mail up first, understand. If you don't . . ."

He was gone. She collapsed in the green chair, on
top of a pile of clothes, talking to herself, or to him,
she wasn't particular about her audience. He heard not
words but the reedy vibrato of her phlegm, saw the
fingers stained with nicotine, the jiggle of sallow chin-
flesh, the MOD teeth. My mother.

Boz turned his eyes to the scaly wall where roseate
AFTER winked to a tawdry BEFORE, and Jesus,
squeezing a bleeding organ in his right hand, forgave
the world for yellow bricks that stretched as far as the
eye could see.

"The work she comes home with you wouldn't believe. I told Lottie, it's a crime, she should complain.
How old is she? Twelve years old. If it had been
Shrimp, if it had been you, I wouldn't say a word, but
she has her mother's health, she's very delicate. And
the exercises they make them do, it's not decent for
a child. I'm not against sex, I always let you and Milly
do whatever you wanted. I turned my head. But that
sort of thing should be private between two people.
The things you see, and I mean right out on the street.
They don't even go into a doorway now. So I tried to
make Lottie see reason, I was very calm, I didn't raise
my voice. Lottie doesn't want it herself, you know,
she's being pressured by the school. How often would
she be able to see her? Weekends. And one month in

the summer. It's all Shrimp's doing. I said to Shrimp, if you want to be a ballet dancer then you go ahead and be a ballet dancer but leave Amparo alone. The man came from the school, and he was very smooth and Lottie signed the papers, I could have cried. Of course it was all arranged. They waited till I was out of the house. She's your child, I told her, leave me out of it. If that's what you want for her, the kind of future you think she deserves. You should hear the stories she comes home with. Twelve years old! It's Shrimp, taking her to those movies, taking her to the park. Of course you can see all of that on television too, that Channel 5, I don't know why they . . . But I suppose it's none of my business. No one cares what you think when you're old. Let her go to the Lowen School, it won't break my heart." She kneaded the left side of her dress illustratively: her heart.

"We could use the room here, though you won't hear me complaining about that. Mrs. Miller said we could apply for a larger apartment, there's five of us, and now six with you, but if I said yes and we moved and then Amparo goes off to this school, we'd just have to move back here, because the requirement there is for five people. Besides it would mean moving all the way to Queens. Now if Lottie were to have another, but of course her health isn't up to it, not to speak of the mental thing. And Shrimp? Well, I don't have to go into that. So I said no, let's stay put. Besides, if we did go and then had to come back here, we probably wouldn't have the luck to get the same apartment again. I don't deny that there are lots of things wrong with it, but still. Try and get water after four o'clock, like sucking a dry tit."

Hoarse laughter, another cigarette. Having broken the thread of thought, she found herself lost in the labyrinth: her eyes darted around the room, little cultured pearls that bounced off into every corner.

Boz had not listened to the monologue, but he was aware of the panic that welled up to fill the sudden wonderful silence. Living with Milly he'd forgotten this side of things, the causeless incurable terrors. Not just his mother's: everyone who lived below 34th.

Mrs. Hanson slurped her Koffee. The sound (her own sound, *she* made it) reassured her and she started talking again, making more of her own sounds. The panic ebbed. Boz closed his eyes.

"That Mrs. Miller means well, of course, but she doesn't understand my situation. What do you think she said I should do, what do you think? Visit that death-house on 12th Street! Said it would be an inspiration. Not to me, to *them*. Seeing someone at my age with my energy and the head of a family. My age! You'd think I was ready to turn to dust like one of those what-do-you-call-its. I was born in 1967, the year the first man landed on the moon. Nineteen sixty-seven. I'm not even sixty, but suppose I were, is there a law against it? Listen, as long as I can make it up those stairs they don't have to worry about me! Those elevators are a crime. I can't even remember the last time . . . No, wait a minute, I can. You were eight years old, and every time I took you inside you'd start to cry. You used to cry about everything though. It's my own fault, spoiling you, and your sisters went right along. That time I came home and you were in Lottie's clothes, lipstick and everything, and to think she helped you. Well, I stopped that! If it had been Shrimp I could understand. Shrimp's that way herself. I always said to Mrs. Holt when she was alive, she had very old-fashioned ideas, Mrs. Holt, that as long as Shrimp had what she wanted it was no concern of hers or mine. And anyhow you'll have to admit that she was a homely girl, while Lottie, oh my, Lottie was so beautiful. Even in high school. She'd spend all her time in front of a mirror and you could hardly blame her. Like a movie star."

She lowered her voice, as though confiding a secret to the olive-drab film of dehydrated vegetable oil on her Koffee.

"And then to go and do that. I couldn't believe my eyes when I saw him. Is it prejudice to want something better for your children? Then I'm prejudiced. A good-looking boy, I don't deny that, and even smart in his way I suppose. He wrote poems to her. In Spanish, so I wouldn't be able to understand them. I told her, it's your life, Lottie, go ahead and ruin it any way you like, but don't tell me I'm prejudiced. You children never heard me use words like that and you never will. I may not have more than a high school education but I know the difference between . . . right and wrong. At the wedding she wore this blue dress and I never said a word about how short it was. So beautiful. It still makes me cry." She paused. Then, with great emphasis, as though this were the single unassailable conclusion that these many evidences remorselessly required of her: "He was always very polite."

Another longer pause.

"You're not listening to me, Boz."

"Yes I am. You said he was always very polite."

"Who?"

Boz searched through his inner family album for the face of anyone who might have behaved politely to his mother.

"My brother-in-law?"

Mrs. Hanson nodded. "Exactly. Juan. And she also said why didn't I try religion." She shook her head in a pantomime of amazement that such things could be allowed.

"She? Who?"

The dry lips puckered with disappointment. The discontinuity had been intended, a trap, but Boz had slipped past. She knew he wasn't listening, but she couldn't prove it.

"Mrs. Miller. She said it would be good for me. I told her one religious nut in the family is enough, and besides I don't call that religion. I mean, I enjoy a stick of Oraline as much as anyone, but religion has to come from the heart." Again she rumpled the violet, orange, and heather-gold flames of her bodice. Down below there somewhere it filled up with blood and squirted it out into the arteries: her heart.

"Are you still that way?" she asked.

"Religious? No, I was off that before I got married. Milly's dead against it too. It's all chemistry."

"Try and tell that to your sister."

"Oh, but for Shrimp it's a meaningful experience. She understands about the chemistry. She just doesn't care, so long as it works."

Boz knew better than to take sides in any family quarrel. Once already in his life he had had to slip loose from those knots, and he knew their strength.

Mickey returned with the mail, laid it on the TV, and was out the door before his grandmother could invent new errands.

One envelope.

"Is it for me?" Mrs. Hanson asked. Boz didn't stir. She took a deep wheezing breath and pushed herself up out of the chair.

"It's for Lottie," she announced, opening the envelope. "It's from the Alexander Lowen School. Where Amparo wants to go."

"What's it say?"

"They'll take her. She has a scholarship for one year. Six thousand dollars."

"Jesus. That's great."

Mrs. Hanson sat down on the couch, across Boz's ankles, and cried. She cried for well over five minutes. Then the kitchen timer went off: "As the World Turns." She hadn't missed an installment in years and neither had Boz. She stopped crying. They watched the program.

Sitting there pinned beneath his mother's weight, warmed by her flesh, Boz felt good. He could shrink down to the size of a postage stamp, a pearl, a pea, a wee small thing, mindless and happy, non-existent, utterly lost in the mail.

III

Shrimp was digging God, and God (she felt sure) was digging Shrimp: her, here on the roof of 334; Him, out there in the russet smogs of dusk, in the lovely poisons of the Jersey air, everywhere. Or maybe it wasn't God but something moving more or less in that direction. Shrimp wasn't sure.

Boz, dangling his feet over the ledge, watched the double moiré patterns of her skin and her shift. The spiral patterns of the cloth moved widdershins, the flesh patterns stenciled beneath ran deasil. The March wind fluttered the material and Shrimp swayed and the spirals spun, vortices of gold and green, lyric illusions.

Off somewhere on another roof an illegal dog yapped. Yap, yap, yap; I love you, I love you, I love you.

Usually Boz tried to stay on the surface of something nice like this, but tonight he was exiled to inside of himself, redefining his problem and coming to grips with it realistically. Basically (he decided) the trouble lay in his own character. He was weak. He had let Milly have her own way in everything until she'd forgotten that Boz might have his own legitimate demands. Even Boz had forgotten. It was a one-sided relationship. He felt he was vanishing, melting into air, sucked down into the green-gold whirlpool. He felt like shit. The pills had taken him in exactly the wrong direction, and Shrimp, out there in St. Theresa country, was no aid or comfort.

The russet dimmed to a dark mauve and then it was night. God veiled His glory and Shrimp came down. "Poor Boz," she said.

"Poor Boz," he agreed.

"On the other hand you've gotten away from this." Her hand whisked away the East Village roofscape and every ugliness. A second, more impatient whisk, as though she'd found the whole mess glued to her hand. In fact, it had *become* her hand, her arm, the whole stiff contraption of flesh she had managed for three hours and fifteen minutes to escape.

"And poor Shrimp."

"Poor Shrimp too," he agreed.

"Because *I'm* stuck here."

"This morning who was telling me it isn't where you live, it's *how* you live?"

She shrugged a sharp-edged scapula. She hadn't been speaking of the building but of her own body, but it would have taken too much trouble to explain that to blossoming Narcissus. She was annoyed with Boz for dwelling on *his* miseries, *his* inner conflicts. She had her own dissatisfactions that she wanted to discuss, hundreds.

"Your problem is very simple, Boz. Once you face it. Your problem is that basically you're a Republican."

"Oh, come off it, Shrimp!"

"Honestly. When you and Milly started living together, Lottie and I couldn't believe it. It had always been clear as day to us."

"Just because I have a pretty face doesn't mean—"

"Oh, Boz, you're being dense. You know that has nothing to do with it one way or the other. And I'm not saying you should vote Republican because I do. But I can read the signs. If you'd look at yourself with a little psychoanalysis you'd be forced to see how much you've been repressing."

He flared up. It was one thing to be called a Republican, but no one was going to call him repressed. "Well, shit on you, sister. If you want to know my party, I'll tell you. When I was thirteen I used to jerk off while I watched you undress, and believe me, it takes a pretty dedicated Democrat to do that."

"That's nasty," she said.

It was nasty, and as untrue as it was nasty. He'd fantasized often enough about Lottie, about Shrimp never. Her short thin brittle body appalled him. She was a gothic cathedral bristling with crockets and pinnacles, a forest of leafless trees; he wanted nice sunshiny cortiles and flowery glades. She was a Dürer engraving; he was a landscape by Domenichino. Screw Shrimp? He'd as soon turn Republican, even if she was his own sister.

"Not that I'm against Republicanism," he added diplomatically. "I'm no Puritan. I just don't enjoy having sex with other guys."

"You've never given it a chance." She spoke in an aggrieved tone.

"Sure I have. Plenty of times."

"Then why is your marriage breaking up?"

Tears started dripping. He cried all the time nowadays, like an air conditioner. Shrimp, skilled in compassion, wept right along with him, wrapping a length of wiry arm around his bare, exquisite shoulders.

Snuffling, he threw back his head, Flip-flop of auburn, big brave smile. "How about the party?"

"Not for me, not tonight. I'm feeling too religious and holy sort of. Maybe later perhaps."

"Aw, Shrimp."

"Really." She wrapped herself in her arms, stuck out her chin, waited for him to plead.

The dog in the distances made new noises.

"One time, when I was a kid . . . right after we moved here, in fact . . ." Boz began dreamily.

But he could see she wasn't listening.

Dogs had just been made finally illegal, and the dog owners were doing Anne-Frank numbers to protect their pups from the city Gestapo. They stopped walking them on the streets, so the roof of 334, which the Park Commission had declared to be a playground (they'd built a cyclone fence all round the edge to give it a playground atmosphere), got to be ankle-deep in dogshit. A war developed between the kids and dogs to see who the roof would belong to. The kids would hunt down off-leash dogs, usually at night, and throw them over the edge. German shepherds fought back the hardest. Boz had seen a shepherd take one of Milly's cousins down to the pavement with him.

All the things that happen and seem so important at the time, and yet you just forget them, one after another. He felt an elegant, controlled sadness, as though, were he to sit down now and work at it, he might write a fine, mature piece of philosophy.

"I'm going to sail away now. Okay?"

"Enjoy yourself," Shrimp said.

He touched her ear with his lips, but it wasn't, even in a brotherly sense, a kiss. A sign, rather, of the distance between them, like the signs on highways that tell you how far it is in miles to New York City.

The party was not by any means a form of insanity, but Boz enjoyed himself in a quiet decorative way, sitting on a bench and looking at knees. Then Williken the photographer from 334 came over and told Boz about Nuancism, Williken being a Nuancist from way back when, how it was overdue for a renaissance. He looked older than Boz remembered him, parched and fleshless and pathetically forty-three.

"Forty-three is the best age," Williken said again, having at last disposed of the history of art to his satisfaction.

"Better than twenty-one?" Which was Boz's age, of course.

Williken decided this was a joke, and coughed. (Williken smoked tobacco.) Boz looked away, and caught the fellow with the red beard eyeing him. A small gold earring twinkled in his left ear.

"Twice as good," Williken said, "and then a bit." Since this was a joke too, he coughed again.

He was (the red beard, the gold earring) next to Boz the best-looking person there. Boz got up, with a pat to the old man's frayed and folded hands.

"And how old are you?" he asked the red beard, the gold earring.

"Six foot two. Yourself?"

"I'm versatile, pretty much. Where do you live?"

"The East Seventies. Yourself?"

"I've been evacuated." Boz struck a pose: Sebastian (Guido's) spreading himself open, flowerlike, to receive the arrows of men's admiration. Oh, Boz could charm the plaster off the walls! "Are you a friend of January's?"

"A friend of a friend, but that friend didn't show. Yourself?"

"The same thing, sort of."

Danny (his name was Danny) grabbed a handful of the auburn hair.

"I like your knees," Boz said.

"You don't think they're too bushy?"

"No, I like bushy knees."

When they left January was in the bathroom. They shouted their good-bys through the paper panel. All the way home—going down the stairs, in the street, in the subway, in the elevator of Danny's building—they kissed and touched and rubbed up against each other, but though this was exciting to Boz in a psychological way, it *didn't* give him a hard-on.

Nothing gave Boz a hard-on.

While Danny, behind the screen, stirred the instant milk over the hotcoil, Boz, alone in all that double bed, watched the hamsters in their cage. The hamsters were screwing in the jumpy, jittery way that hamsters have, and the lady hamster said, "Shirk, shirk, shirk." All nature reproached Boz.

"Sweetener?" Danny asked, emerging with the cups.

"Thanks just the same. I shouldn't be wasting your time like this."

"Who's to say the time's been wasted? Maybe in another half-hour . . ." The mustache detached itself from the beard: a smile.

Boz smoothed his pubic hairs sadly, ruefully, wobbled the oblivious soft cock. "No, it's out of commission tonight."

"Maybe a bit of roughing up? I know guys who—"

Boz shook his head. "It wouldn't help."

"Well, drink your Koffee. Sex isn't that important, believe me. There are other things."

The hamster said, "Shirk! Shirk, shirk."

"I suppose not."

"It isn't," Danny insisted. "Are you always impotent?" There, he had said the dreaded word.

"God, no!" (The horror of it!)

"So? One off-night is nothing to worry about. It happens to me all the time and *I* do it for a living. I'm a hygiene demonstrator."

"You?"

"Why not? A Democrat by day, and a Republican in my spare time. By the way, how are you registered?"

Boz shrugged. "What difference does it make if you don't vote?"

"Stop feeling sorry for yourself."

"I'm a Democrat actually, but before I got married I was Independent. That's why, tonight, I never thought, when I came home with you, that—I mean, you're damned good looking, Danny."

Danny blushed agreement. "Get off it. So tell me, what's wrong with your marriage?"

"You wouldn't want to hear about it," Boz said, and then he went through the whole story of Boz and Milly: of how they had had a beautiful relationship, of how that relationship had then soured, of how he didn't understand why.

"Have you see a counselor?" Danny asked.

"What good would that do?"

Danny had manufactured a tear of real compassion, and he lifted Boz's chin to make certain he would notice. "You should. Your marriage still means a *lot* to you, and if something's gone wrong, you should at least know what. I mean, it might just be something stupid, like getting your metabolic cycles synchronized."

"You're right, I guess."

Danny bent over and squeezed Boz's calf earnestly. "Of course I'm right. Tell you what, I know someone who's supposed to be terrific. On Park Avenue. I'll give you his number." He kissed Boz quickly on the nose, just in time for the tear of his empathy to plop on Boz's cheek.

Later, after one last determined effort, Danny, in nothing but his transparency, saw Boz down to the moat, which (also) was defunct.

When they had kissed good-by and while they were still shaking hands, Boz asked, as though off-handedly, as though he had been thinking of anything else for the last half-hour: "By the way, you wouldn't have worked at Erasmus Hall, would you?"

"No. Why? Did you go there? I wouldn't have been teaching anywhere in your time."

"No. I have a friend who works there. At Washington Irving?"

"I'm out in Bedford-Stuyvesant, actually." The admission was not without its pennyworth of chagrin. "But what's his name? Maybe we met at a union meeting, or something like that."

"It's a she—Milly Hanson."

"Sorry, never heard of her. There are a lot of us, you know. This is a big city." In every direction the pavement and the walls agreed.

Their hands unclasped. Their smiles faded, and they became invisible to each other, like boats that draw apart, moving across the water into heavy mists.

IV

---

277 Park Avenue, where McGonagall's office was, was
a dowdy sixtyish affair that had been a bit player back
in the glass-and-steel boom. But then came the
ground-test tremors of '96 and it had to be wrapped.
Now it had the look, outside, of Milly's last-year dirty-
yellow Wooly © waistcoat. That, plus the fact that
McGonagall was an old-fashioned type Republican
(a style that still mostly inspired distrust), made it
hard for him to get even the official Guild minimum
for his services. Not that it made much difference for
them—after the first fifty dollars the Board of Education would pay the rest under its sanity-and-health
clause.

The waiting room was simply done up with paper
mattresses and a couple authenticated Saroyans to
cheer up the noonday-white walls: an

Alice

and:

Fashionwise Milly was doing an imitation of maiden
modesty in her old Pan Am uniform, a blue-gray gauzy
jerkin over crisp businesslike pajamas. Boz, meanwhile,

was sporting creamy street shorts and a length of the same blue-gray gauze knotted round his throat. When he moved it fluttered after him like a shadow. Between them they were altogether tout ensemble, a picture. They didn't talk. They waited in the room designed for that purpose.

Half a damned hour.

The entrance to McGonagall's office was something from the annals of the Met. The door sublimed into flame, and they passed through, a Pamina, a Tamino, accompanied appropriately by flute and drum, strings and horns. A fat man in a white shift welcomed them mutely into his bargain-rate temple of wisdom, clasping first Pamina's, then Tamino's hands in his. A sensitivist obviously.

He pressed his pink-frosted middle-aged face close to Boz's, as though he were reading its fine print. "You're Boz," he said reverently. Then with a glance in her direction: "And you're Milly."

"No," she said peevishly (it was that half-hour), "I'm Boz, and she's Milly."

"Sometimes," McGonagall said, letting go, "the best solution is divorce. I want you both to understand that if that should be my opinion in your case, I won't hesitate to say so. If you're annoyed that I kept you waiting so long, tant pis, since it was for a good reason. It rids us of our company manners from the start. And what is the first thing you say when you come in here? That your husband is a woman! How did it make you feel, Boz, to know that Milly would like to cut off your balls and wear them herself?"

Boz shrugged, long suffering, ever-likable. "I thought it was funny."

"Ha," laughed McGonagall, "that's what you

thought. But what did you *feel?* Did you want to strike her? Were you afraid? Or secretly pleased?"

"That's it in a nutshell."

McGonagall's living body sank into something pneumatic and blue and floated there like a giant white squid bobbing on the calm surface of a summer sea. "Well then, tell me about your sex life, Mrs. Hanson."

"Our sex life is pretty," Milly said.

"Adventurous," Boz continued.

"And quite frequent." She folded her pretty, faultless arms.

"When we're together," Boz added. A grace note of genuine self-pity decorated the flat irony of the statement. This soon he felt his insides squeezing some idle tears from the appropriate glands; while, in other glands, Milly had begun to churn up petty grievances into a lovely smooth yellow anger. In this, as in so many other ways, they achieved a kind of symmetry between them, they made a pair.

"Your jobs?"

"All that kind of thing is on our profiles," Milly said. "You've had a month to look at them. A half-hour, at the very least."

"But on your profile, Mrs. Hanson, there's no mention of this remarkable reluctance of yours, this grudging every word." He lifted two ambiguous fingers, scolding and blessing her in a single gesture. Then, to Boz: "What do you do, Boz?"

"Oh, I'm strictly a husband. Milly's the breadwinner."

They both looked at Milly.

"I demonstrate sex in the high schools," she said.

"Sometimes," McGonagall said, spilling sideways meditatively over his blue balloon (like all very clever fat men he knew how to pretend to be Buddha), "what are thought to be marital difficulties have their origin in *job* problems."

Milly smiled an assured porcelain smile. "The city tests us every semester on job satisfaction, Mr. Mc-Gonagall. Last time I came out a little high on the ambition scale, but not above the mean score for those who eventually have moved on into administrative work. Boz and I are here because we can't spend two hours together without starting to fight. I can't sleep in the same bed any more, and he gets heartburn when we eat together."

"Well, let's assume for now that you are adjusted to your job. How about you, Boz? Have you been happy being 'just a husband'?"

Boz fingered the gauze knotted round his throat. "Well, no . . . I guess I'm not completely *happy* or we wouldn't be here. I get—oh, I don't know—restless. Sometimes. But I know I wouldn't be any happier working at a job. Jobs are like going to church: it's nice once or twice a year to sing along and eat something and all that, but unless you really believe there's something holy going on, it gets to be a drag going in every single week."

"Have you ever had a real job?"

"A couple times. I hated it. I think most people must hate their jobs. I mean, why else do they pay people to work?"

"Yet something *is* wrong, Boz. Something is missing from your life that ought to be there."

"Something. I don't know what." He looked down-hearted.

McGonagall reached out for his hand. Human contact was of fundamental importance in McGonagall's business. "Children?" he asked, turning to Milly, after this episode of warmth and feeling.

"We can't afford children."

"Would you want them, if you felt you could afford them?"

She pursed her lips. "Oh yes, very much."

"*Lots* of children?"

"Really!"

"There are people, you know, who do want lots of children, who'd have as many as they could if it weren't for the REGENTS system."

"My mother," Boz volunteered, "had four kids. They all came before the Genetic Testing Act, of course, except for me, and I was only allowed then because Jimmy, her oldest one, got killed in a riot, or a dance, or something, when he was fourteen."

"Do you have pets at home?" McGonagall's drift was clear.

"A cat," Boz said, "and a rubber plant."

"Who takes care of the cat mostly?"

"I do, but that's because I'm there through the day. Since I've been gone Milly had to take care of Tabby. It must be lonely for her. For old Tabbycat."

"Kittens?"

Boz shook his head.

"No," Milly said. "I had her spayed."

Boz could almost hear McGonagall thinking: Oh ho! He knew how the session would continue from this point, and that the heat was off him and on Milly. McGonagall might be right, or he might not, but he had an idea between his jaws and he wasn't letting loose: Milly needed to have a baby (a woman's fulfillment); Boz, well, it looked like Boz was going to be a mother.

Sure enough, by the end of the session Milly was spread out on the pliant white floor, back uparched, screaming ("Yes, a baby! I want a baby! Yes, a baby!

A baby!") and having hysterical simulated birth spasms. It was beautiful. Milly hadn't broken down, really broken all the way down, and cried in how long? Years. It was one hundred per cent beautiful.

Afterwards they decided to go down by the stairs, which were dusty and dark and tremendously erotic. They made it on the twenty-eighth floor landing and, their legs all atremble, again on the twelfth. The juice shot out of him in dazzling gigantic hiccoughs, like milk spurting out of a full-to-the-top two-quart container, so much they neither could believe it: a heavenly breakfast, a miracle proving their existence, and a promise they were both determined to keep.

It wasn't all sweetness and roses, by any means. They had more paper work to do than from all the 1040 Forms they'd ever prepared. Plus: visits to a pregnancy counselor; to the hospital to get the prescriptions they both had to start taking; then reserving a bottle at Mount Sinai for after Milly's fourth month (the city would pay for that, so she could stay on the job); and the final solemn moment at the REGENTS office when Milly drank the first bitter glass of the anticontraceptive agent. (She was sick the rest of the day, but did she complain? Yes.) For two weeks after that she couldn't drink anything that came out of the tap in the apartment, until, happy day, her morning test showed a positive reading.

They decided it would be a girl: Loretta, after Boz's sister. They redecided, later, on: Aphra, Murray, Algebra, Sniffles (Boz's preferences), and Pamela, Grace, Lulu, and Maureen (Milly's preferences).

Boz knitted a kind of blanket.

The days grew longer and the nights shorter. Then vice versa. Peanut (which was her name whenever they couldn't decide what her name really would be) was scheduled to be decanted the night before Xmas, 2025.

But the important thing, beyond the microchemistry of where babies come from, was the problem of psychological adjustment to parenthood, by no means a simple thing.

This is the way McGonagall put it to Boz and Milly during their last private counseling session:

"The way we work, the way we talk, the way we watch television or walk down the street, even the way we fuck, or maybe that especially—each of those is part of the problem of identity. We can't do any of those things *authentically* until we find out who we really are and *be* that person, inside and out, instead of the person other people want us to be. Usually those other people, if they want us to be something we aren't, are using us as a laboratory for working out their own identity problems.

"Now Boz, we've seen how you're expected, a hundred tiny times a day, to seem to be one kind of person in personal relationships and a completely different kind of person at other times. Or to use your own words—you're 'just a husband.' This particular way of sawing a person in two got started in the last century, with automation. First jobs became easier, and then scarcer—especially the kinds of jobs that came under the heading of a 'man's work.' In every field men were working side by side with women. For some men the only way to project a virile image was to wear levis on the weekends and to smoke the right brand of cigarette. Marlboros, usually." His lips tightened and his fingers flexed delicately, as again, in his mouth and in his lungs, desire contested with will in the endless, ancient battle: with just such a gesture would a stylite have spoken of the temptations of the flesh, rehearsing the old pleasures only to reject them.

"What this meant, in psychological terms, was that men no longer needed the same kind of uptight, aggressive character structure, any more than they needed the bulky, Greek-wrestler physiques that went along with that kind of character. Even as sexual plumage that kind of body became unfashionable. Girls began to prefer slender, short ectomorphs. The ideal couples were those, like the two of you as a matter of fact, who mirrored each other. It was a kind of movement inward from the poles of sexuality.

"Today, for the first time in human history, men are free to express the essentially *feminine* component in their personality. In fact, from the economic point of view, it's almost required of them. Of course I'm not talking about homosexuality. A man can be *feminized* well beyond the point of transvestism without losing his preference for cunt, a preference which is an *inescapable* consequence of having a cock."

He paused to appreciate his own searing honesty— a Republican speaking at a testimonial dinner for Adlai Stevenson!

"Well, this is pretty much what you must have heard all through high school, but it's one thing to understand something intellectually and quite another to feel it in your body. What most men felt *then*—the ones who allowed themselves to go along with the feminizing tendencies of the age—was simply a crushing, horrible, total guilt, a guilt that became, eventually, a much worse burden than the initial repression. And so the Sexual Revolution of the sixties was followed by the dreary Counter-Revolution of the seventies and eighties, when I grew up. Let me tell you, though I'm sure you've been told many times, that it was simply awful. *All* the men dressed in black or gray or possibly, the adventuresome ones, a muddy brown. They had short haircuts and walked—you can see it in the movies they made then—like early-model robots. They had made such an effort to deny what was happening that they'd become frozen from the waist down. It got so bad that at one point there were four TV series about zombies.

"I wouldn't be going over this ancient history except that I don't think young people your age realize how lucky you are having missed that. Life still has problems—or I'd be out of work—but at least people today who want to solve them have a chance.

"To get back to the decision you're facing, Boz. It was in that same period, the early eighties (in Japan, of course, since it would surely have been illegal in the States then), that the research was done that allowed feminization to be more than a mere cosmetic process. Even so, it was years before these techniques became at all widespread. Only in the last two decades, really. Before our time, every man had been obliged, for simple *biological* reasons, to deny his own deep-rooted maternal instincts. Motherhood is basically a psychosocial, and not a sexual, phenomenon. Every child, be he boy or girl, grows up by learning to emulate his mother. He (or she) plays with dolls and cooks mud pies—if he lives somewhere where mud is available. He rides the shopping cart through the supermarket, like a little kangaroo. And so on. It's only natural for men, when they grow up, to wish to be mothers themselves, if their social and economic circumstances allow it—that is to say, if they have the leisure, since the rest can now be taken care of.

"In short, Milly, Boz needs more than your love, or any woman's love, or any man's love, for that matter.

Like you, he needs another *kind* of fulfillment. He needs, as you do, a child. He needs, even more than you do, the experience of motherhood."

V

In November, at Mount Sinai, Boz had the operation —and Milly too, of course, since she had to be the donor. Already he'd undergone the series of implantations of plastic "dummies" to prepare the skin of his chest for the new glands that would be living there— and to prepare Boz himself spiritually for his new condition. Simultaneously a course of hormone treatments created a new chemical balance in his body so that the mammaries would be incorporated into its working order and yield from the first a nourishing milk.

Motherhood (as McGonagall had often explained) to be a truly meaningful and liberating experience had to be entered into wholeheartedly. It had to become part of the structure of nerve and tissue, not just a process or a habit or a social role.

Every hour of that first month was an identity crisis. A moment in front of a mirror could send Boz off into fits of painful laughter or precipitate him into hours of gloom. Twice, returning from her job, Milly was convinced that her husband had buckled under the strain, but each time her tenderness and patience through the night saw Boz over the hump. In the morning they would go to the hospital to see Peanut floating in her bottle of brown glass, pretty as a water lily. She was completely formed now and a human being just like her mother and father. At those moments Boz couldn't understand what all his agonizing had been about. If anyone ought to have been upset, it should have been Milly, for there she stood, on the threshold of parenthood, slim-bellied, with tubes of liquid silicone for breasts, robbed by the hospital and her husband of the actual experience of maternity. Yet she seemed to possess only reverence for this new life they had created between them. It was as though Milly, rather than Boz, were Peanut's father, and birth were a mystery she might admire from a distance but never wholly, never intimately, share.

Then, precisely as scheduled, at seven o'clock of the evening of December 24, Peanut (who was stuck with this name now for good and forever, since they'd never been able to agree on any other) was released from the brown glass womb, tilted topsy-turvy, tapped on the back. With a fine, full-throated yell (which was to be played back for her every birthday till she was twenty-one years old, the year she rebelled and threw the tape in an incinerator), Peanut Hanson joined the human race.

The one thing he had not been expecting, the wonderful thing, was how busy he had to be. Till now his concern had always been to find ways to fill the vacant daylight hours, but in the first ecstasies of his new selflessness there wasn't time for half of all that needed doing. It was more than a matter of meeting Peanut's needs, though these were prodigious from the beginning and grew to heroic proportions. But with his daughter's birth he had been converted to an eclectic, new-fangled form of conservationism. He started doing real cooking again, and this time without the grocery bills rocketing. He studied Yoga with a handsome young yogi on Channel 3. (There was no time, of course, under the new regime for the four o'clock art movies.) He cut back his Koffee intake to a single cup with Milly at breakfast.

What's more, he kept his zeal alive week after week after month after month. In a modest, modified form he never entirely abandoned the vision, if not always the reality, of a better, richer, fuller, and more responsible life pattern.

Peanut, meanwhile, grew. In two months she doubled her weight from six pounds two ounces to twelve pounds four ounces. She smiled at faces, and developed a repertoire of interesting sounds. She ate—first only a teaspoon or so—Banana-food and Pear-food and cereals. Before long she had dabbled in every flavor of vegetable Boz could find for her. It was only the beginning of what would be a long and varied career as a consumer.

One day early in May, after a chill, rainy spring, the temperature bounced up suddenly to 70°. A sea wind had rinsed the sky from its conventional dull gray to baby blue.

Boz decided that the time had come for Peanut's first voyage into the unknown. He unsealed the door to the balcony and wheeled the little crib outside.

Peanut woke. Her eyes were hazel with tiny flecks of gold. Her skin was as pink as a shrimp bisque. She rocked her crib into a good temper. Boz watched the little fingers playing scales on the city's springtime airs, and catching her gay spirits, he sang to her, a strange silly song he remembered his sister Lottie singing to Amparo, a song that Lottie had heard her mother sing to Boz:

> Pepsi cola hits the spot.
> Two full glasses, thanks a lot.
> Lost my savior, lost my zest,
> Lost my lease, I'm going west.

A breeze ruffled Peanut's dark silky hair, touched Boz's heavier auburn curls. The sunlight and air were like the movies of a century ago, so impossibly clean. He just closed his eyes and practiced his breathing.

At two o'clock, punctual as the news, Peanut started crying. Boz lifted her from the crib and gave her his breast. Except when he left the apartment nowadays, Boz didn't bother with clothing. The little mouth closed round his nipple and the little hands gripped the soft flesh back from the tit. Boz felt a customary tingle of pleasure, but this time it didn't fade away when Peanut settled into a steady rhythm of sucking and swallowing, sucking and swallowing. Instead it spread across the surface and down into the depths of his breast; it blossomed inward to his chest's core. Without stiffening, his cock was visited by tremors of delicate pleasure, and this pleasure traveled, in waves, into his loins and down through the muscles of his legs. For a while he thought he would have to stop the feeding, the sensation became so intense, so exquisite, so much.

He tried that night to explain it to Milly, but she displayed no more than a polite interest. She'd been elected, a week before, to an important post in her union, and her head was still filled with the grim, gray pleasure of ambition satisfied, of having squeezed a toe onto the very first rung of the ladder. He decided it would not be nice to carry on at greater length, so he saved it up for the next time Shrimp came by. Shrimp had had three children over the years (her REGENTS scores were so good that her pregnancies were subsidized by the National Genetics Council), but a sense of emotional self-defense had always kept Shrimp from relating too emphatically to the babies during her year-long stints of motherhood (after which

they were sent to the Council's schools in Wyoming
and Utah). She assured Boz that what he'd felt that
afternoon on the balcony had been nothing extraordinary, it happened to her all the time, but Boz knew
that it had been the very essence of unusualness. It
was, in Lord Krishna's words, a peak experience, a
glimpse behind the veil.

Finally, he realized, it was his own moment and
could not be shared any more than it could be, in just
the same way, repeated.

It never was repeated, that moment, even approxi-
mately. Eventually he was able to forget what it had
been like and only remembered the remembering of it.

Some years later Boz and Milly were sitting out on
their balcony at sunset.

Neither had changed radically since Peanut's birth.
Boz was perhaps a bit heavier than Milly, but it would
have been hard to say whether this was from his having gained or Milly having lost. Milly was a supervisor
now, and had a seat, besides, on three different com-
mittees.

Boz said, "Do you remember our special building?"

"What building is that?"

"The one over there. With the three windows." Boz
pointed to the right where gigantic twin apartments
framed a vista westward of rooftops, cornices, and wa-
tertanks. Some of the buildings probably dated back to
the New York of Boss Tweed; none were new.

Milly shook her head. "There are lots of buildings."

"The one just in back of the right-hand corner of
that big yellow-brick thing with the funny temple hiding its watertank. See it?"

"Mm. There?"

"Yes. You don't remember it?"

"Vaguely. No."

"We'd just moved in here, and we couldn't really afford the place, so for the first year it was practically bare. I kept after you about our buying a houseplant, and you said we'd have to wait. Does it start to come back?"

"Mistily."

"Well, the two of us would come out here regularly and look out at the different buildings and try and figure out exactly which street each of them would be on and whether we knew any of them from sidewalk level."

"I remember now! That's the one where the windows were always closed. But that's all I remember about it."

"Well, we made up a story about it. We said that after maybe five years one of the windows would be opened just enough so we'd be able to see it from here, an inch or two. Then the next day it would be closed again."

"And then?" She was by now genuinely and pleasantly puzzled.

"And then, according to our story, we'd watch it very carefully every day to see if that window was ever opened again. That's how it became our houseplant. It was something we looked after the same way."

"*Did* you keep watching it, in fact?"

"Sort of. Not every day. Every now and then."

"Was that the whole story?"

"No. The end of the story was that one day, maybe another five years later, we'd be walking along an unfamiliar street and we'd recognize the building and go up and ring the bell and the super would answer it and we'd ask him why, five years before, that window had been open."

"And what would he say?" From her smile it was clear that she remembered, but she asked out of respect for the wholeness of the tale.

"That he hadn't thought anyone had ever noticed. And break into tears. Of gratitude."

"It's a pretty story. I should feel guilty for having forgotten it. Whatever made you think of it today?"

"That's the real end of the story. The window was open. The middle window."

"Really? It's closed now."

"But it was open this morning. Ask Peanut. I pointed it out to her so I'd have a witness."

"It's a happy ending, certainly." She touched the back of her hand to his cheek where he was experimenting with sideburns.

"I wonder why it was open, though. After all this time."

"Well, in five years we can go and ask."

He turned, smiling, to face her, and with the same gesture, touched her cheek, gently, and just for now they were happy. They were together again, on the balcony, on a summer evening, and they were happy.

Boz and Milly. Milly and Boz.

NINE LIVES

URSULA K. Le GUIN

Some people may sincerely believe the world desperately needs many copies of really exceptional people. . . . Moreover, given the widespread development of the safe clinical procedures for handling human eggs, cloning experiments would not be prohibitively expensive. . . . A human being born of clonal reproduction most likely will appear on the earth within the next twenty to fifty years. . . .

The first reaction of most people to the arrival of these asexually produced children, I suspect, would be one of despair. The nature of the bond between parents and their children, not to mention everyone's values about the individual's uniqueness, could be changed beyond recognition. . . .

—James D. Watson, "Moving
Toward the Clonal Man" *

* The Atlantic, May 1971, p. 52.

Articles about cloning in the popular press have evoked images centering around the duplication of famous figures; cloned Einsteins, cloned Hitlers, cloned Ringo Starrs. Fanciful possibilities have been discussed in essays and in fiction: that the cloned person will relive the life of his or her "twin"; that wealthy or evil people will seek immortality by transplanting their brains into cloned bodies; that entire societies of people cloned for specialized tasks will develop.

It is probably more likely that in time people will be cloned for more mundane reasons. For example, parents who have lost a child and cannot have another might want a clone of the dead child. Although the clone would be a different individual, he would be in a real sense their lost child. He would be an exact twin of the child. Cloning on a wide scale would be risky, however, since diversity in human types is what has enabled us to survive in changing conditions.

Central to any discussion of cloning is the question of identity. Each of us is unique and unlike any other person. How would we react to the possibility of having duplicates of ourselves, or to their presence? Yet we are affected by our environment and culture, not only by the supporting platform of our genetic heritage. Cloned people would be subject to these same conditions. Like identical twins, they must be regarded as different individuals, however alike their inheritance.

It is still possible that members of a clone, because of their similarities, would be closer to each other than they could ever be to others. Ursula K. Le Guin writes of such a clone, the reasons for its existence, and the reactions of two men who must work with the group. The experience of one member of the clone, who eventually comes to be like everyone else, unique and alone, reflects much of human experience in a new light.

She was alive inside but dead outside, her face a black and dun net of wrinkles, tumours, cracks. She was bald and blind. The tremors that crossed Libra's face were mere quiverings of corruption. Underneath, in the black corridors, the halls beneath the skin, there were crepitations in darkness, ferments, chemical nightmares that went on for centuries. "Oh, the damned flatulent planet," Pugh murmured as the dome shook and a boil burst a kilometre to the southwest, spraying silver pus across the sunset. The sun had been setting for the last two days. "I'll be glad to see a human face."

"Thanks," said Martin.

"Yours is human to be sure," said Pugh, "but I've seen it so long I can't see it."

Radvid signals cluttered the communicator which Martin was operating, faded, returned as face and voice. The face filled the screen, the nose of an Assyrian king, the eyes of a samurai, skin bronze, eyes the colour of iron: young, magnificent. "Is that what human beings look like?" said Pugh with awe. "I'd forgotten."

"Shut up, Owen, we're on."

"Libra Exploratory Mission Base, come in please, this is *Passerine* launch."

"Libra here. Beam fixed. Come on down, launch."

"Expulsion in seven E-seconds. Hold on." The screen blanked and sparkled.

"Do they all look like that? Martin, you and I are uglier men than I thought."

"Shut up, Owen. . . ."

For twenty-two minutes Martin followed the landing-craft down by signal and then through the cleared dome they saw it, small star in the blood-coloured east, sinking. It came down neat and quiet, Libra's thin atmosphere carrying little sound. Pugh and Martin closed the headpieces of their imsuits, zipped out of the dome airlocks, and ran with soaring strides, Nijinsky and Nureyev, towards the boat. Three equipment modules came floating down at four-minute intervals from each other and hundred-metre intervals east of the boat. "Come on out," Martin said on his suit radio, "we're waiting at the door."

"Come on in, the methane's fine," said Pugh.

The hatch opened. The young man they had seen on the screen came out with one athletic twist and leaped down on to the shaky dust and clinkers of Libra. Martin shook his hand, but Pugh was staring at the hatch, from which another young man emerged with the same neat twist and jump, followed by a young woman who emerged with the same neat twist, ornamented by a wriggle, and the jump. They were all tall, with bronze skin, black hair, high-bridged noses, epicanthic fold, the same face. They all had the same face. The fourth was emerging from the hatch with a neat twist and jump. "Martin bach," said Pugh, "we've got a clone."

"Right," said one of them, "we're a tenclone. John Chow's the name. You're Lieutenant Martin?"

"I'm Owen Pugh."

"Alvaro Guillen Martin," said Martin, formal, bowing slightly. Another girl was out, the same beautiful face; Martin stared at her and his eye rolled like a nervous pony's. Evidently he had never given any thought to cloning, and was suffering technological shock. "Steady," Pugh said in the Argentine dialect, "it's only excess twins." He stood close by Martin's elbow. He was glad himself of the contact.

It is hard to meet a stranger. Even the greatest extrovert meeting even the meekest stranger knows a certain dread, though he may not know he knows it. Will he make a fool of me wreck my image of myself invade me destroy me change me? Will he be different from me? Yes, that he will. There's the terrible thing: the strangeness of the stranger.

After two years on a dead planet, and the last half year isolated as a team of two, oneself and one other, after that it's even harder to meet a stranger, however welcome he may be. You're out of the habit of difference, you've lost the touch; and so the fear revives, the primitive anxiety, the old dread.

The clone, five males and five females, had got done in a couple of minutes what a man might have got done in twenty: greeted Pugh and Martin, had a glance at Libra, unloaded the boat, made ready to go. They went, and the dome filled with them, a hive of golden bees. They hummed and buzzed quietly, filled up all silences, all spaces with a honey-brown swarm of human presence. Martin looked bewilderedly at the long-limbed girls, and they smiled at him, three at once. Their smile was gentler than that of the boys, but no less radiantly self-possessed.

"Self-possessed," Owen Pugh murmured to his friend, "that's it. Think of it, to be oneself ten times over. Nine seconds for every motion, nine ayes on every vote. It would be glorious!" But Martin was asleep. And the John Chows had all gone to sleep at once. The dome was filled with their quiet breathing. They were young, they didn't snore. Martin sighed and snored, his Hershey-bar-coloured face relaxed in the dim afterglow of Libra's primary, set at last. Pugh had cleared the dome and stars looked in, Sol among them, a great company of lights, a clone of splendours.

Pugh slept and dreamed of a one-eyed giant who chased him through the shaking halls of Hell.

From his sleeping bag Pugh watched the clone's awakening. They all got up within one minute except for one pair, a boy and a girl, who lay snugly tangled and still sleeping in one bag. As Pugh saw this there was a shock like one of Libra's earthquakes inside him, a very deep tremor. He was not aware of this, and in fact thought he was pleased at the sight; there was no other such comfort on this dead hollow world. More power to them, who made love. One of the others stepped on the pair. They woke and the girl sat up flushed and sleepy, with bare golden breasts. One of her sisters murmured something to her; she shot a glance at Pugh and disappeared in the sleeping bag; from another direction came a fierce stare, from still another direction a voice: "Christ, we're used to having a room to ourselves. Hope you don't mind, Captain Pugh."

"It's a pleasure," Pugh said half-truthfully. He had to stand up then, wearing only the shorts he slept in, and he felt like a plucked rooster, all white scrawn and pimples. He had seldom envied Martin's compact brownness so much. The United Kingdom had come through the Great Famines well, losing less than half its population: a record achieved by rigorous food control. Black-marketeers and hoarders had been executed. Crumbs had been shared. Where in richer lands most had died and a few had thriven, in Britain fewer died and none throve. They all got lean. Their sons were lean, their grandsons lean, small, brittle-boned, easily infected. When civilization became a matter of standing in lines, the British had kept queue, and so had replaced the survival of the fittest with the survival of the fair-minded. Owen Pugh was a scrawny little man. All the same, he was there.

At the moment he wished he wasn't.

At breakfast a John said, "Now if you'll brief us, Captain Pugh—"

"Owen, then."

"Owen, we can work out our schedule. Anything new on the mine since your last report to your Mission? We saw your reports when *Passerine* was orbiting Planet V, where they are now."

Martin did not answer, though the mine was his discovery and project, and Pugh had to do his best. It was hard to talk to them. The same faces, each with the same expression of intelligent interest, all leaned towards him across the table at almost the same angle. They all nodded together.

Over the Exploitation Corps insignia on their tunics each had a name band, first name John and last name Chow of course, but the middle names different. The men were Aleph, Kaph, Yod, Gimel, and Samedh; the women Sadhe, Daleth, Zayin, Beth, and Resh. Pugh tried to use the names but gave it up at once; he could not even tell sometimes which one had spoken, for all the voices were alike.

Martin buttered and chewed his toast, and finally interrupted: "You're a team. Is that it?"

"Right," said two Johns.

"God, what a team! I hadn't seen the point. How much do you each know what the others are thinking?"

"Not at all, properly speaking," replied one of the girls, Zayin. The others watched her with the proprietary, approving look they had. "No ESP, nothing fancy. But we think alike. We have exactly the same equipment. Given the same stimulus, the same problem, we're likely to be coming up with the same reactions and solutions at the same time. Explanations are easy—don't even have to make them, usually. We seldom misunderstand each other. It does facilitate our working as a team."

"Christ yes," said Martin. "Pugh and I have spent seven hours out of ten for six months misunderstanding each other. Like most people. What about emergencies, are you as good at meeting the unexpected problem as a nor . . . an unrelated team?"

"Statistics so far indicate that we are," Zayin answered readily. Clones must be trained, Pugh thought, to meet questions, to reassure and reason. All they said had the slightly bland and stilted quality of answers furnished to the Public. "We can't brainstorm as singletons can, we as a team don't profit from the interplay of varied minds; but we have a compensatory advantage. Clones are drawn from the best human material, individuals of IIQ 99th percentile, Genetic Constitution alpha double A, and so on. We have more to draw on than most individuals do."

"And it's multiplied by a factor of ten. Who is—who was John Chow?"

"A genius surely," Pugh said politely. His interest in cloning was not so new and avid as Martin's.

"Leonardo Complex type," said Yod. "Biomath, also a cellist, and an undersea hunter, and interested in structural engineering problems, and so on. Died before he'd worked out his major theories."

"Then you each represent a different facet of his mind, his talents?"

"No," said Zayin, shaking her head in time with several others. "We share the basic equipment and tendencies, of course, but we're all engineers in Planetary Exploitation. A later clone can be trained to develop other aspects of the basic equipment. It's all training; the genetic substance is identical. We are John Chow. But we were differently trained."

Martin looked shell-shocked. "How old are you?"

"Twenty-three."

"You say he died young—had they taken germ cells from him beforehand or something?"

Gimel took over: "He died at twenty-four in an air-car crash. They couldn't save the brain, so they took some intestinal cells and cultured them for cloning. Reproductive cells aren't used for cloning, since they have only half the chromosomes. Intestinal cells happen to be easy to despecialize and reprogram for total growth."

"All chips off the old block," Martin said valiantly. "But how can . . . some of you be women . . . ?"

Beth took over: "It's easy to program half the clonal mass back to the female. Just delete the male gene from half the cells and they revert to the basic, that is, the female. It's trickier to go the other way, have to hook in artificial Y chromosomes. So they mostly clone from males, since clones function best bisexually."

Gimel again: "They've worked these matters of technique and function out carefully. The taxpayer wants the best for his money, and of course clones are expensive. With the cell manipulations, and the incubation in Ngama Placentae, and the maintenance and training of the foster-parent groups, we end up costing about three million apiece."

"For your next generation," Martin said, still struggling, "I suppose you . . . you breed?"

"We females are sterile," said Beth with perfect equanimity; "you remember that the Y chromosome was deleted from our original cell. The males can interbreed with approved singletons, if they want to. But to get John Chow again as often as they want, they just reclone a cell from this clone."

Martin gave up the struggle. He nodded and chewed cold toast. "Well," said one of the Johns, and all changed mood, like a flock of starlings that change course in one wingflick, following a leader so fast that no eye can see which leads. They were ready to go. "How about a look at the mime? Then we'll unload the equipment. Some nice new models in the roboats; you'll want to see them. Right?" Had Pugh or Martin not agreed they might have found it hard to say so. The Johns were polite but unanimous; their decisions carried. Pugh, Commander of Libra Base 2, felt a qualm. Could he boss around this superman/woman-entity-of-ten? and a genius at that? He stuck close to Martin as they suited for outside. Neither said anything.

Four apiece in the three large airjets, they slipped off north from the dome, over Libra's dun rugose skin, in starlight.

"Desolate," one said.

It was a boy and girl with Pugh and Martin. Pugh wondered if these were the two that had shared a sleeping bag last night. No doubt they wouldn't mind if he asked them. Sex must be as handy as breathing to them. Did you two breathe last night?

"Yes," he said, "it is desolate."

"This is our first time Off, except training on Luna." The girl's voice was definitely a bit higher and softer.

"How did you take the big hop?"

"They doped us. I wanted to experience it." That was the boy; he sounded wistful. They seemed to have more personality, only two at a time. Did repetition of the individual negate individuality?

"Don't worry," said Martin, steering the sled, "you can't experience no-time because it isn't there."

"I'd just like to once," one of them said. "So we'd know."

The Mountains of Merioneth showed leprotic in starlight to the east, a plume of freezing gas trailed silvery from a vent-hole to the west, and the sled tilted groundward. The twins braced for the stop at one moment, each with a slight protective gesture to the other. Your skin is my skin, Pugh thought, but literally, no metaphor. What would it be like, then, to have someone as close to you as that? Always to be answered when you spoke, never to be in pain alone. Love your neighbour as you love yourself. . . . That hard old problem was solved. The neighbour was the self: the love was perfect.

And here was Hellmouth, the mine.

Pugh was the Exploratory Mission's ET geologist, and Martin his technician and cartographer; but when in the course of a local survey Martin had discovered the U-mine, Pugh had given him full credit, as well as the onus of prospecting the lode and planning the Exploitation Team's job. These kids had been sent out from Earth years before Martin's reports got there, and had not known what their job would be until they got here. The Exploitation Corps simply sent out teams regularly and blindly as a dandelion sends out its seeds, knowing there would be a job for them on Libra or the next planet out or one they hadn't even heard about yet. The Government wanted uranium too urgently to wait while reports drifted home across the light-years. The stuff was like gold, old-fashioned but essential, worth mining extraterrestrially and shipping interstellar. Worth its weight in people, Pugh thought sourly, watching the tall young men and women go one by one, glimmering in starlight, into the black hole Martin had named Hellmouth.

As they went in, their homeostatic forehead-lamps

brightened. Twelve nodding gleams ran along the moist, wrinkled walls. Pugh heard Martin's radiation counter peeping twenty to the dozen up ahead. "Here's the dropoff," said Martin's voice in the suit intercom, drowning out the peeping and the dead silence that was around them. "We're in a side-fissure; this is the main vertical vent in front of us." The black void gaped, its far side not visible in the headlamp beams. "Last vulcanism seems to have been a couple of thousand years ago. Nearest fault is twenty-eight kilos east, in the Trench. This region seems to be as safe seismically as anything in the area. The big basalt-flow overhead stabilizes all these substructures, so long as it remains stable itself. Your central lode is thirty-six metres down and runs in a series of five bubble-caverns northeast. It is a lode, a pipe of very high-grade ore. You saw the percentage figures, right? Extraction's going to be no problem. All you've got to do is get the bubbles topside."

"Take off the lid and let 'em float up." A chuckle. Voices began to talk, but they were all the same voice and the suit radio gave them no location in space. "Open the thing right up. —Safer that way. —But it's a solid basalt roof, how thick, ten metres here? —Three to twenty, the report said. —Blow good ore all over the lot. —Use this access we're in, straighten it a bit and run slider-rails for the robos. —Import burros. —Have we got enough propping material? —What's your estimate of total payload mass, Martin?"

"Say over five million kilos and under eight."

"Transport will be here in ten E-months. —It'll have to go pure. —No, they'll have the mass problem in NAFAL shipping licked by now; remember it's been sixteen years since we left Earth last Tuesday. —Right, they'll send the whole lot back and purify it in Earth orbit. —Shall we go down, Martin?"

"Go on. I've been down."

The first one—Aleph? (Heb., the ox, the leader)—swung on to the ladder and down; the rest followed. Pugh and Martin stood at the chasm's edge. Pugh set his intercom to exchange only with Martin's suit, and noticed Martin doing the same. It was a bit wearing, this listening to one person think aloud in ten voices, or was it one voice speaking the thoughts of ten minds?

"A great gut," Pugh said, looking down into the black pit, its veined and warted walls catching stray gleams of head-lamps far below. "A cow's bowel. A bloody great constipated intestine."

Martin's counter peeped like a lost chicken. They stood inside the dead but epileptic planet, breathing oxygen from tanks, wearing suits impermeable to corrosives and harmful radiations, resistant to a two hundred-degree range of temperatures, tear-proof, and as shock-resistant as possible given the soft vulnerable stuff inside.

"Next hop," Martin said, "I'd like to find a planet that has nothing whatever to exploit."

"You found this."

"Keep me home next time."

Pugh was pleased. He had hoped Martin would want to go on working with him, but neither of them was used to talking much about their feelings, and he had hesitated to ask. "I'll try that," he said.

"I hate this place. I like caves, you know. It's why I came in here. Just spelunking. But this one's a bitch. Mean. You can't ever let down in here. I guess this lot can handle it, though. They know their stuff."

"Wave of the future, whatever," said Pugh.

The wave of the future came swarming up the ladder, swept Martin to the entrance, gabbled at and around him: "Have we got enough material for supports? —If we convert one of the extractor-servos to anneal, yes. —Sufficient if we miniblast? —Kaph can calculate stress."

Pugh had switched his intercom back to receive them; he looked at them, so many thoughts jabbering in an eager mind, and at Martin standing silent among them, and at Hellmouth, and the wrinkled plain. "Settled! How does that strike you as a preliminary schedule, Martin?"

"It's your baby," Martin said.

Within five E-days the Johns had all their material and equipment unloaded and operating, and were starting to open up the mine. They worked with total efficiency. Pugh was fascinated and frightened by their effectiveness, their confidence, their independence. He was no use to them at all. A clone, he thought, might indeed be the first truly stable, self-reliant human being. Once adult it would need nobody's help. It would be sufficient to itself physically, sexually, emotionally, intellectually. Whatever he did, any member of it would always receive the support and approval of his peers, his other selves. Nobody else was needed.

Two of the clone stayed in the dome doing calculations and paperwork, with frequent sled-trips to the mine for measurements and tests. They were the mathematicians of the clone, Zayin and Kaph. That is, as Zayin explained, all ten had had thorough mathematical training from age three to twenty-one, but from twenty-one to twenty-three she and Kaph had gone on with math while the others intensified study in other specialities, geology, mining, engineering, electronic engineering, equipment robotics, applied atomics, and so on. "Kaph and I feel," she said, "that we're the element of the clone closest to what John Chow was in his singleton lifetime. But of course he was principally in biomath, and they didn't take us far in that."

"They needed us most in this field," Kaph said, with the patriotic priggishness they sometimes evinced.

Pugh and Martin soon could distinguish this pair from the others, Zayin by gestalt, Kaph only by a discolored left fourth fingernail, got from an ill-aimed hammer at the age of six. No doubt there were many such differences, physical and psychological, among them; nature might be identical, nurture could not be. But the differences were hard to find. And part of the difficulty was that they never really talked to Pugh and Martin. They joked with them, were polite, got along fine. They gave nothing. It was nothing one could complain about; they were very pleasant, they had the standardized American friendliness. "Do you come from Ireland, Owen?"

"Nobody comes from Ireland, Zayin."

"There are lots of Irish-Americans."

"To be sure, but no more Irish. A couple of thousand in all the island, the last I knew. They didn't go in for birth control, you know, so the food ran out. By the Third Famine there were no Irish left at all but the priesthood, and they were all celibate, or nearly all."

Zayin and Kaph smiled stiffly. They had no experience of either bigotry or irony. "What are you then, ethnically?" Kaph asked, and Pugh replied, "A Welshman."

"Is it Welsh that you and Martin speak together?"

None of your business, Pugh thought, but said, "No, it's his dialect, not mine: Argentinean. A descendant of Spanish."

"You learned it for private communication?"

"Whom had we here to be private from? It's just

that sometimes a man likes to speak his native language."

"Ours is English," Kaph said unsympathetically. Why should they have sympathy? That's one of the things you give because you need it back.

"Is Wells quaint?" asked Zayin.

"Wells? Oh, Wales, it's called. Yes. Wales is quaint." Pugh switched on his rock-cutter, which prevented further conversation by a synapse-destroying whine, and while it whined he turned his back and said a profane word in Welsh.

That night he used the Argentine dialect for private communication. "Do they pair off in the same couples or change every night?"

Martin looked surprised. A prudish expression, unsuited to his features, appeared for a moment. It faded. He too was curious. "I think it's random."

"Don't whisper, man, it sounds dirty. I think they rotate."

"On a schedule?"

"So nobody gets omitted."

Martin gave a vulgar laugh and smothered it. "What about us? Aren't we omitted?"

"That doesn't occur to them."

"What if I proposition one of the girls?"

"She'd tell the others and they'd decide as a group."

"I am not a bull," Martin said, his dark, heavy face heating up. "I will not be judged—"

"Down, down, *machismo*," said Pugh. "Do you mean to proposition one?"

Martin shrugged, sullen. "Let 'em have their incest."

"Incest is it, or masturbation?"

"I don't care, if they'd do it out of earshot!"

The clone's early attempts at modesty had soon worn off, unmotivated by any deep defensiveness of

self or awareness of others. Pugh and Martin were
daily deeper swamped under the intimacies of its constant emotional-sexual-mental interchange: swamped
yet excluded.

"Two months to go," Martin said one evening.

"To what?" snapped Pugh. He was edgy lately, and
Martin's sullenness got on his nerves.

"To relief."

In sixty days the full crew of their Exploratory Mission were due back from their survey of the other
planets of the system. Pugh was aware of this.

"Crossing off the days on your calendar?" he jeered.

"Pull yourself together, Owen."

"What do you mean?"

"What I say."

They parted in contempt and resentment.

Pugh came in after a day alone on the Pampas, a vast
lava-plain the nearest edge of which was two hours
south by jet. He was tired but refreshed by solitude.
They were not supposed to take long trips alone, but
lately had often done so. Martin stooped under bright
lights, drawing one of his elegant, masterly charts:
this one was of the whole face of Libra, the cancerous
face. The dome was otherwise empty, seeming dim and
large as it had before the clone came. "Where's the
golden horde?"

Martin grunted ignorance, crosshatching. He
straightened his back to glance round at the sun,
which squatted feebly like a great red toad on the
eastern plain, and at the clock, which said 18:45.
"Some big quakes today," he said, returning to his
map. "Feel them down there? Lot of crates were
falling around. Take a look at the seismo."

The needle jigged and wavered on the roll. It never

stopped dancing here. The roll had recorded five quakes of major intensity back in midafternoon; twice the needle had hopped off the roll. The attached computer had been activated to emit a slip reading, "Epicenter 61′ N by 42′ 4″ E."

"Not in the Trench this time."

"I thought it felt a bit different from usual. Sharper."

"In Base One I used to lie awake all night feeling the ground jump. Queer how you get used to things."

"Go spla if you didn't. What's for dinner?"

"I thought you'd have cooked it."

"Waiting for the clone."

Feeling put upon, Pugh got out a dozen dinnerboxes, stuck two in the Instobake, pulled them out. "All right, here's dinner."

"Been thinking," Martin said, coming to the table. "What if some clone cloned itself? Illegally. Made a thousand duplicates—ten thousand. Whole army. They could make a tidy power-grab, couldn't they?"

"But how many millions did this lot cost to rear? Artificial placentae and all that. It would be hard to keep secret, unless they had a planet to themselves. . . . Back before the Famines, when Earth had national governments, they talked about that: clone your best soldiers, have whole regiments of them. But the food ran out before they could play that game."

They talked amicably, as they used to do.

"Funny," Martin said, chewing. "They left early this morning, didn't they?"

"All but Kaph and Zayin. They thought they'd get the first payload aboveground today. What's up?"

"They weren't back for lunch."

"They won't starve, to be sure."

"They left at seven."

"So they did." Then Pugh saw it. The air-tanks held eight hours' supply.

"Kaph and Zayin carried out spare cans when they left. Or they've got a heap out there."

"They did, but they brought the whole lot in to recharge." Martin stood up, pointing to one of the stacks of stuff that cut the dome into rooms and alleys.

"There's an alarm signal on every imsuit."

"It's not automatic."

Pugh was tired and still hungry. "Sit down and eat, man. That lot can look after themselves."

Martin sat down, but did not eat. "There was a big quake, Owen. The first one. Big enough it scared me."

After a pause Pugh sighed and said, "All right."

Unenthusiastically, they got out the two-man sled that was always left for them, and headed it north. The long sunrise covered everything in poisonous red jello. The horizontal light and shadow made it hard to see, raised walls of fake iron ahead of them through which they slid, turned the convex plain beyond Hellmouth into a great dimple full of bloody water. Around the tunnel entrance a wilderness of machinery stood, cranes and cables and servos and wheels and diggers and robocarts and sliders and control-huts, all slanting and bulking incoherently in the red light. Martin jumped from the sled, ran into the mine. He came out again, to Pugh. "Oh God, Owen, it's down," he said. Pugh went in and saw, five metres from the entrance, the shiny, moist, black wall that ended the tunnel. Newly exposed to air, it looked organic, like visceral tissue. The tunnel entrance, enlarged by blasting and double-tracked for robocarts, seemed unchanged until he noticed thousands of tiny spiderweb cracks in the walls. The floor was wet with some sluggish fluid.

"They were inside," Martin said.

"They may be still. They surely had extra aircans—"

"Look, Owen, look at the basalt flow, at the roof; don't you see what the quake did, look at it."

The low hump of land that roofed the caves still had the unreal look of an optical illusion. It had reversed itself, sunk down, leaving a vast dimple or pit. When Pugh walked on it he saw that it too was cracked with many tiny fissures. From some a whitish gas was seeping, so that the sunlight on the surface of the gas-pool was shafted as if by the waters of a dim red lake.

"The mine's not on the fault. There's no fault here!"

Pugh came back to him quickly. "No, there's no fault, Martin. Look, they surely weren't all inside together."

Martin followed him and searched among the wrecked machines dully, then actively. He spotted the airsled. It had come down heading south, and stuck at an angle in a pothole of colloidal dust. It had carried two riders. One was half sunk in the dust, but his suitmeters registered normal functioning; the other hung strapped on to the tilted sled. Her imsuit had burst open on the broken legs, and the body was frozen hard as any rock. That was all they found. As both regulation and custom demanded, they cremated the dead at once with the laser-guns they carried by regulation and had never used before. Pugh, knowing he was going to be sick, wrestled the survivor on to the two-man sled and sent Martin off to the dome with him. Then he vomited and flushed the waste out of his suit, and finding one four-man sled undamaged, followed after Martin, shaking as if the cold of Libra had got through to him.

The survivor was Kaph. He was in deep shock. They found a swelling on the occiput that might mean concussion, but no fracture was visible.

Pugh brought two glasses of food-concentrate and two chasers of aquavit. "Come on," he said. Martin obeyed, drinking off the tonic. They sat down on crates near the cot and sipped the aquavit.

Kaph lay immobile, face like beeswax, hair bright black to the shoulders, lips stiffly parted for faintly gasping breaths.

"It must have been the first shock, the big one," Martin said. "It must have slid the whole structure sideways. Till it fell in on itself. There must be gas layers in the lateral rocks, like those formations in the Thirty-First Quadrant. But there wasn't any sign—" As he spoke the world slid out from under them. Things leaped and clattered, hopped and jigged, shouted Ha! Ha! Ha! "It was like this at fourteen hours," said Reason shakily in Martin's voice, amidst the unfastening and ruin of the world. But Unreason sat up, as the tumult lessened and things ceased dancing, and screamed aloud.

Pugh leaped across his spilled aquavit and held Kaph down. The muscular body flailed him off. Martin pinned the shoulders down. Kaph screamed, struggled, choked; his face blackened. "Oxy," Pugh said, and his hand found the right needle in the medical kit as if by homing instinct; while Martin held the mask he struck the needle home to the vagus nerve, restoring Kaph to life.

"Didn't know you knew that stunt," Martin said, breathing hard.

"The Lazarus Jab; my father was a doctor. It doesn't often work," Pugh said. "I want that drink I spilled. Is the quake over? I can't tell."

"Aftershocks. It's not just you shivering."

"Why did he suffocate?"

"I don't know, Owen. Look in the book."

Kaph was breathing normally and his colour was restored; only the lips were still darkened. They poured a new shot of courage and sat down by him again with their medical guide. "Nothing about cyanosis or asphyxiation under 'Shock' or 'Concussion.' He can't have breathed in anything with his suit on. I don't know. We'd get as much good out of *Mother Mog's Home Herbalist.* . . . 'Anal Hemorrhoids,' fy!" Pugh pitched the book to a crate-table. It fell short, because either Pugh or the table was still unsteady.

"Why didn't he signal?"

"Sorry?"

"The eight inside the mine never had time. But he and the girl must have been outside. Maybe she was in the entrance, and got hit by the first slide. He must have been outside, in the control-hut maybe. He ran in, pulled her out, strapped her on to the sled, started for the dome. And all that time never pushed the panic button in his imsuit. Why not?"

"Well, he'd had that whack on his head. I doubt he ever realized the girl was dead. He wasn't in his senses. But if he had been I don't know if he'd have thought to signal us. They looked to one another for help."

Martin's face was like an Indian mask, grooves at the mouth-corners, eyes of dull coal. "That's so. What must he have felt, then, when the quake came and he was outside, alone—"

In answer Kaph screamed.

He came up off the cot in the heaving convulsions of one suffocating, knocked Pugh right down with his flailing arm, staggered into a stack of crates and fell to the floor, lips blue, eyes white. Martin dragged him back on to the cot and gave him a whiff of oxygen, then knelt by Pugh, who was sitting up, and wiped at his cut cheekbone. "Owen, are you all right, are you going to be all right, Owen?"

"I think I am," Pugh said. "Why are you rubbing that on my face?"

It was a short length of computer-tape, now spotted with Pugh's blood. Martin dropped it. "Thought it was a towel. You clipped your cheek on that box there."

"Is he out of it?"

"Seems to be."

They stared down at Kaph lying stiff, his teeth a white line inside dark parted lips.

"Like epilepsy. Brain damage maybe?"

"What about shooting him full of meprobamate?"

Pugh shook his head. "I don't know what's in that shot I already gave him for shock. Don't want to overdose him."

"Maybe he'll sleep it off now."

"I'd like to myself. Between him and the earthquake I can't seem to keep on my feet."

"You got a nasty crack there. Go on, I'll sit up a while."

Pugh cleaned his cut cheek and pulled off his shirt, then paused.

"Is there anything we ought to have done—have tried to do—"

"They're all dead," Martin said heavily, gently.

Pugh lay down on top of his sleeping bag, and one instant later was wakened by a hideous, sucking, struggling noise. He staggered up, found the needle, tried three times to jab it in correctly and failed, began to massage over Kaph's heart. "Mouth-to-mouth," he said, and Martin obeyed. Presently Kaph drew a harsh

breath, his heartbeat steadied, his rigid muscles began
to relax.

"How long did I sleep?"

"Half an hour."

They stood up sweating. The ground shuddered, the
fabric of the dome sagged and swayed. Libra was dancing her awful polka again, her *Totentanz*. The sun,
though rising, seemed to have grown larger and redder;
gas and dust must have been stirred up in the feeble
atmosphere.

"What's wrong with him, Owen?"

"I think he's dying with them."

"Them—But they're dead, I tell you."

"Nine of them. They're all dead, they were crushed
or suffocated. They were all him, he is all of them.
They died, and now he's dying their deaths one by
one."

"Oh pity of God," said Martin.

The next time was much the same. The fifth time
was worse, for Kaph fought and raved, trying to speak
but getting no words out, as if his mouth were stopped
with rocks or clay. After that the attacks grew weaker,
but so did he. The eighth seizure came at about four-
thirty; Pugh and Martin worked till five-thirty doing
all they could to keep life in the body that slid without protest into death. They kept him, but Martin
said, "The next will finish him." And it did; but Pugh
breathed his own breath into the inert lungs, until he
himself passed out.

He woke. The dome was opaqued and no light on.
He listened and heard the breathing of two sleeping
men. He slept, and nothing woke him till hunger did.

The sun was well up over the dark plains, and the
planet had stopped dancing. Kaph lay asleep. Pugh
and Martin drank tea and looked at him with proprietary triumph.

When he woke Martin went to him: "How do you feel, old man?" There was no answer. Pugh took Martin's place and looked into the brown, dull eyes that gazed towards but not into his own. Like Martin he quickly turned away. He heated food-concentrate and brought it to Kaph. "Come on, drink."

He could see the muscles in Kaph's throat tighten. "Let me die," the young man said.

"You're not dying."

Kaph spoke with clarity and precision: "I am nine-tenths dead. There is not enough of me left alive."

That precision convinced Pugh, and he fought the conviction. "No," he said, peremptory. "They are dead. The others. Your brothers and sisters. You're not them, you're alive. You are John Chow. Your life is in your own hands."

The young man lay still, looking into a darkness that was not there.

Martin and Pugh took turns taking the Exploitation hauler and a spare set of robos over to Hellmouth to salvage equipment and protect it from Libra's sinister atmosphere, for the value of the stuff was, literally, astronomical. It was slow work for one man at a time, but they were unwilling to leave Kaph by himself. The one left in the dome did paperwork, while Kaph sat or lay and stared into his darkness and never spoke. The days went by, silent.

The radio spat and spoke: the Mission calling from ship. "We'll be down on Libra in five weeks, Owen. Thirty-four E-days nine hours I make it as of now. How's tricks in the old dome?"

"Not good, chief. The Exploit team were killed, all but one of them, in the mine. Earthquake. Six days ago."

The radio crackled and sang starsong. Sixteen-second lag each way; the ship was out around Planet II now. "Killed, all but one? You and Martin were unhurt?"

"We're all right, chief."

Thirty-two seconds.

"*Passerine* left an Exploit team out here with us. I may put them on the Hellmouth project then, instead of the Quadrant Seven project. We'll settle that when we come down. In any case you and Martin will be relieved at Dome Two. Hold tight. Anything else?"

"Nothing else."

Thirty-two seconds.

"Right then. So long, Owen."

Kaph had heard all this, and later on Pugh said to him, "The chief may ask you to stay here with the other Exploit team. You know the ropes here." Knowing the exigencies of Far Out life, he wanted to warn the young man. Kaph made no answer. Since he had said, "There is not enough of me left alive," he had not spoken a word.

"Owen," Martin said on suit intercom, "he's spla. Insane. Psycho."

"He's doing very well for a man who's died nine times."

"Well? Like a turned-off android is well? The only emotion he has left is hate. Look at his eyes."

"That's not hate, Martin. Listen, it's true that he has, in a sense, been dead. I can't imagine what he feels. But it's not hatred. He can't even see us. It's too dark."

"Throats have been cut in the dark. He hates us because we're not Aleph and Yod and Zayin."

"Maybe. But I think he's alone. He doesn't see us or hear us, that's the truth. He never had to see anyone else before. He never was alone before. He had himself to see, talk with, live with, nine other selves all his life. He doesn't know how you go it alone. He must learn. Give him time."

Martin shook his heavy head. "Spla," he said. "Just remember when you're alone with him that he could break your neck one-handed."

"He could do that," said Pugh, a short, soft-voiced man with a scarred cheekbone; he smiled. They were just outside the dome airlock, programming one of the servos to repair a damaged hauler. They could see Kaph sitting inside the great half-egg of a dome like a fly in amber.

"Hand me the insert pack there. What makes you think he'll get any better?"

"He has a strong personality, to be sure."

"Strong? Crippled. Nine-tenths dead, as he put it."

"But he's not dead. He's a live man: John Kaph Chow. He had a jolly queer upbringing, but after all every boy has got to break free of his family. He will do it."

"I can't see it."

"Think a bit, Martin bach. What's this cloning for? To repair the human race. We're in a bad way. Look at me. My IIQ and GC are half this John Chow's. Yet they wanted me so badly for the Far Out Service that when I volunteered they took me and fitted me out with an artificial lung and corrected my myopia. Now if there were enough good sound lads about would they be taking one-lunged short-sighted Welshmen?"

"Didn't know you had an artificial lung."

"I do then. Not tin, you know. Human, grown in a tank from a bit of somebody; cloned, if you like. That's how they make replacement organs, the same general idea as cloning, but bits and pieces instead of whole people. It's my own lung now, whatever. But what I am saying is this, there are too many like me these days, and not enough like John Chow. They're trying to raise the level of the human genetic pool, which is a mucky little puddle since the population crash. So then if a man is cloned, he's a strong and clever man. It's only logic, to be sure."

Martin grunted; the servo began to hum.

Kaph had been eating little; he had trouble swallowing his food, choking on it, so that he would give up trying after a few bites. He had lost eight or ten kilos. After three weeks or so, however, his appetite began to pick up, and one day he began to look through the clone's possessions, the sleeping bags, kits, papers which Pugh had stacked neatly in a far angle of a packing-crate alley. He sorted, destroyed a heap of papers and oddments, made a small packet of what remained, then relapsed into his walking coma.

Two days later he spoke. Pugh was trying to correct a flutter in the tape-player, and failing; Martin had the jet out, checking their maps of the Pampas. "Hell and damnation!" Pugh said, and Kaph said in a toneless voice, "Do you want me to do that?"

Pugh jumped, controlled himself, and gave the machine to Kaph. The young man took it apart, put it back together, and left it on the table.

"Put on a tape," Pugh said with careful casualness, busy at another table.

Kaph put on the topmost tape, a chorale. He lay down on his cot. The sound of a hundred human voices singing together filled the dome. He lay still, his face blank.

In the next days he took over several routine jobs, unasked. He undertook nothing that wanted initiative, and if asked to do anything he made no response at all.

"He's doing well," Pugh said in the dialect of Argentina.

"He's not. He's turning himself into a machine. Does what he's programmed to do, no reaction to anything else. He's worse off than when he didn't function at all. He's not human any more."

Pugh sighed. "Well, good night," he said in English. "Good night, Kaph."

"Good night," Martin said; Kaph did not.

Next morning at breakfast Kaph reached across Martin's plate for the toast. "Why don't you ask for it," Martin said with the geniality of repressed exasperation. "I can pass it."

"I can reach it," Kaph said in his flat voice.

"Yes, but look. Asking to pass things, saying good night or hello, they're not important, but all the same when somebody says something a person ought to answer. . . ."

The young man looked indifferently in Martin's direction; his eyes still did not seem to see clear through to the person he looked towards. "Why should I answer?"

"Because somebody has said something to you."

"Why?"

Martin shrugged and laughed. Pugh jumped up and turned on the rock-cutter.

Later on he said, "Lay off that, please, Martin."

"Manners are essential in small isolated crews, some kind of manners, whatever you work out together. He's been taught that, everybody in Far Out knows it. Why does he deliberately flout it?"

"Do you tell yourself good night?"

"So?"

"Don't you see Kaph's never known anyone but himself?"

Martin brooded and then broke out, "Then by God this cloning business is all wrong. It won't do. What are a lot of duplicate geniuses going to do for us when they don't even know we exist?"

Pugh nodded. "It might be wiser to separate the clones and bring them up with others. But they make such a grand team this way."

"Do they? I don't know. If this lot had been ten average inefficient ET engineers, would they all have been in the same place at the same time? Would they all have got killed? What if, when the quake came and things started caving in, what if all those kids ran the same way, farther into the mine, maybe, to save the one that was farthest in? Even Kaph was outside and went in. . . . It's hypothetical. But I keep thinking, out of ten ordinary confused guys, more might have got out."

"I don't know. It's true that identical twins tend to die at about the same time, even when they have never seen each other. Identity and death, it is very strange. . . ."

The days went on, the red sun crawled across the dark sky, Kaph did not speak when spoken to, Pugh and Martin snapped at each other more frequently each day. Pugh complained of Martin's snoring. Offended, Martin moved his cot clear across the dome and also ceased speaking to Pugh for some while. Pugh whistled Welsh dirges until Martin complained, and then Pugh stopped speaking for a while.

The day before the Mission ship was due, Martin announced he was going over to Merioneth.

"I thought at least you'd be giving me a hand with the computer to finish the rock-analyses," Pugh said, aggrieved.

"Kaph can do that. I want one more look at the Trench. Have fun," Martin added in dialect, and laughed, and left.

"What is that language?"

"Argentinean. I told you that once, didn't I?"

"I don't know." After a while the young man added, "I have forgotten a lot of things, I think."

"It wasn't important, to be sure," Pugh said gently, realizing all at once how important this conversation was. "Will you give me a hand running the computer, Kaph?"

He nodded.

Pugh had left a lot of loose ends, and the job took them all day. Kaph was a good co-worker, quick and systematic, much more so than Pugh himself. His flat voice, now that he was talking again, got on the nerves; but it didn't matter, there was only this one day left to get through and then the ship would come, the old crew, comrades and friends.

During tea-break Kaph said, "What will happen if the Explore ship crashes?"

"They'd be killed."

"To you, I mean."

"To us? We'd radio SOS all signals, and live on half rations till the rescue cruiser from Area Three Base came. Four and a half E-years away it is. We have life-support here for three men for, let's see, maybe between four and five years. A bit tight, it would be."

"Would they send a cruiser for three men?"

"They would."

Kaph said no more.

"Enough cheerful speculations," Pugh said cheerfully, rising to get back to work. He slipped sideways and the chair avoided his hand; he did a sort of half-pirouette and fetched up hard against the dome-hide. "My goodness," he said, reverting to his native idiom, "what is it?"

"Quake," said Kaph.

The teacups bounced on the table with a plastic cackle, a litter of papers slid off a box, the skin of the dome swelled and sagged. Underfoot there was a huge noise, half-sound, half-shaking, a subsonic boom.

Kaph sat unmoved. An earthquake does not frighten a man who died in an earthquake.

Pugh, white-faced, wiry black hair sticking out, a frightened man, said, "Martin is in the Trench."

"What trench?"

"The big fault line. The epicenter for the local quakes. Look at the seismograph." Pugh struggled with the stuck door of a still-jittering locker.

"Where are you going?"

"After him."

"Martin took the jet. Sleds aren't safe to use during quakes. They go out of control."

"For God's sake, man, shut up."

Kaph stood up, speaking in a flat voice as usual. "It's unnecessary to go out after him now. It's taking an unnecessary risk."

"If his alarm goes off, radio me," Pugh said, shut the headpiece of his suit, and ran to the lock. As he went out Libra picked up her ragged skirts and danced a belly-dance from under his feet clear to the red horizon.

Inside the dome, Kaph saw the sled go up, tremble like a meteor in the dull red daylight, and vanish to the northeast. The hide of the dome quivered, the earth coughed. A vent south of the dome belched up a slow-flowing bile of black gas.

A bell shrilled and a red light flashed on the central control board. The sign under the light read Suit Two, and scribbled under that, A.G.M. Kaph did not turn the signal off. He tried to radio Martin, then Pugh, but got no reply from either.

When the aftershocks decreased he went back to

work and finished up Pugh's job. It took him about two hours. Every half hour he tried to contact Suit One, and got no reply, then Suit Two, and got no reply. The red light had stopped flashing after an hour.

It was dinnertime. Kaph cooked dinner for one, and ate it. He lay down on his cot.

The aftershocks had ceased except for faint rolling tremors at long intervals. The sun hung in the west, oblate, pale-red, immense. It did not sink visibly. There was no sound at all.

Kaph got up and began to walk about the messy, half-packed-up, overcrowded, empty dome. The silence continued. He went to the player and put on the first tape that came to hand. It was pure music, electronic, without harmonies, without voices. It ended. The silence continued.

Pugh's uniform tunic, one button missing, hung over a stack of rock-samples. Kaph stared at it a while.

The silence continued.

The child's dream: There is no one else alive in the world but me. In all the world.

Low, north of the dome, a meteor flickered.

Kaph's mouth opened as if he were trying to say something, but no sound came. He went hastily to the north wall and peered out into the gelatinous red light.

The little star came in and sank. Two figures blurred the airlock. Kaph stood close beside the lock as they came in. Martin's imsuit was covered with some kind of dust so that he looked raddled and warty like the surface of Libra. Pugh had him by the arm.

"Is he hurt?"

Pugh shucked his suit, helped Martin peel off his. "Shaken up," he said, curt.

"A piece of cliff fell on to the jet," Martin said, sitting down at the table and waving his arms. "Not while I was in it, though. I was parked, see, and poking about that carbon-dust area when I felt things bumping. So I went out onto a nice bit of early igneous I'd noticed from above, good footing and out from under the cliffs. Then I saw this bit of the planet fall off onto the flyer, quite a sight it was, and after a while it occurred to me the spare aircans were in the flyer, so I leaned on the panic button. But I didn't get any radio reception, that's always happening here during quakes, so I didn't know if the signal was getting through either. And things went on jumping around and pieces of the cliff coming off. Little rocks flying around, and so dusty you couldn't see a metre ahead. I was really beginning to wonder what I'd do for breathing in the small hours, you know, when I saw old Owen buzzing up the Trench in all that dust and junk like a big ugly bat—"

"Want to eat?" said Pugh.

"Of course I want to eat. How'd you come through the quake here, Kaph? No damage? It wasn't a big one actually, was it, what's the seismo say? My trouble was I was in the middle of it. Old Epicenter Alvaro. Felt like Richter Fifteen there—total destruction of planet—"

"Sit down," Pugh said. "Eat."

After Martin had eaten a little his spate of talk ran dry. He very soon went off to his cot, still in the remote angle where he had removed it when Pugh complained of his snoring. "Good night, you one-lunged Welshman," he said across the dome.

"Good night."

There was no more out of Martin. Pugh opaqued the dome, turned the lamp down to a yellow glow less than a candle's light, and sat doing nothing, saying nothing, withdrawn.

The silence continued.

"I finished the computations."

Pugh nodded thanks.

"The signal from Martin came through, but I couldn't contact you or him."

Pugh said with effort, "I should not have gone. He had two hours of air left even with only one can. He might have been heading home when I left. This way we were all out of touch with one another. I was scared."

The silence came back punctuated now by Martin's long, soft snores.

"Do you love Martin?"

Pugh looked up with angry eyes: "Martin is my friend. We've worked together, he's a good man." He stopped. After a while he said, "Yes, I love him. Why did you ask that?"

Kaph said nothing, but he looked at the other man. His face was changed, as if he were glimpsing something he had not seen before; his voice too was changed. "How can you . . . ? How do you . . . ?"

But Pugh could not tell him. "I don't know," he said, "it's practice, partly. I don't know. We're each of us alone, to be sure. What can you do but hold your hand out in the dark?"

Kaph's strange gaze dropped, burned out by its own intensity.

"I'm tired," Pugh said. "That was ugly, looking for him in all that black dust and muck, and mouths opening and shutting in the ground. . . . I'm going to bed. The ship will be transmitting to us by six or so." He stood up and stretched.

"It's a clone," Kaph said. "The other Exploit team they're bringing with them."

"Is it, then?"

"A twelve clone. They came out with us on the *Passerine*."

Kaph sat in the small yellow aura of the lamp seeming to look past it at what he feared: the new clone, the multiple self of which he was not part. A lost piece of a broken set, a fragment, inexpert at solitude, not knowing even how you go about giving love to another individual, now he must face the absolute, closed self-sufficiency of the clone of twelve; that was a lot to ask of the poor fellow, to be sure. Pugh put a hand on his shoulder in passing. "The chief won't ask you to stay here with a clone. You can go home. Or since you're Far Out maybe you'll come on farther out with us. We could use you. No hurry deciding. You'll make out all right."

Pugh's quiet voice trailed off. He stood unbuttoning his coat, stooped a little with fatigue. Kaph looked at him and saw the thing he had never seen before: saw him: Owen Pugh, the other, the stranger who held his hand out in the dark.

"Good night," Pugh mumbled, crawling into his sleeping bag and half asleep already, so that he did not hear Kaph reply after a pause, repeating, across darkness, benediction.

CALL ME JOE

POUL ANDERSON

Evolution never stands still. We are in a state of constant change. Possibly the change is too slow for the untrained observer to detect. But it is there. It has been there for one hundred thousand or more years and it has accelerated greatly since the industrial revolution. It is heading for an endpoint or climax within the next century.
> —Dandridge M. Cole, *Beyond Tomorrow* *

One reason for the ease with which human beings change habitats is that they exhibit a rather low degree of biological specialization. They can walk, run, creep, climb, and swim. They can live on an exclusively carnivorous diet, an exclusively herbivorous one, or almost any kind of mixed alimentation. They can function and proliferate amid the sands of the Sahara or the fogs of Iceland, in the tropical

* Amherst, Wis.: Amherst Press, 1965, p. 120.

forest or on the polar ice, at high altitudes in the Andes or below sea level around the Dead Sea.
—René Dubos, *Beast or Angel?* *

Except for a few hardy individuals, groups, and cultures, humankind's tendency has been to alter its environment rather than to adapt to it. Given a choice, most of us would prefer to protect ourselves with dwelling places, clothing, heating or air conditioning, and transportation, rather than to go without these things in order to become stronger or to produce healthier descendants. If we are ever to live on the moon or in space, we shall have to take much of our environment with us, although our bodies too will begin to change in their new surroundings. Both scientists and science fiction writers have even discussed the possibility of "terraforming" or altering other worlds to be more like the earth.

Yet we have been willing to change ourselves for various reasons. Strenuous physical activity may be unnecessary for many in a technological world, but athletic experiences can be enjoyable in themselves. One could stay inside much of the time, but there is pleasure in feeling sunshine and breezes or in watching snow fall. If we had the ability to alter our bodies greatly, it is possible, for example, that those who love swimming and scuba diving might wish to live in the sea permanently with changed bodies. By adapting ourselves, rather than changing our surroundings to suit only our convenience, we open ourselves to new experiences.

We might even choose to alter ourselves or breed others able to exist in completely inhospitable environments. How would such beings react to the new settings? Would they still be human, and would we regard them as human? How would our species, which has had such a poor history of dealing with ethnic and racial differences, deal with these beings?

Poul Anderson writes of one man created for an alien

* New York: Charles Scribner's Sons, 1974, p. 23.

world, and another who suffers physical disabilities. Although scientists have since learned that Jupiter is quite unlike the planet in the story (though a planet like this may exist elsewhere in our galaxy), the tale is still a strong and moving depiction of possible future experience on a strange world.

The wind came whooping out of eastern darkness, driving a lash of ammonia dust before it. In minutes, Edward Anglesey was blinded.

He clawed all four feet into the broken shards which were soil, hunched down and groped for his little smelter. The wind was an idiot bassoon in his skull. Something whipped across his back, drawing blood, a tree yanked up by the roots and spat a hundred miles. Lightning cracked, immensely far overhead where clouds boiled with night.

As if to reply, thunder toned in the ice mountains and a red gout of flame jumped and a hillside came booming down, spilling itself across the valley. The earth shivered.

Sodium explosion, thought Anglesey in the drumbeat noise. The fire and the lightning gave him enough illumination to find his apparatus. He picked up tools in muscular hands, his tail gripped the trough, and he battered his way to the tunnel and thus to his dugout.

It had walls and roof of water, frozen by sun-remoteness and compressed by tons of atmosphere jammed onto every square inch. Ventilated by a tiny smokehole, a lamp of tree oil burning in hydrogen made a dull light for the single room.

Anglesey sprawled his slate-blue form on the floor, panting. It was no use to swear at the storm. These ammonia gales often came at sunset, and there was nothing to do but wait them out. He was tired, anyway.

It would be morning in five hours or so. He had hoped to cast an axhead, his first, this evening, but maybe it was better to do the job by daylight.

He pulled a dekapod body off a shelf and ate the meat raw, pausing for long gulps of liquid methane from a jug. Things would improve once he had proper tools; so far, everything had been painfully grubbed and hacked to shape with teeth, claws, chance icicles, and what detestably weak and crumbling fragments remained of the spaceship. Give him a few years and he'd be living as a man should.

He sighed, stretched, and lay down to sleep.

Somewhat more than one hundred and twelve thousand miles away, Edward Anglesey took off his helmet.

He looked around, blinking. After the Jovian surface, it was always a little unreal to find himself here again, in the clean quiet orderliness of the control room.

His muscles ached. They shouldn't. He had not really been fighting a gale of several hundred miles an hour, under three gravities and a temperature of 140 Absolute. He had been here, in the almost nonexistent pull of Jupiter V, breathing oxynitrogen. It was Joe who lived down there and filled his lungs with hydrogen and helium at a pressure which could still only be estimated because it broke aneroids and deranged piezoelectrics.

Nevertheless, his body felt worn and beaten. Tension, no doubt—psychosomatics. After all, for a good many hours now he had, in a sense, been Joe, and Joe had been working hard.

With the helmet off, Anglesey held only a thread of identification. The esprojector was still tuned to Joe's brain but no longer focused on his own. Somewhere in the back of his mind, he knew an indescribable feeling of sleep. Now and then, vague forms or colors drifted in the soft black—dreams? Not impossible that

Joe's brain should dream a little when Anglesey's mind wasn't using it.

A light flickered red on the esprojector panel, and a bell whined electronic fear. Anglesey cursed. Thin fingers danced over the controls of his chair, he slewed around and shot across to the bank of dials. Yes— there—K-tube oscillating again! The circuit blew out. He wrenched the faceplate off with one hand and fumbled in a drawer with the other.

Inside his mind, he could feel the contact with Joe fading. If he once lost it entirely, he wasn't sure he could regain it. And Joe was an investment of several million dollars and quite a few highly skilled man-years.

Anglesey pulled the offending K-tube from its socket and threw it on the floor. Glass exploded. It eased his temper a bit, just enough so he could find a replacement, plug it in, switch on the current again—as the machine warmed up, once again amplifying, the Joe-ness in the back alleys of his brain strengthened.

Slowly, then, the man in the electric wheelchair rolled out of the room, into the hall. Let somebody else sweep up the broken tube. To hell with it. To hell with everybody.

Jan Cornelius had never been farther from Earth than some comfortable lunar resort. He felt much put upon that the Psionics Corporation should tap him for a thirteen-month exile. The fact that he knew as much about esprojectors and their cranky innards as any other man alive was no excuse. Why send anyone at all? Who cared?

Obviously the Federation Science Authority did. It had seemingly given those bearded hermits a blank check on the taxpayer's account.

Thus did Cornelius grumble to himself, all the long hyperbolic path to Jupiter. Then the shifting accelerations of approach to its tiny inner satellite left him too wretched for further complaint.

And when he finally, just prior to disembarkation, went up to the greenhouse for a look at Jupiter, he said not a word. Nobody does, the first time.

Arne Viken waited patiently while Cornelius stared. *It still gets me, too,* he remembered. *By the throat. Sometimes I'm afraid to look.*

At length Cornelius turned around. He had a faintly Jovian appearance himself, being a large man with an imposing girth. "I had no idea," he whispered. "I never thought . . . I had seen pictures, but—"

Viken nodded. "Sure, Dr. Cornelius. Pictures don't convey it."

Where they stood, they could see the dark broken rock of the satellite, jumbled for a short way beyond the landing slip and then chopped off sheer. This moon was scarcely even a platform, it seemed, and cold constellations went streaming past it, around it. Jupiter lay across a fifth of that sky, softly ambrous, banded with colors, spotted with the shadows of planet-sized moons and with whirlwinds as broad as Earth. If there had been any gravity to speak of, Cornelius would have thought, instinctively, that the great planet was falling on him. As it was, he felt as if sucked upward, his hands were still sore where he had grabbed a rail to hold on.

"You live here . . . all alone . . . with this?" He spoke feebly.

"Oh, well, there are some fifty of us all told, pretty congenial," said Viken. "It's not so bad. You sign up for four-cycle hitches—four ship arrivals—and believe it or not, Dr. Cornelius, this is my third enlistment."

The newcomer forbore to inquire more deeply. There was something not quite understandable about the men on Jupiter V. They were mostly bearded, though otherwise careful to remain neat; their low-gravity movements were somehow dreamlike to watch; they hoarded their conversation, as if to stretch it through the year and month between ships. Their monkish existence had changed them—or did they take what amounted to vows of poverty, chastity, and obedience because they had never felt quite at home on green Earth?

Thirteen months! Cornelius shuddered. It was going to be a long cold wait, and the pay and bonuses accumulating for him were scant comfort now, four hundred and eighty million miles from the sun.

"Wonderful place to do research," continued Viken. "All the facilities, hand-picked colleagues, no distractions . . . and of course—" He jerked his thumb at the planet and turned to leave.

Cornelius followed, wallowing awkwardly. "It is very interesting, no doubt," he puffed. "Fascinating. But really, Dr. Viken, to drag me way out here and make me spend a year-plus waiting for the next ship . . . to do a job which may take me a few weeks—"

"Are you sure it's that simple?" asked Viken gently. His face swiveled around, and there was something in his eyes that silenced Cornelius. "After all my time here, I've yet to see any problem, however complicated, which when you looked at it the right way didn't become still more complicated."

They went through the ship's air lock and the tube joining it to the station entrance. Nearly everything was underground. Rooms, laboratories, even halls had a degree of luxuriousness—why, there was a fireplace with a real fire in the common room! God alone knew what *that* cost!

Thinking of the huge chill emptiness where the king planet laired, and of his own year's sentence, Cornelius decided that such luxuries were, in truth, biological necessities.

Viken showed him to a pleasantly furnished chamber which would be his own. "We'll fetch your luggage soon, and unload your psionic stuff. Right now, everybody's either talking to the ship's crew or reading his mail."

Cornelius nodded absently and sat down. The chair, like all low-gee furniture, was a mere spidery skeleton, but it held his bulk comfortably enough. He felt in his tunic, hoping to bribe the other man into keeping him company for a while. "Cigar? I brought some from Amsterdam."

"Thanks." Viken accepted with disappointing casualness, crossed long thin legs and blew grayish clouds.

"Ah . . . are you in charge here?"

"Not exactly. No one is. We do have one administrator, the cook, to handle what little work of that type may come up. Don't forget, this is a research station, first, last, and always."

"What is your field, then?"

Viken frowned. "Don't question anyone else so bluntly, Dr. Cornelius," he warned. "They'd rather spin the gossip out as long as possible with each newcomer. It's a rare treat to have someone whose every last conceivable reaction hasn't been— No, no apologies to me. 'S all right. I'm a physicist, specializing in the solid state at ultra-high pressures." He nodded at the wall. "Plenty of it to be observed—there!"

"I see." Cornelius smoked quietly for a while. Then: "I'm supposed to be the psionics expert, but frankly, at present I've no idea why your machine should misbehave as reported."

"You mean those, uh, K-tubes have a stable output on Earth?"

"And on Luna, Mars, Venus . . . everywhere, apparently, but here." Cornelius shrugged. "Of course, psibeams are always persnickety, and sometimes you get an unwanted feedback when— No. I'll get the facts before I theorize. Who are your psimen?"

"Just Anglesey, who's not a formally trained esman at all. But he took it up after he was crippled, and showed such a natural aptitude that he was shipped out here when he volunteered. It's so hard to get anyone for Jupiter V that we aren't fussy about degrees. At that, Ed seems to be operating Joe as well as a Ps.D. could."

"Ah, yes. Your pseudojovian. I'll have to examine that angle pretty carefully too," said Cornelius. In spite of himself, he was getting interested. "Maybe the trouble comes from something in Joe's biochemistry. Who knows? I'll let you into a carefully guarded little secret, Dr. Viken: psionics is not an exact science."

"Neither is physics," grinned the other man. After a moment, he added more soberly: "Not my brand of physics, anyway. I hope to make it exact. That's why I'm here, you know. It's the reason we're all here."

Edward Anglesey was a bit of a shock the first time, He was a head, a pair of arms, and a disconcertingly intense blue stare. The rest of him was mere detail, enclosed in a wheeled machine.

"Biophysicist originally," Viken had told Cornelius. "Studying atmospheric spores at Earth Station when he was still a young man—accident, crushed him up, nothing below his chest will ever work again. Snappish type, you have to go slow with him."

Seated on a wisp of stool in the esprojector control room, Cornelius realized that Viken had been soft-pedaling the truth.

Anglesey ate as he talked, gracelessly, letting the chair's tentacles wipe up after him. "Got to," he explained. "This stupid place is officially on Earth time, GMT. Jupiter isn't. I've got to be here whenever Joe wakes, ready to take him over."

"Couldn't you have someone spell you?" asked Cornelius.

"Bah!" Anglesey stabbed a piece of prot and waggled it at the other man. Since it was native to him, he could spit out English, the common language of the station, with unmeasured ferocity. "Look here. You ever done therapeutic esping? Not just listening in, or even communication, but actual pedagogic control?"

"No, not I. It requires a certain natural talent, like yours." Cornelius smiled. His ingratiating little phrase was swallowed without being noticed by the scored face opposite him. "I take it you mean cases like, oh, re-educating the nervous system of a palsied child?"

"Yes, yes. Good enough example. Has anyone ever tried to suppress the child's personality, take him over in the most literal sense?"

"Good God, no!"

"Even as a scientific experiment?" Anglesey grinned. "Has any esprojector operative ever poured on the juice and swamped the child's brain with his own thoughts? Come on, Cornelius, I won't snitch on you."

"Well . . . it's out of my line, you understand." The psionicist looked carefully away, found a bland meter face and screwed his eyes to that. "I have, uh, heard something about . . . well, yes, there were attempts made in some pathological cases to, uh, bull through . . . break down the patient's delusions by sheer force—"

"And it didn't work," said Anglesey. He laughed. "It can't work, not even on a child, let alone an adult with a fully developed personality. Why, it took a decade of refinement, didn't it, before the machine was debugged to the point where a psychiatrist could even 'listen in' without the normal variation between his pattern of thought and the patient's . . . without that variation setting up an interference scrambling the very thing he wanted to study. The machine has to make automatic compensations for the differences between individuals. We still can't bridge the differences between species.

"If someone else is willing to cooperate, you can very gently guide his thinking. And that's all. If you try to seize control of another brain, a brain with its own background of experience, its own ego—you risk your very sanity. The other brain will fight back instinctively. A fully developed, matured, hardened human personality is just too complex for outside control. It has too many resources, too much hell the subconscious can call to its defense if its integrity is threatened. Blazes, man, we can't even master our own minds, let alone anyone else's!"

Anglesey's cracked-voice tirade broke off. He sat brooding at the instrument panel, tapping the console of his mechanical mother.

"Well?" said Cornelius after a while.

He should not, perhaps, have spoken. But he found it hard to remain mute. There was too much silence— half a billion miles of it, from here to the sun. If you closed your mouth five minutes at a time, the silence began creeping in like fog.

"Well," gibed Anglesey. "So our pseudojovian, Joe,

has a physically adult brain. The only reason I can control him is that his brain has never been given a chance to develop its own ego. I am Joe. From the moment he was 'born' into consciousness, I have been there. The psibeam sends me all his sense data and sends him back my motor-nerve impulses. Nevertheless, he has that excellent brain, and its cells are recording every trace of experience, even as yours and mine; his synapses have assumed the topography which is my 'personality pattern.'

"Anyone else, taking him over from me, would find it was like an attempt to oust me myself from my own brain. It couldn't be done. To be sure, he doubtless has only a rudimentary set of Anglesey-memories—I do not, for instance, repeat trigonometric theorems while controlling him—but he has enough to be, potentially, a distinct personality.

"As a matter of fact, whenever he wakes up from sleep—there's usually a lag of a few minutes, while I sense the change through my normal psi faculties and get the amplifying helmet adjusted—I have a bit of a struggle. I feel almost a . . . a resistence . . . until I've brought his mental currents completely into phase with mine. Merely dreaming has been enough of a different experience to—" Anglesey didn't bother to finish the sentence.

"I see," murmured Cornelius. "Yes, it's clear enough. In fact, it's astonishing that you can have such total contact with a being of such alien metabolism."

"I won't for much longer," said the esman sarcastically, "unless you can correct whatever is burning out those K-tubes. I don't have an unlimited supply of spares."

"I have some working hypotheses," said Cornelius, "but there's so little known about psibeam transmission—is the velocity infinite or merely very great, is the beam strength actually independent of distance? How about the possible effects of transmission . . . oh, through the degenerate matter in the Jovian core? Good Lord, a planet where water is a heavy mineral and hydrogen is a metal! What do we know?"

"We're supposed to find out," snapped Anglesey. "That's what this whole project is for. Knowledge. Bull!" Almost, he spat on the floor. "Apparently what little we have learned doesn't even get through to people. Hydrogen is still a gas where Joe lives. He'd have to dig down a few miles to reach the solid phase. And I'm expected to make a scientific analysis of Jovian conditions!"

Cornelius waited it out, letting Anglesey storm on while he himself turned over the problem of K-tube oscillation:

"They don't understand back on Earth. Even here they don't. Sometimes I think they refuse to understand. Joe's down there without much more than his bare hands. He, I, we started with no more knowledge than that he could probably eat the local life. He has to spend nearly all his time hunting for food. It's a miracle he's come as far as he has in these few weeks— made a shelter, grown familiar with the immediate region, begun on metallurgy, hydrurgy, whatever you want to call it. What more do they want me to do, for crying in the beer?"

"Yes, yes—" mumbled Cornelius. "Yes, I—"

Anglesey raised his white bony face. Something filmed over in his eyes.

"What—" began Cornelius.

"Shut up!" Anglesey whipped the chair around, groped for the helmet, slapped it down over his skull. "Joe's waking. Get out of here."

"But if you'll only let me work while he sleeps, how can I—"

Anglesey snarled and threw a wrench at him. It was a feeble toss, even in low-gee. Cornelius backed toward the door. Anglesey was tuning in the esprojector. Suddenly he jerked.

"Cornelius!"

"Whatisit?" The psionicist tried to run back, overdid it, and skidded in a heap to end up against the panel.

"K-tube again." Anglesey yanked off the helmet. It must have hurt like blazes, having a mental squeal build up uncontrolled and amplified in your own brain, but he said merely, "Change it for me. Fast. And then get out and leave me alone. Joe didn't wake up of himself. Something crawled into the dugout with me—I'm in trouble down there!"

It had been a hard day's work, and Joe slept heavily. He did not wake until the hands closed on his throat.

For a moment, then, he knew only a crazy smothering wave of panic. He thought he was back on Earth Station, floating in null-gee at the end of a cable while a thousand frosty stars haloed the planet before him. He thought the great I-beam had broken from its moorings and started toward him, slowly, but with all the inertia of its cold tons, spinning and shimmering in the earthlight, and the only sound himself, screaming and screaming in his helmet, trying to break from the cable. The beam nudged him ever so gently, but it kept on moving. He moved with it. He was crushed against the station wall—nuzzled into it—his mangled suit frothed as it tried to seal its wounded self. There was blood mingled with the foam—his blood! *Joe* roared.

His convulsive reaction tore the hands off his neck and sent a black shape spinning across the dugout. It struck the wall, thunderously, and the lamp fell to the floor and went out.

Joe stood in darkness, breathing hard, aware in a vague fashion that the wind had died from a shriek to a low snarling while he slept.

The thing he had tossed away mumbled in pain and crawled along the wall. Joe felt through lightlessness after his club.

Something else scrabbled. The tunnel! They were coming through the tunnel! Joe groped blind to meet them. His heart drummed thickly and his nose drank an alien stench.

The thing that emerged, as Joe's hands closed on it, was only about half his size, but it had six monstrously taloned feet and a pair of three-fingered hands that reached after his eyes. Joe cursed, lifted it while it writhed, and dashed it to the floor. It screamed, and he heard bones splinter.

"Come on, then!" Joe arched his back and spat at them, like a tiger menaced by giant caterpillars.

They flowed through his tunnel and into the room, a dozen of them entered while he wrestled one that had curled itself around his shoulders and anchored its sinuous body with claws. They pulled at his legs, trying to crawl up on his back. He struck out with claws of his own, with his tail, rolled over and went down beneath a heap of them and stood up with the heap still clinging to him.

They swayed in darkness. The legged seething of them struck the dugout wall. It shivered, a rafter cracked, the roof came down. Anglesey stood in a pit, among broken ice plates, under the wan light of a sinking Ganymede.

He could see now that the monsters were black in color and that they had heads big enough to accommodate some brain, less than human but probably more than apes. There were a score of them or so, they struggled from beneath the wreckage and flowed at him with the same shrieking malice.

Why?

Baboon reaction, thought Anglesey somewhere in the back of himself. See the stranger, fear the stranger, hate the stranger, kill the stranger. His chest heaved, pumping air through a raw throat. He yanked a whole rafter to him, snapped it in half, and twirled the iron-hard wood.

The nearest creature got its head bashed in. The next had its back broken. The third was hurled with shattered ribs into a fourth, they went down together. Joe began to laugh. It was getting to be fun.

"Yeee-ow! Ti-i-i-iger!" He ran across the icy ground, toward the pack. They scattered, howling. He hunted them until the last one had vanished into the forest.

Panting, Joe looked at the dead. He himself was bleeding, he ached, he was cold and hungry and his shelter had been wrecked . . . but he'd whipped them! He had a sudden impulse to beat his chest and howl. For a moment, he hesitated—why not? Anglesey threw back his head and bayed victory at the dim shield of Ganymede.

Thereafter he went to work. First build a fire, in the lee of the spaceship—which was little more by now than a hill of corrosion. The monster pack cried in darkness and the broken ground; they had not given up on him, they would return.

He tore a haunch off one of the slain and took a bite. Pretty good. Better yet if properly cooked. Heh!

They'd made a big mistake in calling his attention to their existence! He finished breakfast while Ganymede slipped under the western ice mountains. It would be morning soon. The air was almost still, and a flock of pancake-shaped skyskimmers, as Anglesey called them, went overhead, burnished copper color in the first pale dawn streaks.

Joe rummaged in the ruins of his hut until he had recovered the water-smelting equipment. It wasn't harmed. That was the first order of business, melt some ice and cast it in the molds of ax, knife, saw, hammer he had painfully prepared. Under Jovian conditions, methane was a liquid that you drank and water was a dense hard mineral. It would make good tools. Later on he would try alloying it with other materials.

Next—yes. To hell with the dugout, he could sleep in the open again for a while. Make a bow, set traps, be ready to massacre the black caterpillars when they attacked him again. There was a chasm not far from here, going down a long way toward the bitter cold of the metallic-hydrogen strata: a natural icebox, a place to store the several weeks' worth of meat his enemies would supply. This would give him leisure to— Oh, a hell of a lot!

Joe laughed exultantly and lay down to watch the sunrise.

It struck him afresh how lovely a place this was. See how the small brilliant spark of the sun swam up out of eastern fog-banks colored dusky purple and veined with rose and gold; see how the light strengthened until the great hollow arch of the sky became one shout of radiance; see how the light spilled warm and living over a broad fair land, the million square miles of rustling low forests and wave-blinking lakes and

feather-plumed hydrogen geysers; and see, see, see how
the ice mountains of the west flashed like blued steel!

Anglesey drew the wild morning wind deep into his
lungs and shouted with a boy's joy.

"I'm not a biologist myself," said Viken carefully.
"But maybe for that reason I can better give you the
general picture. Then Lopez or Matsumoto can answer
any questions of detail."

"Excellent." Cornelius nodded. "Why don't you assume I am totally ignorant of this project? I very
nearly am, you know."

"If you wish." Viken laughed.

They stood in an outer office of the xenobiology section. No one else was around, for the station's clocks
said 1730 GMT and there was only one shift. No
point in having more, until Anglesey's half of the en-
terprise had actually begun gathering quantitative data.

The physicist bent over and took a paperweight off
a desk. "One of the boys made this for fun," he said,
"but it's a pretty good model of Joe. He stands about
five feet tall at the head."

Cornelius turned the plastic image over in his hands.
If you could imagine such a thing as a feline centaur
with a thick prehensile tail—The torso was squat, long-
armed, immensely muscular; the hairless head was
round, wide-nosed, with big deep-set eyes and heavy
jaws, but it was really quite a human face. The overall color was bluish gray.

"Male, I see," he remarked.

"Of course. Perhaps you don't understand. Joe is the
complete pseudojovian—as far as we can tell, the final
model, with all the bugs worked out. He's the answer
to a research question that took fifty years to ask."
Viken looked sidewise at Cornelius. "So you realize
the importance of your job, don't you?"

"I'll do my best," said the psionicist. "But if . . . well, let's say that tube failure or something causes you to lose Joe before I've solved the oscillation problem. You do have other pseudos in reserve, don't you?"

"Oh, yes," said Viken moodily. "But the cost— We're not on an unlimited budget. We do go through a lot of money, because it's expensive to stand up and sneeze this far from Earth. But for that same reason our margin is slim."

He jammed hands in pockets and slouched toward the inner door, the laboratories, head down and talking in a low, hurried voice:

"Perhaps you don't realize what a nightmare planet Jupiter is. Not just the surface gravity—a shade under three gees, what's that?—but the gravitational potential, ten times Earth's. The temperature. The pressure . . . above all, the atmosphere, and the storms, and the darkness!

"When a spaceship goes down to the Jovian surface, it's a radio-controlled job; it leaks like a sieve, to equalize pressure, but otherwise it's the sturdiest, most utterly powerful model ever designed; it's loaded with every instrument, every servo-mechanism, every safety device the human mind has yet thought up to protect a million-dollar hunk of precision equipment.

"And what happens? Half the ships never reach the surface at all. A storm snatches them and throws them away, or they collide with a floating chunk of Ice VII —small version of the Red Spot—or, so help me, what passes for a flock of birds rams one and stoves it in!

"As for the fifty per cent which do land, it's a one-way trip. We don't even try to bring them back. If the stresses coming down haven't sprung something, the corrosion has doomed them anyway. Hydrogen at Jovian pressure does funny things to metals.

"It cost a total of—about five million dollars—to set

Joe, one pseudo, down there. Each pseudo to follow will cost, if we're lucky, a couple of million more."

Viken kicked open the door and led the way through. Beyond was a big room, low-ceilinged, coldly lit and murmurous with ventilators. It reminded Cornelius of a nucleonics lab; for a moment he wasn't sure why, then he recognized the intricacies of remote control, remote observation, walls enclosing forces which could destroy the entire moon.

"These are required by the pressure, of course," said Viken, pointing to a row of shields. "And the cold. And the hydrogen itself, as a minor hazard. We have units here duplicating conditions in the Jovian, uh, stratosphere. This is where the whole project really began."

"I've heard something about that," nodded Cornelius. "Didn't you scoop up air-borne spores?"

"Not I." Viken chuckled. "Totti's crew did, about fifty years ago. Proved there was life on Jupiter. A life using liquid methane as its basic solvent, solid ammonia as a starting point for nitrate synthesis—the plants use solar energy to build unsaturated carbon compounds, releasing hydrogen; the animals eat the plants and reduce those compounds again to the saturated form. There is even an equivalent of combustion. The reactions involve complex enzymes and . . . well, it's out of my line."

"Jovian biochemistry is pretty well understood, then."

"Oh, yes. Even in Totti's day, they had a highly developed biotic technology: Earth bacteria had already been synthesized and most gene structures pretty well mapped. The only reason it took so long to diagram Jovian life processes was the technical difficulty, high pressure and so on."

"When did you actually get a look at Jupiter's surface?"

"Gray managed that, about thirty years ago. Set a televisor ship down, a ship that lasted long enough to flash him quite a series of pictures. Since then, the technique has improved. We know that Jupiter is crawling with its own weird kind of life, probably more fertile than Earth. Extrapolating from the air-borne microorganisms, our team made trial syntheses of metazoans and—"

Viken sighed. "Damn it, if only there were intelligent native life! Think what they could tell us, Cornelius, the data, the— Just think back how far we've gone since Lavoisier, with the low-pressure chemistry of Earth. Here's a chance to learn a high-pressure chemistry and physics at least as rich with possibilities!"

After a moment, Cornelius murmured slyly, "Are you certain there aren't any Jovians?"

"Oh, sure, there could be several billion of them." Viken shrugged. "Cities, empires, anything you like. Jupiter has the surface area of a hundred Earths, and we've only seen maybe a dozen small regions. But we do know there aren't any Jovians using radio. Considering their atmosphere, it's unlikely they ever would invent it for themselves—imagine how thick a vacuum tube has to be, how strong a pump you need! So it was finally decided we'd better make our own Jovians."

Cornelius followed him through the lab into another room. This was less cluttered, it had a more finished appearance: the experimenter's haywire rig had yielded to the assured precision of an engineer.

Viken went over to one of the panels which lined the walls and looked at its gauges. "Beyond this lies another pseudo," he said. "Female, in this instance.

She's at a pressure of two hundred atmospheres and a temperature of 194 Absolute. There's a . . . an umbilical arrangement, I guess you'd call it, to keep her alive. She was grown to adulthood in this, uh, fetal stage—we patterned our Jovians after the terrestrial mammal. She's never been conscious, she won't ever be till she's 'born.' We have a total of twenty males and sixty females waiting here. We can count on about half reaching the surface. More can be created as required.

"It isn't the pseudos that are so expensive, it's their transportation. So Joe is down there alone till we're sure that his kind can survive."

"I take it you experimented with lower forms first," said Cornelius.

"Of course. It took twenty years, even with forced-catalysis techniques, to work from an artificial air-borne spore to Joe. We've used the psibeam to control everything from pseudo-insects on up. Interspecies control is possible, you know, if your puppet's nervous system is deliberately designed for it and isn't given a chance to grow into a pattern different from the esman's."

"And Joe is the first specimen who's given trouble?"

"Yes."

"Scratch one hypothesis." Cornelius sat down on a workbench, dangling thick legs and running a hand through thin sandy hair. "I thought maybe some physical effect of Jupiter was responsible. Now it looks as if the difficulty is with Joe himself."

"We've all suspected that much," said Viken. He struck a cigarette and sucked in his cheeks around the smoke. His eyes were gloomy. "Hard to see how. The biotics engineers tell me *Pseudocentaurus sapiens* has been more carefully designed than any product of natural evolution."

"Even the brain?"

"Yes, It's patterned directly on the human, to make psibeam control possible, but there are improvements —greater stability."

"There are still the psychological aspects, though," said Cornelius. "In spite of all our amplifiers and other fancy gadgets, psi is essentially a branch of psychology, even today . . . or maybe it's the other way around. Let's consider traumatic experiences. I take it the . . . the adult Jovian fetus has a rough trip going down?"

"The ship does," said Viken. "Not the pseudo itself, which is wrapped up in fluid just like you were before birth."

"Nevertheless," said Cornelius, "the two-hundred-atmospheres pressure here is not the same as whatever unthinkable pressure exists down on Jupiter. Could the change be injurious?"

Viken gave him a look of respect. "Not likely," he answered. "I told you the J-ships are designed leaky. External pressure is transmitted to the, uh, uterine mechanism through a series of diaphragms, in a gradual fashion. It takes hours to make the descent, you realize."

"Well, what happens next?" went on Cornelius. "The ship lands, the uterine mechanism opens, the umbilical connection disengages, and Joe is, shall we say, born. But he has an adult brain. He is not protected by the only half-developed infant brain from the shock of sudden awareness."

"We thought of that," said Viken. "Anglesey was on the psibeam, in phase with Joe, when the ship left this moon. So it wasn't really Joe who emerged, who perceived. Joe has never been much more than a biological waldo. He can only suffer mental shock to the extent that Ed does, because it *is* Ed down there!"

"As you will," said Cornelius. "Still, you didn't plan for a race of puppets, did you?"

"Oh, heavens, no," said Viken. "Out of the question. Once we know Joe is well established, we'll import a few more esmen and get him some assistance in the form of other pseudos. Eventually females will be sent down, and uncontrolled males, to be educated by the puppets. A new generation will be born normally— Well, anyhow, the ultimate aim is a small civilization of Jovians. There will be hunters, miners, artisans, farmers, housewives, the works. They will support a few key members, a kind of priesthood. And that priesthood will be esp-controlled, as Joe is. It will exist solely to make instruments, take readings, perform experiments, and tell us what we want to know!"

Cornelius nodded. In a general way, this was the Jovian project as he had understood it. He could appreciate the importance of his own assignment.

Only, he still had no clue to the cause of that positive feedback in the K-tubes.

And what could he do about it?

His hands were still bruised. *Oh, God,* he thought with a groan, for the hundredth time, *does it affect me that much? While Joe was fighting down there, did I really hammer my fists on metal up here?*

His eyes smoldered across the room, to the bench where Cornelius worked. He didn't like Cornelius, fat cigar-sucking slob, interminably talking and talking. He had about given up trying to be civil to the Earthworm.

The psionicist laid down a screwdriver and flexed cramped fingers. "Whuff!" He smiled. "I'm going to take a break."

The half-assembled esprojector made a gaunt backdrop for his wide soft body, where it squatted toad-

fashion on the bench. Anglesey detested the whole
idea of anyone sharing this room, even for a few hours
a day. Of late he had been demanding his meals
brought here, left outside the door of his adjoining
bedroom-bath. He had not gone beyond for quite
some time now.

And why should I?

"Couldn't you hurry it up a little?" snapped Anglesey.

Cornelius flushed. "If you'd had an assembled spare
machine, instead of loose parts—" he began. Shrug-
ging, he took out a cigar stub and relit it carefully; his
supply had to last a long time. Anglesey wondered if
those stinking clouds were blown from his mouth of
malicious purpose. *I don't like you, Mr. Earthman
Cornelius, and it is doubtless quite mutual.*

"There was no obvious need for one, until the other
esmen arrive," said Anglesey in a sullen voice. "And
the testing instruments report this one in perfectly
good order."

"Nevertheless," said Cornelius, "at irregular intervals it goes into wild oscillations which burn out the
K-tube. The problem is why. I'll have to try out this
new machine as soon as it is ready, but frankly, I don't
believe the trouble lies in electronic failure at all—or
even in unsuspected physical effects."

"Where, then?" Anglesey felt more at ease as the
discussion grew purely technical.

"Well, look. What exactly is the K-tube? It's the
heart of the esprojector. It amplifies your natural
psionic pulses, uses them to modulate the carrier wave,
and shoots the whole beam down at Joe. It also picks
up Joe's resonating impulses and amplifies them for
your benefit. Everything else is auxiliary to the K-
tube."

"Spare me the lecture," snarled Anglesey.

"It was only rehearsing the obvious," said Cornelius, "because every now and then it is the obvious answer which is hardest to see. Maybe it isn't the K-tube which is misbehaving. Maybe it is you."

"What?" The white face gaped at him. A dawning rage crept red across its thin bones.

"Nothing personal intended," said Cornelius hastily. "But you know what a tricky beast the subconscious is. Suppose, just as a working hypothesis, that way down underneath, you don't want to be on Jupiter. I imagine it is a rather terrifying environment. Or there may be some obscure Freudian element involved. Or, quite simply and naturally, your subconscious may fail to understand that Joe's death does not entail your own."

"Um-m-m—" *Mirabile dictu*, Anglesey remained calm. He rubbed his chin with one skeletal hand. "Can you be more explicit?"

"Only in a rough way," replied Cornelius. "Your conscious mind sends a motor impulse along the psi-beam to Joe. Simultaneously, your subconscious mind, being scared of the whole business, emits the glandular-vascular-cardiac-visceral impulses associated with fear. These react on Joe, whose tension is transmitted back along the beam. Feeling Joe's somatic fear symptoms, your subconscious gets still more worried, thereby increasing the symptoms. Get it? It's exactly similar to ordinary neurasthenia, with this exception: that since there is a powerful amplifier, the K-tube, involved, the oscillations can build up uncontrollably within a second or two. You should be thankful the tube does burn out—otherwise your brain might do so!"

For a moment Anglesey was quiet. Then he laughed. It was a hard, barbaric laughter. Cornelius started as it struck his eardrums.

"Nice idea," said the esman. "But I'm afraid it won't fit all the data. You see, I like it down there. I like being Joe."

He paused for a while, then continued in a dry impersonal tone: "Don't judge the environment from my notes. They're just idiotic things like estimates of wind velocity, temperature variations, mineral properties—insignificant. What I can't put in is how Jupiter looks through a Jovian's infrared-seeing eyes."

"Different, I should think," ventured Cornelius after a minute's clumsy silence.

"Yes and no. It's hard to put into language. Some of it I can't, because r .n hasn't got the concepts. But . . . oh, I can't describe it. Shakespeare himself couldn't. Just remember that everything about Jupiter which is cold and poisonous and gloomy to us is right for Joe."

Anglesey's tone grew remote, as if he spoke to himself:

"Imagine walking under a glowing violet sky, where great flashing clouds sweep the earth with shadow and rain strides beneath them. Imagine walking on the slopes of a mountain like polished metal, with a clean red flame exploding above you and thunder laughing in the ground. Imagine a cool wild stream, and low trees with dark coppery flowers, and a waterfall, methanefall . . . whatever you like . . . leaping off a cliff, and the strong live wind shakes its mane full of rainbows! Imagine a whole forest, dark and breathing, and here and there you glimpse a pale-red wavering will-o'-the-wisp, which is the life radiation of some fleet shy animal, and . . . and—"

Anglesey croaked into silence. He stared down at his clenched fists, then he closed his eyes tight and tears ran out between the lids.

"Imagine being *strong!*"

Suddenly he snatched up the helmet, crammed it on his head and twirled the control knobs. Joe had been sleeping, down in the night, but Joe was about to wake up and—roar under the four great moons till all the forest feared him?

Cornelius slipped quietly out of the room.

In the long brazen sunset light, beneath dusky cloud banks brooding storm, he strode up the hill-slope with a sense of day's work done. Across his back, two woven baskets balanced each other, one laden with the pungent black fruit of the thorntree and one with cable-thick creepers to be used as rope. The ax on his shoulder caught the waning sunlight and tossed it blindingly back.

It had not been hard labor, but weariness dragged at his mind and he did not relish the household chores yet to be performed, cooking and cleaning and all the rest. Why couldn't they hurry up and get him some helpers?

His eyes sought the sky, resentfully. Moon Five was hidden—down here, at the bottom of the air ocean, you saw nothing but the sun and the four Galilean satellites. He wasn't even sure where Five was just now, in relation to himself . . . *wait a minute, it's sunset here, but if I went out to the viewdome I'd see Jupiter in the last quarter, or would I, oh, hell, it only takes us half an Earth-day to swing around the planet anyhow—*

Joe shook his head. After all this time, it was still damnably hard, now and then, to keep his thoughts straight. *I, the essential I, am up in heaven, riding Jupiter V between cold stars. Remember that. Open your eyes, if you will, and see the dead control room superimposed on a living hillside.*

He didn't, though. Instead, he regarded the boulders strewn wind-blasted gray over the tough mossy vegetation of the slope. They were not much like Earth rocks, nor was the soil beneath his feet like terrestrial humus.

For a moment Anglesey speculated on the origin of the silicates, aluminates, and other stony compounds. Theoretically, all such materials should be inaccessibly locked in the Jovian core, down where the pressure got vast enough for atoms to buckle and collapse. Above the core should lie thousands of miles of allotropic ice, and then the metallic-hydrogen layer. There should not be complex minerals this far up, but there were.

Well, possibly Jupiter had formed according to theory, but had thereafter sucked enough cosmic dust, meteors, gases, and vapors down its great throat of gravitation, to form a crust several miles thick. Or more likely the theory was altogether wrong. What did they know, what *could* they know, the soft pale worms of Earth?

Anglesey stuck his—Joe's—fingers in his mouth and whistled. A baying sounded in the brush, and two midnight forms leaped toward him. He grinned and stroked their heads; training was progressing faster than he'd hoped, with these pups of the black caterpillar beasts he had taken. They would make guardians for him, herders, servants.

On the crest of the hill, Joe was building himself a home. He had logged off an acre of ground and erected a stockade. Within the grounds there now stood a lean-to for himself and his stores, a methane well, and the beginnings of a large comfortable cabin.

But there was too much work for one being. Even with the half-intelligent caterpillars to help, and with

cold storage for meat, most of his time would still go
to hunting. The game wouldn't last forever, either; he
had to start agriculture within the next year or so—
Jupiter year, twelve Earth years, thought Anglesey.
There was the cabin to finish and furnish; he wanted
to put a waterwheel, no, methane wheel in the river to
turn any of a dozen machines he had in mind, he
wanted to experiment with alloyed ice and—

And, quite apart from his need of help, why should
he remain alone, the single thinking creature on an
entire planet? He was a male in this body, with male
instincts—in the long run, his health was bound to
suffer if he remained a hermit, and right now the
whole project depended on Joe's health.

It wasn't right!

*But I am not alone. There are fifty men on the satel-
lite with me. I can talk to any of them, any time I
wish. It's only that I seldom wish it, these days. I
would rather be Joe.*

*Nevertheless . . . I, the cripple, feel all the tiredness,
anger, hurt, frustration, of that wonderful biological
machine called Joe. The others don't understand.
When the ammonia gale flays open his skin, it is I who
bleed.*

Joe lay down on the ground, sighing. Fangs flashed
in the mouth of the black beast which humped over
to lick his face. His belly growled with hunger, but he
was too tired to fix a meal. Once he had the dogs
trained—

Another pseudo would be so much more rewarding
to educate.

He could almost see it, in the weary darkening of
his brain. Down there, in the valley below the hill, fire
and thunder as the ship came to rest. And the steel
egg would crack open, the steel arms—already crum-

bling, puny work of worms!—lift out the shape within and lay it on the earth.

She would stir, shrieking in her first lungful of air, looking about with blank mindless eyes. And Joe would come carry her home. And he would feed her, care for her, show her how to walk—it wouldn't take long, an adult body would learn those things very fast. In a few weeks she would even be talking, be an individual, a soul.

Did you ever think, Edward Anglesey, in the days when you also walked, that your wife would be a gray four-legged monster?

Never mind that. The important thing was to get others of his kind down here, female and male. The station's niggling little plan would have him wait two more Earth years, and then send him only another dummy like himself, a contemptible human mind looking through eyes which belonged rightfully to a Jovian. It was not to be tolerated!

If he weren't so tired—

Joe sat up. Sleep drained from him as the realization entered. *He* wasn't tired, not to speak of. Anglesey was. Anglesey, the human side of him, who for months had slept only in catnaps, whose rest had lately been interrupted by Cornelius—it was the human body which drooped, gave up, and sent wave after soft wave of sleep down the psibeam to Joe.

Somatic tension traveled skyward; Anglesey jerked awake.

He swore. As he sat there beneath the helmet, the vividness of Jupiter faded with his scattering concentration, as if it grew transparent; the steel prison which was his laboratory strengthened behind it. He was losing contact— Rapidly, with the skill of experience, he brought himself back into phase with the neural currents of the other brain. He willed sleepiness on Joe, exactly as a man wills it on himself.

And, like any other insomniac, he failed. The Joe-body was too hungry. It got up and walked across the compound toward its shack.

The K-tube went wild and blew itself out.

The night before the ships left, Viken and Cornelius sat up late.

It was not truly a night, of course. In twelve hours the tiny moon was hurled clear around Jupiter, from darkness back to darkness, and there might well be a pallid little sun over its crags when the clocks said witches were abroad in Greenwich. But most of the personnel were asleep at this hour.

Viken scowled. "I don't like it," he said. "Too sudden a change of plans. Too big a gamble."

"You are only risking—how many?—three male and a dozen female pseudos," Cornelius replied.

"And fifteen J-ships. All we have. If Anglesey's notion doesn't work, it will be months, a year or more, till we can have others built and resume aerial survey."

"But if it does work," said Cornelius, "you won't need any J-ships, except to carry down more pseudos. You will be too busy evaluating data from the surface to piddle around in the upper atmosphere."

"Of course. But we never expected it so soon. We were going to bring more esmen out here, to operate some more pseudos—"

"But they aren't *needed,*" said Cornelius. He struck a cigar to life and took a long pull on it, while his mind sought carefully for words. "Not for a while, anyhow. Joe has reached a point where, given help, he can leap several thousand years of history—he may even have a radio of sorts operating in the fairly near future, which would eliminate the necessity of much of your esping. But without help, he'll just have to mark time. And it's stupid to make a highly trained human esman perform manual labor, which is all that the other pseudos are needed for at this moment. Once the Jovian settlement is well established, certainly, then you can send down more puppets."

"The question is, though," persisted Viken, "can Anglesey himself educate all those pseudos at once? They'll be helpless as infants for days. It will be weeks before they really start thinking and acting for themselves. Can Joe take care of them meanwhile?"

"He has food and fuel stored for months ahead," said Cornelius. "As for what Joe's capabilities are, well, hm-m-m . . . we just have to take Anglesey's judgment. He has the only inside information."

"And once those Jovians do become personalities," worried Viken, "are they necessarily going to string along with Joe? Don't forget, the pseudos are not carbon copies of each other. The uncertainty principle assures each one a unique set of genes. If there is only one human mind on Jupiter, among all those aliens—"

"One *human* mind?" It was barely audible. Viken opened his mouth inquiringly. The other man hurried on.

"Oh, I'm sure Anglesey can continue to dominate them," said Cornelius. "His own personality is rather—tremendous."

Viken looked startled. "You really think so?"

The psionicist nodded. "Yes. I've seen more of him in the past weeks than anyone else. And my profession naturally orients me more toward a man's psychology than his body or his habits. You see a waspish cripple. I see a mind which has reacted to its physical handicaps by developing such a hellish energy, such an inhuman power of concentration, that it almost frightens me. Give that mind a sound body for its use and nothing is impossible to it."

"You may be right, at that," murmured Viken after a pause. "Not that it matters. The decision is taken, the rockets go down tomorrow. I hope it all works out."

He waited for another while. The whirring of ventilators in his little room seemed unnaturally loud, the colors of a girlie picture on the wall shockingly garish. Then he said slowly, "You've been rather closed-mouthed yourself, Jan. When do you expect to finish your own esprojector and start making the tests?"

Cornelius looked around. The door stood open to an empty hallway, but he reached out and closed it before he answered with a slight grin: "It's been ready for the past few days. But don't tell anyone."

"How's that?" Viken started. The movement, in low-gee, took him out of his chair and halfway across the table between the men. He shoved himself back and waited.

"I have been making meaningless tinkering motions," said Cornelius, "but what I waited for was a highly emotional moment, a time when I can be sure Anglesey's entire attention will be focused on Joe. This business tomorrow is exactly what I need."

"Why?"

"You see, I have pretty well convinced myself that the trouble in the machine is psychological, not physical. I think that for some reason, buried in his subconscious, Anglesey doesn't want to experience Jupiter. A conflict of that type might well set a psionic amplifier circuit oscillating."

"Hm-m-m." Viken rubbed his chin. "Could be. Lately Ed has been changing more and more. When he first came here, he was peppery enough, and he would at least play an occasional game of poker. Now he's pulled so far into his shell you can't even see him. I never thought of it before, but . . . yes, by God, Jupiter must be having some effect on him."

"Hm-m-m." Cornelius nodded. He did not elaborate—did not, for instance, mention that one altogether uncharacteristic episode when Anglesey had tried to describe what it was like to be a Jovian.

"Of course," said Viken thoughtfully, "the previous men were not affected especially. Nor was Ed at first, while he was still controlling lower-type pseudos. It's only since Joe went down to the surface that he's become so different."

"Yes, yes," said Cornelius hastily. "I've learned that much. But enough shop talk—"

"No. Wait a minute." Viken spoke in a low, hurried tone, looking past him. "For the first time, I'm starting to think clearly about this . . . never really stopped to analyze it before, just accepted a bad situation. There is something peculiar about Joe. It can't very well involve his physical structure, or the environment, because lower forms didn't give this trouble. Could it be the fact that—Joe is the first puppet in all history with a potentially human intelligence?"

"We speculate in a vacuum," said Cornelius. "Tomorrow, maybe, I can tell you. Now I know nothing."

Viken sat up straight. His pale eyes focused on the other man and stayed there, unblinking. "One minute," he said.

"Yes?" Cornelius shifted, half rising. "Quickly, please. It is past my bedtime."

"You know a good deal more than you've admitted," said Viken. "Don't you?"

"What makes you think that?"

"You aren't the most gifted liar in the universe. And then—you argued very strongly for Anglesey's scheme, this sending down the other pseudos. More strongly than a newcomer should."

"I told you, I want his attention focused elsewhere when—"

"Do you want it that badly?" snapped Viken.

Cornelius was still for a minute. Then he sighed and leaned back.

"All right," he said. "I shall have to trust your discretion. I wasn't sure, you see, how any of you old-time station personnel would react. So I didn't want to blabber out my speculations, which may be wrong. The confirmed facts, yes, I will tell them; but I don't wish to attack a man's religion with a mere theory."

Viken scowled. "What the devil do you mean?"

Cornelius puffed hard on his cigar, its tip waxed and waned like a miniature red demon star. "This Jupiter V is more than a research station," he said gently. "It is a way of life, is it not? No one would come here for even one hitch unless the work was important to him. Those who re-enlist, they must find something in the work, something which Earth with all her riches cannot offer them. No?"

"Yes," answered Viken. It was almost a whisper. "I didn't think you would understand so well. But what of it?"

"Well, I don't want to tell you, unless I can prove it, that maybe this has all gone for nothing. Maybe you have wasted your lives and a lot of money, and will have to pack up and go home."

Viken's long face did not flicker a muscle. It seemed to have congealed. But he said calmly enough: "Why?"

"Consider Joe," said Cornelius. "His brain has as

much capacity as any adult human's. It has been recording every sense datum that came to it, from the
moment of 'birth'—making a record in itself, in its
own cells, not merely in Anglesey's physical memory
bank up here. Also, you know, a thought is a sense
datum too. And thoughts are not separated into neat
little railway tracks; they form a continuous field.
Every time Anglesey is in rapport with Joe, and thinks,
the thought goes through Joe's synapses as well as his
own—and every thought carries its own associations,
and every associated memory is recorded. Like if Joe
is building a hut, the shape of the logs might remind
Anglesey of some geometric figure, which in turn
would remind him of the Pythagorean theorem—"

"I get the idea," said Viken in a cautious way.
"Given time, Joe's brain will have stored everything
that ever was in Ed's."

"Correct. Now a functioning nervous system with
an engrammatic pattern of experience—in this case, a
nonhuman nervous system—isn't that a pretty good
definition of a personality?"

"I suppose so—good Lord!" Viken jumped. "You
mean Joe is—taking over?"

"In a way. A subtle, automatic, unconscious way."
Cornelius drew a deep breath and plunged into it.
"The pseudojovian is so nearly perfect a life form:
your biologists engineered into it all the experience
gained from nature's mistakes in designing us. At
first, Joe was only a remote-controlled biological machine. Then Anglesey and Joe became two facets of a
single personality. Then, oh, very slowly, the stronger,
healthier body . . . more amplitude to its thoughts . . .
do you see? Joe is becoming the dominant side. Like
this business of sending down the other pseudos—
Anglesey only thinks he has logical reasons for want-

ing it done. Actually, his 'reasons' are mere rationalizations for the instinctive desires of the Joe-facet.

"Anglesey's subconscious must comprehend the situation, in a dim reactive way; it must feel his human ego gradually being submerged by the steamroller force of Joe's instincts and Joe's wishes. It tries to defend its own identity, and is swatted down by the superior force of Joe's own nascent subconscious.

"I put it crudely," he finished in an apologetic tone, "but it will account for that oscillation in the K-tubes."

Viken nodded, slowly, like an old man. "Yes, I see it," he answered. "The alien environment down there ...the different brain structure...good God! Ed's being swallowed up in Joe! The puppet master is becoming the puppet!" He looked ill.

"Only speculation on my part," said Cornelius. All at once, he felt very tired. It was not pleasant to do this to Viken, whom he liked. "But you see the dilemma, no? If I am right, then any esman will gradually become a Jovian—a monster with two bodies, of which the human body is the unimportant auxiliary one. This means no esman will ever agree to control a pseudo—therefore, the end of your project."

He stood up. "I'm sorry, Arne. You made me tell you what I think, and now you will lie awake worrying, and I am maybe quite wrong and you worry for nothing."

"It's all right," mumbled Viken. "Maybe you're not wrong."

"I don't know." Cornelius drifted toward the door. "I am going to try to find some answers tomorrow. Good night."

The moon-shaking thunder of the rockets, crash, crash, crash, leaping from their cradles, was long past.

Now the fleet glided on metal wings, with straining secondary ramjets, through the rage of the Jovian sky.

As Cornelius opened the control-room door, he looked at his telltale board. Elsewhere a voice tolled the word to all the stations, *one ship wrecked, two ships wrecked*, but Anglesey would let no sound enter his presence when he wore the helmet. An obliging technician had haywired a panel of fifteen red and fifteen blue lights above Cornelius' esprojector, to keep him informed, too. Ostensibly, of course, they were only there for Anglescy's bencfit, though the csman had insisted he wouldn't be looking at them.

Four of the red bulbs were dark and thus four blue ones would not shine for a safe landing. A whirlwind, a thunderbolt, a floating ice meteor, a flock of manta-like birds with flesh as dense and hard as iron—there could be a hundred things which had crumpled four ships and tossed them tattered across the poison forests.

Four ships, hell! Think of four living creatures, with an excellence of brain to rival your own, damned first to years in unconscious night and then, never awakening save for one uncomprehending instant, dashed in bloody splinters against an ice mountain. The wasteful callousness of it was a cold knot in Cornelius' belly. It had to be done, no doubt, if there was to be any thinking life on Jupiter at all; but then let it be done quickly and minimally, he thought, so the next generation could be begotten by love and not by machines!

He closed the door behind him and waited for a breathless moment. Anglesey was a wheelchair and a coppery curve of helmet, facing the opposite wall. No movement, no awareness whatsoever. Good!

It would be awkward, perhaps ruinous, if Anglesey learned of this most intimate peering. But he needn't, ever. He was blindfolded and ear-plugged by his own concentration.

Nevertheless, the psionicist moved his bulky form with care, across the room to the new esprojector. He did not much like his snooper's role, he would not have assumed it at all if he had seen any other hope. But neither did it make him feel especially guilty. If what he suspected was true, then Anglesey was all unawares being twisted into something not human; to spy on him might be to save him.

Gently, Cornelius activated the meters and started his tubes warming up. The oscilloscope built into Anglesey's machine gave him the other man's exact alpha rhythm, his basic biological clock. First you adjusted to that, then you discovered the subtler elements by feel, and when your set was fully in phase you could probe undetected and—

Find out what was wrong. Read Anglesey's tortured subconscious and see what there was on Jupiter that both drew and terrified him.

Five ships wrecked.

But it must be very nearly time for them to land. Maybe only five would be lost in all. Maybe ten would get through. Ten comrades for—Joe?

Cornelius sighed. He looked at the cripple, seated blind and deaf to the human world which had crippled him, and felt a pity and an anger. It wasn't fair, none of it was.

Not even to Joe. Joe wasn't any kind of soul-eating devil. He did not even realize, as yet, that he was Joe, that Anglesey was becoming a mere appendage. He hadn't asked to be created, and to withdraw his human counterpart from him would very likely be to destroy him.

Somehow, there were always penalties for everybody when men exceeded the decent limits.

Cornelius swore at himself, voicelessly. Work to do. He sat down and fitted the helmet on his own head. The carrier wave made a faint pulse, inaudible, the trembling of neurones low in his awareness. You couldn't describe it.

Reaching up, he tuned to Anglesey's alpha. His own had a somewhat lower frequency, it was necessary to carry the signals through a heterodyning process. Still no reception ... well, of course he had to find the exact wave form, timbre was as basic to thought as to music. He adjusted the dials slowly, with enormous care.

Something flashed through his consciousness, a vision of clouds roiled in a violet-red sky, a wind that galloped across horizonless immensity—he lost it. His fingers shook as he tuned back.

The psibeam between Joe and Anglesey broadened. It took Cornelius into the circuit. He looked through Joe's eyes, he stood on a hill and stared into the sky above the ice mountains, straining for sign of the first rocket; and simultaneously, he was still Jan Cornelius, blurrily seeing the meters, probing about for emotions, symbols, any key to the locked terror in Anglesey's soul.

The terror rose up and struck him in the face.

Psionic detection is not a matter of passive listening in. Much as a radio receiver is necessarily also a weak transmitter, the nervous system in resonance with a source of psionic-spectrum energy is itself emitting. Normally, of course, this effect is unimportant; but when you pass the impulses, either way, through a set of heterodyning and amplifying units, with a high negative feedback—

In the early days, psionic psychotherapy vitiated itself because the amplified thoughts of one man, entering the brain of another, would combine with the latter's own neural cycles according to the ordinary vector laws. The result was that both men felt the new beat frequencies as a nightmarish fluttering of their very thoughts. An analyst, trained into self-control, could ignore it; his patient could not, and reacted violently.

But eventually the basic human wave-timbres were measured, and psionic therapy resumed. The modern esprojector analyzed an incoming signal and shifted its characteristics over to the "listener's" pattern. The *really* different pulses of the transmitting brain, those which could not possibly be mapped onto the pattern of the receiving neurones—as an exponential signal cannot very practicably be mapped onto a sinusoid— those were filtered out.

Thus compensated, the other thought could be apprehended as comfortably as one's own. If the patient were on a psibeam circuit, a skilled operator could tune in without the patient being necessarily aware of it. The operator could either probe the other man's thoughts or implant thoughts of his own.

Cornelius' plan, an obvious one to any psionicist, had depended on this. He would receive from an unwitting Anglesey-Joe. If his theory was right and the esman's personality was being distorted into that of a monster—his thinking would be too alien to come through the filters. Cornelius would receive spottily or not at all. If his theory was wrong, and Anglesey was still Anglesey, he would receive only a normal human stream-of-consciousness, and could probe for other trouble-making factors.

His brain roared!

What's happening to me?

For a moment, the interference which turned his thoughts to saw-toothed gibberish struck him down with panic. He gulped for breath, there in the Jovian wind, and his dreadful dogs sensed the alienness in him and whined.

Then, recognition, remembrance, and a blaze of anger so great that it left no room for fear. Joe filled his lungs and shouted it aloud, the hillside boomed with echoes:

"Get out of my mind!"

He felt Cornelius spiral down toward unconsciousness. The overwhelming force of his own mental blow had been too much. He laughed, it was more like a snarl, and eased the pressure.

Above him, between thunderous clouds, winked the first thin descending rocket flare.

Cornelius' mind groped back toward the light. It broke a watery surface, the man's mouth snapped after air and his hands reached for the dials, to turn his machine off and escape.

"Not so fast, you." Grimly, Joe drove home a command that locked Cornelius' muscles rigid. "I want to know the meaning of this. Hold still and let me look!" He smashed home an impulse which could be rendered, perhaps, as an incandescent question mark. Remembrance exploded in shards through the psionicist's forebrain.

"So. That's all there is? You thought I was afraid to come down here and be Joe, and wanted to know why? But I told you I wasn't!"

I should have believed—whispered Cornelius.

"Well, get out of the circuit, then." Joe continued growling it vocally. "And don't ever come back in the control room, understand? K-tubes or no, I don't want to see you again. And I may be a cripple, but I can still take you apart cell by cell. Now—sign off—leave me alone. The first ship will be landing in minutes."

You a cripple . . . you, Joe Anglesey?

"What?" The great gray being on the hill lifted his barbaric head as if to sudden trumpets. "What do you mean?"

Don't you understand? said the weak, dragging thought. *You know how the esprojector works. You know I could have probed Anglesey's mind in Anglesey's brain without making enough interference to be noticed. And I could not have probed a wholly nonhuman mind at all, nor could it have been aware of me. The filters would not have passed such a signal. Yet you felt me in the first fractional second. It can only mean a human mind in a nonhuman brain.*

You are not the half-corpse on Jupiter V any longer. You're Joe—Joe Anglesey.

"Well, I'll be damned," said Joe. "You're right."

He turned Anglesey off, kicked Cornelius out of his mind with a single brutal impulse, and ran down the hill to meet the spaceship.

Cornelius woke up minutes afterward. His skull felt ready to split apart. He groped for the main switch before him, clashed it down, ripped the helmet off his head and threw it clanging on the floor. But it took a little while to gather the strength to do the same for Anglesey. The other man was not able to do anything for himself.

They sat outside sickbay and waited. It was a harshly lit barrenness of metal and plastic, smelling of antiseptics—down near the heart of the satellite, with miles of rock to hide the terrible face of Jupiter.

Only Viken and Cornelius were in that cramped little room. The rest of the station went about its business mechanically, filling in the time till it could learn what had happened. Beyond the door, three biotechnicians, who were also the station's medical staff,

fought with death's angel for the thing which had
been Edward Anglesey.

"Nine ships got down," said Viken dully. "Two
males, seven females. It's enough to start a colony."

"It would be genetically desirable to have more,"
pointed out Cornelius. He kept his own voice low, in
spite of its underlying cheerfulness. There was a certain awesome quality to all this.

"I still don't understand," said Viken.

"Oh, it's clear enough—now. I should have guessed
it before, maybe. We had all the facts, it was only
that we couldn't make the simple, obvious interpretation of them. No, we had to conjure up Frankenstein's
monster."

"Well," Viken's words grated, "we have played
Frankenstein, haven't we? Ed is dying in there."

"It depends on how you define death." Cornelius
drew hard on his cigar, needing anything that might
steady him. His tone grew purposely dry of emotion.

"Look here. Consider the data. Joe, now: a creature
with a brain of human capacity, but without a mind—
a perfect Lockean *tabula rasa*, for Anglesey's psibeam
to write on. We deduced, correctly enough—if very
belatedly—that when enough had been written, there
would be a personality. But the question was: whose?
Because, I suppose, of normal human fear of the unknown, we assumed that any personality in so alien a
body had to be monstrous. Therefore it must be hostile to Anglesey, must be swamping him—"

The door opened. Both men jerked to their feet.

The chief surgeon shook his head. "No use. Typical
deep-shock traumata, close to terminus now. If we
had better facilities, maybe—"

"No," said Cornelius. "You cannot save a man who
has decided not to live any more."

"I know." The doctor removed his mask. "I need a cigarette. Who's got one?" His hands shook a little as he accepted it from Viken.

"But how could he—decide—anything?" choked the physicist. "He's been unconscious ever since Jan pulled him away from that . . . that thing."

"It was decided before then," said Cornelius. "As a matter of fact, that hulk in there on the operating table no longer has a mind. I know. I was there." He shuddered a little. A stiff shot of tranquilizer was all that held nightmare away from him. Later he would have to have that memory exorcised.

The doctor took a long drag of smoke, held it in his lungs a moment, and exhaled gustily. "I guess this winds up the project," he said. "We'll never get another esman."

"I'll say we won't." Viken's tone sounded rusty. "I'm going to smash that devil's engine myself."

"Hold on a minute!" exclaimed Cornelius. "Don't you understand? This isn't the end. It's the beginning!"

"I'd better get back," said the doctor. He stubbed out his cigarette and went through the door. It closed behind him with a deathlike quietness.

"What do you mean?" Viken said it as if erecting a barrier.

"Won't you understand?" roared Cornelius. "Joe has all Anglesey's habits, thoughts, memories, prejudices, interests . . . oh, yes, the different body and the different environment, they do cause some changes— but no more than any man might undergo on Earth. If you were suddenly cured of a wasting disease, wouldn't you maybe get a little boisterous and rough? There is nothing abnormal in it. Nor is it abnormal to want to stay healthy—no? Do you see?"

Viken sat down. He spent a while without speaking.

Then, enormously slow and careful: "Do you mean Joe is Ed?"

"Or Ed is Joe. Whatever you like. He calls himself Joe now, I think—as a symbol of freedom—but he is still himself. What *is* the ego but continuity of existence?

"He himself did not fully understand this. He only knew—he told me, and I should have believed him—that on Jupiter he was strong and happy. Why did the K-tube oscillate? A hysterical symptom! Anglesey's subconscious was not afraid to stay on Jupiter—it was afraid to come back!

"And then, today, I listened in. By now, his whole self was focused on Joe. That is, the primary source of libido was Joe's virile body, not Anglesey's sick one. This meant a different pattern of impulses—not too alien to pass the filters, but alien enough to set up interference. So he felt my presence. And he saw the truth, just as I did.

"Do you know the last emotion I felt, as Joe threw me out of his mind? Not anger any more. He plays rough, him, but all he had room to feel was joy.

"I knew how strong a personality Anglesey had! Whatever made me think an overgrown child-brain like Joe's could override it? In there, the doctors—bah! They're trying to salvage a hulk which has been shed because it is useless!"

Cornelius stopped. His throat was quite raw from talking. He paced the floor, rolled cigar smoke around his mouth but did not draw it any farther in.

When a few minutes had passed, Viken said cautiously. "All right. You should know—as you said, you were there. But what do we do now? How do we get in touch with Ed? Will he even be interested in contacting us?"

"Oh, yes, of course," said Cornelius. "He is still himself, remember. Now that he has none of the cripple's frustrations, he should be more amiable. When the novelty of his new friends wears off, he will want someone who can talk to him as an equal."

"And precisely who will operate another pseudo?" asked Viken sarcastically. "I'm quite happy with this skinny frame of mine, thank you!"

"Was Anglesey the only hopeless cripple on Earth?" asked Cornelius quietly.

Viken gaped at him.

"And there are aging men, too," went on the psionicist, half to himself. "Someday, my friend, when you and I feel the years close in, and so much we would like to learn—maybe we, too, would enjoy an extra lifetime in a Jovian body." He nodded at his cigar. "A hard, lusty, stormy kind of life, granted—dangerous, brawling, violent—but life as no human, perhaps, has lived it since the days of Elizabeth the First. Oh, yes, there will be small trouble finding Jovians."

He turned his head as the surgeon came out again.

"Well?" croaked Viken.

The doctor sat down. "It's finished," he said.

They waited for a moment, awkwardly.

"Odd," said the doctor. He groped after a cigarette he didn't have. Silently, Viken offered him one. "Odd. I've seen these cases before. People who simply resign from life. This is the first one I ever saw that went out smiling—smiling all the time."

THE IMMORTALS

JAMES GUNN

The "natural" outcome of a bad hand of genetic cards, or of many other of life's mishaps and misfortunes, is a level of pain and distress that cries out for artificial relief; just as we build fires and weave clothing to keep out nature's chills. And we must learn how not to burn or suffocate ourselves in the process.

—Joshua Lederberg *

What was settled before, by chance or ineluctable circumstance, now becomes within our own power to regulate, and presents us with the need to take decisions—a task which many people find burdensome. Constant decision-making is the price of freedom. Part of the problem which faces us is to devise adequate institutions for taking the

* In the Foreword to *The Ethics of Genetic Conrtol* by Joseph Fletcher, Garden City, N.Y.: Doubleday Anchor Books, 1974, p. vi.

broader social decisions with which the mushrooming of
biological knowledge most certainly is about to face us.
—Gordon Rattray Taylor,
The Biological Time Bomb *

Science fiction since Frankenstein has often been concerned with the possible evils of new discoveries. The
pace of biological development has emphasized these fears
in the mind of the public.

Of great concern is the type of society these advances
might create. We are already faced with difficult problems. Kidney patients, in areas where there are few dialy-
sis machines, have had their cases reviewed by physicians
who must decide which of them will live or die. Organ
transplantation has raised fears that there might be a lack
of proper safeguards involving the donor of the needed
organ. Treatment for hemophiliacs is costly, and many
cannot afford it.

More important for most people is day-to-day medical
care. Who should pay for it? Who should receive it?
Why do so many who need care lack it? As for new
discoveries, how will they be made available to those who
need them?

Conceive of a society in which only certain people will
be cared for medically. Wealthy or powerful individuals
already are likely to receive better medical care than most
people do. In the case of medical advances, might they
not wish to control these discoveries, perhaps by buying
off or regulating researchers?

James Gunn deals with many biological themes. At
the center of his story are the Cartwrights, a family of
mutants whose blood can give the recipient immortality.
We also see a corrupt society in which only a few control
the tools which could help everyone.

* New York: New American Library, 1968, pp. 16–17.

The clinic was deserted.

Harry Elliott smothered a yawn as he walked slowly toward the draped operating table under the cold, glareless light at the back of the big room tiled in antiseptic white and flooded with invisible, germ-killing ultraviolet. He lit the candelabra of bunsen burners standing on each side of the table and turned on the ventilators under the mural of Immortality slaying Death with a hypodermic. The air, straight from the Medical Center, was pure, disease-free, and aromatic with the hospital incense of alcohol and ether.

Science, surgery, and salvation—the clinic had something for everybody.

It was going to be another ordinary day, Harry decided. Soon would come the shrill cacophony of six o'clock, and the factories would release their daily human floods into the worn channels between the high walls. For an hour or two, then, he would be busy.

But it was a good shift. He was busy only between six and curfew. Other times he could sneak a view of the *Geriatrics Journal* or flip a few reels of text over the inner surface of his glasses. He didn't need them for seeing—if he had he would have used contact lenses—but they were handy for viewing and they made a man look professional and older.

At eighteen that was important to Harry....

Sunday was bad. But then Sunday was a bad day for everybody.

He would be glad when it was over. One more week and he would be back on duty inside. Six more months

185

and he would have his residency requirements completed. As soon as he passed his boards—it was unthinkable that he would not pass—there would be no more clinics.

It was all very well to administer to the masses—that was what the oath of Hippocrates was about, partly—but a doctor had to be practical. There just wasn't enough medical care to go around. Curing an ear infection here, a case of gonorrhea there, was like pouring antibiotics into the river. The results were unnoticeable.

With those who had a chance at immortality, it was different. Saving a life meant something. It might even mean a reprieve for himself, when he needed it. And reprieves had been stretched into immortality.

The prognosis, though, was unfavorable. A man's best hope was to make something of himself worth saving. Then immortality would be voted him by a grateful electorate. That was why Harry had decided to specialize in geriatrics. Later, when he had more leisure and laboratory facilities, he would concentrate on the synthesis of the *elixir vitae*. Success would mean immortality not only for himself but for everybody. Even if he did not succeed within a lifetime, if his research was promising there would be reprieves.

But it was the synthesis that was important. The world could not continue to depend upon the Cartwrights. They were too selfish. They preferred to hide their own accidental immortality rather than contribute harmless amounts of blood at regular intervals. If Fordyce's statistical analysis of Locke's investigations were correct, there were enough Cartwrights alive to grant immortality to 50,000 mortals—and that number would increase geometrically as more Cartwrights were born. One day a baby would inherit life as its birthright, and not death.

If the Cartwrights were not so selfish . . . As it was, there had been only enough of them discovered to provide immortality for a hundred to two hundred persons; nobody knew exactly how many. And the tame Cartwrights were so infertile that their numbers increased very slowly. They could contribute only a limited quantity of the precious blood. From this could be extracted only a small amount of the gamma globulin that carried the immunity factor. Even at closely calculated minimal dosages, the shots could not be stretched beyond a small group of essential persons, because the immunity to death was passive. It was good for no more than thirty to forty days.

But once the blood protein was synthesized . . .

Harry had an idea of how it might be done—by taking apart the normal gamma globulin molecule and then putting it back together again, atom by atom. With radiation and the new quick freeze, absolute, he could do it. Once he got his hands on a research grant and laboratory facilities . . .

He walked slowly toward the street entrance, past the consultation rooms with their diagnostic couches on both sides of the long clinic hallway. He paused between the giant Aesculapian staffs that supported the lintel of the doorway, just before he reached the moving curtain of air that kept out the heat of summer, the cold of winter, and the dust and disease of the city. At this stage in his career, it was folly to think of research grants. They were for older, tried researchers, not for callow residents, nor even eager young specialists.

The clinic was built out from the Medical Center wall. Opposite was the high wall of a factory that made armored cars for export to the suburbs. That's where the Center got its ambulances. A little farther along the Medical Center wall was a second, smaller outbuilding. On its roof was a neon sign: BLOOD BOUGHT HERE. Beside its door would be another, smaller sign: "We Are Now Paying $5 a Pint."

In a few minutes the blood-bank technicians would be busy inserting needles into scarred antecubital veins as the laborers were set free by the quitting whistles. They would pour through the laboratory, spending their life resources prodigally, coming back, many of them, to give another pint before two weeks had elapsed, much less two months. No use trying to keep track of them. They would do anything: trade identity cards, scuff up their inner arms so that the previous needle hole would not show, swear that the scars were from antibiotic shots. . . .

And then they would gulp down their orange juice —some of the children did it mostly for that because they had never tasted orange juice before—grab their five dollars and head for the nearest shover of illicit antibiotics and nostrums. Or they would give it to some neighborhood leech for rubbing salve on some senile invalid or for chanting runes over some dying infant.

Well, they were essential. He had to remember that. They were a great pool of immunities. They had been exposed to all the diseases bred of poverty, ignorance, and filth from which the squires had been protected. The squires needed the citizens' gamma globulins, their antigens. The squires needed the serums manufactured in citizen bodies, the vaccines prepared from their reactions.

A remarkable teacher had once shocked him into awareness by saying: "Without filth there is no cleanliness; without disease there is no health." Harry remembered that in his contacts with the citizens. It helped.

Past the blood bank, the Center wall curved away. Beyond was the city. It was not dying; it was dead.

Wooden houses had subsided into heaps of rotten lumber. Brick tenements had crumbled; here and there a wall tottered against the sky. Aluminum and magnesium walls were dented and pierced. Decay was everywhere.

But, like green shoots pushing through the forest's mat of dead leaves, the city was being born again. A two-room shack was built with scavenged boards. A brick bungalow stood behind tenement ruins. Metal walls became rows of huts.

The eternal cycle, Harry thought. Out of death, life. Out of life, destruction. Only man could evade it.

All that remained of the original city were the walled factories and the vast hospital complexes. Behind their protective walls, they stood tall and strong and faceless. On the walls, armored guard houses glinted in the orange-red fire of the declining sun.

As Harry stood there, the whistles began to blow— all tones and volumes of them, making a strange, shrill counterpoint, suited to sunset in the city. It was primitive and stirring, like a savage ceremony to propitiate the gods and insure the sun's return.

The gates rolled up and left openings in the factory walls. Laborers spilled out into the street: all kinds of them, men and women, children and ancients, sickly and strong. Yet there was a sameness to them. They were ragged and dirty and diseased; they were the city dwellers.

They should have been miserable, but they were usually happy. They would look up at the blue sky, if the smog had not yet crept up from the river, and laugh, for no reason at all. The children would play tag between their parents' legs, yelling and giggling. Even the ancients would smile indulgently.

It was the healthy squires who were sober and concerned. Well, it was natural. Ignorance can be happy; the citizens need not be concerned about good health or immortality. It was beyond them. They could appear on a summer day like the May fly and flutter about gaily and die. But knowledge had to worry; immortality had its price.

Remembering that always made Harry feel better. Seeing the great hordes of citizens with no chance for immortality made him self-conscious about his advantages. He had been raised in a suburban villa far from the city's diseases and carcinogens. From infancy he had received the finest of medical care. He had been through four years of high school, eight years of medical school, and almost three years of residency training.

That gave him a head start toward immortality. It was right that he should pay for it with concern.

Where did they all come from? He thought: they must breed like rabbits in those warrens. Where did they all go to? Back into the wreckage of the city, like the rats and the vermin.

He shuddered. Really, they were almost another race.

Tonight, though, they weren't laughing and singing. Even the children were silent. They marched down the street soberly, almost the only sound the tramp of their bare feet on the cracked pavement. Even the doors of the blood bank weren't busy.

Harry shrugged. Sometimes they were like this. The reason would be something absurd—a gang fight, company trouble, some dark religious rite that could never really be stamped out. Maybe it had something to do with the phases of the moon.

He went back into the clinic to get ready. The first patient was a young woman. She was an attractive creature with blond hair worn long around her shoulders and a ripe body—if you could ignore the dirt and the odor that drifted even into the professional chamber behind the consultation room.

He resisted an impulse to have her disrobe. Not because of any consequences—what was a citizen's chastity? A mythical thing like the unicorn. Besides, they expected it. From the stories the other doctors told, he thought they must come to the clinic for that purpose. But there was no use tempting himself. He would feel unclean for days.

She babbled as they always did. She had sinned against nature. She had not been getting enough sleep. She had not been taking her vitamins regularly. She had bought illicit terramycin from a shover for a kidney infection. It was all predictable and boring.

"I see," he kept muttering. And then, "I'm going to take a diagnosis now. Don't be frightened."

He switched on the diagnostic machine. A sphygmomanometer crept up snakelike from beneath the Freudian couch and encircled her arm. A mouthpiece slipped between her lips. A stethoscope counted her pulse. A skull cap fitted itself to her head. Metal caps slipped over her fingertips. Bracelets encircled her ankles. A band wrapped itself around her hips. The machine punctured, withdrew samples, counted, measured, listened, compared, correlated. . . .

In a moment it was over. Harry had his diagnosis. She was anemic; they all were. They couldn't resist that five dollars.

"Married?" he asked.

"Nah?" she said hesitantly.

"Better not waste any time. You're pregnant."

"Prag-nant?" she repeated.

"You're going to have a baby."

A joyful light broke across her face. "Aw! Is that all! I thought maybe it was a too-more. A baby I can take care of nicely. Tell me, Doctor, will it be boy or girl?"

"A boy," Harry said wearily. *The slut!* Why did it always irritate him so?

She got up from the couch with a lithe, careless grace. "Thank you, Doctor. I will go to tell Georgie. He will be angry for a little, but I know how to make him glad.

There were others waiting in the consultation rooms, contemplating their symptoms. Harry checked the panel: a woman with pleurisy, a man with cancer, a child with rheumatic fever.... But Harry stepped out into the clinic to see if the girl dropped anything into the donation box as she passed. She didn't. Instead, she paused by the shover hawking his wares just outside the clinic door.

"Get your aureomycin here," he ranted, "your penicillin, your terramycin. A hypodermic with every purchase. Good health! Good health! Stop those sniffles before they lay you low, low, low. Don't let that infection cost you your job, your health, your life. Get your filters, your antiseptics, your vitamins. Get your amulets, your good-luck charms. I have here a radium needle which has already saved thirteen lives. And here is an ampule of *elixir vitae*. Get your ilotycin here..."

The girl bought an amulet and hurried off to Georgie. A lump of anger burned in Harry's throat.

The throngs were still marching silently in the street. In the back of the clinic a woman was kneeling at the operating table. She took a vitamin pill and a paper cup of tonic from the dispensary.

Behind the walls the sirens started. Harry turned toward the doorway. The gate in the Medical Center wall rolled up.

First came the outriders on their motorcycles. The people in the street scattered to the walls on either side, leaving a lane down the center of the street. The outriders brushed carelessly close to them—healthy young squires, their nose filters in place, their goggled eyes haughty, their guns slung low on their hips.

That would have been something, Harry thought enviously—to have been a company policeman. There was a dash to them, a hint of violence. They were hell on wheels. And if they were one-tenth as successful with women as they were reputed to be, there was no woman—from citizen through technician and nurse up to their suburban peers—who was immune to them.

Well, let them have the glamour and the women. He had taken the safer and more certain route to immortality. Few company policemen made it.

After the outriders came an ambulance, its armored ports closed, its automatic 40-millimeter gun roaming restlessly for a target. More outriders covered the rear. Above the convoy a helicopter swooped low.

Something glinted in the sunlight, became a line of small round objects beneath the helicopter, dropping in an arc toward the street. One after another they broke with fragile, popping sounds. They strung up through the convoy.

Like puppets when the puppeteer has released the strings, the outriders toppled to the street, skidding limply as their motorcycles slowed and stopped on their single wheels.

The ambulance could not stop. It rolled over one of the fallen outriders and crashed into a motorcycle, bulldozing it out of the way. The 40-millimeter gun had jerked erratically to fix its radar sight on the helicopter, but the plane was skimming the rooftops. Before the gun could get the range the plane was gone.

Harry smelled something sharply penetrating. His head felt swollen and light. The street tilted and then straightened.

In the midst of the crowd beyond the ambulance an arm swung up. Something dark sailed through the air and smashed against the top of the ambulance. Flames splashed across it. They dripped down the sides, ran into gun slits and observation ports, were drawn into the air intake.

A moment followed in which nothing happened. The scene was like a frozen tableau—the ambulance and the motorcycles balanced in the street, the outriders and some of the nearest citizens crumpled and twisted on the pavement, the citizens watching, the flames licking up toward greasy, black smoke. . . .

The side door of the ambulance fell open. A medic staggered out, clutching something in one hand, beating at flames on his white jacket with the other.

The citizens watched silently, not moving to help or hinder. From among them stepped a dark-haired man. His hand went up. It held something limp and dark. The hand came down against the medic's head.

No sound came from Harry over the roar of the idling motorcycles and ambulance. The pantomime continued, and he was part of the frozen audience as the medic fell and the man stooped, patted out the flames with his bare hands, picked the object out of the medic's hand, and looked at the ambulance door.

There was a girl standing there, Harry noticed. From this distance Harry could tell little more than that she was dark-haired and slender.

The flames on the ambulance had burnt themselves out. The girl stood in the doorway, not moving. The man beside the fallen medic looked at her, started to hold out a hand, stopped, let it drop, turned, and faded back into the crowd.

Less than two minutes had passed since the sirens began.

Silently the citizens pressed forward. The girl turned and went back into the ambulance. The citizens stripped the outriders of their clothing and weapons, looted the ambulance of its black bag and medical supplies, picked up their fallen fellows, and disappeared.

It was like magic. One moment the street was full of them. The next moment they were gone. The street was empty of life.

Behind the Medical Center walls the sirens began again.

It was like a release. Harry began running down the street, his throat swelling with shouts. There were no words to them.

Out of the ambulance came a young boy. He was slim and small—no more than seven years old. He had blond hair, cut very short, and dark eyes in a tanned face. He wore a ragged T-shirt that once might have been white and a pair of blue jeans cut off above the knees.

He reached an arm back into the ambulance. A yellowed claw came out to meet it, and then an arm. The arm was a gnarled stick encircled with ropy blue veins like lianas. It was attached to a man on stiff, stiltlike legs. He was very old. His hair was thin, white silk. His scalp and face were wrinkled parchment. A tattered tunic fell from bony shoulders, around his permanently bent back, and was caught in folds around his loins.

The boy led the old man slowly and carefully into the ruined street, because the man was blind, his eyelids flat and dark over empty sockets. The old man bent painfully over the fallen medic. His fingers explored the medic's skull. Then he moved to the outrider who had been run over by the ambulance. The man's chest was crushed; a pink froth edged his lips as punctured lungs gasped for breath.

He was as good as dead. Medical science could do nothing for injuries that severe, that extensive.

Harry reached the old man, seized him by one bony shoulder. "What do you think you're doing?" he asked.

The old man didn't move. He held to the outrider's hand for a moment and then creaked to his feet. "Healing," he answered in a voice like the whisper of sandpaper.

"That man's dying," Harry said.

"So are we all," said the old man.

Harry glanced down at the outrider. Was he breathing easier, or was that illusion?

It was then the stretcher bearers reached them.

Harry had a difficult time finding the Dean's office. The Medical Center covered hundreds of city blocks, and it had grown under a strange stimulus of its own. No one had ever planned for it to be so big, but it had sprouted an arm here when demand for medical care and research outgrew the space available, a wing there, and arteries through and under and around. . . .

He followed the glowing guidestick through the unmarked corridors, and tried to remember the way. But it was useless. He inserted the stick into the lock on an armored door. The door swallowed the stick and opened. As soon as Harry had entered, the door swung shut and locked. He was in a bare anteroom. On a metal bench bolted to the floor along one wall sat the boy and the old man from the ambulance. The boy looked up at Harry curiously and then his gaze returned to his folded hands. The old man rested against the wall.

A little farther along the bench was a girl. She looked like the girl who had stood in the doorway of the ambulance, but she was smaller than he had thought and younger. Her face was pale. Only her blue eyes were vivid as they looked at him with a curious appeal and then faded. His gaze dropped to her figure; it was boyish and unformed, clad in a simple brown dress belted at the waist. She was no more than twelve or thirteen years old, he thought.

The reception box had to repeat the question twice: "Name?"

"Dr. Harry Elliott," he said.

"Advance for confirmation."

He went to the wall beside the far door and put his right hand against the plate set into it. A light flashed into his right eye, comparing retinal patterns.

"Deposit all metal objects in the receptacle," the box said.

Harry hesitated, and then pulled his stethoscope out of his jacket pocket, removed his watch, emptied his trouser pockets of coins and pocketknife and hypo-spray.

Something clicked. "Nose filters," the box said.

Harry put those into the receptacle, too. The girl was watching him, but when he looked at her, her eyes moved away. The door opened. He went through the doorway. The door closed behind him.

Dean Mock's office was a magnificent room, thirty feet long and twenty feet wide. It was decorated in mid-Victorian style. The furniture all looked like real antiques, especially the yellow-oak rolltop desk and the mahogany instrument cabinet.

The room looked rich and impressive. Personally, though, Harry preferred Twentieth Century Modern. Its clean chromium-and-glass lines were esthetically pleasing; moreover, they were from the respectable first days of medical science—that period when mankind first began to realize that good health was not merely an accident, that it could be bought if men were willing to pay the price.

Harry had seen Dean Mock before, but never to speak to. His parents couldn't understand that. They thought he was the peer of everyone in the Medical Center because he was a doctor. He kept telling them how big the place was, how many people it contained: 75,000, 100,000—only the statisticians knew how many. It didn't do any good; they still couldn't understand. Harry had given up trying.

The Dean didn't know Harry. He sat behind the rolltop desk in his white jacket and studied Harry's record cast up on the frosted glass insert. He was good at it, but you couldn't deceive a man who had studied like that for ten years in this Center alone.

The Dean's black hair was thinning. He was almost eighty years old now, but he didn't look it. He came of good stock, and he had had the best of medical care. He was good for another twenty years, Harry estimated, without longevity shots. By that time, surely, with his position and his accomplishments, he would be voted a reprieve.

Once, when a bomb had exploded in the power room, some of the doctors had whispered in the safe darkness that Mock's youthful appearance had a more reasonable explanation than heredity, but they were wrong. Harry had searched the lists, and Mock's name wasn't on them.

Mock looked up quickly and caught Harry staring at him. Harry glanced away, but not before he had seen in Mock's eyes a look of—what?—fright? desperation?

Harry couldn't understand it. The raid had been daring, this close to the Center walls, but nothing new. There had been raids before; there would be raids again. Any time there is something valuable, lawless men will try to steal it. In Harry's day it happened to be medicine.

Mock said abruptly, "Then you saw the man? You could recognize him if you saw him again, or if you had a good solidograph?"

"Yes, sir," Harry said. Why was Mock making such a production out of it? He had already been over this with the head resident and the chief of the company police.

"Do you know Governor Weaver?" Mock asked.

"An Immortal!"

"No, no," Mock said impatiently. "Do you know where he lives?"

"In the Governor's mansion. Forty miles from here, almost due west."

"Yes, yes," Mock said. "You're going to carry a message to him, a message. The shipment has been hijacked. Hijacked." Mock had a nervous habit of repeating words. Harry had to listen intently to keep from being distracted. "It will be a week before another shipment is ready, a week. How we will get it to him I don't know. I don't know." The last statement was muttered to himself.

Harry tried to make sense out of it. Carry a message to the Governor? "Why don't you call him?" he said, unthinking.

But the question only roused Mock out of his introspection. "The underground cables are cut. Cut. No use repairing them. Repair men get shot. And even if they're fixed, they're only cut again next night. Radio and television are jammed. Get ready. You'll have to hurry to get out the southwest gate before curfew."

"A pass will get me through," Harry said, uncomprehending. Was Mock going insane?

"Didn't I tell you? Tell you?" Mock passed the back of his hand across his forehead as if to clear away cobwebs. "You're going alone, on foot, dressed as a citizen. A convoy would be cut to pieces. To pieces. We've tried. We've been out of touch with the Governor for three weeks. Three weeks! He must be getting impatient. Never make the Governor impatient. It isn't healthy."

For the first time Harry really understood what the Dean was asking him to do. The Governor! He had it in his power to cut half a lifetime off Harry's personal quest for immortality. "But my residency—"

Mock looked wise. "The Governor can do you more good than a dozen boards. More good."

Harry caught his lower lip between his teeth and counted off on his fingers. "I'll need nose filters, a small medical kit, a gun—"

Mock was shaking his head. "None of those. Out of character. If you reach the Governor's mansion, it will be because you pass as a citizen, not because you defend yourself well or heal up your wounds afterward. And a day or two without filters won't reduce your life expectancy appreciably. Well, Doctor? Will you get through?"

"As I hope for immortality!" Harry said earnestly.

"Good, good. One more thing. You'll take along with you the people you saw in the anteroom. The boy's name is Christopher; the old man calls himself Pearce. He's some kind of neighborhood leech. The Governor has asked for him."

"A leech?" Harry said incredulously.

Mock shrugged. His expression said that he considered the exclamation impertinent, but Harry could not restrain himself, and he said, "If we made an example of a few of these quacks—"

"The clinics would be more crowded than they are now. Now. They serve a good purpose. Besides, what can we do? He doesn't claim to be a physician. He calls himself a healer. He doesn't drug, operate, advise, or manipulate. Sick people come to him and he touches them. Touches them. Is that practicing medicine?"

Harry shook his head.

"What if the sick people claim to be helped? Pearce claims nothing. Nothing. He charges nothing. Nothing. If the sick people are grateful, if they want to give him something, who is to stop them?"

Harry sighed. "I'll have to sleep. They'll get away."

Mock jeered, "A feeble old man and a boy?"

"The girl's lively enough."

"Marna?" Mock reached into a drawer and brought out a hinged silver circle. He tossed it to Harry. Harry caught it and looked at it.

"It's a bracelet. Put it on."

It looked like nothing more than a bracelet. Harry shrugged, slipped it over his wrist, and clamped it shut. For a moment it seemed too big, and then it tightened. His wrist tingled where the bracelet touched him.

"It's tuned to the one on the girl's wrist. Tuned. When the girl moves away from you, her wrist will tingle. The farther she goes, the more it will hurt. After a little she will come back. I'd put bracelets on the boy and the old man, but they only work in pairs. Pairs. If someone tries to remove the bracelet forcibly, the girl will die. Die. It links itself to the nervous system. The Governor has the only key."

Harry stared at Mock. "What about mine?"

"The same. For you it's a warning device."

Harry took a deep breath and looked down at his wrist. The silver gleamed now like a snake's flat eyes.

"Why didn't you have one on the medic?"

"We did. We had to amputate his arm to get it off." Mock turned to his desk and started the microfilmed reports flipping past the window again. In a moment he looked up and seemed startled that Harry had not moved. "Still here? Get started. Wasted too much time now if you're going to beat curfew."

Harry turned and started toward the door through which he had come.

"Watch out for ghouls," Dean Mock called after him. "And mind the head-hunters."

By the time they reached the southwest gate, Harry had evolved a method of progress for his little group that was mutually unsatisfactory.

"Hurry up," he would say. "There's only a few minutes left before curfew."

The girl would look at him and look away. Pearce, already moving more rapidly than Harry had expected, would say, "Patience. We'll get there."

None of them would speed up. Harry would walk

ahead rapidly, outdistancing the others. His wrist would begin to tingle, then to smart, to burn, and to hurt. The farther he left Marna behind, the worse his pain grew. Only the thought that her waist felt just as bad sustained him.

After a little the pain would begin to ebb. He knew then, without looking, that she had broken. When he would turn, she would be twenty feet behind him, no closer, willing to accept that much pain to keep from coming nearer to him.

Then he would have to stop and wait for the old man. Once she walked on past, but after a little she could stand the pain no more, and she returned. After that she stopped when he did.

It was a small triumph for Harry, but something to strengthen him when he started thinking about the deadly thing on his wrist and the peculiar state of the world, in which the Medical Center had been out of touch with the Governor's mansion for three weeks, in which a convoy could not get through, in which a message had to be sent by a foot messenger.

Under other conditions, Harry might have thought Marna a lovely thing. She was slim and graceful, her skin was clear, her features were regular and pleasing, and the contrast between her dark hair and her blue eyes was striking. But she was young and spiteful and linked to him by a hateful condition. They had been thrown together too intimately too soon; and besides, she was only a child.

They reached the gate with only a minute to spare.

On either side of them the chain-link double fence stretched as far as Harry could see. There was no end to it, really; it completely encircled the town. At night it was electrified, and savage dogs roamed the space between the fences.

Somehow citizens still got out. They formed outlaw bands that attacked defenseless travelers. That would be one of the dangers.

The head guard at the gate was a dark-skinned, middle-aged squire. At sixty he had given up any hopes for immortality; he intended to get what he could out of this life. That included bullying his inferiors.

He looked at the blue, daylight-only pass, and then at Harry. "Topeka? On foot." He chuckled. It made his big belly shake until he had to cough. "If the ghouls don't get you, the head-hunters will. The bounty on heads is twenty dollars now. Outlaw heads only—but then, heads don't talk. Not if they're detached from bodies. Of course, that's what you're figuring on doing—joining a wolf pack." He spat on the sidewalk beside Harry's foot.

Harry jerked back his foot in revulsion. The guard's eyes brightened.

"Are you going to let us through?" Harry asked.

"Let you through?" Slowly the guard looked at his wrist watch. "Can't do that. Past curfew. See?"

Automatically Harry bent over to look. "But we got here before curfew—" he began. The guard's fist hit him just above the left ear and sent him spinning away.

"Get back in there and stay in there, you filthy citizens!" the guard shouted.

Harry's hand went to his pocket where he kept the hypospray, but it was gone. Words that would blast the guard off his post and into oblivion trembled on his lips, but he dared not utter them. He wasn't Dr. Elliot any more, not until he reached the Governor's mansion. He was Harry Elliott, citizen, fair game for any man's fist, who should consider himself lucky it was only a fist.

"Now," the guard said suggestively, "if you were to leave the girl as security—" He coughed.

Marna shrank back. She touched Harry accidentally. It was the first time they had touched, in spite of a more intimate linkage that joined them in pain and release, and something happened to Harry. His body recoiled automatically from the touch, as it would from a scalding sterilizer. Marna stiffened, aware of him.

Harry, disturbed, saw Pearce shuffling toward the guard, guided by his voice. Pearce reached out, his hand searching. He touched the guard's tunic, then his arm, and worked his way down the arm to the hand. Harry stood still, his hand doubled into a fist at his side, waiting for the guard to hit the old man. But the guard gave Pearce the instinctive respect due age and only looked at him curiously.

"Weak lungs," Pearce whispered. "Watch them. Pneumonia might kill before antibiotics could help. And in the lower left lobe, a hint of cancer—"

"Aw, now!" The guard jerked his hand away, but his voice was frightened.

"X-ray," Pearce whispered. "Don't wait."

"There—there ain't nothing wrong with me," the guard stammered. "You—you're trying to scare me." He coughed.

"No exertion. Sit down. Rest."

"Why, I'll—I'll—" He began coughing violently. He jerked his head at the gate. "Go on," he said, choking. "Go out there and die."

The boy Christopher took the old man's hand and led him through the open gateway. Harry caught Marna's upper arm—again the contact—and half helped her, half pushed her through the gate, keeping his eye warily on the guard. But the man's eyes were turned inward toward something far more vital to himself.

As soon as they were through, the gate slammed down behind them and Harry released Marna's arm as if it were distasteful to hold it. Fifty yards beyond, down the right-hand lanes of the disused six-lane divided highway, Harry said, "I suppose I ought to thank you."

Pearce whispered, "That would be polite."

Harry rubbed his head where the guard had hit him. It was swelling. He wished for a medical kit. "How can I be polite to a charlatan?"

"Politeness does not cost."

"Still—to lie to the man about his condition. To say —cancer—" Harry had a hard time saying it. It was a bad word—it was the one disease, aside from death itself, for which medical science had found no final cure.

"Was I lying?"

Harry stared sharply at the old man and then shrugged. He looked at Marna. "We're all in this together. We might as well make it as painless as possible. If we try to get along together, we might even all make it alive."

"Get along?" Marna said. Harry heard her speak for the first time; her voice was low and melodious, even in anger. "With this?" She held up her arm. The silver bracelet gleamed in the last red rays of the sun.

Harry said harshly, raising his wrist, "You think it's any better for me?"

Pearce whispered, "We will cooperate, Christopher and I—I, Dr. Elliott, because I am too old to do anything else, and Christopher because he is young and discipline is good for the young."

Christopher grinned. "Grampa used to be a doctor before he learned how to be a healer."

"Pride dulls the senses and warps the judgment," Pearce said softly.

Harry held back a comment. Now was no time to argue about medicine and quackery.

The road was deserted. The once magnificent pavement was cracked and broken. Grass sprouted tall and thick in the cracks. The weeds stood like young trees along both edges, here and there the big, brown faces of sunflowers, fringed in yellow, nodding peacefully.

Beyond were the ruins of what had once been called the suburbs. The distinction between them and the city had been only a line drawn on a map; there had been no fences then. When they had gone up, the houses outside had soon crumbled.

The real suburbs were far out. First it was turnpike time to the city that had become more important than distance; then helicopter time. Finally time had run out for the city. It had become so obviously a sea of carcinogens and disease that the connection to the suburbs had been broken. Shipments of food and raw materials went in and shipments of finished materials came out, but nobody went there any more—except to the medical centers. They were located in the cities because their raw material was there: the blood, the organs, the diseases, the bodies for experiment. . . .

Harry walked beside Marna, ahead of Christopher and Pearce, but the girl didn't look at him. She walked on, her eyes straight ahead, as if she were alone. Harry said finally, "Look, it's not my fault. I didn't ask for this. Can't we be friends?"

She glanced at him just once. "No!"

His lips tightened, and he dropped away. He let his wrist tingle. What did he care if a thirteen-year-old girl disliked him?

The western sky was fading from scarlet into lavender and purple. Nothing moved in the ruins or along the road. They were alone in an ocean of desolation. They might have been the last people on a ruined earth.

Harry shivered. Soon it would be hard to keep to the road. "Hurry," he said to Pearce, "if you don't want to spend the night out here with the ghouls and the head-hunters."

"There are worse companions," Pearce whispered.

By the time they reached the motel, the moonless night was completely upon them and the old suburbs were behind. The sprawling place was dark except for a big neon sign that said "MOTEL," a smaller sign that said "Vacancy," and, at the gate in the fence that surrounded the whole place, a mat that said "Welcome." On a frosted glass plate were the words "Push button."

Harry was about to push the button when Christopher said urgently, "Dr. Elliott, look!" He pointed toward the fence at the right with a stick he had picked up half a mile back.

"What?" Harry snapped. He was tired and nervous and dirty. He peered into the darkness. "A dead rabbit."

"Christopher means the fence is electrified," Marna said, "and the mat you're standing on is made of metal. I don't think we should go in here."

"Nonsense!" Harry said sharply. "Would you rather stay out here at the mercy of whatever roams the night? I've stopped at these motels before. There's nothing wrong with them."

Christopher held out his stick. "Maybe you'd better push the button with this."

Harry frowned, took the stick, and stepped off the mat. "Oh, all right," he said ungraciously. At the second try, he pushed the button.

The frosted glass plate became a television eye. "Who rings?"

"Four travelers bound for Topeka," Harry said. He held up the pass in front of the eye. "We can pay."

"Welcome," said the speaker. "Cabins thirteen and fourteen will open when you deposit the correct amount of money. What time do you wish to be awakened?"

Harry looked at his companions. "Sunrise," he said.

"Good night," said the speaker. "Sleep tight."

The gate rolled up. Christopher led Pearce around the welcome mat and down the driveway beyond. Marna followed. Irritated, Harry jumped over the mat and caught up with them.

A single line of glass bricks along the edge of the driveway glowed fluorescently to point out the way they should go. They passed a tank trap and several machine-gun emplacements, but the place was deserted.

When they reached cabin 13, Harry said, "We won't need the other one; we'll stay together." He put three twenty-dollar uranium pieces into the coin slot.

"Thank you," the door said. "Come in."

As the door opened, Christopher darted inside. The small room held a double bed, a chair, a desk, and a floor lamp. In the corner was a small partitioned bathroom with an enclosed shower, a lavatory, and a toilet. The boy went immediately to the desk, removed a plastic menu card from it, and returned to the door. He helped Pearce enter the room and then waited by the door until Harry and Marna were inside. He cracked the menu card into two pieces. As the door swung shut, he slipped one of the pieces between the door and the jamb. As he started back toward Pearce, he stumbled against the lamp and knocked it over. It crashed and went out. They were left with only the illumination from the bathroom light.

"Clumsy little fool!" Harry said.

Marna was at the desk, writing. She turned and handed the paper to Harry. He edged toward the light and looked at it. It said:

Christopher has broken the eye, but the room is still bugged. We can't break that without too much suspicion. Can I speak to you outside?

"That is the most ridiculous—" Harry began.

"This seems adequate," Pearce whispered. "You two can sleep in fourteen." His blind face was turned intently toward Harry.

Harry sighed. He might as well humor them. He opened the door and stepped into the night with Marna. The girl moved close to him, put her arms around his neck and her cheek against his. Without his volition, his arms went around her waist. Her lips moved against his ear; a moment later he realized that she was speaking.

"I do not like you, Dr. Elliott, but I do not want us all killed. Can you afford another cabin?"

"Of course, but—I'm not going to leave those two alone."

"It would be foolish for us not to stick together. Please, now. Ask no questions. When we go in fourteen, take off your jacket and throw it casually over the lamp. I'll do the rest."

Harry let himself be led to the next cabin. He fed the door. It greeted them and let them in. The room was identical with 13. Marna slipped a piece of plastic between the door and the jamb as the door closed. She looked at Harry expectantly.

He shrugged, took off his jacket, and tossed it over the lamp. The room took on a shadowy and sinister appearance. Marna knelt, rolled up a throw rug, and pulled down the covers on the bed. She went to the wall phone, gave it a little tug, and the entire flat vision plate swung out on hinges. She reached into it, grabbed something, and pulled it out. There seemed to be hundreds of turns of copper wire on a spool.

Marna went to the shower enclosure, unwinding wire as she went. She stood outside the enclosure and fastened one end of the wire to the hot-water faucet. Then she strung it around the room like a spider's web, broke it off, and fastened the end to the drain in the shower floor. She threaded the second piece of wire through the room close to but not touching the first wire.

Careful not to touch the wires, she reached into the shower enclosure and turned on the hot-water faucet. It gurgled, but no hot water came out. She tiptoed her way out between the wires, picked up the throw rug, and tossed it on the bed.

"Well, 'night," she said, motioning Harry toward the door and gesturing for him to be careful of the wires. When Harry reached the door without mishap, Marna turned off the lamp and removed the jacket.

She let the door slam behind them and gave a big sigh of relief.

"Now you've fixed it!" Harry whispered savagely. "I can't take a shower, and I'll have to sleep on the floor."

"You wouldn't want to take a shower anyway," Marna said. "It would be your last one. All of them are wired. You can have the bed if you want it, although I'd advise you to sleep on the floor with the rest of us."

Harry couldn't sleep. First it had been the room, shadowed and silent, and then the harsh breathing of the old man and the softer breaths of Christopher and

Marna. As a resident, he was not used to sleeping in the same room with other persons.

Then his arm had tingled—not much, but just enough to keep him awake. He had got out of bed and crawled to where Marna was lying on the floor. She, too, had been awake. Silently he had urged her to share the bed with him, gesturing that he would not touch her. He had no desire to touch her, and if he had, he swore by Hippocrates that he would restrain himself. He only wanted to ease the tingling under the bracelet so that he could go to sleep.

She motioned that he could lie on the floor beside her, but he shook his head. Finally she relented enough to move to the floor beside the bed. By lying on his stomach and letting his arm dangle, Harry relieved the tingling and fell into an uneasy sleep.

He had dreams. There was one in which he was performing a long and difficult lung resection. The microsurgical controls slipped in his sweaty fingers; the scalpel sliced through the aorta. The patient started up on the operating table, the blood spurting from her heart. It was Marna. She began to chase him down long, hospital halls.

The overhead lights kept getting farther and farther apart until Harry was running in complete darkness through warm, sticky blood that rose higher and higher until it closed over his head.

Harry woke up, smothering, fighting against something that enveloped him completely, relentlessly. There was a sound of scuffling nearby. Something spat and crackled. Someone cursed.

Harry fought, futilely. Something ripped. Again. Harry caught a glimpse of a grayer darkness, struggled toward it, and came out through a long rip in the taut blanket, which had been pulled under the bed on all four sides.

"Quick!" Christopher said, folding up his pocket-knife. He headed for the door where Pearce was already standing patiently.

Marna picked up a metal leg which had been un-screwed from the desk. Christopher slipped the chair out from under the door knob and silently opened the door. He led Pearce outside, and Marna followed. Dazedly, Harry came after her.

In cabin 14 someone screamed. Something flashed blue. A body fell. Harry smelled the odor of burning flesh.

Marna ran ahead of them toward the gate. She rested the ferule of the desk leg on the ground and let the metal bar fall toward the fence. The fence spat blue flame, which ran, crackling, down the desk leg. The leg glowed redly and sagged. Then everything went dark, including the neon sign above them and the light at the gate.

"Help me!" Marna panted.

She was trying to lift the gate. Harry put his hands underneath and lifted. The gate moved a foot and stuck.

Up the drive someone yelled hoarsely, without words. Harry strained at the gate. It yielded, rolled up silently. He put up his hand to hold it up while Marna got through, and then Pearce and the boy. Harry edged under and let the gate drop.

A moment later the electricity flickered on again. The desk leg melted through and dropped away.

Harry looked back. Coming toward them was a motorized wheelchair. In it was something lumpy and monstrous, a nightmarish menace—until Harry recognized it for what it was: a basket case, a quadruple amputee complicated by a heart condition. An artificial heart-and-lung machine rode on the back of the wheelchair like a second head. Behind galloped a gangling scarecrow creature with hair that flowed out behind. It wore a dress in imitation of a woman. . . .

Harry stood there watching, fascinated, while the wheelchair stopped beside one of the gun emplacements. Wires reached out from one of the chair arms like Medusan snakes, inserted themselves into control plugs. The machine gun started to chatter. Something plucked at Harry's sleeve.

The spell was broken. He turned and ran into the darkness.

Half an hour later he was lost. Marna, Pearce, and the boy were gone. All he had left was a tired body, an arm that burned, and a wrist that hurt worse than anything he could remember.

He felt his upper arm. His sleeve was wet. He brought his fingers to his nose. Blood. The bullet had creased him.

He sat disconsolately on the edge of the turnpike, the darkness as thick as soot around him. He looked at the fluorescent dial of his watch. Three-twenty. A couple of hours until sunrise. He sighed and tried to ease the pain in his wrist by rubbing around the bracelet. It seemed to help. In a few minutes it dropped to a tingle.

"Dr. Elliott," someone said softly.

He turned. Relief and something like joy flooded through his chest. There, outlined against the dim starlight, were Christopher, Marna, and Pearce.

"Well," Harry said gruffly, "I'm glad you didn't try to escape."

"We wouldn't do that, Dr. Elliott," Christopher said.

"How did you find me?" Harry asked.

Marna silently held up her arm.

The bracelet. Of course. He had given them too

much credit, Harry thought sourly. Marna sought him out because she could not help herself, and Christopher, because he was out here alone with a senile old man to take care of and he needed help.

Although, honesty forced him to admit, it had been himself and not Christopher and Pearce who had needed help back there a mile or two. If they had depended on him, their heads would be drying in the motel's dry-storage room, waiting to be turned in for the bounty. Or their still-living bodies would be on their way to some organ bank somewhere.

"Christopher," Harry said to Pearce, "must have been apprenticed to a bad-debt evader."

Pearce accepted it for what it was: a compliment and an apology. "Dodging the collection agency traps and keeping out of the way of the health inspector," he whispered, "make growing up in the city a practical education. . . . You're hurt."

Harry started. How did the old man know? Even with eyes, it was too dark to see more than silhouettes. Harry steadied himself. It was an instinct, perhaps. Diagnosticians got it, sometimes, he was told, after they had been practicing for years. They could smell disease before the patient lay down on the couch. From the gauges they got only confirmation.

Or maybe it was simpler than that. Maybe the old man smelled the blood with a nose grown keen to compensate for his blindness.

The old man's fingers were on his arm, surprisingly gentle. Harry pulled his arm away roughly. "It's only a crease."

Pearce's fingers found his arm again. "It's bleeding. Find some dry grass, Christopher."

Marna was close. She had made a small, startled movement toward him when Pearce had discovered his wound. Harry could not accept her actions for sympathy; her hate was too tangible. Perhaps she was wondering what she would do if he were to die.

Pearce ripped the sleeve away.

"Here's the grass, Grampa," Christopher said.

How did the boy find dry grass in the dark? "You aren't going to put that on the wound!" Harry said quickly.

"It will stop the bleeding," Pearce whispered.

"But the germs—"

"Germs can't hurt you—unless you want them to."

He put the grass on the wound and bound it with the sleeve. "That will be better soon."

He would take it off, Harry told himself, as soon as they started walking. Somehow, though, it was easier to let it alone now that the harm was done. After that he forgot about it.

When they were walking again, Harry found himself beside Marna. "I suppose you got your education dodging health inspectors in the city, too?" he said drily.

She shook her head. "No. There's never been much else to do. Ever since I can remember I've been trying to escape. I got free once." Her voice was filled with remembered happiness. "I was free for twenty-four hours, and then they found me."

"But I thought—" Harry began. "Who are you?"

"Me? I'm the Governor's daughter."

Harry recoiled. It was not so much the fact, but the bitterness with which she spoke that impressed him.

Sunrise found them on the turnpike. They had passed the last ruined motel. Now, on either side of the turnpike, were rolling, grassy hills, valleys filled with trees, and the river winding muddily beside them, sometimes so close they could have thrown a stone into it, sometimes turning beyond the hills out of sight.

The day was warm. Above them the sky was blue, with only a trace of fleecy cloud on the western horizon. Occasionally a rabbit would hop across the road in front of them and vanish into the brush on the other side. Once they saw a deer lift its head beside the river and stare at them curiously.

Harry stared back with hunger in his eyes.

"Dr. Elliott," Christopher said.

Harry looked at him. In the boy's soiled hand was an irregular lump of solidified brown sugar. It was speckled with lint and other unidentifiable additions, but at the moment it was the most desirable object Harry could think of. His mouth watered, and he swallowed hard. "Give it to Pearce and the girl. They'll need their strength. And you, too."

"That's all right," Christopher said. "I have more." He held up three other pieces in his other hand. He gave one to Marna and one to Pearce. The old man bit into his with the stubs that served him as teeth.

Harry picked off the largest pieces of foreign matter, and then could restrain his hunger no longer. It was an unusually satisfying breakfast.

They kept walking, not moving rapidly but steadily. Pearce never complained. He kept his bent old legs tottering forward, and Harry gave up trying to move him faster.

They passed a hydroponic farm with an automated canning factory close beside it. No one moved around either building. Only the belts turned, carrying the tanks toward the factory to be harvested, or away from it refilled with nutrients, replanted with new crops.

"We should get something for lunch," Harry said.

It would be theft, but it would be in a good cause. He could get his pardon directly from the Governor.

"Too dangerous," Christopher said.

"Every possible entrance," Marna said, "is guarded by spy beams and automatic weapons."

"Christopher will get us a good supper," Pearce whispered.

They saw a suburban villa on a distant hill, but there was no one in sight around it. They plodded on along the grass-grown double highway toward Lawrence.

Suddenly Christopher said, "Down! In the ditch beside the road!"

This time Harry moved quickly, without questions. He helped Pearce down the slope—the old man was very light—and threw himself down into the ditch beside Marna. A minute later they heard motors race by not far away. After they passed, Harry risked a glance above the top of the ditch. A group of motorcycles dwindled on the road toward the city. "What was that?" Harry asked, shaken.

"Wolf pack!" Marna said, hatred and disgust mingled in her voice.

"But they looked like company police," Harry said.

"When they grow up they will be company policemen," Marna said.

"I thought the wolf packs were made up of escaped citizens," Harry said.

Marna looked at him scornfully. "Is that what they tell you?"

"A citizen," Pearce whispered, "is lucky to stay alive when he's alone. A group of them wouldn't last a week."

They got back up on the turnpike and started walking again. Christopher was nervous as he led Pearce.

He kept turning to look behind him and glancing from side to side. Soon Harry was edgy too.

"Down!" Christopher shouted.

Something whistled a moment before Harry was struck a solid blow in the middle of the back as he was throwing himself to the pavement. It knocked him hard to the ground. Marna screamed.

Harry rolled over, wondering if his back was broken. Christopher and Pearce were on the pavement beside him, but Marna was gone.

A rocket blasted a little ahead and above them. Then another. Pearce looked up. A powered glider zoomed toward the sky. Marna was dangling from it, her body twisting and struggling to get free. From a second glider swung empty talons—padded hooks which had closed around Marna and had almost swooped up Harry.

Harry got to his knees, clutching his wrist. It was beginning to send stabs of pain up his arms, like a prelude to a symphony of anguish. The only thing that kept him from falling to the pavement in writhing torment was the black anger that surged through his veins and fought off weakness. He shook his fist at the turning gliders, climbing on smoking jets.

"Dr. Elliott!" Christopher said urgently.

Harry looked toward the voice with blurred eyes. The boy was in the ditch again. So was the old man.

"They'll be back! Get down!" Christopher said.

"But they've got Marna!" Harry said.

"It won't help if you get killed."

One glider swooped like a hawk toward a mouse. The other, carrying Marna, continued to circle as it climbed. Harry rolled toward the ditch. A line of chattering bullets chipped at the pavement where he had been.

"I thought," he gasped, "they were trying to abduct us."

"They hunt heads, too," Christopher said.

"Anything for a thrill," Pearce whispered.

"I never did anything like that," Harry moaned. "I never knew anyone who did."

"You were busy," Pearce said.

It was true. Since he was four years old he had been in school constantly, the last part of that time in medical school. He had been home only for a brief day now and then; he scarcely knew his parents any more. What would he know of the pastimes of young squires? But this—this wolf-pack business! It was a degradation of life that filled him with horror.

The first glider was now a small cross in the sky; Marna, a speck hanging from it. It straightened and glided toward Lawrence. The second followed.

Suddenly Harry began beating the ground with his aching arm. "Why did I dodge? I should have let myself be captured with her. She'll die."

"She's strong," Pearce whispered, "stronger than you or Christopher, stronger than almost anyone. But sometimes strength is the cruelest thing. Follow her. Get her away."

Harry looked at the bracelet from which pain lanced up his arm and through his body. Yes, he could follow her. As long as he could move, he could find her. But feet were so slow against glider wings.

"The motorcycles will be coming back," Christopher said. "The gliders will have radioed them."

"But how do we capture a motorcycle?" Harry asked. The pain wouldn't let him think clearly.

Christopher had already pulled up his T-shirt. Around his thin waist was wrapped turn after turn of nylon cord. "Sometimes we fish," he said. He stretched the cord across the two-lane pavement in the concealment of grass grown tall in a crack. He motioned Harry to lie flat on the other side. "Let them pass, all but the last one," he said. "Hope that he's a straggler, far enough behind so that the others won't notice when we stand up. Wrap the cord around your waist. Get it up where it will catch him around the chest."

Harry lay beside the pavement. His left arm felt like a swelling balloon, and the balloon was filled with pain. He looked at it once, curiously, but it was still the same size.

After an eternity came the sound of motors, many of them. As the first ones passed, Harry cautiously lifted his head. Yes, there was a straggler. He was about a hundred feet behind the others; he was speeding now to catch up.

The others passed. When the straggler got within twenty feet Harry jumped up, bracing himself against the impact. Christopher sprang up at the same instant. The young squire had time only to look surprised before he hit the cord. The cord pulled Harry out into the middle of the pavement, his heels skidding. Christopher had tied his end to the trunk of a young tree.

The squire smashed into the pavement. The motorcycle slowed and stopped. Beyond, far down the road, the others had not looked back.

Harry untangled himself from the cord and ran to the squire. He was about as old as Harry, and as big. He had a harelip and a withered leg. He was dead. The skull was crushed.

Harry closed his eyes. He had seen men die before, but he had never been the cause of it. It was like breaking his Hippocratic oath.

"Some must die," Pearce whispered. "It is better for the evil to die young."

Harry stripped quickly and got into the squire's clothes and goggles. He strapped the pistol down on his hip and turned to Christopher and Pearce. "What about you?"

"We won't try to escape," Pearce said.

"I don't mean that. Will you be all right?"

Pearce put a hand on the boy's shoulder. "Christopher will take care of me. And he will find you after you have rescued Marna."

The confidence in Pearce's voice strengthened Harry. He did not pause to question that confidence. He mounted the motorcycle, settled himself into the saddle seat, and turned the throttle. The motorcycle took off violently.

It was tricky, riding on one wheel, but he had had experience on similar vehicles in the subterranean Medical Center thoroughfares.

His arm hurt, but it was not like it had been before when he was helpless. Now it was a guidance system. As he rode, he could feel the pain lessen. That meant he was getting closer to Marna.

It was night before he found her. The other motorcycles had completely outdistanced him, and he had swept past the side road several miles before the worsening pain warned him. He cruised back and forth before he finally located the curving ramp that led across the cloverleaf ten miles east of Lawrence.

From this a ruined asphalt road turned east, and the pain in Harry's arm had dropped to an ache. The road ended in an impenetrable thicket. Harry stopped just before he crashed into it. He sat immobile on the seat, thinking.

He hadn't considered what he was going to do when he found Marna; he had merely taken off in hot pursuit, driven partly by the painful bracelet on his wrist, partly by his emotional involvement with the girl.

Somehow—he could scarcely trace back the involutions of chance to its source—he had been trapped into leading this pitiful expedition from the Medical Center to the Governor's mansion. Moment by moment it had threatened his life—and not, unless all his hopes were false, just a few years but eternity. Was he going to throw it away here on a quixotic attempt to rescue a girl from the midst of a pack of cruel young wolves?

But what would he do with the thing on his wrist? What of the Governor? And what of Marna?

"Ralph?" someone asked out of the darkness, and the decision was taken out of his hands.

"Yeth," he lisped. "Where ith everybody?"

"Usual place—under the bank."

Harry moved toward the voice, limping. "Can't thee a thing."

"Here's a light."

The trees lighted up, and a black form loomed in front of Harry. Harry blinked once, squinted, and hit the squire with the edge of his palm on the fourth cervical vertebra. As the man dropped, Harry picked the everlight out of the air, and caught the body. He eased the limp form into the grass and felt the neck. It was broken, but the squire was still breathing. He straightened the head so that there would be no pressure on nerve tissue, and looked up.

Light glimmered and flickered somewhere ahead. There was no movement, no sound; apparently no one had heard him. He flicked the light on, saw the path, and started through the young forest.

The campfire was built under a clay overhang so that it could not be seen from above. Roasting over it was a whole young deer being slowly turned on a spit by one of the squires. Harry found time to recognize the empty ache in his midriff for what it was: hunger.

The rest of the squires sat in a semicircle around the fire. Marna was seated on the far side, her hands bound behind her. Her head was raised; her eyes searched the darkness around the fire. What was she looking for? Of course—for him. She knew by the bracelet on her wrist that he was near.

He wished that he could signal her, but there was no way. He studied the squires: one was an albino; a second, a macrocephalic; a third, a spastic. The others may have had physical impairments that Harry could not see—all except one, who seemed older than the rest and leaned against the edge of the clay bank. He was blind, but inserted surgically into his eye sockets were electrically operated binoculars. He carried a power pack on his back with leads to the binoculars and to an antenna in his coat.

Harry edged cautiously around the forest edge beyond the firelight toward where Marna was sitting.

"First the feast," the albino gloated, "then the fun."

The one who was turning the spit said, "I think we should have the fun first—then we'll be good and hungry."

They argued back and forth, good-naturedly for a moment and then, as others chimed in, with more heat. Finally the albino turned to the one with the binoculars. "What do you say, Eyes?"

In a deep voice, Eyes said, "Sell the girl. Young parts are worth top prices."

"Ah," said the albino slyly, "but you can't see what

a pretty little thing she is, Eyes. To you she's only a pattern of white dots against a gray kinescope. To us she's white and pink and black and—"

"One of these days," Eyes said in a calm voice, "you'll go too far."

"Not with her, I won't—"

A stick broke under Harry's foot. Everyone stopped talking and listened. Harry eased his pistol out of its holster.

"Is that you, Ralph?" the albino said.

"Yeth," Harry said, limping out into the edge of the firelight, but keeping his head in the darkness, his pistol concealed at his side.

"Can you imagine?" the albino said. "The girl says she's the Governor's daughter."

"I am," Marna said clearly. "He will have you cut to pieces slowly for what you are going to do."

"But I'm the Governor, dearie," said the albino in a falsetto, "and I don't give a—"

Eyes interrupted, "That's not Ralph. His leg's all right."

Harry cursed his luck. The binoculars were equipped to pick up X-ray reflections as well as radar. "Run!" he shouted in the silence that followed.

His first shot was for Eyes. The man was turning so that it struck his power pack. He began screaming and clawing at the binoculars that served him for eyes. But Harry wasn't watching. He was releasing the entire magazine into the clay bank above the fire. Already loosened by the heat from the fire, the bank collapsed, smothering the fire and burying several of the squires sitting close to it.

Harry dived to the side. Several bullets went through the space he had just vacated.

He scrambled for the forest and started running.

He kept slamming into trees, but he picked himself up and ran again. Somewhere he lost his everlight. Behind, the pursuit thinned and died away.

He ran into something that yielded before him. It fell to the ground, something soft and warm. He tripped over it and toppled, his fist drawn back.

"Harry!" Marna said.

His fist turned into a hand that went out to her, pulled her tight. "Marna!" he sobbed. "I didn't know. I didn't think I could do it. I thought you were—"

Their bracelets clinked together. Marna, who had been soft beneath him, suddenly stiffened, pushed him off. "Let's not get slobbery about it," she said angrily. "I know why you did it. Besides, they'll hear us."

Harry drew a quick, outraged breath and then let it come out in a sigh. What was the use? She'd never believe him—why should she? He wasn't sure himself. Now that it was over and he had time to realize the risks he had taken, he began to shiver. He sat there in the dark forest, his eyes closed, and tried to control his shaking.

Marna put her hand out hesitantly and touched his arm. She started to say something, stopped, and the moment was past.

"B-b-brat-t-t!" he chattered. "N-n-nasty—un-ungrateful b-b-brat!" And then the shakes were gone.

She started to move. "Sit still!" he whispered. "We've got to wait until they give up the search."

At least he had eliminated the greatest danger: Eyes with his radar, X-ray vision that was just as good by night as by day.

They sat in the darkness and waited, listening to the forest noises. An hour passed. Harry was going to say that perhaps it was safe to move, when he heard something rustling nearby. Animal, or human enemy? Marna, who had not touched him again or spoken, clutched his upper arm with a panic-strengthened hand. Harry doubled his fist and drew back his arm.

"Dr. Elliott?" Christopher whispered. "Marna?"

Relief surged over Harry like a warm, life-giving current. "You wonderful little imp! How did you find us?"

"Grampa helped me. He has a sense for that. I have a little, but he's better. Come." Harry felt a small hand fit itself into his.

Christopher began to lead them through the darkness. At first Harry was distrustful, and then, as the boy kept them out of bushes and trees, he moved more confidently. The hand became something he could trust. He knew how Pearce felt, and how bereft he must be now.

Christopher led them a long way before they reached another clearing. A bed of coals glowed dimly beneath a sheltering bower of green leaves. Pearce sat near the fire, slowly turning a spit fashioned from a green branch. It rested on two forked sticks. On the spit two skinned rabbits were golden brown and sizzling.

Pearce's sightless face turned as they entered the clearing. "Welcome back," he said.

Harry felt a warmth inside him that was like coming home. "Thanks," he said huskily.

Marna fell to her knees in front of the fire, raising her hands to it to warm them. Rope dangled from them, frayed in the center where she had methodically picked it apart while she had waited by another fire. She must have been cold, Harry thought, and I let her shiver through the forest while I was warm in my jacket. But there was nothing to say.

When Christopher removed the rabbits from the spit, they almost fell apart. He wrapped four legs in damp green leaves and tucked them away in a cool hollow between two tree roots. "That's for breakfast," he said.

The four of them fell to work on the remainder. Even without salt, it was the most delicious meal Harry had ever eaten. When it was finished, he licked his fingers, sighed, and leaned back on a pile of old leaves. He felt more contented than he could ever remember being. He was a little thirsty, because he had refused to drink from the brook that ran through the woods close to their improvised camp, but he could stand that. A man couldn't surrender all his principles. It would be ironic to die of typhoid so close to his chance at immortality.

That the Governor would confer immortality upon him—or at least put him into a position where he could earn it—he did not doubt. After all, he had saved the Governor's daughter.

Marna was a pretty little thing. It was too bad she was still a child. An alliance with the Governor's family would not hurt his chances. Perhaps in a few years— He put the notion away from him. Marna hated him.

Christopher shoveled dirt over the fire with a large piece of bark. Harry sighed again and stretched luxuriously. Sleeping would be good tonight.

Marna had washed at the brook. Her face was clean and shining. "Will you sleep here beside me?" Harry asked her, touching the dry leaves. He held up his bracelet apologetically. "This thing keeps me awake when you're very far away."

She nodded coldly and sat down beside him—but far enough away so that they did not touch.

Harry said, "I can't understand why we've run across so many teratisms. I can't remember ever seeing one in my practice at the Medical Center."

"You were in the clinics?" Pearce asked. And without waiting for an answer he went on, "Increasingly, the practice of medicine becomes the treatment of monsters. In the city they would die; in the suburbs they are preserved to perpetuate themselves. Let me look at your arm."

Harry started. Pearce had said it so naturally that for a moment he had forgotten that the old man couldn't see. The old man's gentle fingers untied the bandage and carefully pulled the matted grass away. "You won't need this any more."

Harry put his hand wonderingly to the wound. It had not hurt for hours. Now it was only a scar. "Perhaps you really were a doctor. Why did you give up practice?"

Pearce whispered, "I grew tired of being a technician. Medicine had become so desperately complicated that the relationship between doctor and patient was not much different from that between mechanic and patient."

Harry objected: "A doctor has to preserve his distance. If he keeps caring, he won't survive. He must become callous to suffering, inured to sorrow, or he couldn't continue in a calling so intimately associated with them."

"No one ever said," Pearce whispered, "that it was an easy thing to be a doctor. If he stops caring, he loses not only his patient but his own humanity. But the complication of medicine had another effect. It restricted treatment to those who could afford it. Fewer and fewer people grew healthier and healthier. Weren't the rest human, too?"

Harry frowned. "Certainly. But it was the wealthy contributors and the foundations that made it all possible. They had to be treated first so that medical research could continue."

Pearce whispered, "And so society was warped all out of shape; everything was sacrificed to the god of medicine—all so that a few people could live a few years longer. Who paid the bill?

"And the odd outcome was that those who received care grew less healthy, as a class, than those who had to survive without it. Premies were saved to reproduce their weaknesses. Faults that would have proved fatal in childhood were repaired so that the patient reached maturity. Non-survival traits were passed on. Physiological inadequates multiplied, requiring greater care—"

Harry sat upright. "What kind of medical ethics are those? Medicine can't count the cost or weigh the value. Its business is to treat the sick—"

"Those who can afford it. If medicine doesn't evaluate, then someone else will: power or money or groups. One day I walked out on all that. I went among the citizens, where the future was, where I could help without discrimination. They took me in; they fed me when I was hungry, laughed with me when I was happy, cried with me when I was sad. They cared, and I helped them as I could."

"How?" Harry asked. "Without a diagnostic machine, without drugs or antibiotics."

"The human mind," Pearce whispered, "is still the best diagnostic machine. And the best antibiotic. I touched them. I helped them to cure themselves. So I became a healer instead of a technician. Our bodies want to heal themselves, you know, but our minds give counter-orders and death-instructions."

"Witch doctor!" Harry said scornfully.

"Yes. Always there have been witch doctors. Healers. Only in my day have the healer and the doctor become two persons. In every other era the people with the healing touch were the doctors. They existed then; they exist now. Countless cures are testimony. Only today do we call it superstition. And yet we know that some doctors, no wiser or more expert than others, have a far greater recovery rate. Some nurses— not always the most beautiful ones—inspire in their patients a desire to get well.

"It takes you two hours to do a thorough examination; I can do it in two seconds. It may take you months or years to complete a treatment; I've never taken longer than five minutes."

"But where's your control?" Harry demanded. "How can you prove you've helped them? If you can't trace cause and effect, if no one else can duplicate your treatment, it isn't science. It can't be taught."

"When a healer is successful, he knows," Pearce whispered. "So does his patient. As for teaching—how do you teach a child to talk?"

Harry shrugged impatiently. Pearce had an answer for everything. There are people like that, so secure in their mania that they can never be convinced that the rest of the world is sane. Man had to depend on science—not on superstition, not on faith healers, not on miracle workers. Or else he was back in the Dark Ages.

He lay back in the bed of leaves, feeling Marna's presence close to him. He wanted to reach out and touch her, but he didn't.

Else there would be no law, no security, no immortality. . . .

The bracelet awoke him. It tingled. Then it began to hurt. Harry put out his hand. The bed of leaves beside him was warm, but Marna was gone.

"Marna!" he whispered. He raised himself on one elbow. In the starlight that filtered through the trees above, he could just make out that the clearing was empty of everyone but himself. The places where Pearce and the boy had been sleeping were empty. "Where is everybody?" he said, more loudly.

He cursed under his breath. They had picked their time and escaped. But why, then, had Christopher found them in the forest and brought them here? And what did Marna hope to gain? Make it to the mansion alone?

He started up. Something crunched in the leaves. Harry froze in that position. A moment later he was blinded by a brilliant light.

"Don't move!" said a high-pitched voice. "I will have to shoot you. And if you try to dodge, the Snooper will follow." The voice was cool and precise. The hand that held the gun, Harry thought, would be as cool and accurate as the voice.

"I'm not moving," Harry said. "Who are you?"

The voice ignored him. "There were four of you. Where are the other three?"

"They heard you coming. They're hanging back, waiting to rush you."

"You're lying," the voice said contemptuously.

"Listen to me!" Harry said urgently. "You don't sound like a citizen. I'm a doctor—ask me a question about medicine, anything at all. I'm on an urgent mission. I'm taking a message to the Governor."

"What is the message?"

Harry swallowed hard. "The shipment was hijacked. There won't be another ready for a week."

"What shipment?"

"I don't know. If you're a squire, you've got to help me."

"Sit down." Harry sat down. "I have a message for you. Your message won't be delivered."

"But—" Harry started up.

From somewhere behind the light came a small explosion—little more than a sharply expelled breath. Something stung Harry in the chest. He looked down. A tiny dart clung there between the edges of his jacket. He tried to reach for it and couldn't. His arm wouldn't move. His head wouldn't move either. He toppled over onto his side, not feeling the impact. Only his eyes, his ears, and his lungs seemed unaffected. He lay there, paralyzed, his mind racing.

"Yes," the voice said calmly, "I am a ghoul. Some of my friends are head-hunters, but I hunt bodies and bring them in alive. The sport is greater. So is the profit. Heads are worth only twenty dollars; bodies are worth more than a hundred. Some with young organs like yours are worth much more.

"Go, Snooper. Find the others."

The light went away. Something crackled in the brush and was gone. Slowly Harry made out a black shape that seemed to be sitting on the ground about ten feet away.

"You wonder what will happen to you," the ghoul said. "As soon as I find your companions, I will paralyze them, too, and summon my stretchers. They will carry you to my helicopter. Then, since you came from Kansas City, I will take you to Topeka."

A last hope died in Harry's chest.

"That works best, I've found," the high-pitched voice continued. "Avoids complications. The Topeka hospital I do business with will buy your bodies, no questions asked. You are permanently paralyzed, so you will never feel any pain, although you will not lose consciousness. That way the organs never deteriorate. If you're a doctor, as you said, you know what I mean. You may know the technical name for the poison in the dart; all I know is that it was synthesized from the poison of the digger wasp. By use of intravenous feeding, these eminently portable organ banks have been kept alive for years until their time comes. . . ."

The voice went on, but Harry didn't listen. He was thinking that he would go mad. They often did. He had seen them lying on slabs in the organ bank, and their eyes had been quite mad. Then he had told himself that the madness was why they had been put there, but now he knew the truth. He would soon be one of them.

Perhaps he would strangle before he reached the hospital, before they got the tube down his throat and the artificial respirator on his chest and the tubes into his arms. They strangled sometimes, even under care.

He would not go mad, though. He was too sane. He might last for months.

He heard something crackle in the brush. Light flashed across his eyes. Something moved. Bodies thrashed. Someone grunted. Someone else yelled. Something went *pouf!* Then the sounds stopped, except for someone panting.

"Harry!" Marna said anxiously. "Harry! Are you all right?"

The light came back as the squat Snooper shuffled into the little clearing again. Pearce moved painfully through the light. Beyond him was Christopher and Marna. On the ground near them was a twisted creature. Harry couldn't figure out what it was, and then he realized it was a dwarf, a gnome, a man with thin, little legs and a twisted back and a large, lumpy head. Black hair grew sparsely on top of the head, and the eyes looked out redly, hating the world.

"Harry!" Marna said again, a wail this time.

He didn't answer. He couldn't. It was a momentary flash of pleasure, not being able to answer, and then it was buried in a flood of self-pity.

Marna picked up the dart gun and threw it deep into the brush. "What a filthy weapon!"

Reason returned to Harry. They had not escaped after all. Just as he had told the ghoul, they had only faded away so that they could rescue him if an opportunity came. But they had returned too late.

The paralysis was permanent; there was no antidote. Perhaps they would kill him. How could he make them understand that he wanted to be killed?

He blinked his eyes rapidly.

Marna had moved to him. She cradled his head in her lap. Her hand moved restlessly, soothing his hair.

Carefully, Pearce removed the dart from his chest and shoved it deep into the ground. "Be calm," he said. "Don't give up. There is no such thing as permanent paralysis. If you will try, you can move your little finger." He held up Harry's hand, patted it.

Harry tried to move his finger, but it was useless. What was the matter with the old quack? Why didn't he kill him and get it over with? Pearce kept talking, but Harry did not listen. What was the use of hoping? It only made the pain worse.

"A transfusion might help," Marna said.

"Yes," Pearce agreed. "Are you willing?"

"You know what I am?"

"Of course. Christopher, search the ghoul. He will have tubing and needles on him for emergency treatment of his victims." Pearce spoke to Marna again.

"There will be some commingling. The poison will enter your body."

Marna's voice was bitter. "You couldn't hurt me with cyanide."

There were movements and preparations. Harry couldn't concentrate on them. Things blurred. Time passed like the slow movement of a glacier.

As the first gray light of morning came through the trees, Harry felt life moving painfully in his little finger. It was worse than anything he had ever experienced, a hundred times worse than the pain from the bracelet. The pain spread to his other fingers, to his feet, up his legs and arms toward his trunk. He wanted to plead with Pearce to restore the paralysis, but by the time his throat relaxed, the pain was almost gone.

When he could sit up, he looked around for Marna. She was leaning back against a tree trunk, her eyes closed, looking paler than ever. "Marna!" he said. Her eyes opened wearily; an expression of joy flashed across them as they focused on him, and then they clouded.

"I'm all right," she said.

Harry scratched his left elbow where the needle had been. "I don't understand—you and Pearce—you brought me back from that—but—"

"Don't try to understand," she said. "Just accept it."

"It's impossible," he muttered. "What are you?"

"The Governor's daughter."

"What else?"

"A Cartwright," she said bitterly.

His mind recoiled. One of the Immortals! He was not surprised that her blood had counteracted the poison. Cartwright blood was specific against any foreign substance. He thought of something. "How old are you?"

"Seventeen," she said. She looked down at her slim figure. "We mature late, we Cartwrights. That's why Weaver sent me to the Medical Center—to see if I was fertile. A fertile Cartwright can waste no breeding time."

There was no doubt: she hated her father. She called him Weaver. "He will have you bred," Harry repeated stupidly.

"He will try to do it himself," she said without emotion. "He is not very fertile; that is why there are only three of us—my grandmother, my mother, and me. Then we have some control over conception—particularly after maturity. We don't want his children, even though they might make him less dependent on us. I'm afraid"—her voice broke—"I'm afraid I'm not mature enough."

"Why didn't you tell me before?" Harry demanded.

"And have you treat me like a Cartwright?" Her eyes glowed with anger. "A Cartwright isn't a person, you know. A Cartwright is a walking blood bank, a living fountain of youth, something to be possessed, used, guarded, but never really allowed to live. Besides"—her head dropped—"you don't believe me. About Weaver."

"But he's the Governor!" Harry exclaimed. He saw her face and turned away. How could he explain? You had a job and you had a duty. You couldn't go back on those. And then there were the bracelets. Only the Governor had the key. They couldn't go on for long linked together like that. They would be separated again, by chance or by force, and he would die.

He got to his feet. The forest reeled for a moment, and then settled back. "I owe you thanks again," he said to Pearce.

"You fought hard to preserve your beliefs," Pearce

whispered, "but there was a core of sanity that fought with me, that said it was better to be a whole man with crippled beliefs than a crippled man with whole beliefs."

Harry stared soberly at the old man. He was either a real healer who could not explain how he worked his miracles, or the world was a far crazier place than Harry had ever imagined. "If we start moving now," he said, "we should be in sight of the mansion by noon."

As he passed the dwarf, he looked down, stopped, and looked back at Marna and Pearce. Then he stooped, picked up the misshapen little body, and walked toward the road.

The helicopter was beside the turnpike. "It would be only a few minutes if we flew," he muttered.

Close behind him Marna said, "We aren't expected. We would be shot down before we got within five miles."

Harry strapped the dwarf into the helicopter seat. The ghoul stared at him out of hate-filled eyes. Harry started the motor, pressed the button on the autopilot marked "Return," and stepped back. The helicopter lifted, straightened, and headed southeast.

Christopher and Pearce were waiting on the pavement when Harry turned. Christopher grinned suddenly and held out a rabbit leg. "Here's breakfast."

They marched down the turnpike toward Lawrence.

The Governor's mansion was built on the top of an L-shaped hill that stood tall between two river valleys. Once it had been the site of a great university, but taxes for supporting such institutions had been diverted into more vital channels. Private contributions had dwindled as the demands of medical research and medical care had intensified. Soon there was no interest in educational fripperies, and the university died.

The Governor had built his mansion there some seventy-five years ago when Topeka became unbearable. Long before that it had become a lifetime office —and the Governor would live forever.

The state of Kansas was a barony—a description that would have meant nothing to Harry, whose knowledge of history was limited to the history of medicine. The Governor was a baron, and the mansion was his keep. His vassals were the suburban squires; they were paid with immortality or its promise. Once one of them had received an injection, he had two choices: remain loyal to the Governor and live forever, barring accidental death, or die within thirty days.

The Governor had not received a shipment for four weeks. The squires were getting desperate.

The mansion was a fortress. Its outer walls were five-foot-thick pre-stressed concrete faced with five-inch armor plate. A moat surrounded the walls; it was stocked with piranha.

An inner wall rose above the outside one. The paved, unencumbered area between the two could be flooded with napalm. Inside the wall were hidden guided-missile nests.

The mansion rose, ziggurat fashion, in terraced steps. On each rooftop was a hydroponic farm. At the summit of the buildings was a glass penthouse; the noon sun turned it into silver. On a mast towering above, a radar dish rotated.

Like an iceberg, most of the mansion was beneath the surface. It went down through limestone and granite a mile deep. The building was almost a living creature; automatic mechanisms controlled it, brought in air, heated and cooled it, fed it, watered it, watched for enemies and killed them if they got too close. . . .

It could be run by a single hand. At the moment it was.

There was no entrance to the place. Harry stood in front of the walls and waved his jacket. "Ahoy, the mansion! A message for the Governor from the Medical Center. Ahoy, the mansion!"

"Down!" Christopher shouted.

An angry bee buzzed past Harry's ear and then a whole flight of them. Harry fell to the ground and rolled. In a little while the bees stopped.

"Are you hurt?" Marna asked quickly.

Harry lifted his face out of the dust. "Poor shots," he said grimly. "Where did they come from?"

"One of the villas," Christopher said, pointing at the scattered dwellings at the foot of the hill.

"The bounty wouldn't even keep them in ammunition," Harry said.

In a giant, godlike voice, the mansion spoke: "Who comes with a message for me?"

Harry shouted from his prone position, "Dr. Harry Elliott. I have with me the Governor's daughter Marna and a leech. We're under fire from one of the villas."

The mansion was silent. Slowly then a section of the inside wall swung open. Something flashed into the sunlight, spurting flame from its tail. It darted downward. A moment later a villa lifted into the air and fell back, a mass of rubble.

Over the outer wall came a crane arm. From it dangled a large metal car. When it reached the ground a door opened.

"Come into my presence," the mansion said.

The car was dusty. So was the penthouse where they were deposited. The vast swimming pool was dry; the cabanas were rotten; the flowers and bushes and palm trees were dead.

In the mirror-surfaced central column, a door gaped at them like a dark mouth. "Enter," said the door.

The elevator descended deep into the ground. Harry's stomach surged uneasily; he thought the car would never stop, but eventually the doors opened. Beyond was a spacious living room, decorated in shades of brown. One entire wall was a vision screen.

Marna ran out of the car. "Mother!" she shouted. "Grandmother!" She raced through the apartment. Harry followed her more slowly.

There were six bedrooms opening off a long hall. At the end of it was a nursery. On the other side of the living room were a dining room and a kitchen. Every room had a wall-wide vision screen. Every room was empty.

"Mother?" Marna said again.

The dining-room screen flickered. Across the huge screen flowed the giant image of a creature who lolled on pneumatic cushions. It was a thing incredibly fat, a sea of flesh rippling and surging. Although it was naked, its sex was a mystery. The breasts were great pillows of fat, but there was a sprinkling of hair between them. Its face, moon though it was, was small on the fantastic body; in it eyes were stuck like raisins.

It drew sustenance out of a tube; then, as it saw them, it pushed the tube away with one balloonlike hand. It giggled; the giggle was godlike.

"Hello, Marna," it said in the mansion's voice. "Looking for somebody? Your mother and your grandmother thwarted me, you know. Sterile creatures! I connected them directly to the blood bank; now there will be no delay about blood—"

"You'll kill them!" Marna gasped.

"Cartwrights? Silly girl! Besides, this is our bridal night, and we would not want them around, would we, Marna?"

Marna shrank back into the living room, but the creature looked at her from that screen, too. It turned its raisin eyes toward Harry. "You are the doctor with the message. Tell me."

Harry frowned. "You—are Governor Weaver?"

"In the flesh, boy." The creature chuckled. It made waves of fat surge across its body and back again.

Harry took a deep breath. "The shipment was hijacked. It will be a week before another shipment is ready."

Weaver frowned and reached a stubby finger toward something beyond the camera's range. "There!" He looked back at Harry and smiled the smile of an idiot. "I just blew up Dean Mock's office. He was inside it at the time. It's justice, though. He's been sneaking shots of elixir for twenty years."

"Elixir? But—!" The information about Mock was too unreal to be meaningful; Harry didn't believe it. It was the mention of elixir that shocked him.

Weaver's mouth made an "O" of sympathy. "I've shocked you. They tell you the elixir has not been synthesized. It was. Some one hundred years ago by a doctor named Russell Pearce. You were planning on synthesizing it, perhaps, and thereby winning yourself immortality as a reward. No—I'm not telepathic. Fifty out of every one hundred doctors dream that dream. I'll tell you, Doctor—I am the electorate. I decide who shall be immortal, and it pleases me to be arbitrary. Gods are always arbitrary. That is what makes them gods. I could give you immortality. I will; I will. Serve me well, Doctor, and when you begin to age, I will make you young again. I could make you dean of the Medical Center. Would you like that?"

Weaver frowned again. "But no—you would sneak elixir, like Mock, and you would not send me the shipment when I need it for my squires." He scratched between his breasts. "What will I do?" He wailed. "The loyal ones are dying off. I can't give them their shots, and then their children are ambushing their parents. Whitey crept up on his father the other day; sold him to a junk collector. Old hands keep young hands away from the fire. But the old ones are dying off, and the young ones don't need the elixir, not yet. They will, though. They'll come to me on their knees, begging, and I'll laugh at them and let them die. That's what gods do, you know."

Weaver scratched his wrist. "You're still shocked about the elixir. You think we should make gallons of it, keep everybody young forever. Now think about it! We know that's absurd, eh? There wouldn't be enough of anything to go around. And what would be the value of immortality if everybody lived forever?" His voice changed suddenly, became businesslike. "Who hijacked the shipment? Was it this man?"

A picture flashed on the lower quarter of the screen.

"Yes," Harry said. His brain was spinning. Illumination and immortality, all in one breath. It was coming too fast. He didn't have time to react.

Weaver rubbed his doughy mouth. "Cartwright! How can he do it?" There was a note of godlike fear in the voice. "To risk—forever. He's mad—that's it, the man is mad. He wants to die." The great mass of flesh shivered; the body rippled. "Let him try me. I'll give him death." He looked at Harry again and scratched his neck. "How did you get here, you four?"

"We walked," Harry said tightly.

"Walked? Fantastic!"

"Ask a motel manager just this side of Kansas City, or a pack of wolves that almost got away with Marna, or a ghoul that paralyzed me. They'll tell you we walked."

Weaver scratched his mountainous belly. "Those wolf packs. They can be a nuisance. They're useful, though. They keep the countryside tidy. But if you were paralyzed, why is it you are here instead of waiting to be put to use on some organ-bank slab?"

"The leech gave me a transfusion from Marna." Too late Harry saw Marna motioning for him to be silent.

Weaver's face clouded. "You've stolen my blood! Now I can't bleed her for a month. I will have to punish you. Not now, but later when I have thought of something fitting the crime."

"A month is too soon," Harry said. "No wonder the girl is pale if you bleed her every month. You'll kill her."

"But she's a Cartwright," Weaver said in astonishment, "and I need the blood."

Harry's lips tightened. He held up the bracelet on his wrist. "The key, sir?"

"Tell me," Weaver said, scratching under one breast, "is Marna fertile?"

"No, sir." Harry looked levelly into the eyes of the Governor of Kansas. "The key?"

"Oh, dear," Weaver said. "I seem to have misplaced it. You'll have to wear the bracelets yet a bit. Well, Marna. We will see how it goes tonight, eh, fertile or no? Find something suitable for a bridal night, will you? And let us not mar the occasion with weeping and moaning and screams of pain. Come reverently and filled with a great joy, as Mary came unto God."

"If I have a child," Marna said, her face white, "it will have to be a virgin birth."

The sea of flesh surged with anger. "Perhaps there will be screams tonight. Yes. Leech! You—the obscenely old person with the boy. You are a healer."

"So I have been called," Pearce whispered.

"They say you work miracles. Well, I have a miracle for you to work." Weaver scratched the back of one hand. "I itch. Doctors have found nothing wrong with me, and they have died. It drives me mad."

"I cure by touch," Pearce said. "Every person cures himself; I only help."

"No man touches me," Weaver said. "You will cure me by tonight. I will not hear of anything else. Otherwise I will be angry with you and the boy. Yes, I will be very angry with the boy if you do not succeed."

"Tonight," Pearce said, "I will work a miracle for you."

Weaver smiled and reached out for a feeding tube. His dark eyes glittered like black marbles in a huge dish of custard. "Tonight, then!" The image vanished from the screen.

"A grub," Harry whispered. "A giant white grub in the heart of a rose. Eating away at it, blind, selfish, and destructive."

"I think of him," Pearce said, "as a fetus who refuses to be born. Safe in the womb, he destroys the mother, not realizing that he is thereby destroying himself." He turned slightly toward Christopher. "There is an eye?"

Christopher looked at the screen. "Every one."

"Bugs."

"All over."

Pearce said, "We will have to take the chance that he will not audit the recordings, or that he can be distracted long enough to do what must be done."

Harry looked at Marna and then at Pearce and Christopher. "What can we do?"

"You're willing?" Marna said. "To give up immortality? To risk everything?"

Harry grimaced. "What would I be losing? A world like this—"

"What is the situation?" Pearce whispered. "Where is Weaver?"

Marna shrugged helplessly. "I don't know. My mother and grandmother never knew. He sends the elevator. There are no stairs, no other exits. And the elevators are controlled from a console beside his bed. There are thousands of switches. They also control the rest of the building, the lights, water, air, heat, and food supplies. He can release toxic or anesthetic gases or flaming gasoline. He can set off charges not only here but in Topeka and Kansas City, or send rockets to attack other areas. There's no way to reach him."

"You will reach him," Pearce whispered.

Marna's eyes lighted up. "If there were some weapon I could take— But there's an inspection in the elevator—magnetic and fluoroscopic detectors."

"Even if you could smuggle in a knife, say," Harry said, frowning, "it would be almost impossible to hit a vital organ. And even though he isn't able to move his body, his arms must be fantastically strong."

"There is, perhaps, one way," Pearce said. "If we can find a piece of paper, Christopher will write it out for you."

The bride waited near the elevator doors. She was dressed in white satin and old lace. The lace was pulled up over the head for a veil. In front of the living-room screen, in a brown velour Grand Rapids overstuffed

chair, sat Pearce. At his feet, leaning against his bony
knee, was Christopher.

The screen flickered, and Weaver was there, grin-
ning his divine-idiot's grin. "You're impatient, Mama.
It pleases me to see you so eager to rush into the arms
of your bridegroom. The wedding carriage arrives."

The doors of the elevator sighed open. The bride
stepped into the car. As the doors began to close,
Pearce got to his feet, pushing Christopher gently to
one side, and said, "You seek immortality, Weaver,
and you think you have found it. But what you have
is only a living death. I am going to show you the only
real immortality. . . ."

The car dropped. It plummeted to the tune of the
wedding march from Lohengrin. Detectors probed at
the bride and found only cloth. The elevator began to
slow. After it came to a full stop, the doors remained
closed for a moment, and then, squeaking, they
opened.

The stench of decay flowed into the car. For a
moment the bride recoiled, and then she stepped forward out of the car. The room had once been a marvelous mechanism: a stainless steel womb. Not much
bigger than the giant pneumatic mattress that occupied the center, the room was completely automatic.
Temperature regulators kept it at blood heat. Food
came directly from the processing rooms through the
tubes without human aid. Sprays had been installed
for water to sweep dirt and refuse to collectors around
the edge of the room that would dispose of it. An overhead spray was to wash the creature who occupied the
mattress. Around the edges of the mattress, like a great
circular organ with ten thousand keys, was a complex
control console. Directly over the mattress, on the
ceiling, was a view screen.

Some years before, apparently, a waterpipe had broken, through some shift in the earth, and a small leak or a hard freeze had made the rock swell. The cleansing sprays no longer worked, and the occupant of the room either was afraid to have intruders trace the trouble, or he no longer cared.

The floor was littered with decaying food, with cans and wrappers, with waste matter. As the bride stepped into the room a multitude of cockroaches scattered. Mice scampered into hiding places.

The bride pulled the long white-satin skirt up above her hips. She unwound a thin, nylon cord from her waist. There was a loop fastened into the end. She shook it out until it hung free.

She had seen that Weaver was watching the overhead screen with almost hypnotic concentration. Pearce was talking. "Aging is not a physical disease; it is mental. The mind grows tired and lets the body die. Only half the Cartwrights' immunity to death lies in their blood; the other half is their unflagging will to live.

"You are one hundred and fifty-three years old. I tended your father, who died before you were born. I gave him, unwittingly, a transfusion of Marshall Cartwright's blood."

Weaver whispered, "But that would make you—" His voice was thin and high; it was not godlike at all. It was ridiculous coming from that vast mass of flesh.

"Almost two hundred years old," Pearce said. His voice was stronger, richer, deeper—no longer a whisper. "Without ever a transfusion of Cartwright blood, ever an injection of the *elixir vitae*. The effective mind can achieve conscious control of the autonomic nervous system, of the very cells that make up the blood stream and the body."

The bride craned her neck to see the screen on the ceiling. Pearce looked odd. He was taller. His legs were straight and muscular. His shoulders were broader. As the bride watched, muscle and flesh and fat built up beneath his skin, firming it, smoothing out wrinkles. The facial bones receded beneath young flesh and skin. Silky white hair thickened and grew darker.

"You wonder why I stayed old," Pearce said, and his voice was resonant and powerful. "It is something one does not use for oneself. It comes through giving, not taking."

His sunken eyelids grew full, paled, opened. And Pearce looked out at Weaver, tall, strong, and straight —no more than thirty, surely. There was power latent in that face—power leashed, under control. Weaver recoiled from it.

Then, onto the screen, walked Marna.

Weaver's eyes bulged. His head swiveled toward the bride. Harry tossed off the veil and swung the looped cord lightly between two fingers. The importance of his next move was terrifying. The first throw had to be accurate, because he might never have a chance for another. His surgeon's fingers were deft, but he had never thrown a lariat. Christopher had described how he should do it, but there had been no chance to practice.

And if he were dragged within reach of those doughy arms! A hug would smother him.

And in that startled moment, Weaver's head lifted with surprise and his hand stabbed toward the console. Harry flipped the cord. The loop dropped over Weaver's head and tightened around his neck.

Quickly Harry wrapped the cord several times around his hand and pulled it tight. Weaver jerked against it, tightening it further. The thin cord disap-

peared into the neck's soft flesh. Weaver's stubby
fingers clawed at it, tearing the skin, as his body
thrashed on the mattress.

He had, Harry thought crazily, an Immortal at the
end of his fishing line—a great white whale struggling
to free itself so that it could live forever, smacking the
pneumatic waves with fierce lunges and savage tugs.
For him it became dreamlike and unreal.

Weaver, by some titanic effort, had turned over. He
had his hands around the cord now. He rose onto soft,
flowing knees and pulled at the cord, dragging Harry
forward toward the mattress. Weaver's eyes were beginning to bulge out of his pudding-face.

Harry dug his heels into the floor. Weaver came
up, like the whale leaping its vast bulk incredibly out
of the water, and stood, shapeless and monstrous, his
face purpling. Then, deep inside, the heart gave up,
and the body sagged. It flowed like a melting wax
image back to the mattress on which it had spent almost three-quarters of a century.

Harry dazedly unwrapped the cord from his hand.
It had cut deep into the skin; blood welled out. He
didn't feel anything as he dropped the cord. He shut
his eyes and shivered.

After a period of time that he never remembered,
he heard someone calling him. "Harry!" It was
Marna's voice. "Are you all right? Harry, please!"

He took a deep breath. "Yes. Yes, I'm all right."

"Go to the console," said the young man who had
been Pearce. "You'll have to find the right controls,
but they should be marked. We've got to release
Marna's mother and grandmother. And then we've got
to get out of here ourselves. Marshall Cartwright is
outside, and I think he's getting impatient."

Harry nodded, but still he waited. It would take a

strong man to go out into a world where immortality was fact rather than a dream. He would have to live with it and its problems. And they would be greater than anything he had imagined.

He moved forward to begin the search.

THE WEARIEST
RIVER

THOMAS N. SCORTIA

I find myself surprised by the thought that dying is an all-right thing to do, but perhaps it should not surprise. It is, after all, the most ancient and fundamental of biologic functions, with its mechanisms worked out with the same attention to detail, the same provision for the advantage of the organism, the same abundance of genetic information for guidance through the stages, that we have long since become accustomed to finding in all the crucial acts of living.

—Lewis Thomas, *The Lives of a Cell* *

Human stupidity is formidable, but not invincible, and sooner or later most of us will set our sights on immortality and transhumanity. . . . Only a few would-be martyrs will insist on their right to rot.

—R. C. W. Ettinger, *Man Into Superman* †

* New York: Viking Press, 1974, p. 51.
† New York: St. Martin's Press, 1972, pp. 226–227.

The dream of immortality has a central place in our myths and legends. It has been seen as a blessing by some and as a curse by others. Seeing clearly that everything sooner or later comes to an end in this world, many people trust in some sort of life after death. Although there is evidence that the actual process of dying involves a feeling of peace and well-being, the thought of one's personal extinction remains a fearful prospect. Old age, once honored in societies where few reached it, and still respected in some, is a state many of us wish to circumvent in a society which emphasizes youth and discards its aged. It is seen only as the prelude to death.

According to some, immortality, or at the very least an extension of the human life span, is possible. Several theories seeking to explain the aging process have been developed. One theory is chemist Johan Bjorksten's "cross-linkage" hypothesis. Bjorksten believes that aging is caused by the formation of bridges between protein molecules which cannot be broken by cell enzymes. This phenomenon is especially noticeable in collagen, the most common form of protein in the body. Another chemist, Denham Harman, has proposed the "free radical" theory, in which unmated atoms or parts of molecules (free radicals) cause destructive chemical reactions in the body. A third theory holds that failure of the body's immune system brings about aging. Other theories range from the notion that certain diets might prolong life to the more likely idea that death is somehow "programmed" into our genes.

In spite of humanity's preoccupation with aging and death, and the fact that dubious therapies such as cellular injection are sought by many, little research has been done in this area until recently. In addition, as Osborn Segerberg, Jr., points out in The Immortality Factor (New York: Dutton, 1974), "little thought has been given to what a world of immortals would be like. There has been no planning on the part of governments, insurance companies, or pension programs for even a modest extension of lifespan."

James Gunn, at the conclusion of his story, regards the prospect of immortality with a bit of hope. Thomas N. Scortia presents an alternately bleak vision of an immortalist world, a story of chilling plausibility rather than of easy pessimism.

. . . old men must die, or the world would grow mouldy, would only breed the past again.

—ALFRED, LORD TENNYSON, Becket

n the middle of the already decaying city, he screamed.

It was a quiet scream, filled with an anguish that spoke of centuries of pain to come. It tore at his throat, ripping its silent pain through his larynx and venting its violence on a frozen air, expending its energy in a terrible internal spasm of sorrow for the thousands of robot creatures about him.

They were human—these creatures in the city—and that was the terrible thing about it. They were flesh and squirming viscera and pulsing blood and lymph and they were totally . . . completely . . . agonizingly unaware of him, of what he had done to them.

Unware that in their newfound centuries of life, they were destroyed—as was he.

He moved through their midst, positioning each foot carefully in front of the other, painfully aware of the effort to coordinate this simple, unelaborated, primitive complex that was his body.

How terrible, he thought, to be trapped forever in this thing with two legs and two arms and quivering gonads and peripheral functional parts that stir like the passing fantasy of fern fronds before the winds of the most casual physical impulse.

How terrible, how terrible, how terrible.

How terrible to be trapped in this body, this husk with fingers that articulate with a clumsy intent, with legs that flex at the slightest effort, with stomach that churns and growls and aches, with head that swivels idiotically on corded neck and eyes that peer and burn and water and blink and see little beyond the images a few feet from them. Forever? Surely not forever?

"Hey man," his mortal friend said. (What was this word "friend"? He wasn't quite sure that it fitted the semantic content of the present situation.) "Hey man, you look spaced out. Real spaced out."

"I am," he said. (Was that his voice? Did it belong to him? Was it a part of his total structure? The resonance, the vibration, the feeling of articulation? Am I what I say—me? Was that Hopkins? No, "What I do is me; for that I came.")

Truth, undying truth . . . "I caught this morning morning's minion, kingdom of daylight's dauphin . . ."

"I am in a bad way," he said slowly. "I am remembering."

"That's a bad scene," his friend said. "Can't have that."

"It's too terrible," he said. "I remember. Oh, God, I remember."

"We gotta fix that. That's the word. Fix and the world fixes you."

True, true, true. Paradissium Ammisam. But who knows what things in the chemical delirium of life may come? It is the end, it is the end.

"I gotta go," he said. It was an intense demand, a full and compelling thing. He shouldn't have had the beer. The beer was all wrong. The beer was yin and not enough yang . . . pang . . . it had invaded his turgid loins to . . .

"Gotta urinate," he said.

"Merry, sir. Drink is the provoker of two things, sir. Urine and lechery, sir. It both giveth the desire and taketh away the ability." That was . . . that was . . . the porter. The mad porter. Macbeth and "Tomorrow, and tomorrow, and tomorrow, Creeps in this petty pace from day to . . ."

"I gotta go," he repeated. "This fragile, clumsy, intangible, awkward, painful, lewd, disorganized body has generated excessive fluid as a part of its purine metabolism and out of all this I must void a certain discrete amount of urea. I did not say uric acid since uric acid is exclusively the end product of the purine metabolism of birds and of the mammals; only the noble Dalmatian—the dog, that is—has uric acid as the end product of its purine metabolism. That, of course, is exactly, precisely the way it should be."

"In the alley, babe. In the alley and we're away like the b. a. bird to the pad, the living machine."

They went and he did and they did.

In the end by devious routes . . . by hyperspace tube?

By walking? By teleportation? By finding the yellow brick road into the center of the simple intricacies of a Klein bottle or perhaps only a prosaic tesseract, they came to the palace, the place, the pit, the pad, where they lived, the non-Policyholders, fleeing from reality.

And Gloria said "Hello" and Glenda said "Hi" and Geraldine said "Far out" and Gervais said "You freaks" and he wondered . . . here is the family and the family is all g, completely g, they glory in g, and the final g is . . . must be God.

"And here's the hepatitis express," somebody named g said and there was a wonder in the constricting live rubber thing on his arm and the bite that pierced the blue veins surrounded with a wealth, a tapestry, a blue-and-black universe of hematomata.

And . . .

And . . .

And . . .

"For a time," he said, "I was possessed by a completely irrational fear."

"It's all right," Gloria said.

That was the way it was in the first century, in the formative century, when he—fabricator of immortality—fled like the rest to an endless fantasy of drugs. For them, it was boredom. For him, the heavy weight of guilt.

Now, two and a half centuries later . . .

Malcolm, who was now nearly three hundred years old and looked—for the evening at least—perhaps forty, sat at the center table in the Meatrack, waiting for his female customer. The small vial containing the single amber capsule of death felt like a pound weight in his pocket. It was one of his few remaining ambers until he could see Nordling again.

Nordling, he thought wearily. Nordling, death's deputy, right hand of the Angel of Death; Nordling, who brewed the one sure exit in this life of pain and endless decay. Malcolm really didn't need Nordling, he told himself. After all, he could make the rather simple polynucleic acid endotoxin himself, but there was still the emotional reluctance to have anything ever to do again with that deadly science of creation. Hence Nordling, and before him what seemed an endless line of suppliers, all dead or immobilized in the Kraals now.

Malcolm had told Bobby, his runner, that he did not like making the contact in such a public place as the Meatrack, but the man had refused to see him elsewhere. He badly needed the money to pay the interest to the barracudas for the money he had borrowed. *Funny*, he thought. *It's the young ones who come to me now.* Well, not so odd actually, when you considered the meaning of life after fifty in this decaying city that existed under the benevolent tyranny of the Company.

He lifted the coffee cup to his lips and sipped cautiously. It was much too hot, as though the waiter thought the temperature might disguise the harsh taste of roasted grain. He sat the cup precisely in its cracked saucer to the left of his plate and stirred it patiently, thinking of Eliot's Prufrock, "I have measured out my life with coffee spoons."

He sighed, remembering when there was a time for poetry and even love in the days before the world had filled with the aged and the fierce young ones treading hotly on their heels, before the drug scene, before the passion of the gorgons. There had been fine dining places in the city—he remembered them from two centuries before—where one might enjoy the pleasurable graces of a culture that still held itself a few footsteps above the survival level. Now . . . ?

> The muttering retreats
> Of restless nights in one-night cheap hotels
> And sawdust restaurants with oyster-smells . . .

Only the smells here were of burned food and the stench of decaying garbage drifting in from the open alley door. He had become obsessed with Prufrock lately. He wondered if anyone else even remembered Eliot's aging drab. Prufrock, he thought, seemed the perfect anthem for the city and the people in it.

He nervously scanned the faces of a new group that entered the curtained door, searching for some sign of recognition on the faces of the women. They were all high on alkaloids, he saw. The Meatrack was one of the few remaining public restaurants in the city and existed perilously by virtue of a platoon of bullyboys who policed the immediate area and warred with the indigenous gangs. The extra expense of protection found its reflection in their prices.

He was contemplating the limp vegesteak on his

plate (fifteen dollars for eight ounces) and idly pawing through the soya gravy when the waiter behind him, obviously high on some psychedelic drug, slipped on a piece of discarded food and dumped a pitcher of precious water on him. Malcolm jumped to his feet, realizing that in seconds he would be compromised.

His make-up ran in an instant. The smooth thirtyish face that he had so carefully built up earlier that evening dissolved in running primary colors and the protein-based tissue firmer lapsed into a semigelatinous liquid that slumped down his cheeks. In an instant, amid the young and not-so-young diners, he dissolved and became what he was, one of the old ones, the hated, feared and loved old ones and . . . worse . . . several youngish people at the near table recognized him.

"Look, look," the girl at the next table said. Her pupils were widely dilated, magnifying her eyes.

"Malcolm," the girl next to her breathed and then squealed a high ecstatic squeal.

The mid-thirties blond man next to her glared and half rose, his biceps in the clinging gauze-thin shirt bulging with the unconscious need to attack.

"It's Malcolm, Malcolm, Malcolm," other female voices around the room breathed and he knew that he had been found out.

He pushed from the chair quickly. He threw a wad of credits onto the table, scarcely noticing the wide contemptuous eyes of his waiter, who had moments before been relatively deferential. Malcolm looked wildly about the dusty dining room, seeing hate-filled male eyes, lust-filled female eyes, dull eyes, abnormally bright eyes. Only one understanding glance met his and he recognized Felice, a dancer at his club, her dirty yellow-white hair framing sagging jowls and a pain-filled expression. The drunken young man with her reached out to touch her liver-spotted hand and she turned away, withdrawing her sympathy from him in the instant. The young man glared at him. Malcolm guessed from his youth that he was not a Policyholder, that he had not yet received the Heinholtz treatment. This, of course, made him very vulnerable and overly cautious in his reactions. Malcolm had little to fear from him.

The waiter snapped, "Take your money, damn it."

Malcolm stared at his six-foot bulky body, with the tight muscles and the first signs of a bulging stomach. The young ones didn't keep themselves in shape anymore. Well, why should they work at it? There were so few of them and little competition. Besides which the standards had changed dramatically in his time so that the lame and the halt and the disfigured became invested with a special beauty all their own.

"Keep it," he said. "You earned it."

"Look, mister," the man said, "get out of here fast. I'll show you the back door. We don't want any more trouble with the constables. We got enough trouble now on the streets."

Malcolm paused to consider his offer. Yes, it would perhaps be better to leave by the rear entrance now that he was unmasked.

"Show me the way," he said tiredly, throwing down his napkin and placing his hand unconsciously on the younger man's arm.

"Don't touch me," the young man said with distaste. "I'm trying to save your life. So don't touch me."

Malcolm followed him to the rear of the small café while the girls ohed and ahed at his shambling figure and the men held themselves in tight reserve. Had he been a woman, he thought, the situation would have been completely reversed. He felt the physical texture of the young men's hate and he thought, *Never mind, in another thirty or fifty years you will join me and the young men who are left will hate you and loathe you and I will be here in the fading vigor of my fourth century to mock you and gloat at how the world has turned and the prince has become the frog.*

Once through the kitchen and into the cloying darkness of the alley, he paused and rested against the decaying brick of the building. The waiter turned in the yellow glow of the doorway and snapped, "Old man, you move on. If you want to get yourself killed, do me the favor of doing it a few blocks from here. You owe me that much."

"Yes," Malcolm said tiredly, "yes, I owe you that much." He started slowly down the alley.

At the opposite end of the alley he heard excited voices and a sudden whooping sound. *Like hounds after the aging stallion,* he thought.

Or wolves.

They thought they had been wolves—Gloria, Gervais, all the rest. Just because they were mortal and did not fear death. Instead they embarked on a kind of spiritual immortality, taunting physical death.

"Have you ever felt that way?" Malcolm asked. "That sense of panic, of complete disorientation?"

"We all get it," Glenda said, embracing him. "I wonder that you don't get it more often." (They didn't know about him, that he did not share their cherished mortality.)

"I don't like it," he said.

"None of us do," Gervais said. He was the big one, the strong one of the family, and even when he wasn't trying to show off, his most casual move brought great biceps bulging against his knit shirt. He was reddish

blond and in the open throat of his shirt a crinkly mass
of red-blond hair writhed on his chest like the snakes
of Medusa's head. His arms were peppered with freckles and freckles spotted the backs of his fingers. He
had a turned-up nose and nostrils wide and flared and
he looked into distances not easily perceived by the
others.

"We are," Gervais said, "an enclave of wolves. In
the midst of the sheep flocking to the Company and
its immortal pablum, we are wolves."

"I have a confession," Malcolm said. "I've run from
it too long and there's no respite in the family. The
weight of guilt is too much."

"You're spaced out," Gervais said. "Why should
you have more guilt than I have guilt or she has guilt?"

"Because," Malcolm said, "I am a stranger and
afraid in a world I surely made."

"I like you," Gloria said. "You're a classicist and
I've always liked classicists. How old are you?"

"Much older than you," Malcolm said.

"How old?"

"A century, at least."

They drew back from him then, the whole family,
and Gervais said, "You didn't tell us."

"I couldn't," he said plaintively.

"You took a policy?" Gloria accused.

"Long ago," he said. "Rather, I wrote the policy."

Glenda said, "That's impossible. Heinholtz wrote
the policy and he gave his formula to the Company
and the Company has come to own the world, but
Heinholtz is dead or worse . . . in the Kraals."

"If it were only true," Malcolm said.

"You can't be that old," Geraldine said.

"I am, I am," he said.

"You sicken me," Gervais said. "We'll all die soon."

"But you won't," Glenda said.

"I've tried to," he said. "I've gone your drug trip and I've swallowed your own private brand of immortality and I've tried."

"But you'll still live," Gervais accused.

"Forgive me, forgive me, forgive me," Malcolm pleaded.

"I sicken unto death at the sight of you," Gervais said, posturing.

Malcolm felt a dull sense of futility. He was getting high again as they all were. It was no use, no possible way of assuaging his guilt for what he had brought on the world.

Outside, the first signs of decay were creeping over the city. The Company existed, the single most potent financial force on the globe, and there was no hope, not so long as humans held to life and other humans disavowed life. It was all a dead end, the people outside embracing the treatment and these poor creatures fleeing into a dream existence in which they fancied themselves wolves among sheep.

Enclave of wolves, he thought bitterly. Everyone knows that on the North American continent wolves are extinct.

A sad good-by to the family of g's, he thought. It was a lost period of his immortal life. But now there were other wolves . . .

Malcolm ran down the alley behind the Meatrack as fast as his tired legs would carry him. If only he could come on a patrol of the Company constables, he thought.

"There he is," a bull voice yelled.

"Get him and let's do him," another yelled, his voice chemically blurred.

He tried to run faster. The alley's mouth was a

thousand miles away and the searing breath was already tearing at his throat. He had been in such situations before and had managed to escape. Thank God, he was not that attenuated. Not like the rank on rank of oldsters in the Kraals on the edge of the city. The endless rows of weak and pulsing oldsters who could not die, who could not be killed. All because of him, that being who was Malcolm in an avatar long ago, before the world had sunk into the corruption of the present, the decay of now.

He broke from the alleyway and looked to the right and left. They would soon be upon him and he had no more strength. (What demands can you make on a body nearly three centuries old? True, he had preserved it in a fashion that the other oldsters without his specialized knowledge had not been able, but it remained a three-century-old body and the end was in sight . . . distant and prolonged but definitely in sight.)

At the alley's entrance, his foot caught in a chuckhole in the macadam and he fell sprawling. His outthrust hand skidded across the gritty pavement, leaving layers of skin behind. He felt the sudden tingling as the friction wound gathered quickly and began to heal. Then the five men tumbled from the alley's mouth and were upon him. He raised his arm to ward off the blows. They would have knives. Everyone had knives, knowing that they would wound and rend and cause pain but would not kill.

The young ones did have knives and they used them. His outstretched hand took one that pierced his palm. Another thrust at his chest and buried itself an inch deep. A third in a grimy hand buried itself in his belly as he screamed with pain. The attack had been silent to this point. His scream alarmed them.

"He'll bring the constables," one yelled. A second aimed a kick at his ribs and he fell back gasping. He heard a distant grinding and suddenly the attack was over.

The twelve-wheeled lorry came from a side street, its hard plastic wheels grinding at the scattered litter of the street. Its multiple red lights plucked at the decaying buildings on either side. They saw him even before he saw them and pulled toward him. *Thank God*, he thought, *constables*.

"Damned old fool," a voice said. "Know better than to come downtown."

A bulky body leaped from the lorry, scattering garbage before a booted foot, and grabbed him. "Inside, gran'pa," the man snorted. "Inside or we'll let them spread your immortal guts over the pavement."

He needed no second urging. He bustled into the lorry and the armored door closed behind him. Seconds later, the lorry turret ground out twenty degrees to face the gang of youngsters.

"Back," an amplified voice said. "The Company is marshaling the block."

"Give us the raunchy bastard," a voice yelled from the group.

"Back," the lorry's amplified voice shouted again. A thick tubular structure emerged from the turret and seconds later the chemical match of the flame thrower ignited. The young men saw the first glow and broke in frantic retreat..

"Thank God," a voice from within the lorry said. "I don't think I can torch another one this evening."

"Mary-waist," another voice snorted in contempt.

The sergeant in charge of the lorry turned to Malcolm. He wore a heavy grenade launcher as a side arm. "How are you, old man?" he demanded.

Malcolm inspected his body. The wound on his hand was now only a faint pink scar. The one in his belly still ached but his exploring fingers told him that it had closed cleanly. The pain was another matter from this and the shattered ribs. It would abate eventually, he knew, but it would probably never completely disappear. For every wound the fast-healing scar tissue developed tiny points of pressure on nerve endings. He could not be wounded or killed but each breach of the quick-healing walls of his body left its legacy of unending dull pain.

The lorry began to move, gaining speed to thirty miles an hour as they threaded their way down the boulevard past the shattered walls of abandoned highrises and piles of debris stacked beside the curb. Of all the streets in the city, the boulevard was still relatively clear.

The constable sergeant took his name and asked his residence. Malcolm attempted to thank him.

"I get paid," the man said in complete disinterest. "Besides, they couldn't have killed you."

"It wouldn't have been worth living afterward if you hadn't arrived in time," Malcolm said.

"But you would have," the man said in complete detachment. Then, "Stay home at night. Don't go out like that. Next time, we may not be able to rescue you."

"All right, all right," he said. "The young ones haven't got me yet."

"How old are you?" the sergeant asked.

"I'm not ready for the Kraals yet," he snapped, knowing full well that many men a hundred years his junior were already a part of that living death.

"You will be," the sergeant said.

"So will you," he snapped irritably.

"I'll take my chance," the sergeant said. "What do you do?"

"Do?"

"For a living."

"I'm an entertainer," he said. "A dancer."

"Oh," the sergeant said, not bothering to hide the distaste in his voice. "One of those."

"One of those," Malcolm said.

They drove him down the dark and dangerous streets to the club in the Village. He checked the time and thought that if he made it through the show, they might be able to get back to their apartment before the barracudas caught him. He had borrowed the money at Britt's insistence. She loved the precious luxuries of this sad world and who was he to deny her? Now the barracudas were pressing him. If he didn't pay up soon, they would certainly take action against him. What action made him shudder. He cursed himself silently for his weakness, his pathetic need to please Britt, who, after all, would be with him regardless of the favors he lavished on her.

At the alleyway entrance to the club, the sergeant said, "You're clear. You can make it."

"Thank you," he said tiredly.

"What do you do there?" the sergeant asked idly.

"As I told you, I dance," he said.

"I just bet you're light as a leaf on your feet," the man said.

"It isn't that kind of dance," he said.

"I didn't think it was," the man said contemptuously.

Malcolm swung heavily from the lorry, dropping the last foot from the steps in false bravado. The shock of alighting twisted his ankle slightly, but he would be damned if he would let the sergeant see it.

"See you sometime," he said mockingly.

"Not bloody likely," the man's voice came to him. The lorry started, spun its wheels and lumbered down the street, leaving him at the head of the alley. He turned and walked into its shadows.

He entered the stage door and moved through the dim lights to his dressing room, pausing to eye the stage. He was surprised to see that Felice was on and he wondered how she had made it back from the Meatrack in time for the performance. He watched her clumsy movements that contrasted so grotesquely with her partner's, a lean young man with jet black hair and stringy young muscles. He was clad only in a ragged loincloth and she wore a musty lion's mane. The act was quite trite, but the sadomasochistic overtones appealed to the young males in the audience.

He looked out over the club floor. The younger men clustered in the rear, most of them unaccompanied. He watched several sprawled out in the dimness, the young thighs jerking nervously to the music. Several of them had their hands thrust deep in their pockets and he could see the cloth that covered their abdomen squirm with the violence of their parallel play. The aphrodisiac smell of amyl nitrite was oppressive.

"The dead are dancing with the dead," he thought wearily and tried to remember where that had come from. Wilde? Yes, Wilde, he thought.

He made his way through the dusty scenery, past tables of empty bottles that exuded a rank odor and to the rear curtained area that was their dressing room. Britt was already there, changing to her costume. It was a wispy thing of green-and-blue gauze with small starfish clustered about the breasts and pubic region. Under the blue and green lights of the floor, the drinkers of the club would get the illusion of garments floating on vagrant ocean currents. Her long blond hair she had carefully matted with spray so that it drifted like a damp halo about her head. She looked up as he entered and her thick sensuous lips parted moistly.

Her eyes were excited, those marvelous blue eyes that seemed to have a separate existence from her superb flawless skin and straw-blond hair.

"What happened?" she asked.

He told her, watching her eyes grow wide with excitement as her small kitten's tongue extended and licked her lips with a sensuousness that still excited him. During their club act, she quite frequently used that gesture, but then it was for effect . . . studied, carefully structured. Now, it was unconscious as she savored vicariously the terrible danger of being maimed and living on, helpless and shattered in body.

He began to change to his costume. It was equally brief, consisting of a loincloth and a pair of sandals over which plastic scales and long talons had been glued to give the appearance of a monster's feet. He divested himself of his clothing and donned the loincloth, the sandals and finally the chilling sea-creature mask that he wore in the act. Britt came over and helped him position the dorsal fin that protruded from between his shoulder blades and ran down to the base of his spine. He stood in front of the mirror. Of course, under the lights the effect was more exotic.

He secured the net and trident from beside the dressing table and turned as one of the lighting men stuck his head through the curtain to yell, "Get a move on. You're up in five minutes."

Britt came over to him and touched his belly where the scars were still an angry red. She leaned forward and kissed each mark, her eyes suddenly intense. He wondered if she had been taking anything. It was very hard to tell and she had promised him that she wouldn't.

When their music started, she left the dressing area while he made the final adjustments to the mask. Then he walked through the cluttered passageway to the curtains that separated the stage from the back. He peered through the slit in a side hanging and noted that the crowd had increased in the last hour. Whereas the front rows had been largely women, the sexes were now equally mixed, although there was some tendency for the older men to sit to the right of the club with their dates while the older women with their young men were to the left. He supposed the maître d' had arranged this to avoid the friction that had marred the performances in the past.

The music started then, an eerie atonal theme of flute, wood winds and a theremin. It had been mechanically synthesized a year before for their act and the tape was beginning to show signs of wear. It remained, nevertheless, a very effective background. He looked out to watch Britt's first sinuous, gliding steps across the small stage, her hair drifting in the cold blue-green light as though she were underwater. She was a sea thing, sinuous and exotic, her breasts rising and falling with the slow exertion of her body. The dance was deliberately sensuous, showing the fine muscular development of her body. Her near nudity was more suggestive than any more bold show of flesh.

He waited until the flute gave a shrill trill and entered from stage right. He was a sea creature himself now, a thing of grotesque lust, twisting through the stage fronds, his stance a clear menace to the more delicate figure of Britt. He made swimming motions toward her, brandishing his trident, as she fell back in mock terror. He was conscious of the clumsiness of his movements, the lack of grace in his aging body. As the audience leaned forward expectantly, he deliberately exaggerated the clumsiness. He threw the net now, tangling her in its coils and she writhed sensuously. In the next instant he had carried her back against a papier-mâché rock and had imprisoned her in the coils of the net.

Now the erotic play began for which the audience had waited. Slowly with the end of the trident he divested her of her gauze costume, stripping it from her in shreds and scattering the concealing starfish to the floor of the stage. In minutes she was pinioned against the rock, completely nude, her body cringing in mock horror. He continued his slow clumsy dance about her, thrusting out with his trident at intervals to draw a tiny patch of blood. With each rivulet of blood, he heard a whispering gasp from the audience. The women were watching him with bright eyes, the men leaning forward. He caught sight of a white young male face with glazed eyes and a tiny tongue wetting white lips as he stepped back to eye Britt's blood-dotted figure. *Ah*, he thought, *Medusa and the other Gorgons—I am one with you all.*

He was preparing for the final thrust of the trident. To this point the blood had been very real, but secreted in a taped pocket under one arm Britt carried a vial of thick red dye for this final movement. As he drew back for the mock thrust that would penetrate the plastic vial, the feverish young man jumped to his feet and yelled, "Make it real; make it real!" Before Malcolm could recover, the young man had leaped to the low stage and was trying to wrest the trident from him. Club security guards ran from either side for the stage but the whole audience seemed to dissolve suddenly into groups of struggling people.

Malcolm fell back from the young man and aimed a heavy kick at him. The man shrugged it off. He was a Policyholder, Malcolm realized, and almost invulnerable. Any assault—no matter how lethal—would incapacitate him only for minutes during the nervous spasm of regeneration. The security men saw this and fell on him with the electrostingers that they carried in their belts. He writhed under the spasms from the stingers and fell to the stage as Malcolm ran to Britt and freed her from the clinging net. Her eyes were wild and excited at the turmoil over the footlights.

"Let's get out of here before the constables come," he shouted and forced her backstage. The noise of the conflict faded behind the heavy curtains. He forced her into a robe and found a shirt and pantaloons for himself. Once out into the street, he dragged her into a stumbling run. They reached the head of the alley as the lorries loaded with constables approached down the main street.

The seven blocks to their tiny apartment was a time of continuing panic for Malcolm. Had they come upon a street gang, he would not have known what to do. She was so vulnerable, he thought, in her young mortality and so enthralled with the thought of violence.

At the door, he whistled the combination that activated the lock and propelled her inward. She sprawled on the bed while he found quick-healing unguent and touched the wounds his trident had left. They healed quickly as he watched.

She sighed and said, "Take off your clothes."

He eyed her tired flesh and removed his shirt and her eyes brightened. He finished undressing and stood nude before her, his belly drooping with the corduroyed ridges of expansion marks where he had gained and lost weight again and again. His legs were intricate laceries of blue and red capillaries slashed by scars. The flesh of the calves sagged while the heavy muscles of the thighs bulged through the thin skin in stringy masculinity. His chest remained remarkably firm although the nipples had expanded and the fatty deposits about the pectorals were sagging. The scar tissue on his belly was still an angry red mass.

She groaned when she saw his body and threw the robe from herself, positioning herself on the bed, arms and legs akimbo. He thought, *Oh, please, do I have to go through this insane charade?* Only, this was what she wanted, and he was much too old and too tired and too corrupt to argue against it.

In the cupboard he found the ropes and tied her arms to each end of the headboard, feet spread-eagled each to the foot of the bed.

"Make love to me, Mal, Mal, please, baby," she breathed. He found the belt, old and supple black leather, massaged to the delicacy of human skin by a hundred oily hands, and doubled it in his fist as she squirmed below him. He raised his arm and the black thing struck out like a snake. The soft smack of leather against skin was almost a caress. She squirmed in ecstasy as he brought it down again and again. Red welts appeared on her back. Not raw welts but light ones that would fade with the morning. He growled at her because she wanted him to do so.

Then he made love to her, violating her as she squirmed and struggled and climaxed again and again. Later they lay silently in an embrace that was the nearest they ever got to tenderness.

"I wish . . ." she said dreamily.

"Wish what?" he asked.

"I wish you were . . . well . . . different."

"Different?" he asked, knowing well what she meant.

"I mean, not so perfect," she said. "You know, except for age, you're too perfect. I remember Martin. His face was badly burned, the whole side twisted up so that he couldn't smile. There was something so beautiful, so exciting about his face."

"I'm sorry," he said.

"No matter," she said dreamily. "But it would be nice . . . you know, if maybe you had lost an arm or maybe been badly scarred tonight. Oh, I don't know."

"I'm sorry," he said again, beginning to drift off to sleep.

"It's all right; it's all right," she said dreamily. "I still love you." After a long moment, she said, "It's a long time ahead. Maybe something will happen."

"Maybe," he said tiredly as her hand dreamily massaged the decayed mass of flesh about his biceps.

He lay with her breathing heavily in his arms and thought that he would have to find some other way of getting money soon. Customers were hard to contact for the amber capsules. Besides, he thought, there were few enough of the capsules left . . . the one he always carried hidden in his boot heel against the time he might be too badly maimed, the one he kept here in the room and the box of perhaps five he had cached in the cellar of the club where they worked. It was only a matter of time before the Company finally caught up with Nordling, he supposed. That ancient decrepit could barely function now and he took useless chances.

God, he thought, how many had there been before Nordling? He had known them all, helped them begin their operations to synthesize the deadly toxin, the only material that could bring death to a Policyholder. One by one they had been caught and sent to the Kraals' living death. Eventually, Malcolm thought, he too would be caught and there would no longer be any release from the Heinholtz treatment. He would lie in the Kraals as the world decayed, and the Company, mindless in its corporate need to hold power, would flicker out with the world, like some smoky candle guttering in the wind.

Yes, it was inevitable that the Company would find Nordling someday. At the moment he was merely a thorn in its corporate hide, certainly not a major force menacing it. His operations were too restricted, too limited in the number of people he might affect. He had encountered increasing difficulty in getting the raw materials for the synthesis and his production had dropped alarmingly in the last two months. Besides Malcolm there were perhaps a dozen pushers in the city who depended on him and their supply of the amber capsules had become very limited recently, driving the price up severalfold. It was just as well, he thought. With the increasing pressure of the barracudas on him, he needed every extra dollar he could marshal.

Still, he thought dreamily, he would always keep the two capsules in reserve. One for him—he shook his head sadly on the pillow—one for Britt if indeed she should decide to take a policy with the Company. He had tried to talk her out of it, but it seemed certain that she would do it eventually as she neared her traumatic thirtieth birthday. Then, of course, she would eventually want one of the ambers, and no matter how badly now he needed money, he would always keep one in reserve for her.

He drifted into sleep, his mind's eye imaging that

last moment when she too would join him in that death that was denied to all of the oldsters. It would be a tragically beautiful thing, he thought. Exciting in its own way. A part of him twisted at the thought and at the physical evidence of excitement it evoked from his sagging body. Still—he licked his lips dreamily— still it would be an experience the likes of which they had never shared in their childish games of ropes and belts. All of that, he thought, was a mimicking of the pain of death prompted by fear. Fear of death. Well, he remembered that emotion very well . . .

In the beginning his sole motivation was fear. How do you characterize the fear of living? You look at your body and you see it mature, lengthen its bones, grow full and mature, see groin hair form with puberty, the growth of genitals and with them desire, and having reached this point of full and complete development . . .

You feel that you are growing old.

What a terrible, frightening feeling at eighteen to see the inevitable touch of death on your body. For Malcolm the fear of death came very early, much too early, neurotically and compulsively early. Which was why his whole life became deformed. He knew before he went to college what he must do. The state of biochemical and particularly molecular biological knowledge had reached the point where one might conceivably do something about this inevitable death sentence.

So he studied. He raced quickly through his undergraduate work in barely more than two years and entered graduate school, impatient, filled with the need to know, to garner information, to fit all the bits and pieces together, to find the ultimate answer to this terrible compulsion that obsessed him.

After his Ph.D. (that robot period when he

crammed knowledge into his head and recited it back like some giant white-skinned parrot, while he pursued his carefully directed doctoral research) he was free at last, free to do what he wished. Provided, of course, he could find the funding. Well, there was funding, a mass of funding from the pharmaceutical companies that at that moment were swallowing Ph.D.'s like the whale swallowing Jonah. Brakeley Pharmaceuticals (famous for Argomycin) swallowed him but fortunately he found himself in the right compartment of that multiple stomach. They were working on synthetic viruses in the laboratory in Brooklyn where he found himself. Imagine a pharmaceutical company, devoted to fun and profit (oh, yes, very much for profit), manufacturing viruses. Well, of course, it makes sense if one considers that viruses are potential information carriers, as are RNA and DNA. A suitably tailored virus may take its place as a part of the genetic chain, indistinguishable from the natural nucleic acid chain, if one could suppress the naturally generated control factors.

They had the idea of using an artificial virus to counter the natural virus that everyone now knew caused all of the varieties of cancer. The cancer virus was endemic to the cell from birth, suppressed by factors in the body until failure occurred and the virus entered the cell's reproductive mechanism. After this point the cell ceased to follow the ordained plan and grew cancerous. The plan was to balance the natural virus with a tailored one that would unite in the cell with the natural genetic material and cancel out the cancer virus.

Clever. It gave him the chance he needed, the tools he needed. He became interested rather in a virus that would carry the genetic pattern for instant renewal of tissues, for selective acceleration of metabolism, for the removal of all the degenerative processes that collectively spelled old age.

He succeeded. How well he succeeded was truly astonishing. The laboratory animals did not age at first. More . . . they could not be killed. They repaired themselves at a fantastic rate. They were immortal. The Company brass came down from the glass tower in which they lived and marveled at what he had wrought.

It turned out that Brakeley was part of a conglomerate that had been assembled by a manufacturer of industrial cleaning compounds. More, the major stockholders of the parent corporation were also members of the board of a major insurance company in Connecticut. There was a subtle shift in financial alignment. The parent company divested itself of Brakeley by a complicated exchange of paper (completely and piously approved by the SEC) and Brakeley became a part of the Company, the Universal Surety Company.

He was baffled at these maneuvers. He wanted only to pursue the thing he had made. By now the problem had become apparent to him, though not to the enthusiastic corporate officers. (If they recognized the problem, they chose to ignore it in the sugar-plum visions of profit and power.) Still, the laboratory animals—the rats, hamsters, rhesus monkeys—were truly immortal or at least capable of life-spans many multiples of the ordinary. Only, after a stasis period, they didn't stop aging. They aged and they aged and they aged, growing more decrepit, more burdened with the accrued wounds of living, less agile, more needing of attention, but still living. Always living.

Which mattered not a damn to the Company. There was a new type of life insurance. It took time for all the states to approve it. Arkansas was the first.

Then Washington. Surprisingly, California (the center of the national youth cult) was next to last. By this time foreign subsidiaries were busy with the new technique. Pay your monthly premium or sign over a certain percentage of your present and future resources—become a Policyholder (now it was always capitalized)—and life perpetual or at least very much extended became yours.

Malcolm wondered and marveled and feared at this. Surely, there was someone at the top who could see the danger, the terrible danger of this burgeoning policy. But no corporation is ruled by a single man. There is no continuity of personal power even in a near-immortal corporation. One director gave way to another and always there was a board to answer to, innumerable anonymous stockholders to placate, the various autonomous governments whose economies became increasingly immersed in the workings of the Company. Like Juggernaut, the whole process rolled, accelerated and could not be stopped by men of good or ill will.

In due course the Company dominated the world . . . and stagnated it with a vast population of near-immortal but constantly aging men. No one knew how to stop the complex economic machinery that had been started. There was finally an immortal Director and Malcolm took the new toxin to him.

"This is how we end life," he said sadly, tiredly.

"Who are you?" the Director demanded.

"I'm the one who gave you the treatment," Malcolm said.

The Director sneered. "Something as world-shaping as this the product of a single man? Don't be silly. No one man could conceive of the Heinholtz principle and carry it to completion."

"I did," Malcolm challenged.

"Please don't waste my time. I'm very busy," the Director said. "Besides, who wants a toxin that kills when we have eternal life?"

They ushered him out and that day he left the elaborate quarters in Brooklyn that his status in the Company gave him. He left and disappeared and gave up all that he had ever wanted. For a long time he disappeared in the new drug-drenched subculture, trying to forget, trying to drown the sorrows of his aging body (yes, he had been one of the first) in the useless flight from psychological reality.

Eventually he saw that this too was a dead end.

Malcolm was awakened by an insistent pounding on the door. Britt still slept, her body curled into a loose fetal position while her wealth of blond hair sprawled in thick locks over the faintly soiled pillow. He gathered a threadbare seersucker robe about his body and opened the door on its chain. Through the partially open door he recognized Bobby, his runner, fidgeting nervously on the doorstep.

"Sure death," Bobby swore, his teeth chattering against the morning chill. "I ain't gonna stand out here all morning. Why in hell don't you answer your door?"

"I was asleep," Malcolm said irritably.

"Well, I got business for you. Big business."

"How much?"

"Five caps," Bobby said, "and by ten tonight. There's ten thousand total in it."

"Fifteen," Malcolm countered. "You know how short the supply is. I must have that much."

"Twelve," Bobby snorted. "That's all my clients say to settle for."

Malcolm thought. With the barracudas pressing him on the loan interest he'd have to settle for that he decided. "Twelve it is," he agreed finally, "but not the Meatrack again. Say back of the show after the last performance."

Bobby nodded. "I'll be there. Take it easy on the streets this morning. Things are getting tight even this early."

"Thanks," Malcolm said and shut the door. He leaned back against the door and shuddered. He didn't like to get on the streets until afternoon, but he'd have to get to the club and rescue his cache before any of the other personnel showed up. It was bad enough getting to it with only the cleaning women present but later it would be almost impossible. If he could have thought of a better place to hide the capsules, he would have long ago. As it was, the club was about the best place.

As Britt stirred and slowly came awake, he prepared breakfast. He used their last egg with some soya paste and spinach to make an omelet. It was lean enough fare to begin a trying day but until he could get some more money they'd have to make do. The tips at the club had been sparse enough lately and they still had a week to run before payday.

He flipped the omelet expertly with long years of practice, divided it in portions of one-third and two-thirds. The larger portion he carried over to the bed, where Britt was now sitting up, blinking at the light that streamed from the barred window. "Good morning, love," she said between yawns. "Oh, that's nice of you. Only"—she wrinkled her nose—"I'm getting tired of soya omelets."

"There won't be any more for a while," he said. "That was our last egg."

"Oh," she said, looking as if she were about to cry.

"I've got a customer," he said quickly. "Bobby came and they want five caps."

"That's dangerous," she said. "You know how close the constables came the last time you supplied a party. One is bad enough, but a party gets a lot of attention."

"I don't know that it is a party," he said.

"With that many ambers, it's always a party," she said, downing the last of her omelet and making a faint gesture of distaste as she shoved the empty plate across the bed. "Any coffee?"

He shook his head. Her face formed a distinct pout. *Well, hell*, he thought, *what does she expect? I can't keep the place in food when she spends it all on clothes and make-up. Who notices in the dim lights of the club?* But she had to have the best, as though she were under the closest scrutiny.

"We've got some tea," he said. He didn't tell her it was synthetic, hoping that she would not notice. Fortunately she didn't and sat sipping the hot brown liquid as he dressed.

"You're going out?" she asked in sudden alarm.

"To get the caps," he said. "I have to get to the club before the day personnel show up."

"Take care," she said. "If you run into anything, forget the caps and come home."

"We need the money," he said.

The morning sunlight was blinding when he stepped from the apartment onto the street. He looked carefully to the right and left but the alley was deserted. He turned from the alley onto the littered thoroughfare and walked for three blocks before he became aware that the street was peopled largely by oldsters. There were several groups of constables along the way. He wondered what this might signify but he felt relatively safe in such crowds.

He covered the seven blocks to the club in an hour,

pausing periodically to rest. He walked quite regularly, but as he grew older, the fatigue of covering even two blocks weighed heavily on him. At the club, he paused and leaned against the side of the building to get his breath. He was quite unprepared for the appearance of the constable in the door of the club.

"What are you doing here, old man?" the constable demanded.

Malcolm thought of telling him that he worked there, but a sixth sense warned him to be silent. "Resting," he said breathlessly.

"Well, you just move along," the constable said.

He nodded silently and moved away. At the alley, he considered going in the side door, but he saw that there was another constable posted there. His heart sank for a moment. What were they doing? Was it possible . . . ?

"Malcolm, get the hell away from here," a woman's voice said near him. He turned as Felice grabbed his elbow. Her yellowing white hair was badly disarrayed; her bloodshot eyes buried in innumerable folds of flesh were wide and excited. "Them constables is roughing everybody up," she said. "Better get away."

"What's happened?" he demanded.

"They found a bunch of ambers in the basement. One of our people must have hid them there."

"Ambers?" he asked. "Not in the club?"

"Oh, God," she said. "I wished I'd known. What I wouldn't give for just one."

"You don't mean that," he said.

She sighed. "You just don't know how badly I mean it." Her eyes began to mist and in a second she stood blubbering like a small child. "Just that close and I didn't know. I'd never have enough money to buy one and they was that close." She eyed him then with suspicion dawning in her eyes.

He fled, leaving her sobbing like some mechanical doll who had been programmed to endless repetitive sorrow. On the street he was caught up in the flow of traffic. Surprisingly, there were still a large number of oldsters hurrying along and he suddenly realized that a demonstration must be forming. He turned, thinking that he must get away from here. At the opposite end of the street a line of constables was forming, their riot batons linked electrified tip to electrified tip as they moved forward. All of them carried hand-grenade launchers on their belts and several labored under the weight of flame throwers.

He looked to the right and left, hoping somehow that he could evade the cresting flood of humanity. If he could get away, he could still find Nordling. He was only a few blocks away; he never ventured forth now, depending on friends for what food he consumed, living only for the stinking basement under his shack where the filthy glassware sprawled to the ceiling, the Soxhlet extractors gurgling, the calcium-encrusted condenser dripping out its slow amber drops.

The streets were filling rapidly now with the oldsters, many of them lame and hobbling. Most of the men were accompanied by younger women, many of these half supporting their escorts as they converged on the plaza fronting the Company's downtown headquarters. Malcolm could see that another line of constables, armed with grenade launchers and several portable flame throwers, had drawn up in front of the plaza, backed by several armed lorries. The tense group of constables ringed the great obsidian statue in the plaza, its golden-black hands stretching outward over the plaza, cupped to bear the small simulacrum of a limp human form. The Company called it Succor. Malcolm hated its perverse symbolism. Behind the statue two turreted heavy flame throwers crouched menacingly.

Malcolm found himself suddenly halted in a crush of bodies. The square before the plaza was filled with old people, many of them carrying the tattered yellow banners of the Retrenchment Party. They stood silently, waiting. A dreadful menacing silence settled over the plaza.

"Your right to assemble will be protected; now, go home," a voice boomed out from a public-address system. It was the Director's voice. Malcolm had not heard it in years but he recognized it.

Several of the old people hoisted a banner. The wind whopped at it, rippling the words. They shouted: "The World Is Starving. POLICY RETRENCH- MENT NOW!"

"Go home," the Director's voice boomed. "You've had your say. The Company's policies are open to everyone."

A ragged wave of voices flowed from the crowd, old throats crying threats and protest.

"Go home or the constables will take action," the voice shouted.

"Retrenchment now," old voices screamed and withered fists thrust above the crowd like a sudden stand of ancient wheat. The line of constables began to move forward, electrostingers at the ready. From somewhere in the forefront of the crowd a paving brick sailed out and struck one of the constables on the temple. He folded slowly to the pavement. Others were ripping up paving blocks and pieces of macadam. The line of constables faltered before the sudden assault of missiles, then the line hardened and it began to move forward again. Malcolm saw their young eyes, bright and greedy beneath their visors, their faces grimly joyous in anticipation of the attack. Many drew their launchers.

The crowd began to disperse, the old men moving back painfully. How often had he seen this, this silent gathering of misery? The constables began to relax. It was all over, he thought, moving back and trying for a side street that suddenly opened to his left. It was all over, a completely ineffectual, thoroughly futile protest without leaders, without a statement of need. Old men did not make demands, he thought; they merely stood pathetically and waited for someone to succor them.

Pathetic men, he thought. Dead men whose bodies still somehow carried the spastic fire of life. *Like myself,* he thought.

"I am *Lazarus, come from the dead,*" he thought. "*Come back to tell you all, I shall tell you all.*" *I am Lazarus and Prufrock,* his mind said, *and Joseph of Arimathea and the ghost of Caligula and Alastair Crowley, clutching decay to my breast saying, "Look what I have wrought."*

He started to move away, conscious of the black mood of defeat settling over the old men. The first hint of trouble yet to come was a distant murmur that grew louder. He turned to see a crowd of young men spilling into the plaza, their eyes bright with hatred. *Oh, God,* he thought, *I've got to get away from here.*

Too late. The young men converged on the crowd of dispersing oldsters. He heard shouts of "Parasites" and "Leeches" as the two forces converged. In an insane corner of his eye, he saw the constables drawing back. Their faces glowed with anticipation; their eyes were bright with the anticipation of the conflict. He heard the *pop* of a chemical match and knew someone had armed a flame thrower.

Malcolm knew he had to get away. The only channel of escape was the edge of the plaza but this would bring him close to the outer ranks of the constables. He paused in indecision and then decided that he would have to risk it. From the far side of the crowd he heard shouts of rage and cries of pain and he knew that the two mobs had joined in combat. Frustrating, useless carnage but he could not get involved. He began to sprint along the edge of the crowd, his ancient heart laboring with the exertion.

He was abreast of the constables now, passing around their ranks. "You, stop," an officer yelled and he realized that he had been seen. He tried to increase his speed but the young officer almost contemptuously caught up with him and in an instant grabbed him, pinioning his arms to his side.

"Damn, I told you to halt," the officer said and then yelled, "Sergeant, take care of this man."

A constable sergeant ran from the rear ranks and the officer released him as the sergeant menaced him with his electrostinger. He heard screams as the constables opened fire on the mob with launchers. Again and again he heard the whoosh of flame throwers. Over all this came wave on wave of anguished screaming.

"I haven't done anything," Malcolm whined. He tried to appear weak and ineffectual but a part of him was surprised to discover that his cringing stance was not completely an act. He was frightened and the potent muscularity of the sergeant intimidated him.

"Brace," the sergeant said and began to search him. He suddenly remembered that he could not be searched. The man's hands drifted over his body and he bolted, hoping for one insane instant that he might escape. The man launched himself in a low tackle and brought Malcolm to the ground. The impact drove the breath from his body. Hands pulled at his clothing, turning out his pockets, and then the sergeant had the plastic box that he still carried, the box that contained the amber capsule for his client. He shuddered, hoping that the man would not find the one secreted in the hollow heel of his boot.

The man had found what he wanted, however. He shouted and the officer hurried over. "An amber." The officer laughed. "That means a leave for both of us, catching a pusher." He slapped the sergeant on the back and then self-consciously recovered his dignity.

"I'm not a pusher," Malcolm protested.

"Where did you get the amber?" the officer demanded.

"I stole it," Malcolm answered. "One of the men in the crowd dropped it. I picked it up and ran."

"Frankly, old man, I don't believe you," the officer said. "We'll see if the colonel does." He addressed the sergeant, "Take him along."

The sergeant pinioned Malcolm's arms behind him and half dragged him, skirting the strife-torn plaza, to a small compound where there were already several prisoners. Malcolm was thrust behind a fenced and guarded wire barricade that had been thrown up in the last hour. From there he could see the final scenes of the battle between the youngsters and the old men. The constables were breaking it up now and the plaza was dotted with writhing bodies of young and old men, many of them horribly burned in the cross fire from several turreted flame throwers. Some of the bodies were still and he realized that part of the attacking force had been young men who were not Policyholders. Strange that they would risk their lives in such a senseless fight. He could understand the motivation of the young Policyholders. There were few enough resources left in the world with the work force so diminished and the oldsters represented a large unproductive segment. Better in their eyes to carry them all off to the Kraals, where at least in their suspended existence their consumption would be reduced to a minimum.

Guards came now and began to remove prisoners one by one for disposition. He waited his turn impatiently, wondering what would happen. Would they banish him to the Kraals or simply impose a lien on his basic ration? God knows, it was hard enough to exist in this decaying mass of stone and brick that had once been a city but he could survive that with the help of Britt.

When the guard came to the gate and beckoned for him, he came forward hesitantly. He was led through the wire and down a line of constables, now at ease and relaxing, to a camp table where a man with eagles on his fatigue jacket looked soberly at him. "The lieutenant says you're a pusher," the colonel said tiredly.

Malcolm repeated his story. The colonel looked at him as if he didn't exist. Then he leafed through the forged identification papers the lieutenant had taken from Malcolm. "No previous record," the colonel said. "What the hell made you steal this?"

"Wouldn't you have done the same thing?" Malcolm demanded tiredly.

The colonel pursed his lips. "I'm not that old, old man."

"You will be someday," Malcolm said.

The colonel held a whispered conversation with the lieutenant. Finally he looked up and said, "We've had enough trouble today. Your record is clean. I'll make an entry and let you go. The next time you'll be in serious trouble."

"Thank you," Malcolm said. The colonel said nothing.

The lieutenant detailed a man to take him back through the ranks of constables and on the edge of the plaza the man released him. Malcolm sighed, realizing that he had somehow escaped. The forged papers still held up. Well, they had been done by an expert many years ago, just after his surgery, and he had been sure that they would pass. The possession of the amber was another matter and the colonel was too tired of the whole mess apparently to pursue that. He felt a vague unease at how easily he had escaped but he turned and retraced his earlier steps. He still had to see Nordling. Without the money from the order Bobby had brought, he thought fearfully, he would be unable to meet his weekly payments to the barracudas.

It was over a mile to Nordling's house, a decaying brick shack that opened on a street whose walks were piled high with festering garbage. He climbed the splintered steps that popped and creaked under his weight. They had long ago lost any trace of the paint that once protected them and each step Malcolm took caused a cloud of dust and wood powder to puff from the joints of the steps. He tapped the coded tap and saw Nordling's withered hand pull aside a rain-streaked piece of canvas to look out. When Nordling recognized him, he pulled the door half open and spoke. "Inside, inside, don't camp out there. You know how dangerous the streets are."

He led Malcolm through a dank-smelling hall, half denuded of plaster. The walls canted at a distinct angle as though part of the foundation had collapsed. At the head of the basement stairs, Nordling paused and shivered. "I had three young'uns break in last night. Thank God, the locks on the basement are good."

"I need five caps," Malcolm said impatiently.

"I just let you have five a week ago," Nordling whined. "What happened to them?" Malcolm told him. Nordling led the way down the stairs to the basement. He adjusted a mantle light and Malcolm looked around. The place was webbed with cobwebs except for the area where Nordling had set up the apparatus. Malcolm noted the arrangement of glassware —the molecular still, with its rusty vacuum pump; the Soxhlet extractor near at hand, its flash filled with bubbling green-stained ether; the three-necked reactor that produced the final amber material that went into the molecular still. This last step was necessary since secondary contaminants from the reaction canceled the effectiveness of the primary toxin.

"I've got to have the caps," Malcolm insisted.

"Well, if it was anybody but you..." Nordling sniffed. "The danger of getting the materials, not to mention the cost..."

"You've always gotten your money," Malcolm said. "Besides, who set you up in the business to start with?"

"You had your reasons," Nordling said. "Only what if the constables ever—"

"The worst they would do would be to put you in the Kraals and you've been expecting that for years."

"Would too, if it wasn't for the special formula," Nordling said.

"Well, that's payment enough," Malcolm said.

"Sometimes I wish the hell I'd never met you," Nordling said.

"You'd have been in the Kraals long ago if you hadn't," Malcolm said.

Nordling sorted through the contents of a drawer in the rickety table under the still. "Here," he said.

"I've got just five. You'll take all I've got and I bet you didn't bring any money."

Malcolm took the five amber capsules. "You'll get your money," he said. Nordling smiled sourly. "I'll see you to the door," he said.

They ascended the steps from the basement to the hall. Malcolm pushed open the door and stopped. Before he could pull back, the door flew against the wall and a large hand grabbed at him. Behind him, Nordling cried out a high, womanish cry. The hall was filled with constables and the hand that grabbed at Malcolm belonged to the sergeant who had seized him earlier in the day. Felice was with them, screaming, "See, see, I told you he was the one. I followed him. He's the one."

Behind the sergeant, the lieutenant grinned knowingly. "We thought you'd lead us to the supplier," the lieutenant said. "Like a damn fool, you came right to him."

They took them back to the aluminum-and-glass headquarters of the Company, past the torn and blasted plaza where scavengers were still gathering the wounded and the dead. In the subbasements where prisoners were held and interrogated they made both of them strip to their shorts and they were separated. Malcolm found himself imprisoned in a narrow cell with white poured-concrete walls. It was without windows and a merciless white fluorescent light beat down on him, prying its way under his eyes when he lay on the cot suspended from the wall and tried to sleep.

He lost track of time. He might have been there hours or days. He knew only that he was cold and that the single fragile coverlet was insufficient to stop his shivering. Part of the shivering, of course, was reaction. He felt a dull dread oppressing his mind and he knew that it was only a matter of time before they would come for him. He had heard the stories of Company interrogations. In a world where physical damage to the body was repaired in minutes, there was no particular moral onus to torture and the Company had, he heard, developed some very refined ways of handling those from whom it would extract information.

He hoped that they would consider him small fry. Nordling was quite another matter and he imagined that they would expend their best efforts on him. Nordling was not a strong man. It was, therefore, inevitable that he would compromise Malcolm. When they came finally for him, Malcolm supposed that they would have the whole story. They could not afford to release him and he was sure that the Kraals were not for him.

He thought of the alternatives and realized that only his death would satisfy them. So be it. In this terrible world of which he was a part, in which he had played too much of a formative role, it was just as well. He knew now at long last that he would welcome the end of consciousness. Indeed, he should have chosen that way long ago. Now that they had the amber secreted in his boot and he was unable to get to the one in his and Britt's apartment, he was wholly dependent on them. They would give him what he wanted.

He was dozing uneasily when they finally came for him.

The lieutenant and the sergeant lifted him from the bunk and dragged him unprotesting along the sterile corridors to a large room. The colonel sat at a table at one end of the room looking stern and just. They threw him to the floor before the colonel and he raised himself and looked around. When he saw what was affixed to the wall, he retched, shuddering in fear and horror.

It was Nordling, of course. They had been very imaginative with him. Since any physical damage to a man who had received the Heinholtz treatment was quickly repaired, they had found a unique solution.

They had flayed Nordling alive.

They had carefully incised the flesh of his arms and thighs and abdomen and pinned the flesh back with heavy pins to the wall so that the flesh could not close with the tissue underneath. Nordling was pinned like an insect to a drying board, the raw tissue and musculature of his body red and oozing. He lived still and would continue to live but his flesh must be a burning agony.

"Why don't you kill him?" Malcolm demanded.

"No," the colonel said. "We will release him in due course and he will heal."

"Why, why?" Malcolm said.

"Because he had information. He was incapable of developing the process for the toxin in the ambers. No more than the others we have captured. We had to know where he learned the technique."

"Did the others tell you?" Malcolm challenged.

"No," the colonel admitted. "They did not know enough, but Nordling did. He has told us all we want to know."

Malcolm slumped in defeat. Finally he looked up and said, "Take me to the Director."

"The Director knows you are here," the colonel said. "He does not wish to see you. He has given us his orders."

Malcolm began to sob quietly. "To think," he said, "to think that I created all this."

"I don't understand why you should have decided to renounce your identity, to hide and live the way you have done."

"Don't you see the horror?" Malcolm said. "Can't you see why I would be ashamed, feel guilty?"

"You?" the colonel said. "Heinholtz? The man who gave us the treatment, on whose efforts the very existence of the Company is based?"

"There was a time when I wanted that recognition," Malcolm said, "and I couldn't get it."

"But guilt?" the colonel said. "That's a stupid word."

The most terrible invention of Western society, Malcolm thought, is guilt. No Easterner understands the term in the terrible, personal, God-related sense that a Westerner does. He remained afflicted with guilt.

Guilt for what he had done. Guilt for the pride in what he had done.

For in the center of world decay, the final destruction of all that was good and kind and gentle and beautiful in a world webbed with the cobwebs of neglect, what man cannot perversely glory in the knowledge that he had brought the proud race of man to this impasse?

The end objective of power is power. Orwell had said that. The end objective of destruction is destruction; the end objective of decay is decay. It was so simple, so obvious, so terribly real.

And he had brought it to pass. Innocently, naïvely, he had brought it to pass. He had moved among the tattered remnants of his culture and a part of him perversely gloried in what his ego had wrought. Surely, he thought, they will remember that I have passed this way.

Only he remained and remained and remained. He

lived a dozen lives, watched the subtle intrusion of new mores, new needs in the culture that became fragmented between the naturally aging and the aging deathless beings he had created. He watched the ones too debilitated to care for themselves taken off to the Kraals, where they were sustained, washed, urinated, defecated, swabbed and allowed to live and live and live. He watched these and saw the terrible economic drain on the faltering society. Surely, it would be simpler to kill them or let them somehow die. Only power had bred power and the Company was a mindless thing that had tasted power and thirsted for power and would not let power go. There was no end, only the continuing pattern of desperate people paying for life and the Company existing, nurturing, faltering, watching the slow, inevitable decline simply because no one had the power or the inclination to cry "Halt."

In the end he began again to make the toxin. Later he taught others. Someone had to cry "Halt," he decided. Only by this time the cries of "Halt" were feeble and hardly effective.

There was only one way that the machine could run down and he saw that within his lifetime it would. After that, there was little left that even he, perverse and involved as his emotional processes had become, could be proud of.

How to be proud of the slow destruction of a culture?

He recalled the character in a mid-twentieth-century novel—Priam Kurz, he thought—who in one scene broke a rare Han vase, proclaiming that the power of the destroyer was equal to the power of the creator. A wretched, twisted notion. Only, his secret mind whispered, perhaps it was true.

In his own unique way he continued to be a destroyer. Though one cannot truly be said to be a destroyer when what one destroys is destruction itself.

Only it was over now. They had twisted the last truth from Nordling in his agony and . . .

"I'm sorry, Malcolm," Nordling sobbed from his wall of pain. "I tried. I had to tell them."

"It doesn't matter," Malcolm said tiredly. "What will you do now?"

"The Director has ordered that we take you to the Kraals," the colonel said.

"Very well," Malcolm said.

The lieutenant helped him to his feet. The sergeant handed him his clothing and he donned it slowly, painfully. He turned to look at Nordling. Mercifully, he had fainted. "Take him down from there," Malcolm said.

"In due time," the colonel said with no particular interest.

They left the subbasement, the lieutenant leading the way up the dank concrete corridors to the first floor. They took a side entrance and skirted the plaza. Its broad expanse was now mercifully free of the wounded and the dead, but the dirty black slick from the flame throwers stained the plaza and the turrets with the flame throwers were still manned.

At the edge of the plaza a single vehicle waited for them. The sergeant straddled the driver's mount, hand on tiller, and the lieutenant grabbed Malcolm by the loose cloth of his sleeve. "Come on, old man," the lieutenant said. "We've had about enough of you."

Malcolm shivered. After this only the Kraals, the endless imprisonment in a coffinlike cell with liquid nutriments pumping food and oxygen through his dreamless body. Total dreaded immobilization forevermore without even the salve of unconsciousness.

He had sworn this would never happen to him, that the single amber he carried with him would give him the release from this nightmare. If only he could get to the one hidden in the apartment. It was the only way.

He whirled in the last second with all of the energy he could marshal from his aged body. His hand darted out and pulled the lieutenant's launcher from its holster. If the lieutenant had not been so careless he could not have done it. Malcolm fell back, the launcher raised. The projectile blew a hole in the sergeant's chest and he fell over the tiller, his body convulsing with the nervous discharge of healing. In ten minutes he would be whole and . . .

The lieutenant fell back, fear distorting his face. Malcolm fired, and in the instant he fired, he suddenly knew why the lieutenant was so afraid. The projectile shattered his body and blood spurted from a dozen wounds as the man died. He was not a Policyholder, Malcolm saw. He had killed the man and he would not rise again.

Constables were yelling and running toward him. He had to get away. He pushed the convulsing body of the sergeant from the saddle and mounted. A projectile struck his shoulder, the explosion shattering it. Somehow he managed to start the motor and throw it on automatic as another projectile nearly tore off his leg. The carrier was roaring across the plaza now and heading into a side street. In the last instant one of the flame-thrower crews managed to get its turret turned in his direction and a great rolling ball of flame marched smokily down the street. It engulfed the carrier and Malcolm screamed in the searing agony. Somehow, miraculously, the carrier kept moving swiftly up the street.

The carrier ran for several blocks before it struck

the pile of debris where an ancient stone-and-concrete curtain wall had slid from the face of its parent building. He was dimly, painfully aware of the carrier tipping wildly, of his body flying out and over the pile of debris. He struck the ground and his impact dislodged the pile of stone poised precariously over a deep trench. All light faded as he was buried under the rubble.

He lay for hours under the debris, hearing the sound of shouting men and the roar of searching lorries. Somehow, no one thought to investigate the pile of rubble. Several constables mounted the pile and looked about but no one thought to look underneath. He lay, burning, feeling the agony in his body as it slowly healed. It healed so much more slowly than ever before because the damage had been so widespread. After darkness fell and light between the interstices of the stone had faded, he knew that he was well again.

He tried to wiggle under the debris and heard the rattle of brick fragments striking the pavement. He must get back to Britt. They would be searching for him and he must get to the amber before they found him. He might escape with her, hide and start another synthetic existence, but he was too tired. He would rather escape by the only sure path available to him.

He tried again and heard the sliding sound of debris. Suddenly an arm was free and painfully he found purchase and pulled his torso free. Now he could move bricks and stone and mortar fragments with his horribly scarred hands. It took him another fifteen minutes of panting effort to free his legs, the right and the horribly twisted left. Charred clothing fell away from his body as he moved.

He stumbled down the alley. The flesh of his face was puckered and scales of dead skin fell away as he

wiped his hands across his eyes. Somehow he identi-
fied the intersection leading to the apartment and
turned, falling back against a wall as a patrol of two
constables passed.

He moved painfully toward the alleyway and stood
finally before his door, praying that Britt was not
home. He didn't want her to see him this way. He
keyed the door and stepped over the sill, pushing the
heavy drapes aside. Then he leaned back against the
wall and sighed. She wasn't there. He stumbled across
the room and pawed through the clothing in the bottom drawer of his bureau. The small plastic box with
its single amber capsule was there where he had left
it, tucked deep into the sleeve of a shirt.

He whirled as the door opened behind him. She
came in as he feverishly pried open the box and picked
at the capsule in its bed of cotton. His fingers were
puckering with new scar tissue and in his clumsiness
he dropped the capsule. It fell to the carpet as Britt
pushed through the canvas curtains and saw him.

"Oh, Mal," she cried and ran across the room to
him. He was struggling with his hand but the muscles
would not obey. Finally he managed to pick up the
capsule with his other hand.

"No, don't," she yelled, and before he could move,
she was beside him, prying open his fingers. The capsule dropped into her small hand. "No, not that way,"
she cried. "I know what happened. We can get away,
buy new papers. They'll never find you."

She rose and ran across the room to the curtained
commode. Before he could stop her the amber disappeared in a vortex of water.

She was back beside him now, her hands caressing
his body, pulling his remaining clothing from him.
"I love you," she sobbed. "I love you."

She pulled him to the bed, heedless of the litter of

costumes sprawled across it. She was in his arms, kissing his body, caressing him. His eyes saw the gauze and the sea things littering the bed and the monstrous sea-creature mask at one corner.

They were making love then as his inner voice insanely chanted the lines from *Prufrock*:

> We have lingered in the chambers of the sea
> By sea-girls wreathed with seaweed red and brown
> Till human voices wake us and we drown.

The only human voice in the room was hers, muttering with building passion as she kissed his shattered limbs, his hideously scarred face, the terrible warped substance that was his flesh.

"You're so beautiful," she sobbed. "Oh, Mal, Mal, you're so very, very beautiful."

And in the throes of sadness and lust, he wept and kept on weeping throughout it all.

DAY MILLION

FREDERIK POHL

In Poul Anderson's story, we have seen the possibility of creating new bodies to fit alien environments. In time we might also change our bodies to suit certain tasks, for greater strength, or to rid ourselves of certain bodily processes, such as ingestion, that might be deemed inefficient.

Or we might alter ourselves simply for aesthetic reasons, or for fun. This change would undoubtedly affect our conceptions of beauty, our mores, our way of perceiving ourselves and others. In spite of individual and racial differences, we are all basically similar; we have the same bodily equipment. How would biological alteration on a vast scale affect us and our values? Is such change desirable?

Frederik Pohl proceeds on the assumption that widespread biological and social change will occur. His story addresses the mid-twentieth-century male and contrasts the past, present, and future. This seemingly simple love story is a provocative look at a radically different future and a tonic for temporal provincialism.

On this day I want to tell you about, which will be about a thousand years from now, there was a boy, a girl and a love story.

Now although I haven't said much so far, none of it is true. The boy was not what you and I would normally think of as a boy, because he was a hundred and eighty-seven years old. Nor was the girl a girl, for other reasons; and the love story did not entail that sublimation of the urge to rape and concurrent postponement of the instinct to submit which we at present understand in such matters. You won't care much for this story if you don't grasp these facts at once. If, however, you will make the effort, you'll likely enough find it jam-packed, chockful and tiptop-crammed with laughter, tears and poignant sentiment which may, or may not, be worthwhile. The reason the girl was not a girl was that she was a boy.

How angrily you recoil from the page! You say, who the hell wants to read about a pair of queers? Calm yourself. Here are no hot-breathing secrets of perversion for the coterie trade. In fact, if you were to see this girl, you would not guess that she was in any sense a boy. Breasts, two; vagina, one. Hips, Callipygean; face, hairless; supra-orbital lobes, nonexistent. You would term her female at once, although it is true that you might wonder just what species she was a female of, being confused by the tail, the silky pelt or the gill slits behind each ear.

Now you recoil again. Cripes, man, take my word for it. This is a sweet kid, and if you, as a normal male, spent as much as an hour in a room with her, you would bend heaven and earth to get her in the sack.

Dora (we will call her that; her "name" was omicron-Dibase seven-group-totter-oot S Doradus 5314, the last part of which is a color specification corresponding to a shade of green)—Dora, I say, was feminine, charming and cute. I admit she doesn't sound that way. She was, as you might put it, a dancer. Her art involved qualities of intellection and expertise of a very high order, requiring both tremendous natural capacities and endless practice; it was performed in null-gravity and I can best describe it by saying that it was something like the performance of a contortionist and something like classical ballet, maybe resembling Danilova's dying swan. It was also pretty damned sexy. In a symbolic way, to be sure; but face it, most of the things we call "sexy" are symbolic, you know, except perhaps an exhibitionist's open fly. On Day Million when Dora danced, the people who saw her panted; and you would too.

About this business of her being a boy. It didn't matter to her audiences that genetically she was male. It wouldn't matter to you, if you were among them, because you wouldn't know it—not unless you took a biopsy cutting of her flesh and put it under an electron-microscope to find the XY chromosome—and it didn't matter to them because they didn't care. Through techniques which are not only complex but haven't yet been discovered, these people were able to determine a great deal about the aptitudes and easements of babies quite a long time before they were born—at about the second horizon of cell-division, to be exact, when the segmenting egg is becoming a free blastocyst —and then they naturally helped those aptitudes along. Wouldn't we? If we find a child with an aptitude for music we give him a scholarship to Juilliard. If they found a child whose aptitudes were for being a woman, they made him one. As sex had long been dissociated from reproduction this was relatively easy to do and caused no trouble and no, or at least very little, comment.

How much is "very little"? Oh, about as much as would be caused by our own tampering with Divine Will by filling a tooth. Less than would be caused by wearing a hearing aid. Does it still sound awful? Then look closely at the next busty babe you meet and reflect that she may be a Dora, for adults who are genetically male but somatically female are far from unknown even in our own time. An accident of environment in the womb overwhelms the blueprints of heredity. The difference is with us it happens only by accident and we don't know about it except rarely, after close study; whereas the people of Day Million did it often, on purpose, because they wanted to.

Well, that's enough to tell you about Dora. It would only confuse you to add that she was seven feet tall and smelled of peanut butter. Let us begin our story.

On Day Million Dora swam out of her house, entered a transportation tube, was sucked briskly to the surface in its flow of water and ejected in its plume of spray to an elastic platform in front of her—ah—call it her rehearsal hall. "Oh, shit!" she cried in pretty confusion, reaching out to catch her balance and finding herself tumbled against a total stranger, whom we will call Don.

They met cute. Don was on his way to have his legs renewed. Love was the farthest thing from his mind; but when, absent-mindedly taking a short cut across the landing platform for submarinites and finding himself drenched, he discovered his arms full of the loveliest girl he had ever seen, he knew at once they were meant for each other. "Will you marry me?" he asked. She said softly, "Wednesday," and the promise was like a caress.

Don was tall, muscular, bronze and exciting. His name was no more Don than Dora's was Dora, but the personal part of it was Adonis in tribute to his vibrant maleness, and so we will call him Don for short. His personality color-code, in Angstrom units, was 5290, or only a few degrees bluer than Dora's 5314, a measure of what they had intuitively discovered at first sight, that they possessed many affinities of taste and interest.

I despair of telling you exactly what it was that Don did for a living—I don't mean for the sake of making money, I mean for the sake of giving purpose and meaning to his life, to keep him from going off his nut with boredom—except to say that it involved a lot of travelling. He traveled in interstellar space-ships. In order to make a spaceship go really fast about thirty-one male and seven genetically female human beings had to do certain things, and Don was one of the thirty-one. Actually he contemplated options. This involved a lot of exposure to radiation flux—not so much from his own station in the propulsive system as in the spillover from the next stage, where a genetic female preferred selections and the subnuclear particles making the selections she preferred demolished themselves in a shower of quanta. Well, you don't give a rat's ass for that, but it meant that Don had to be clad at all times in a skin of light, resilient, extremely strong copper-colored metal. I have already mentioned this, but you probably thought I

meant he was sunburned.

More than that, he was a cybernetic man. Most of his ruder parts had been long since replaced with mechanisms of vastly more permanence and use. A cadmium centrifuge, not a heart, pumped his blood. His lungs moved only when he wanted to speak out loud, for a cascade of osmotic filters rebreathed oxygen out of his own wastes. In a way, he probably would have looked peculiar to a man from the twentieth century, with his glowing eyes and seven-fingered hands; but to himself, and of course to Dora, he looked mighty manly and grand. In the course of his voyages Don had circled Proxima Centauri, Procyon and the puzzling worlds of Mira Ceti; he had carried agricultural templates to the planets of Canopus and brought back warm, witty pets from the pale companion of Aldebaran. Blue-hot or red-cool, he had seen a thousand stars and their ten thousand planets. He had, in fact, been travelling the starlanes with only brief leaves on Earth for pushing two centuries. But you don't care about that, either. It is people that make stories, not the circumstances they find themselves in, and you want to hear about these two people. Well, they made it. The great thing they had for each other grew and flowered and burst into fruition on Wednesday, just as Dora had promised. They met at the encoding room, with a couple of well-wishing friends apiece to cheer them on, and while their identities were being taped and stored they smiled and whispered to each other and bore the jokes of their friends with blushing repartee. Then they exchanged their mathematical analogues and went away. Dora to her dwelling beneath the surface of the sea and Don to his ship.

It was an idyll, really. They lived happily ever after

—or anyway, until they decided not to bother any more and died.

Of course, they never set eyes on each other again.

Oh, I can see you now, you eaters of charcoal-broiled steak, scratching an incipient bunion with one hand and holding this story with the other, while the stereo plays d'Indy or Monk. You don't believe a word of it, do you? Not for one minute. People wouldn't live like that, you say with an irritated and not amused grunt as you get up to put fresh ice in a stale drink.

And yet there's Dora, hurrying back through the flushing commuter pipes towards her underwater home (she prefers it there; has had herself somatically altered to breathe the stuff). If I tell you with what sweet fulfillment she fits the recorded analogue of Don into the symbol manipulator, hooks herself in and turns herself on . . . if I try to tell you any of that you will simply stare. Or glare; and grumble, what the hell kind of love-making is this? And yet I assure you, friend, I really do assure you that Dora's ecstasies are as creamy and passionate as any of James Bond's lady spies, and one hell of a lot more so than anything you are going to find in "real life." Go ahead, glare and grumble. Dora doesn't care. If she thinks of you at all, her thirty-times-great-great-grandfather, she thinks you're a pretty primordial sort of brute. You are. Why, Dora is farther removed from you than you are from the australopithecines of five thousand centuries ago. You could not swim a second in the strong currents of her life. You don't think progress goes in a straight line, do you? Do you recognize that it is an ascending, accelerating, maybe even exponential curve? It takes hell's own time to get started, but when it goes it goes

like a bomb. And you, you Scotch-drinking steak-eater
in your Relaxacizer chair, you've just barely lighted the
primacord of the fuse. What is it now, the six or
seven hundred thousandth day after Christ? Dora lives
in Day Million. A thousand years from now. Her body
fats are polyunsaturated, like Crisco. Her wastes are
hemodialyzed out of her bloodstream while she sleeps
—that means she doesn't have to go to the bathroom.
On whim, to pass a slow half-hour, she can command
more energy than the entire nation of Portugal can
spend today, and use it to launch a week-end satellite
or remold a crater on the Moon. She loves Don very
much. She keeps his every gesture, mannerism, nu-
ance, touch of hand, thrill of intercourse, passion of
kiss stored in symbolic-mathematical form. And when
she wants him, all she has to do is turn the machine
on and she has him.

And Don, of course, has Dora. Adrift on a sponson
city a few hundred yards over her head or orbiting
Arcturus, fifty light-years away, Don has only to command his own symbol-manipulator to rescue Dora
from the ferrite files and bring her to life for him, and
there she is; and rapturously, tirelessly they ball all
night. Not in the flesh, of course; but then his flesh
has been extensively altered and it wouldn't really be
much fun. He doesn't need the flesh for pleasure.
Genital organs feel nothing. Neither do hands, nor
breasts, nor lips; they are only receptors, accepting and
transmitting impulses. It is the brain that feels, it is
the interpretation of those impulses that makes agony
or orgasm; and Don's symbol-manipulator gives him
the analogue of cuddling, the analogue of kissing, the
analogue of wildest, most ardent hours with the
eternal, exquisite and incorruptible analogue of Dora.
Or Diane. Or sweet Rose, or laughing Alicia; for to

be sure, they have each of them exchanged analogues before, and will again.

Balls, you say, it looks crazy to me. And you—with your after-shave lotion and your little red car, pushing papers across a desk all day and chasing tail all night—tell me, just how the hell do you think you would look to Tiglath-Pileser, say, or Attila the Hun?

WATERSHED

JAMES BLISH

It has been said that we might well blush comparing our own mankind, so full of misshapen subjects, with those animal societies in which, in a hundred thousand individuals, not one will be found lacking in a single antenna. In itself that geometrical perfection is not in the line of our evolution whose bent is toward suppleness and freedom. All the same, suitably subordinated to other values, it may well appear as an indication and a lesson. So far we have certainly allowed our race to develop at random, and we have given too little thought to the question of what medical and moral factors must replace the crude forces of natural selection should we suppress them.

—Pierre Teilhard de Chardin,
The Phenomenon of Man *

James Blish's book The Seedling Stars (Gnome Press, 1957) is a collection of the stories comprising his "pan-

* New York: Harper Torchbooks, 1965, p. 282.

tropy" series. In these stories, the author assumed that humanity would genetically alter itself in order to settle other worlds. He showed the reader altered people in the hostile environment of Ganymede, people living in the trees of a jungle world, and even microscopic people on a world of water. The essential humanity of these characters, in spite of their different shapes and environments, and the fact that they could never survive here on Earth, comes through in these stories.

Here, in the last story of his series, Blish writes of a confrontation between men who have kept our familiar form and those who have been altered.

The murmurs of discontent—Captain Gorbel, being a military man, thought of it as "disaffection" —among the crew of the R.S.S. *Indefeasible* had reached the point where they could no longer be ignored, well before the ship had come within fifty light-years of its objective.

Sooner or later, Gorbel thought, sooner or later this idiotic seal-creature is going to notice them.

Captain Gorbel wasn't sure whether he would be sorry or glad when the Adapted Man caught on. In a way, it would make things easier. But it would be an uncomfortable moment, not only for Hoqqueah and the rest of the pantrope team, but for Gorbel himself. Maybe it would be better to keep sitting on the safety valve until Hoqqueah and the other Altarians were put off on—what was its name again? Oh yes, Earth.

But the crew plainly wasn't going to let Gorbel put it off that long.

As for Hoqqueah, he didn't appear to have a noticing center anywhere in his brain. He was as little discommoded by the emotional undertow as he was by the thin and frigid air the Rigellian crew maintained inside the battlecraft. Secure in his coat of warm blubber, his eyes brown, liquid and merry, he sat in the forward greenhouse for most of each ship's day, watching the growth of the star Sol in the black skies ahead.

And he talked. Gods of all stars, how he talked! Captain Gorbel already knew more about the ancient —the very ancient—history of the seeding program than he had had any desire to know, but there was still more coming. Nor was the seeding program Hoqqueah's sole subject. The Colonization Council delegate had had a vertical education, one which cut in a narrow shaft through many different fields of specialization—in contrast to Gorbel's own training, which had been spread horizontally over the whole subject of spaceflight without more than touching anything else.

Hoqqueah seemed to be making a project of enlarging the Captain's horizons, whether he wanted them enlarged or not.

"Take agriculture," he was saying at the moment. "This planet we're to seed provides an excellent argument for taking the long view of farm policy. There used to be jungles there; it was very fertile. But the people began their lives as farmers with the use of fire, and they killed themselves off in the same way."

"How?" Gorbel said automatically. Had he remained silent, Hoqqueah would have gone on anyhow; and it didn't pay to be impolite to the Colonization Council, even by proxy.

"In their own prehistory, fifteen thousand years before their official zero date, they cleared farmland by burning it off. Then they would plant a crop, harvest it, and let the jungle return. Then they burned the jungle off and went through the cycle again. At the beginning, they wiped out the greatest abundance of game animals Earth was ever to see, just by farming that way. Furthermore the method was totally destructive to the topsoil.

"But did they learn? No. Even after they achieved spaceflight, that method of farming was standard in most of the remaining jungle areas—even though the bare rock was showing through everywhere by that time."

Hoqqueah sighed. "Now, of course, there are no jungles. There are no seas, either. There's nothing but desert, naked rock, bitter cold, and thin, oxygen-poor air—or so the people would view it, if there were any of them left. Tapa farming wasn't solely responsible, but it helped."

Gorbel shot a quick glance at the hunched back of Lieutenant Averdor, his adjutant and navigator. Averdor had managed to avoid saying so much as one word to Hoqqueah or any of the other pantropists from the beginning of the trip. Of course he wasn't required to assume the diplomatic burdens involved— those were Gorbel's crosses—but the strain of dodging even normal intercourse with the seal-men was beginning to tell on him.

Sooner or later, Averdor was going to explode. He would have nobody to blame for it but himself, but that wouldn't prevent everybody on board from suffering from it.

Including Gorbel, who would lose a first-class navigator and adjutant.

Yet it was certainly beyond Gorbel's authority to order Averdor to speak to an Adapted Man. He could only suggest that Averdor run through a few mechanical courtesies, for the good of the ship. The only response had been one of the stoniest stares Gorbel had ever seen, even from Averdor, with whom the captain had been shipping for over thirty Galactic years.

And the worst of it was that Gorbel was, as a human being, wholly on Averdor's side.

"After a certain number of years, conditions change on any planet," Hoqqueah babbled solemnly, waving a flipper-like arm to include all the points of light outside the greenhouse. He was working back to his primary obsession: the seeding program. "It's only logical to insist that man be able to change with them—or, if he can't do that, he must establish himself somewhere else. Suppose he had colonized only the Earth-like planets? Not even those planets remain Earthlike forever, not in the biological sense."

"Why would we have limited ourselves to Earthlike planets in the first place?" Gorbel said. "Not that I know much about the place, but the specs don't make it sound like an optimum world."

"To be sure," Hoqqueah said, though as usual Gorbel didn't know which part of his own comment Hoqqueah was agreeing to. "There's no survival value in pinning one's race forever to one set of specs. It's only sensible to go on evolving with the universe, so as to stay independent of such things as the aging of worlds, or the explosions of their stars. And look at the results! Man exists now in so many forms that there's always a refuge somewhere for any threatened people. That's a great achievement—compared to it, what price the old arguments about sovereignty of form?"

"What, indeed?" Gorbel said, but inside his skull his other self was saying: Ah-ha, he smells the hostility after all. Once an Adapted Man, always an Adapted Man—and always fighting for equality with the basic human form. But it's no good, you seal-snouted bureaucrat. You can argue for the rest of your life, but your whiskers will always wiggle when you talk.

And obviously you'll never stop talking.

"And as a military man yourself, you'd be the first to appreciate the military advantages, Captain," Hoqqueah added earnestly. "Using pantropy, man has seized thousands of worlds that would have been in-accessible to him otherwise. It's enormously increased our chances to become masters of the galaxy, to take most of it under occupation without stealing anyone else's planet in the process. An occupation without dispossession—let alone without bloodshed. Yet if some race other than man should develop imperial ambitions, and try to annex our planets, it will find itself enormously outnumbered."

"That's true," Captain Gorbel said, interested in spite of himself. "It's probably just as well that we worked fast, way back there in the beginning. Before somebody else thought up the method, I mean. But, how come it was us? Seems to me that the first race to invent it should've been a race that had it—if you follow me."

"Not quite, Captain. If you will give me an example—?"

"Well, we scouted a system once where there was a race that occupied two different planets, not both at the same time, but back and forth," Gorbel said. "They had a life-cycle that had three different forms. In the first form they'd winter over on the outermost of the two worlds. Then they'd change to another form that could cross space, mother-naked, without ships, and spend the rest of the year on the inner planet in the third form. Then they'd change back into the second form and cross back to the colder planet.

"It's a hard thing to describe. But the point is, this wasn't anything they'd worked out; it was natural to them. They'd evolved that way." He looked at Averdor again. "The navigation was tricky around there during the swarming season."

Averdor failed to rise to the bait.

"I see; the point is well taken," Hoqqueah said, nodding with grotesque thoughtfulness. "But let me point out to you, Captain, that being already able to do a thing doesn't aid you in thinking of it as something that needs to be perfected. Oh, I've seen races like the one you describe, too—races with poly-

morphism, sexual alteration of generation, metamor-
phosis of the insect life history type, and so on. There's
a planet named Lithia, about forty light-years from
here, where the dominant race undergoes complete
evolutionary recapitulation *after* birth—not before it,
as men do. But why should any of them think of
form-changing as something extraordinary, and to be
striven for? It's one of the commonplaces of their
lives, after all."

A small bell chimed in the greenhouse. Hoqqueah
got up at once, his movements precise and almost
graceful despite his tubbiness. "Thus endeth the day,"
he said cheerfully. "Thank you for your courtesy, Captain."

He waddled out. He would, of course, be back tomorrow.

And the day after that.

And the next day—unless the crewmen hadn't
tarred and feathered the whole bunch by then.

If only, Gorbel thought distractedly, if only the
damned Adapts weren't so quick to abuse their priv-
ileges! As a delegate of the Colonization Council,
Hoqqueah was a person of some importance, and
could not be barred from entering the greenhouse
except in an emergency. But didn't the man know
that he shouldn't use the privilege each and every day,
on a ship manned by basic-form human beings, most
of whom could not enter the greenhouse at all without a direct order?

And the rest of the pantropists were just as bad. As
passengers with the technical status of human beings,
they could go almost anywhere in the ship that the
crew could go—and they did, persistently and un-
apologetically, as though moving among equals. Le-
gally, that was what they were—but didn't they know
by this time that there was such a thing as prejudice?

And that among common spacemen the prejudice against their kind—and against any Adapted Man—always hovered near the borderline of bigotry?

There was a slight hum as Averdor's power chair swung around to face the captain. Like most Rigellian men, the lieutenant's face was lean and harsh, almost like that of an ancient religious fanatic, and the starlight in the greenhouse did nothing to soften it; but to Captain Gorbel, to whom it was familiar down to its last line, it looked especially forbidding now.

"Well?" he said.

"I'd think you'd be fed up to the teeth with that freak by this time," Averdor said without preamble. "Something's got to be done, Captain, before the crew gets so surly that we have to start handing out brig sentences."

"I don't like know-it-alls any better than you do," Gorbel said grimly. "Especially when they talk nonsense—and half of what this one says about space flight is nonsense, that much I'm sure of. But the man's a delegate of the Council. He's got a right to be up here if he wants to."

"You can bar anybody from the greenhouse in an emergency—even the ship's officers."

"I fail to see any emergency," Gorbel said stiffly.

"This is a hazardous part of the galaxy—potentially, anyhow. It hasn't been visited for millennia. That star up ahead has nine planets besides the one we're supposed to land on, and I don't know how many satellites of planetary size. Suppose somebody on one of them lost his head and took a crack at us as we went by?"

Gorbel frowned. "That's reaching for trouble. Besides, the area's been surveyed recently at least once—otherwise we wouldn't be here."

"A sketch job. It's still sensible to take precautions.

If there should be any trouble, there's many a Board of Review that would call it risky to have unreliable second-class human types in the greenhouse when it breaks out."

"You're talking nonsense."

"Dammit, Captain, read between the lines a minute," Averdor said harshly. "I know as well as you do that there's going to be no trouble that we can't handle. And that no reviewing board would pull a complaint like that on you if there were. I'm just trying to give you an excuse to use on the seals."

"I'm listening."

"Good. The *Indefeasible* is the tightest ship in the Rigellian navy, her record's clean, and the crew's morale is almost a legend. We can't afford to start gigging the men for their personal prejudices—which is what it will amount to, if those seals drive them to breaking discipline. Besides, they've got a right to do their work without a lot of seal snouts poking continually over their shoulders."

"I can hear myself explaining that to Hoqqueah."

"You don't need to," Averdor said doggedly. "You can tell him, instead, that you're going to have to declare the ship on emergency status until we land. That means that the pantrope team, as passengers, will have to stick to their quarters. It's simple enough."

It was simple enough, all right. And decidedly tempting.

"I don't like it," Gorbel said. "Besides, Hoqqueah may be a know-it-all, but he's not entirely a fool. He'll see through it easily enough."

Averdor shrugged. "It's your command," he said. "But I don't see what he could do about it even if he did see through it. It'd be all on the log and according to regs. All he could report to the Council would be a suspicion—and they'd probably discount it. Everybody knows that these second-class types are quick to think they're being persecuted. It's my theory that that's why they are persecuted, a lot of the time at least."

"I don't follow you."

"The man I shipped under before I came on board the *Indefeasible*," Averdor said, "was one of those people who don't even trust themselves. They expect everybody they meet to slip a knife into them when their backs are turned. And there are always other people who make it almost a point of honor to knife a man like that, just because he seems to be asking for it. He didn't hold that command long."

"I see what you mean," Gorbel said. "Well, I'll think about it."

But by the next ship's day, when Hoqqueah returned to the greenhouse, Gorbel still had not made up his mind. The very fact that his own feelings were on the side of Averdor and the crew made him suspicious of Averdor's "easy" solution. The plan was tempting enough to blind a tempted man to flaws that might otherwise be obvious.

The Adapted Man settled himself comfortably and looked out through the transparent metal. "Ah," he said. "Our target is sensibly bigger now, eh, Captain? Think of it: in just a few days now, we will be—in the historical sense—home again."

And now it was riddles! "What do you mean?" Gorbel said.

"I'm sorry; I thought you knew. Earth is the home planet of the human race, Captain. There is where the basic form evolved."

Gorbel considered this unexpected bit of informa-

tion cautiously. Even assuming that it was true—and
it probably was; that would be the kind of thing Hoqqueah would know about a planet to which he was
assigned—it didn't seem to make any special difference
in the situation. But Hoqqueah had obviously brought
it out for a reason. Well, he'd be trotting out the
reason, too, soon enough; nobody would ever accuse
the Altarian of being taciturn.

Nevertheless, he considered turning on the screen
for a close look at the planet. Up to now he had felt
not the slightest interest in it.

"Yes, there's where it all began," Hoqqueah said.
"Of course at first it never occurred to those people
that they might produce preadapted children. They
went to all kinds of extremes to adapt their environment instead, or to carry it along with them. But they
finally realized that with the planets, that won't work.
You can't spend your life in a spacesuit, or under a
dome, either.

"Besides, they had had form trouble in their society
from their earliest days. For centuries they were ab-
surdly touchy over minute differences in coloring and
shape, and even in thinking. They had regime after
regime that tried to impose its own concept of the
standard citizen on everybody, and enslaved those who
didn't fit the specs."

Abruptly, Hoqqueah's chatter began to make Gorbel uncomfortable. It was becoming easier and easier
to sympathize with Averdor's determination to ignore
the Adapted Man's existence entirely.

"It was only after they'd painfully taught themselves that such differences really don't matter that
they could go on to pantropy," Hoqqueah said. "It
was the logical conclusion. Of course, a certain continuity of form had to be maintained, and has been

maintained to this day. You cannot totally change the
form without totally changing the thought processes.
If you give a man the form of a cockroach, as one
ancient writer foresaw, he will wind up thinking like
a cockroach, not like a human being. We recognized
that. On worlds where only extreme modifications of
the human form would make it suitable—for instance,
a planet of the gas giant type—no seeding is attempted. The Council maintains that such worlds are
the potential property of other races than the human,
races whose psychotypes would not have to undergo
radical change in order to survive there."

Dimly, Captain Gorbel saw where Hoqqueah was
leading him, and he did not like what he saw. The
seal-man, in his own maddeningly indirect way, was
arguing his right to be considered an equal in fact
as well as in law. He was arguing it, however, in a
universe of discourse totally unfamiliar to Captain
Gorbel, with facts whose validity he alone knew and
whose relevance he alone could judge. He was in
short, loading the dice, and the last residues of Gorbel's tolerance were evaporating rapidly.

"Of course there was resistance back there at the
beginning," Hoqqueah said. "The kind of mind that
had only recently been persuaded that colored men
are human beings was quick to take the attitude that
an Adapted Man—any Adapted Man—was the social
inferior of the 'primary' or basic human type, the type
that lived on Earth. But it was also a very old idea on
the Earth that basic humanity inheres in the mind,
not in the form.

"You see, Captain, all this might still have been
prevented had it been possible to maintain the attitude that changing the form even in part makes a
man less of a man than he was in the 'primary' state.

But the day has come when that attitude is no longer tenable—a day that is the greatest of all moral watersheds for our race, the day that is to unite all our divergent currents of attitudes toward each other into one common reservoir of brotherhood and purpose. You and I are very fortunate to be on the scene to see it."

"Very interesting," Gorbel said coldly. "But all those things happened a long time ago, and we know very little about this part of the galaxy these days. Under the circumstances—which you'll find clearly written out in the log, together with the appropriate regulations—I'm forced to place the ship on emergency alert beginning tomorrow, and continuing until your team disembarks. I'm afraid that means that henceforth all passengers will be required to stay in quarters."

Hoqqueah turned and arose. His eyes were still warm and liquid, but there was no longer any trace of merriment in them.

"I know very well what it means," he said. "And to some extent I understand the need—though I had been hoping to see the planet of our birth first from space. But I don't think you quite understood me, Captain. The moral watershed of which I spoke is not in the past. It is now. It began the day that the Earth itself became no longer habitable for the so-called basic human type. The flowing of the streams toward the common reservoir will become bigger and bigger as word spreads through the galaxy that Earth itself has been seeded with Adapted Men. With that news will go a shock of recognition—the shock of realizing that the 'basic' types are now, and have been for a long time, a very small minority, despite their pretensions."

Was Hoqqueah being absurd enough to threaten—
an unarmed, comical seal-man shaking a fist at the
captain of the *Indefeasible?* Or—

"Before I go, let me ask you this one question, Captain. Down there is your home planet, and my team
and I will be going out on its surface before long. Do
you dare to follow us out of the ship?"

"And why should I?" Gorbel said.

"Why, to show the superiority of the basic type,
Captain," Hoqqueah said softly. "Surely you cannot
admit that a pack of seal-men are your betters, on
your own ancestral ground!"

He bowed and went to the door. Just before he
reached it, he turned and looked speculatively at Gorbel and at Lieutenant Averdor, who was staring at him
with an expression of rigid fury.

"Or can you?" he said. "It will be interesting to see
how you manage to comport yourselves as a minority.
I think you lack practice."

He went out. Both Gorbel and Averdor turned
jerkily to the screen, and Gorbel turned it on. The
image grew, steadied, settled down.

When the next trick came on duty, both men were
still staring at the vast and tumbled desert of the
Earth.

FURTHER
READING

NONFICTION

Ettinger, R. C. W. *Man Into Superman*. New York: St. Martin's Press, 1972.

Etzioni, Amitai. *Genetic Fix*. Harper Colophon Books, 1975.

Feinberg, Gerald. *The Prometheus Project*. Garden City, N.Y.: Doubleday Anchor Books, 1969.

Fishlock, David. *Man Modified*. New York: Funk & Wagnalls, 1969.

Fletcher, Joseph. *The Ethics of Genetic Control: Ending Reproductive Roulette*. Garden City, N.Y.: Doubleday Anchor Books, 1974.

Gabor, Dennis. *Innovations: Scientific, Technological, and Social*. New York: Oxford University Press, 1970.

Handler, Philip, ed. *Biology and the Future of Man*. New York: Oxford University Press, 1970.

Harrington, Alan. *The Immortalist*. New York: Avon, 1970.

Kavaler, Lucy. *Freezing Point*. New York: John Day, 1970.

Kent, Saul. *Future Sex*. New York: Warner Paperback Library, 1974.

Luria, S. E. *Life: The Unfinished Experiment*. New York: Scribner's, 1973.

Rosenfeld, Albert. *The Second Genesis: The Coming Control of Life.* New York: Vintage, 1975.

Rostand, Jean. *Humanly Possible.* New York: Saturday Review Press, 1973.

Segerberg, Osborn, Jr. *The Immortality Factor.* New York: Dutton, 1974.

Still, Henry. *Man-Made Men.* New York: Hawthorn, 1973.

Taylor, Gordon Rattray. *The Biological Time Bomb.* New York: New American Library, 1968.

Thomas, Lewis. *The Lives of a Cell.* New York: Viking, 1974.

Tuccille, Jerome. *Here Comes Immortality.* New York: Stein & Day, 1973.

Watson, James D. *The Double Helix.* New York: Signet, 1968.

FICTION: Novels and Subjects

Aldiss, Brian. *Hothouse.* London: Faber & Faber, 1962. (Far-future biological change)

Anderson, Poul. *Brain Wave.* New York: Ballantine, 1954. (Increased intelligence)

Anderson, Poul. *Twilight World.* New York: Torquil Books, 1961. (Mutants)

Bass, T. J. *The Godwhale.* New York: Ballantine, 1974. (Cyborgs)

Bass, T. J. *Half Past Human.* New York: Ballantine, 1969. (Genetic engineering)

Beresford, J. D. *The Hampdenshire Wonder.* New York: Arno Press, 1975. (Mutants)

Blish, James. *The Seedling Stars.* New York: Gnome Press, 1957. (Genetic engineering and biological alteration)

Blish, James. *Titan's Daughter.* New York: Berkley, 1961. (Genetic engineering)

Blish, James, and Norman L. Knight. *A Torrent of Faces.* Garden City, N. Y.: Doubleday, 1967. (Overpopulation and genetic engineering)

Bodelson, Anders. *Freezing Down.* New York: Harper & Row, 1971. (Cryonics)

Brunner, John. *The Whole Man.* New York: Ballantine, 1964. (Mutants and future medicine)

Budrys, Algis. *Who?* New York: Pyramid, 1958. (Cyborgs)

Clarke, Arthur C. *The City and the Stars.* New York: Harcourt, 1956. (Immortality, results of evolution in the far future)

Clarke, Arthur C. *The Deep Range.* New York: Harcourt, 1957. (Marine biology)

Clarke, Arthur C. *2001: A Space Odyssey.* New York: New American Library, 1968. (Human evolution is seen as an experiment conducted by an advanced alien civilization. The experiment includes an elaborate trap set by an extraterrestrial intelligence to obtain the result, a current human specimen, which is then transformed into a new form of life.)

deCamp, L. Sprague, and P. Schuyler Miller. *Genus Homo.* Reading, Pa.: Fantasy Press, 1950. (Evolution)

Dick, Philip K. *Ubik.* Garden City, N. Y.: Doubleday, 1969. (Cryonics)

Disch, Thomas M. *Camp Concentration.* Garden City, N. Y.: Doubleday, 1969. (Human experimentation)

Frank, Pat. *Mr. Adam.* Philadelphia: Lippincott, 1946. (Mutants)

Gunn, James. *The Immortals.* New York: Bantam, 1962. (Immortality, future medicine, mutants, organ transplantation)

Harrison, Harry. *Make Room! Make Room!* Garden City, N. Y.: Doubleday, 1966. (Overpopulation; the film *Soylent Green* was based on this novel.)

Huxley, Aldous. *Brave New World*. Garden City, N. Y.: Doubleday, 1932. (Biological engineering, alternate modes of reproduction)

Meredith, Richard C. *We All Died at Breakaway Station*. New York: Ballantine, 1969. (Cyborgs)

Nourse, Alan E. *The Bladerunner*. New York: Ballantine, 1975. (Future medicine)

Nourse, Alan E. *Star Surgeon*. New York: McKay, 1960. (Future medicine)

Padgett, Lewis. *Mutant*. New York: Simon & Schuster, 1953. (Mutants)

Sheckley, Robert. *Immortality, Inc.* New York: Bantam, 1959. (Immortality)

Shiras, Wilmar H. *Children of the Atom*. New York: Gnome Press, 1953. (Mutants)

Silverberg, Robert. *Master of Life and Death*. New York: Ace, 1957. (Euthanasia, bioethics)

Silverberg, Robert. *Tower of Glass*. New York: Scribner's, 1970. (Androids)

Simak, Clifford. *Why Call Them Back from Heaven?* Garden City, N. Y.: Doubleday, 1967. (Cryonics)

Smith, Cordwainer. *Nostrilia*. New York: Ballantine, 1975. (Biological engineering, immortality)

Stapledon, Olaf. *Last and First Men*. New York: Dover, 1968. (Participant evolution)

Stapledon, Olaf. *Odd John*. New York: Dover, 1972. (Mutants)

Stapledon, Olaf. *Sirius*. New York: Dover, 1972. (Biological engineering involving animals. The main character is an intelligent dog.)

Sturgeon, Theodore. *More Than Human*. New York: Farrar, 1953. (Mutants)

Sturgeon, Theodore. *Venus Plus X*. New York: Pyramid, 1960. (Biological alteration, alternate modes of reproduction)

Taine, John. *Seeds of Life*. Reading, Pa.: Fantasy Press, 1951. (Biological engineering)

van Vogt, A. E. *Slan*. New York: Simon & Schuster, 1951. (Mutants)

Vance, Jack. *To Live Forever*. New York: Ballantine, 1956. (Immortality)

Wallace, F. L. *Address: Centauri*. New York: Gnome Press, 1955. (Mutants, cyborgs, future medicine)

Weinbaum, Stanley G. *The New Adam*. New York: Avon, 1967. (Mutants)

Wells, H. G. *The Island of Dr. Moreau*. New York: Ace, 1958. (Biological engineering)

Wells, H. G. *The Time Machine*. New York: Airmont Books, 1964. (Divergent evolution)

Wilhelm, Kate. *Where Late the Sweet Birds Sang*. New York: Harper & Row, 1976. (Cloning)

Wolfe, Bernard. *Limbo*. New York: Random House, 1952. (Cyborgs)

Wright, S. Fowler. *The World Below*. New York: Longmans, Green, 1930. (Evolutionary change)

Wylie, Philip. *Gladiator*. New York: Knopf, 1930. (Biological engineering)

Wyndham, John. *Re-birth*. New York: Ballantine, 1955. (Mutants)

Wyndham, John. *The Trouble with Lichen*. London: Joseph, 1959. (Immortality)

Zelazny, Roger. *Isle of the Dead*. New York: Ace, 1969. (Immortality)

Zelazny, Roger. *This Immortal*. New York: Ace, 1966. (Immortality)

FICTION: Anthologies

Conklin, Groff, ed. *Science Fiction Adventures in Mutation.* New York: Vanguard Press, 1955.

Dann, Jack. *Immortal.* Harper & Row (to be published).

Dickson, Gordon R. *Mutants.* New York: Macmillan, 1970.

Nolan, William F., ed. *The Pseudo-People.* Los Angeles: Sherbourne Press, 1965.

Scortia, Thomas N., and George Zebrowski, eds. *Human-Machines: The Cyborg in Science Fiction.* New York: Vintage, 1975.

Silverberg, Robert, ed. *Mutants.* New York: Thomas Nelson, 1974.

Zebrowski, George. *Biogenesis.* Santa Cruz: Unity Press (to be published).

SHORT FICTION

Asimov, Isaac. "Founding Father," 1965. Reprinted in *SF: Authors' Choice,* ed. by Harry Harrison, Berkley, 1968.

Ballard, J. G. "Billenium," 1960. Reprinted in *Billenium* by J. G. Ballard, Berkley, 1962.

Ballard, J. G. "Prima Belladonna," 1956. Reprinted in *Billenium.*

Ballard, J. G. "The Voices of Time," 1961. Reprinted in *The Voices of Time and Other Stories* by J. G. Ballard, Berkley, 1962.

Bernott, Joan. "The Test-Tube Creature, Afterward," 1972. Appeared in *Again, Dangerous Visions,* ed. by Harlan Ellison, Doubleday, 1972.

Brown, Fredric. "Keep Out," 1954. Reprinted in *Science Fiction Adventures in Mutation*.

Byram, George. "The Wonder Horse," 1957. Reprinted in *SF: 58*, ed. by Judith Merril, Gnome Press, 1958.

Davis, Chan. "Letter to Ellen," 1947. Reprinted in *Science-Fiction Thinking Machines*, ed. by Groff Conklin, Vanguard Press, 1954.

de Camp, L. Sprague. "Hyperpilosity," 1938. Reprinted in *Omnibus of Science Fiction*, ed. by Groff Conklin, Crown, 1952.

Dick, Philip K. "Oh, To Be a Blobel," 1964. Reprinted in *The Preserving Machine* by Philip K. Dick, Ace, 1969.

Guin, Wyman. "Volpa," 1956. Reprinted in *Living Way Out* by Wyman Guin, Avon, 1967.

Farmer, Philip José. "Seventy Years of Decpop," 1972. Reprinted in *Best Science Fiction for 1973*, ed. by Forrest J. Ackerman, Ace, 1973.

Heard, H. F. "Cyclops," 1952. Appeared in *Future Tense*, ed. by Kendell Foster Crossen, Greenberg, Publishers, 1952.

Heinlein, Robert A. "Jerry Was a Man," 1947. Reprinted in *Assignment in Eternity* by Robert A. Heinlein, Fantasy Press, 1953.

Herbert, Frank. "Greenslaves," 1965. Reprinted in *On Our Way to the Future*, ed. by Terry Carr, Ace, 1970.

Huxley, Julian. "The Tissue-Culture King," 1927. Reprinted in *Time Probe: The Sciences in Science Fiction*, ed. by Arthur C. Clarke, Dell, 1966.

Kaempffert, Waldemar. "The Diminishing Draft," 1918. Reprinted in *Big Book of Science Fiction*, ed. by Groff Conklin, Crown, 1950.

Keyes, Daniel. "Flowers for Algernon," 1959. Reprinted in *Fifth Annual of The Year's Best SF*, ed. by Judith Merril, Simon & Schuster, 1960.

King, Vincent. "Defense Mechanism," 1966. Reprinted

in *New Writings in SF 7*, ed. by John Carnell, Bantam, 1971.

Knight, Damon. "The Country of the Kind," 1955. Reprinted in *New Dreams This Morning*, ed. by James Blish, Ballantine, 1966.

Knight, Damon. "Dio," 1957. Reprinted in *Alpha Four*, ed. by Robert Silverberg, Ballantine, 1974.

Knight, Damon. "Mary," 1964. Reprinted in *A Day in the Life*, ed. by Gardner R. Dozois, Harper & Row, 1972.

Kornbluth, C. M. "The Marching Morons," 1951. Reprinted in *The Science Fiction Hall of Fame*, Vol. 2A, ed. by Ben Bova, Doubleday, 1973.

Leiber, Fritz. "Yesterday House," 1952. Reprinted in *Alpha Five*, ed. by Robert Silverberg, Ballantine, 1974.

MacDonald, John D. "A Child is Crying," 1948. Reprinted in *The Shape of Things*, ed. by Damon Knight, Popular Library, 1965.

MacDonald, John D. "Trojan Horse Laugh," 1949. Reprinted in *Tomorrow 1*, ed. by Robert Hoskins, Signet, 1971.

McIntyre, Vonda N. "The Genius Freaks," 1973. Appeared in *Orbit 12*, ed. by Damon Knight, Putnam, 1973.

MacLean, Katherine. "And Be Merry," 1950. Reprinted in *Omnibus of Science Fiction*.

MacLean, Katherine. "The Origin of the Species," 1953. Appeared in *Children of Wonder*, ed. by William Tenn, Simon & Schuster, 1953.

MacLean, Katherine. "Syndrome Johnny," 1951. Reprinted in *SF: Author's Choice*.

Miller, Walter M., Jr. "Conditionally Human," 1952. Reprinted in *Conditionally Human* by Walter M. Miller, Jr., Ballantine, 1962.

Miller, Walter M., Jr. "Dark Benediction," 1951. Reprinted in *Conditionally Human*.

Niven, Larry. "The Defenseless Dead," 1973. Appeared in *Ten Tomorrows*, ed. by Roger Elwood, Gold Medal, 1973.

Niven, Larry. "The Jigsaw Man," 1967. Appeared in *Dangerous Visions*, ed. by Harlan Ellison, Doubleday, 1967.

Nourse, Alan E. "The Coffin Cure," 1951. Reprinted in *Science Fiction Oddities*, ed. by Groff Conklin, Berkley, 1966.

Padgett, Lewis. "When the Bough Breaks," 1941. Reprinted in *The Astounding Science Fiction Anthology*, ed. by John W. Campbell, Jr., Simon & Schuster, 1952.

Pierce, J. R. "The Higher Things," 1970. Appeared in *Nova 1*, ed. by Harry Harrison, Delacorte, 1970.

Pierce, J. R. "Invariant," 1944. Reprinted in *The Astounding Science Fiction Anthology*.

Pohl, Frederik, and C. M. Kornbluth. "The Meeting," 1972. Reprinted in *The Best Science Fiction of the Year*, ed. by Terry Carr, Ballantine, 1973.

Scortia, Thomas N. "Woman's Rib," 1972. Reprinted in *Best Science Fiction Stories of the Year: Second Annual Collection*, ed. by Lester del Rey, Dutton, 1973.

Silverberg, Robert. "Born With the Dead," 1974. Reprinted in *Born With the Dead* by Robert Silverberg, Vintage, 1975.

Silverberg, Robert. "Going," 1971. Reprinted in *Born With the Dead*.

Simak, Clifford. "Desertion," 1944. Appeared in *Big Book of Science Fiction*.

Simak, Clifford. "Eternity Lost," 1949. Reprinted in *The Best Science Fiction Stories: 1950*, ed. by Everett F. Bleiler and T. E. Dikty, Frederick Fell, 1950.

Smith Cordwainer. "A Planet Named Shayol," 1961. Reprinted in *Seventh Annual of The Year's Best SF*, ed. by Judith Merril, Simon & Schuster, 1962.

Spinrad, Norman. "No Direction Home," 1971. Reprinted in *No Direction Home* by Norman Spinrad, Pocket Books, 1975.

Stevens, James. "Syn," 1975. Appeared in *Tomorrow Today*, ed. by George Zebrowski, Unity Press, 1975.

Sturgeon, Theodore. "Maturity," 1947. Reprinted in *Six Great Short Novels of Science Fiction*, ed. by Groff Conklin, Dell, 1954.

Szilard, Leo. "The Mark Gable Foundation," 1961. Reprinted in *The Expert Dreamers*, ed. by Frederik Pohl, Avon, 1962.

Vonnegut, Kurt, Jr. "The Big Trip Up Yonder," 1953. Reprinted in *Assignment in Tomorrow*, ed. by Frederik Pohl, Doubleday, 1954.

Wandrei, Donald. "A Scientist Divides," 1934. Reprinted in *The Best of Science Fiction*, ed. by Groff Conklin, Crown, 1946.

Weinbaum, Stanley G. "The Adaptive Ultimate," 1935. Reprinted in *The Best of Stanley G. Weinbaum*, Ballantine, 1974.

Weinbaum, Stanley G. "Proteus Island," 1936. Reprinted in *The Best of Stanley G. Weinbaum*.

Westlake, Donald. "The Winner," 1970. Appeared in *Nova 1*.

Wilhelm, Kate. "April Fool's Day Forever," 1970. Appeared in *Orbit 7*, ed. by Damon Knight, Putnam, 1970.

Wolfe, Gene. "The Fifth Head of Cerberus," 1972. Reprinted in *The Fifth Head of Cerberus* by Gene Wolfe, Scribner's, 1972.

Zelazny, Roger. "The Keys to December," 1966. Reprinted in *World's Best Science Fiction: 1967*, ed. by Donald A. Wollheim and Terry Carr, Ace, 1967.

ABOUT THE AUTHORS

POUL ANDERSON grew up in Texas and Minnesota. He majored in physics at the University of Minnesota, graduating with honors. His novels include *Brain Wave*, *Three Hearts and Three Lions*, *Tau Zero*, *The Broken Sword*, *Fire Time*, and *A Knight of Ghosts and Shadows*. Among his short-story collections are *Guardians of Time*, *Strangers from Earth*, *Trader to the Stars*, *The Horn of Time*, *The Queen of Air and Darkness and Other Stories*, and *Homeward and Beyond*. He has won five Hugo Awards (given annually by the members of the World Science Fiction Conventions) and two Nebula Awards (given annually by members of the Science Fiction Writers of America). He lives in California with his wife, poet and writer Karen Anderson.

JAMES BLISH was educated at Rutgers and Columbia University. His novels include *And All the Stars a Stage*, *Titan's Daughter*, *The Seedling Stars*, *Jack of Eagles*, *A Torrent of Faces* (with Norman L. Knight), the *Cities in Flight* tetralogy, *Doctor Mirabilis*, and *A Case of Conscience*, which won the Hugo Award for Best Novel of 1958. He was the editor of two anthologies, *New Dreams This Morning* and *Nebula Award Stories Five*, and the author of two volumes of critical essays on science fiction, *The Issue at Hand* and *More Issues at Hand*.

He lived in England with his wife, artist and illustrator Judith Ann Lawrence, until his death in 1975.

THOMAS M. DISCH grew up in Minnesota and attended New York University. His novels include *Camp Concentration, The Genocides, Mankind Under the Leash, Echo Round His Bones,* and *334.* He is the editor of three anthologies, *The Ruins of Earth, Bad Moon Rising,* and *The New Improved Sun.* His short stories have appeared in *Playboy, Mademoiselle, Paris Review, New Worlds,* and various magazines and anthologies. He is also the author of two short-story collections, *Fun With Your New Head* and *Getting Into Death,* and a volume of poetry, *The Right Way to Figure Plumbing.* He lives in New York City.

JAMES GUNN served in the U. S. Navy during World War II. He earned a B. S. in journalism and an M. A. in English from the University of Kansas. His novels include *Star Bridge* (with Jack Williamson), *This Fortress World, Station in Space, The Immortals, The Joy Makers, The Burning,* and *The Listeners.* Among his short-story collections are *Breaking Point, Some Dreams Are Nightmares,* and *The End of the Dreams.* He is the editor of *Nebula Award Stories Ten* and the author of a history of science fiction, *Alternate Worlds.* His stories have been dramatized on NBC Radio and on television's *Desilu Playhouse. The Immortals* became an ABC Movie of the Week and then a television series, *The Immortal.* He is presently a professor of English and journalism at the University of Kansas.

R. A. LAFFERTY is a retired electrical engineer who has spent most of his life in Oklahoma, except for a number of years in Australia, the Dutch East Indies, and New Guinea as a Staff Sergeant during World War II. His novels include *Past Master, Arrive at Easterwine, The Devil Is Dead, Okla Hannali,* and *Fourth Mansions.* He is also the author of many short stories which have appeared in literary magazines and in science fiction magazines and anthologies, as well as in three collections, *Nine Hundred Grandmothers*, *Strange Doings*, and *Does Anyone Else Have Something Further to Add?* He received a Hugo Award in 1973 for his short story "Eurema's Dam."

URSULA K. LE GUIN received her B. A. from Radcliffe College and her M. A. in French and Italian Renaissance Literature from Columbia University. Her novels include *The Wizard of Earthsea*, *The Tombs of Atuan*, *The Farthest Shore*, *City of Illusions*, *The Lathe of Heaven*, *The Left Hand of Darkness*, and *The Dispossessed*. *The Left Hand of Darkness* received both the Hugo and Nebula Awards for Best Novel in 1969; *The Dispossessed* won both awards in 1975. *The Farthest Shore* was given a National Book Award for Children's Literature. Other awards include a Hugo for her novella "The Word for World Is Forest." She lives in Oregon with her husband, historian Charles A. Le Guin.

FREDERIK POHL has been both a writer and editor of science fiction. He has worked as an editor for *Galaxy* magazine, Ballantine Books and Ace Books. He also edited the *Star* series of original science fiction stories for Ballantine during the 1950s. He is presently editing a series of science fiction novels for Bantam Books. His short stories have appeared in *Playboy*, *The Magazine of Fantasy & Science Fiction*, *Analog*, and many other magazines and anthologies, including several "best-of-the-year" collections. His novels include *The Space Merchants*, *Gladiator-at-Law*, *Wolfbane* (all with C. M. Kornbluth), *Starchild*, *Rogue Star* (both with Jack Williamson), *The Age of the Pussyfoot*, and *Man Plus*. His short-story collections include *The Gold at the Starbow's End*, *Day Million*, and *The Best of Frederik Pohl*. He lives in New Jersey.

THOMAS N. SCORTIA was educated at Michigan State University and Washington University. He served in the U. S. Army and was a physiochemist in the aerospace industry. He is considered one of the leading propellant chemists in the country. His novels include *The Prometheus Crisis*, *The Glass Inferno* (both with Frank Robinson), *Artery of Fire*, and *Earthwreck*. *The Glass Inferno* was the basis for the film *The Towering Inferno*. He is the author of several short stories, many of which have appeared in "best-of-the-year" collections. He is the editor of the anthologies *Two Views of Wonder* (with Chelsea Quinn Yarbro), *Human-Machines* (with George Zebrowski), and *Strange Bedfellows*. He is also the author of a short-story collection, *Caution! Inflammable!* He lives in California.

LEONARD TUSHNET was a physician and writer. His stories have appeared in *The Magazine of Fantasy & Science Fiction*, *Forum*, *National Jewish Monthly*, *Mosaic*, *New Mexico Quarterly*, *The Prairie Schooner*, *Jewish Currents*, *Cimarron Review*, *Maelstrom*, and many other publications. His short story "The Little Doctor" was included in *The Best American Short Stories of 1971*. His nonfiction includes *To Die With Honor*, *The Medicine Men*, and *The Uses of Adversity*. He lived in New Jersey until his death in 1974.

KATE WILHELM is the author of many short stories which have appeared in *Orbit*, *Quark*, *The Magazine of Fantasy & Science Fiction*, and other magazines and anthologies. Her novels include *The Killer Thing*, *Let the Fire Fall*, *Margaret and I*, *City of Cain*, and *Where Late the Sweet Birds Sang*. Her short-story collections include *The Downstairs Room*, *The Mile-Long Spaceship*, and *The Infinity Box*. She is the editor of *Nebula Award Stories Nine* and *Clarion Four*. Her story "The Planners" won a Nebula Award. She is married to science fiction writer and editor Damon Knight.

ABOUT THE EDITOR

PAMELA SARGENT received her B.A. and M.A. in philosophy from the State University of New York at Binghamton (Harpur College). She is the author of twenty short stories and a novel, *Cloned Lives* (Fawcett-Gold Medal Books). She is also the editor of *Women of Wonder* and *More Women of Wonder* (Vintage Books). She lives in upstate New York.